PRAISE FOR D.

Somebody That I Used to Know

"Davis thoughtfully tackles the complexities of transracial adoption, friendship, and not giving yourself up for love."

—*School Library Journal* (starred review)

"Davis meaningfully explores the complexities around transracial adoption in ways specific to the Black community. Dylan's friends are well developed and contribute to the storyline and growth of both main characters. The evolution of Dylan and Legend's relationship is a nice, slow burn. A textured story of going from friends to something more, complete with a happily ever after."

—*Kirkus Reviews*

Tiffany Sly Lives Here Now

"Debut author Davis takes an unflinching approach to racism, religion, emotional abuse, and mental illness. Tiffany's circumstances are nightmarish, but the narrative isn't weighed down, in large part because of her integrity, passion, and refusal to be self-pitying."

—*Publishers Weekly*

"Davis's debut novel is an honest, funny, and captivating examination of race, socioeconomics, mental health, and family . . . A dynamic and honest coming-of-age novel with universal appeal that will especially speak to Black girls questioning their place in the world."

—*Kirkus Reviews*

ALSO BY DANA L. DAVIS

Somebody That I Used to Know

Tiffany Sly Lives Here Now

The Voice in My Head

Roman and Jewel

FAKE
Famous

a novel

DANA L. DAVIS

⊞ SKYSCAPE

Published by Skyscape, New York

www.apub.com

Amazon, the Amazon logo, and Skyscape are trademarks of Amazon.com, Inc., or its affiliates.

ISBN-13: 9781542038768 (hardcover)
ISBN-13: 9781542038751 (paperback)
ISBN-13: 9781542038775 (digital)

Cover design by Erin Fitzsimmons
Cover image: © Volodymyr Burdiak, © komkrit Preechachanwate / Shutterstock;
© ohlamour studio / Stocksy United

Printed in the United States of America
First edition

For Carmen and Viana

ONE

*D*ear Universe. Show me something good. That's pretty much what I say every morning. I'm not totally convinced the Universe is listening. Or, since the Universe speaks so many different languages, maybe today when I said *good*, the Universe thought I said, *I'd like to be almost knocked unconscious by a metal hog feeder.*

"See this bump?" I take a step forward, neck extended so the purple bruise on my forehead is on full display. "Outside the chicken coop? Becky *attacked* me during morning chores! I bumped my head running from her. Have a heart. Don't be like Becky."

Her lips curl into a snarl. Dang, that must've pissed her off.

"I mean, I wasn't . . . calling you a chicken."

She pulls her arm back, and suddenly a plastic bottle is soaring at me. I make an attempt to duck, but—BLAM!—it strikes dead center on my forehead, right on the same spot from earlier this morning!

"Ow." I cover my throbbing bruise with the palm of my hand.

"Maybe you should wear a helmet in the morning," Loren calls out from the top bunk of the bed we share, her long fuzzy ponytail flopping from side to side as she stares down at me with a sad shake of her head. "And you know Daeshya doesn't speak English, right?"

"Oh, she understands me." I reach into the crib to pick up the bundle of fat, slobbers, and soggy diaper that is our ten-month-old sister,

Daeshya. She feels as heavy as one of our plastic grain bags stuffed to the brim with field corn. "Don't you, Dae-Dae?"

Daeshya's chubby fingers grab a handful of my messy, kinky curls. "Wed!"

"It's Red. Rrrr. Red." I peel her fingers open and bop her on the nose.

"Why is she sleeping in here, anyway?" Loren yawns, pulling her *Stranger Things* comforter under her chin with one hand and sliding on her thick square-framed glasses with the other. "You guys woke me up like seventeen times last night."

"Helping Mom. You should try it sometime!" I hurl the baby bottle in Loren's direction, but it ricochets off the wood of the bunk and lands on our dusty wool area rug with a thud.

Loren snorts. "Hope you're not signing up for sports at your new college."

"I meant to do that." I reach to grab the bottle. "I'm gonna make sure our brothers are up and moving. Stuff your face with a Pop-Tart or a Cheerio and meet me behind the south barn. Manure drop-off in twenty minutes."

"Why do *we* always get stuck with poop?" Loren whines. "Shouldn't we be making needlepoint coasters, weaving spools of thread onto looms, mashing potatoes for shepherd's pie?"

"We are not the cast of *Anne of Green Gables*." I reposition Daeshya higher on my hip. "Also, what's poop to you is actually—"

"Disgusting?"

"No, I was gonna say fodder for a healthy crop of oats."

Loren groans. "Do you always have to sound like such a farmer?"

"I am a farmer. You are too. Now hurry up and get dressed."

I move into the hallway just as my eleven-year-old brother, Elijah, stumbles out of his bedroom in a tank top, shorts, sunglasses, and a Minecraft backpack slung over his shoulder. His brown skin shines under the hallway lights.

"Elijah, why is your skin . . . shiny?"

"I'm wearing suntan lotion." He rubs his tired eyes with one hand while the other fiddles with his phone.

"Please tell me you're joking."

"I tried to talk him out of dressing like he's going to a pool party, Red." Jaxson's moving down the hall now. The reclaimed floorboards of our old, rustic farmhouse creak and moan underneath him. Thankfully *Jax* is dressed appropriately for a day out in the fields—in jeans and a long-sleeved T-shirt. His coiffed dreads are pulled into a ponytail and somehow maneuvered through the opening of a straw hat, so his hair flails out in all directions on top of his head. "But he said he wanted to get a tan because 'Black people can tan too.'"

Elijah nods like, yeah, that's exactly what he said. "What? They can."

Jax turns to me. "By the way, best sister in the *world*. I need a favor." He rubs his hands together. "You know my friend Chris, right?"

I switch Daeshya from one hip to the other. "Is that the guy with one green eyebrow or the one who barks at people in the hallway at school?"

"Green eyebrow." Jax leans on my shoulder, and his Axe body spray burns my nose. No idea why he thinks he should drown himself in it before detasseling corn, but . . . whatever. "He's working at Wacky Waters all summer. He said he can get me a job there as a lifeguard."

I nod. "But you can't swim."

"What's that got to do with anything?" Jax asks. "It's the kids' section. Two feet of water."

"You're a farmer, not a lifeguard," I point out. "Mom and Dad will say no."

"That's why I need you to ask them *for* me." He grins, exposing a mouthful of silver braces. "They like you better than the rest of us. For real."

"Jax, stop." I roll my eyes. "Mom and Dad like their children all the same."

Elijah and Jaxson exchange looks, then burst into laughter.

"Good one, Red." Jaxson slaps his knee. "Only you can make me laugh this early in the morning."

"Sis, I swear." Elijah lays a hand on my shoulder. "You got major jokes."

I shake him off. "Whatever. You guys suck. And not to make you feel worse than you already should, but if I happen to *see* Green Eyebrow at Wacky Waters today, I'll say hi." I slide my phone out of the back pocket of my jeans and show Elijah and Jaxson a text from my best friend, Melissa. They both lean forward to read.

Wacky Waters today!!! Can't wait to see yooooou!

"What?!" Elijah screeches.

Jax shakes his head. "See? The clear favorite!"

"Mom and Dad have nothing to do with this." I laugh. "My a cappella class is celebrating. We graduated. Most of us are off to college. We deserve a day of fun. Now move. Get to detasseling, detasselers." I stick out my hand. "'Go Farmers' on three. One . . . two . . ."

"I swear, man." Elijah pushes my hand away. "Humans have invented Wi-Fi, but nobody thought to invent a *machine* that detassels corn?" He moves off, muttering under his breath.

Jaxson trails behind, muttering as well.

I watch them go. "Should we tell them there *is* a machine that detassels corn?"

Daeshya blows a spit bubble.

"Good point. Don't tell."

I continue, then push open the bathroom door at the end of the hallway to find Mom. She's already dressed for a day of work at our store, running bathwater and tossing plastic toys into our claw-foot tub. The floor still has the same green and pink tiles from when this house was built in the 1940s. Though Mom calls the colors avocado and rose

4

and says we kids should be thankful we live in such a historically decorated home, I think *historically decorated* is just a phrase she made up.

"Special delivery," I sing, adding fancy runs to the end of my made-up song. "Deliveeery. Eeee. Oooooh yeah."

Daeshya squeals, kicking her little legs and extending her hands with glee, nearly jumping into Mom's outstretched arms.

"Hi, my little ball of sunshine." Mom hugs and kisses Daeshya. "And geez, Red . . ." She glances up at me. "You sound *good*. Make me a playlist of you singing."

"Oh staaahp it, Ma." I pretend to flip my hair over my shoulder. "And when would I have time to make a playlist? After I empty the compost buckets, open the coop, water the plants, candle the eggs, take care of the chicks, wash the pigs, and clean out the barn . . . it's time for school."

"You do way too much around here." Mom groans.

"Wish I could do *more*." I lean up against the wall and sigh. "You and Dad are the ones who do too much around here."

Mom snaps her fingers. "Hey, here's an idea. Let's go see Zay-Zay Waters, live. Wouldn't that be fun? A break from all this hard work?"

"Last time I checked, tickets to a Zay-Zay Waters concert were like five hundred dollars. At least for the seats where you can actually see her."

"Oh." Mom frowns. "How much are the tickets where you can't see her?"

"Free." I whip out my phone, tap the YouTube icon, and find a clip from an episode of *Oh, So You Think You Can Sing Live?* Zay-Zay sometimes sits in as a guest judge. "Check this out."

Zay demonstrates a complicated part of a song to a young singer. Her long blue nails tap out the rhythm while she sings.

Mom studies the screen. "I know you think I'm way off when I say it, but I swear you two *look* alike."

"Mom, bye!" I laugh. "She has waist-length black hair. I have curly red hair. She has millions of dollars. I have ten cents. She's uptown; I'm down on the farm. She also has a smoking-hot boyfriend, and I . . . do not."

"Who cares about all of that? You have similar bone structure. And the skin tone is a perfect match. Besides," she goes on, "that's not even Zay-Zay's hair!"

"But that's definitely her boyfriend." I sigh dreamily. "Koi Kalawai'a and Zay-Zay Waters. They're *perfect*. Relationship goals."

"Nineteen-year-old-millionaire love is the new goal?" Mom laughs as she sets Daeshya gently into the tub. The kid plops right into the water without Mom taking off her diaper. "By the way, how'd Dae sleep?"

She woke up fourteen times.

Threw a bottle at my head fifteen times.

Ripped curtains off the wall.

Stuck her finger in a light socket. I thought she was dead.

"'Twas a peaceful night," I lie. "I think she only woke up . . . once? Maybe? And at sunrise, she hugged me and gave me a kiss."

Mom beams. "How come she always behaves so well with *you?*"

"I have the magic touch?" I change the subject, since lying makes my elbows itch. I scratch at them. "Oh yeah. Eli has on shorts, a tank top, and *suntan* lotion, and is headed out to detassel corn, and Jax wants to be a lifeguard this summer at Wacky Waters."

"Eli will be burnt up and eaten alive by mosquitos." Mom digs Dae's wet diaper out of the tub. "And Jax is a farmer, *not* a lifeguard. He can't even swim."

"I tried to tell him." I wave at Dae. "I'm off to help Dad with the manure delivery. Bye, Dae. Stay sweet." *You little terror.*

She picks up a plastic bath toy and is about to toss it at my head, but I quickly duck into the hallway.

~

The sun is blazing, though it's early morning. Tiny beads of sweat form at my brow as I move around the corner of the farmhouse toward the south barn, where the manure drop-off is happening, my leather boots kicking up dust along the way. Soon, the peaceful quiet of this place will be replaced with a flurry of activity. I can almost hear the kids screaming with glee, smell the many food carts we'll have on the property, and inhale the thrill in the air as pretty much all of Orange City, Iowa, makes its way to the Morgan Family Farm for the three-day event that is the annual Summer Strawberry Festival.

Up ahead, I see a man in a flannel shirt, Levi's, and mud-splattered rubber boots leaning against a dump truck near the fence of the barn. I rush to him. "Hiya." I extend a hand. "Hope you haven't been waiting long."

"What else do you hope?" He pushes off the rear bumper of the truck and sort of scowls at me. "I got a delivery for Ellis Morgan. Been calling his phone. No answer."

I see the fresh pile of manure dumped near the fence.

"I can sign for it," I say.

He glares at me, as if a girl signing for two hundred pounds of manure seems . . . *off* to him. "You work here or somethin'?"

"If you don't get paid, can you really call it work?" When I take the clipboard out of his hands, I notice Loren moving toward us, holding her phone, staring at the screen like she's watching something brand new and exciting. I scribble my signature on the line. "There. All good."

"Is that what you think?" He picks at his teeth and runs a hand through greasy hair that's possibly blond under the thick layers of grime. "I got two more deliveries today. Gon' be late for both now, thanks to y'all."

He snatches back the clipboard, grunts, and climbs into his truck. Before I have a chance to sarcastically tell him to have a nice day, he's driving off. I move to where Loren now sits on our wooden fence, her leather boots dangling off the side as she watches a clip from *Oh, So You Think You Can Sing Live?*

"C'mon, sis. Put that away. The sooner we get started, the sooner we get done."

"One sec." The light from Loren's phone reflects in her glasses as she stares like she's stuck in a trance. "Oh my gosh!" she gasps. "He got the platinum buzzer. He's going to New York City! Look!"

I peer over her shoulder. Sure enough, silver confetti rains down on the boy as he jumps up and down.

I dig my gloves out of the pocket of my jeans. "Let's grab shovels from the barn and start mixing the soil into the manure before Dad gets here."

Loren's eyes are glued to her phone. "He's about to start crying. I can feel it. I love when they cry."

"You have five seconds to put that thing away." I climb onto the fence and stand slowly, lining up my boots on the thin wooden plank like I'm standing on a tightrope. "One . . . two . . . three . . ." I stomp, holding out my arms to keep my balance.

"Hey!" Loren grips the fence with one hand so she doesn't fall. "What's your problem?"

"Four . . . four and a half . . . four and three-quarters." I stomp again. Harder.

"Stop counting! I'm not Daeshya." Loren slides off the fence and lands with a thud. "And you look like Black Dorothy up there. Hey, be careful. Or a tornado is gonna blow you off to Oz."

"I'm down for that." I start singing. *"Somewheeeeeere over the raiin-bow."*

Loren positions her phone in my direction as I sing. "I'm recording this, Mariah Scary."

"Waaaay up hiiigh." I jut out my hip and hold my hand exactly the way Zay-Zay Waters does when she really goes in.

"I know you're only joking, but you sound sooo good." Loren pulls at her fuzzy ponytail with her free hand, looking up at me like I'm something special. "I wish I could sing like you." She points. "But be careful, sis. The fence is broken in that sp—"

Her warning is one second too late. The portion of the fence gives way, my foot slips, and I fall. And honestly, I never thought falling in slow motion was a real thing outside of movie magic. Until this very moment. I fall ever so slowly, and after what feels like minutes instead of seconds, where I'm contemplating the meaning of life—SPLAT—I'm splayed out in the pile of freshly dumped manure, staring up at the sky.

"Oh. My. Ga," Loren whispers.

When I turn to look at her, I can hear the manure squish underneath me. *Ewww.* We stare at one another in total silence. Her, with her eyes stretched as wide as I've ever seen them stretch, and me, with *my* eyes burning from the stench of manure in my lashes. In spite of her jaw-dropped gaze, she's actually still holding up her phone, recording me. For reasons beyond my understanding, I decide to be a good sport and . . . keep on singing.

"Somewhere over the rainbow, smells real bad." I force myself onto my feet so the manure goes *squish, squish* beneath my boots. I strike Zay-Zay Waters's popular pose with my hip jutted out. *"There's some stuff that I landed in. Oops, wish I never haaad."*

Loren howls, bending over in a fit of hysterical laughter. "Screaming!"

"I'm Zay-Zay Waters, ya' heard me." I imitate Zay-Zay's superstrong Brooklyn accent. "Comin' to you live from the Morgan Family Farm in Orange City, Iowa." I shake off a clump of manure. "Lemme know if you think *you* can sing live!!"

"What on earth?"

We turn to see Dad.

"What the heck are y'all doin'?" He yanks off his old, worn Iowa Hawkeyes baseball cap and pulls on the strands of his short fro. The light-brown skin on his face twists to form a disgusted scowl.

Uh-oh.

Loren lowers her phone. "Red . . . fell."

"I did." I clumsily climb my way out of the pile and make a pitiful attempt to shake some off, but it's sorta stuck to me like glue. "Sorry."

"Go on and hose off behind the barn, Red." Dad steps back, like he's afraid I might get manure on *him*. "Then shower inside before you get some sort of incurable bacterial infection." He turns to Loren. "I'm gonna hose down the greenhouse and come back to help." He moves off, his heavy leather boots kicking up dust as he mutters and mumbles to himself. When he disappears around the corner of the hayfield, I turn to Loren.

"That went well."

"If by *well* you mean . . . smell." Loren pushes her glasses back onto her nose. "Then yes. I agree."

I extend my arms, which are covered in manure. "Is it weird that I have the sudden, overwhelming urge to give you a long hug and never let go?"

"Don't you dare touch me!" She stumbles back. "Go hose off and shower, like Dad said! Hurry, before the stench of you makes me drop dead."

"Fine. But *you* better delete that video."

"You kidding?" She stares down at her phone. "Black Dorothy never sounded so good. I'm gonna edit this and save it for forever."

I extend my arms again. "I'mma hug you. Tight."

She recoils. "Fine! I'll delete it!"

"You better!" As I take off toward where we keep the hose behind the barn, a clump of manure slides down my back. I wonder if I'm the first human to fall from a fence into a pile of manure. With the way the Universe works . . . probably not.

TWO

"Why are you at your store?" My best friend Melissa's voice booms through the speaker on my phone.

"It's a long story." I'm rushing down the aisle in our country market, which we call the Big Red Barn, my arm extended so the phone is right in front of my face and Melissa can see me in clear view. "One that involves washing streaks of cow poo off my skin. Wanna hear it?"

"Ew. No." Melissa sprays sunblock onto her face. "Did I mention *Brad* is here and asking about you. 'Cuz he is."

I groan. Poor Brad. Unrequited love since kindergarten. The boy refuses to give up hope.

"Hi, Red."

I turn to see a kid that's always here on Sunday mornings. I think his name is Mendel. He's got little tassels hanging off the sides of his pants and a small disc-shaped hat over the top of his head. He's holding two bags of our homegrown steel-cut oats, a favorite around these parts.

"Melissa, I gotta go. Grabbing the car keys from my mom and then heading out." I hang up the call. "Mendel, right?" I smile down at him.

"My mom told me to come find you. The nice lady checking us out said she had to throw up and ran to the bathroom."

I groan. Erin's almost nine months pregnant. She's always throwing up. "Um. Gimme a second. I'll find someone else to help." I move toward the end of the aisle where we keep the phone and press star-51 to talk into the receiver. "Can we get a checker to the front, please? Checker to the front." My voice booms from the overhead speakers.

"That looks fun," Mendel says. "Can I use it?"

"Menachem Mendel." His mom appears, pushing a small cart filled with fresh produce, her hair covered with a pretty scarf tied at the back. "Don't give Red a hard time." She tosses me a pained-looking smile. I can tell she'd really like to get out of here ASAP. "Is there someone who can ring up our groceries?"

"Of course. I'll grab my mom."

"Thanks so much." Mendel's mom maneuvers her cart into a quick U-turn and travels back down the narrow aisle. The wooden floor slats of our rustic barnyard store go *clickety-clack* as Mendel trails behind her.

I continue on, past the deli section, where our butcher, Andre, is using an electric slicer to cut up deli meats. I wave at him and push through the swinging double doors that lead to the stockroom. The smell of overripe produce and raw meat sorta slams into me as I skirt around wooden crates filled with canned goods. Up ahead, through the dusty window of Mom and Dad's office, I notice Mom sitting at her desk. Our farm manager, Tony, stands in front of her, wiping his eyes from . . . crying. The heck?!

I creep closer, press my back to the door so they can't see me, and peek through the window.

"I understand. I do." Tony wipes at his eyes.

"We're so sorry." Mom's got tears in her eyes too. "If things change for us, we'd love to have you back. You're the perfect farm manager."

They're firing Tony?!

I step forward to knock on the office window and raise my voice so they can hear me through the glass. "Sorry to disturb you," I call out as Mom repositions Daeshya on her lap. I can't believe Tony has to be fired while Daeshya sits there, probably throwing things at him! "I need the keys to the van." Mom waves me in. "Also." I step inside and pull the door shut behind me. "Erin's puking in the bathroom. Again. There's no checker."

"Oh *no*." Mom stands and pries Daeshya's hands out of her long braids. "Can you watch your sister for me until Lyndia gets here? She's having car trouble but is on her way." She speaks to Daeshya. "Go with Red, ok?" Daeshya starts to scream holy terror, arching her back and kicking her little legs in protest.

My phone chimes in my hand. It's a text from Melissa.

I'm putting my phone in a locker. Meet us at the wave pool!

"Um . . ." I try to avoid eye contact with Tony as I take a step toward Mom. "Today's the Aca-pellets trip to Wacky Waters. I'm already late as it is." I pull on my exposed straps to point out I'm wearing my swimsuit under my jean skirt and T-shirt.

"I'm sure Lyndia will be here soon." Mom struggles to manage Daeshya's meltdown. "Please, Red."

My phone buzzes again. I check the text. It's from my other Aca-pellet friend, Eileen.

Do you want us to rent you an innertube for the wave pool? They only have a few left.

I send back a quick text.

Yeah. Grab me one.

I press the button to lock the screen on my phone before extending my arms to Daeshya. "C'mon, girl. Stop all that screaming before we put a muzzle on you." I take her out of Mom's outstretched arms and wrap *my* arm tightly around her, so she can't injure me with her monster-size tantrum. I find a way to grab Tony's arm with my free hand and squeeze. I hope he knows that squeeze means I think him being fired is a serious crime against humanity and also . . . that I'll

13

miss him. As I turn to leave, he grabs me gently by the elbow and squeezes back.

"I'll miss you, too, kid," he whispers.

My eyes well. I quickly rub at them so no tears can escape. "Ready, Daeshya? Let's give Mom some privacy with Tony."

~

"C'mon, Universe," I whisper to myself as I watch my friends' TikTok videos of Wacky Waters. "You were supposed to show me something good today!" I wonder if blood boiling is an actual thing. I should take my temperature and check.

Jaxson stumbles into the living room. His brown skin has been roasted shades darker by the sun. He frowns when he sees me staring out the window like sadness threw up on me.

"Sis?" He plops down onto the couch. "What the heck you doing here?"

"Lyndia's car stopped." Dae crawls around at my feet. "She was supposed to be here *six* hours ago."

"Is she staring at the people fixing her car? Why can't she rideshare it?" Jax grabs the remote off the coffee table.

"It's her parents' Tesla, and it ran out of . . . energy, or whatever Teslas run out of. She has to wait for a tow. She can't just leave the car there." I shake my head. "I tried to get Loren to relieve me. Dad, too . . . but Dae would scream bloody murder if either of them came anywhere near her. Oh, and get this . . ." I pick Daeshya up and place her into her playpen. "They had to fire Tony!"

"Wait, *what*?!" Jax glares at me like I'm the one who fired Tony. "That's the stupidest thing I ever heard. Why they fire Tony?"

"They can't afford to pay him. He was crying when they let him go."

"Tony is my *dude*." Jax yanks his hat off, and his dreads fall onto his shoulders. "So messed up!"

"Super messed up." I move to the couch and slump down next to my brother. I turn to face him. "You smell like burnt corn, grass, Axe body spray, and . . . you just smell. Bad."

"It's a nightmare out there, sis. Like a corn war zone," he grumbles. "Did you ask about me working at Wacky Waters?"

"Don't say Wacky Waters!" The time on my phone turns to 4:00 p.m. I sigh. "I should let it go. I've officially missed the postgraduation a cappella senior trip."

"I'd be hella mad if I was you."

"I'm not mad." I lay my head back and stare at the ceiling. "Mom and Dad are . . . doing the best they can. Sucks is all."

"You better than me." Jaxson is flipping through channels on the TV. "If I was eighteen like you and had just finished high school, I'd be plotting my escape instead of majoring in *farming* and going to a school down the street. Why you doing that? Red, you can sing. Go do something amazing."

"First of all, I'm not majoring in farming. It's agricultural systems management."

Jaxson shrugs like he doesn't get the difference.

"And as far as doing something amazing, being there for your family is the most amazing thing a person can do."

"Girl, you trippin'. I'm deuces after I graduate from high school. Farming is not my jam."

"But . . ." I'm struggling to imagine Jax just leaving Orange City and all his family obligations. "You would abandon the family business?"

"To abandon is to cease support or give up completely." He continues flipping through channels. "I'd still be a part of the farming game. Not one of the key players, though."

I slide off the couch and move to the window, as if standing here and staring outside will make Lyndia magically appear. The window faces our oat fields. To see them flourishing, when last year's crop had so much trouble, makes a weak smile creep onto my face, in spite of the blood-boiling situation. Jax is only fourteen. He'll figure things out. I know I did. The day I decided to go to Northwestern College so I could stick around and help Mom and Dad . . . it was a good day. A right decision. I *am* one of the key players. I have to be.

"Do we have anti-itch cream? And something to make my skin stop burning."

I turn to see a miserable-looking Elijah standing at the doorway, *covered* in bugbites. His skin is scorched about *five* shades darker by the sun and red in spots, especially on his shoulders.

"Elijah, you are a whole mess." Jax rolls his head back and laughs. "Suntan lotion fail."

"I don't think 'I told you so' seems fair," I add.

"Then don't say it," Elijah cries. "Just help meee."

Why is my little brother so hardheaded? *Ugh.* "I'll find some aloe. That might help."

"Yoooo. Wait." Jax sits up. "Zay-Zay Waters wearin' your hair, Red."

Entertainment Now is playing on the screen. Zay-Zay Waters is being followed by dozens of camerapeople into a restaurant, wearing curly red hair . . . almost *exactly* like mine.

"I thought that was you for a sec," Jax says seriously, before turning his attention to his phone. "Oooh. You should make a TikTok doppelgänger account."

"Yeah, you should." Elijah stares at the mounted flat screen. "I never realized you and her look so much *alike*. And check out her forehead!"

Jax and I say *whoa* at exactly the same time. Zay-Zay Waters *also* has a purple bruise on her head. Like . . . literally in the same spot as mine.

"Maybe Zay-Zay ran into a hog feeder while being chased by a crazy chicken too." Jax laughs.

"Red!" Loren stumbles into the living room like a derailed train, knocking over two framed family photos. She pauses to snatch the pictures off the floor. "Super quick. No bigs. No cause for serious alarm." She clumsily places the photos back onto the shelf. "Remember when I was supposed to delete that video of you singing in poo?"

"You mean this one?!" Jax holds up his phone. A TikTok video is playing. A girl sits in her room, her screen split in two, voice booming through the speakers of Jax's phone:

"What exactly was Zay-Zay Waters doing at a farm in Iowa early this morning? I think it's maybe a promo for her upcoming guest appearances on *Oh, So You Think You Can Sing Live?* Let's check it out. Here is my reaction. Watching it now for the first time."

"Wed!" Daeshya points at Jax's phone from her playpen.

Jax turns up the volume, and we all watch as the video Loren recorded this morning plays, with me—*not* Zay-Zay Waters—standing on the fence, falling splat into manure, and standing up to sing.

"There's some stuff that I landed in. Oops, wish I never haaad." In the video, I place a hand on my hip and say, *"I'm Zay-Zay Waters, ya' heard me. Comin' to you live from the Morgan Family Farm in Orange City, Iowa."* I shake off a clump of manure. *"Lemme know if you think you can sing live!!"*

My head swivels around to glare at Loren.

"I sorta . . ." Loren swallows. "Edited it and uploaded it onto TikTok. It . . . *kinda* went viral."

"What do you mean *kinda?*" Jax fiddles with his phone. "The original video has forty-two million views!"

"You're lying," I almost whisper.

"Nope." He holds it up for me to see. "Forty-two million and counting, sis."

I take a step toward Loren and whisper, "I . . . am going to kill you."

"But nobody knows it's you!" Jax stretches out his arms to block me from reaching around him to where Loren is now cowering. "They think it's Zay-Zay."

"Not entirely." Eli calls out, staring down at his own phone. "There's some debate in the comment section. *Some* people are wondering if it's really her or not." He slides his finger up his screen, reading comments. "But the general consensus seems to be that it is Zay-Zay."

"See?" Jax smiles. "You're overreacting. Relax."

He's right. I am overreacting.

"Not to mention, you was killin' it with the vocals," Jax adds, like that's the only important thing. "Red." He steps forward and places a hand on my shoulder. "In spite of the manure bath you were swimming in, you sounded good. Better than good. Why you think people think it's her? It's a vibe. You got star quality. Can't you see?"

"I'm here. I'm here." Lyndia rushes into the living room and stops cold. Her smile flips upside down. "Whoa." She holds out her hand like she's testing the air or something. "The energy in here feels bloated and gassy. Are you kids eating enough fiber?" She tosses her purse into the corner and reaches into the playpen to grab Daeshya, who squeals with excitement at the sight of her. "Seriously, kids. Exhale. Eat an apple. It's a beautiful day." She quickly heads off with Dae in her arms and disappears down the hallway.

Lyndia's right. It *is* a beautiful day. I point my finger at Loren, trying to stand as tall and as menacing as my five feet, four inches will allow. "Delete the video."

"I tried," she says sadly. "But it's already been copied like hundreds of times. So I figured, what's the point?"

"The point is"—I force a calm, even tone—"if they can trace the original, it leads back to me."

"Which is a bad thing why?" Jax scratches at his head. "Don't you wanna be famous?"

I sigh. "I don't wanna be Zay-Zay Waters's look-alike." I roll my eyes at the thought. "I got bigger fish to fry. Real fish. Like the annual Strawberry Festival. *That* should be the thing we're all focused on."

"You're right." Loren nods. "I'll delete it."

"Thank you." I exhale, relieved. "And then it'll probably be buried among all the other viral Zay-Zay Waters videos. Right?"

Eli, Jaxson, and Loren exchange looks.

"I mean . . . sure?" Eli says.

"Possibly," Loren adds.

"Maybe." Jax grimaces. "But to be safe." He takes my phone from me.

I frown. "What are you doing?"

"Making your social media accounts private. For now." He hands it back to me. "This way, people can't find you when Zay-Zay reveals it's *not* her swimming in manure. Give it a few weeks before you make your accounts public again, and file this under 'What are the odds?' Trust me, you good, sis."

Jax is right. I'm officially deciding to file this under "What are the odds?" and move on.

It's the best advice my little brother has ever given me.

THREE

"M oonlight Sonata" plays softly through my speakers. I switch off the phone alarm and peel back my heavy comforter. "C'mon, Universe," I whisper. "Show me something good. But nothing too crazy, ok?" I had to make changes to my morning mantra. Can't have the Universe thinking *good* means *manure bath on TikTok*. Last week's nightmare must never be repeated. I swing my legs off the bed and bang my fist on the slats of wood under the top bunk. "Loren, you up? You're helping me and Mom open the store."

"I'm up, I'm up," Loren mumbles.

I slide into a pair of crumpled jeans, smooth out the wrinkles on the She-Ra T-shirt I wore to bed, and step into my leather cowboy boots. "Gonna check on the boys and see if Mom needs help with Daeshya."

Loren yawns in response.

I move into the hallway and bang on Jax and Eli's door. "Rise and shine, you guys!"

I continue on, pushing into the bathroom at the end of the hall. The morning sun is shining through the frosted glass of the old wood-framed window, casting rays of light onto the rusted porcelain tub and toilet. I squint from the sudden brightness and grab my toothbrush out of the pink cup on the sink. Seven days since I went viral. It seems like a dream. Was it?

Someone knocks.

"I'm in here!" I call out, my mouth full of toothpaste. But the door pushes open anyway, and a sleepy Loren stumbles inside. "Hey!" I rinse out my mouth with water before turning to her and wiping off my chin with a paper towel. "What happened to respecting privacy?"

"In a house with one properly working bathroom and seven people?" She laughs as she pulls the plastic shower curtain back and flips on the water. "Good one."

I wet my hair under the faucet and squeeze it dry with a towel.

"Red, can you, like, get out?"

In the mirror above the sink, I see Loren's head, covered with a purple shower cap, peeking around the curtain.

"Byeeee." She waves. "Shut the door on your way, please and thanks."

I step into the hallway, pulling the door closed as Loren's morning screeching of BLT songs begins. Or whatever that group's called. That's not real music. Zay-Zay Waters is real music.

"Together with you, until forever, I do."

As I move down the stairs, past our small den, and into the kitchen, I sing "Together with You," one of Zay-Zay's duets with her boyfriend, Koi Kalawai'a.

"You said you loved me, I knew it toooo."

My phone's on the counter, so I type a search as I sing: *Zay-Zay Waters in manure.*

There it is. The original video is gone, but the copies have millions and *millions* of views. Me, singing in manure, went . . . viral? *Unbelievable.* I read some of the comments.

Zay-Zay so funny!

Love her.

Love Zay with red hair. Too cute!

I think that was fake manure!

I think it was a fake Zay-Zay!

No, no. It's her! Different hair color. But look at the bump on her head!
It's def her. Why you think she's been MIA? She's embarrassed!
Yeah! Only a fool would play around in manure!

Hey, I'm no fool! But Zay-Zay *has* been MIA. Not a post. An interview. Absolutely no sight of her. Is she on vacation? When she reemerges . . . will she out me?

I grab a tray of banana-nut muffins and my jar of overnight oats from inside the fridge.

"Together with you, until forever I do."

I attempt the insane run she does at the end. Eh. Not too bad. Nowhere close to the way Zay-Zay kills it. I can sing all right, it's true. But Zay-Zay Waters can *sang*. I toss a few muffins into a paper bag.

"You said you loved me, I knew it tooooo."

"Girl, you know you can sang." The sound of Dad's heavy boots reverberates in the kitchen as his tall, six-feet-six frame moves down the wooden staircase.

"I'm messin' around." I turn to face Dad. "It's nothing."

"Have you heard me singing in the shower? *That's* nothing."

"That . . . actually hurts my ears."

We both laugh as Dad pulls his standard leather outback hat over his head and hands me the machine shed remote. "Make sure you lock everything back up so Norman won't . . ." Dad slaps himself on the forehead. "Dang it. I keep forgetting."

"I forget too." Norman always liked to hide out in the machine shed. "The other day I set out his food bowl."

Dad kinda groans, like talking about our dead American bulldog is not something he's interested in doing. He moves toward the door. "You mind helping me at the hog barn this morning? Slaughter today."

The things that happen on slaughter day have made me give up eating any sort of animal. Period. Being a vegetarian farmer is not all that odd. But being a vegetarian pig *slaughterer*? A girl's gotta draw the line somewhere. "Can't Jax help?"

"Jax?" Dad chuckles. "Threw up last time. Cried too. We're on a time crunch, and with my arm in this cast, I need real help. How about this? Grab the tractor, bone saw, and chains for the pulley. Drive it all over to the barn, and get the hot water bath ready. Sound good?"

Jobs that don't include splattered pig blood all over my clothes? "Sounds great. These things I can do."

"Don't forget to add pine needles to the water. I keep 'em stashed in the back shed in one of the grain bags. It helps the hair come off the hog before we—"

"Dad." I make a disgusted face. "Spare me the details."

"Appreciate you." He winces as he adjusts his sling, and I swear for a split second, I see the entire world on his shoulders. Like he's Atlas, the Titan in Greek mythology, condemned to hold up the sky for eternity. But instead of having the whole sky in his hands, he's got the entire Morgan Family Farm on his *back*. "All right, kiddo. See you over at the barn."

He pushes out the side screen door, and it slams shut after him. I turn to face where I would usually lay out Norman's food bowls and swallow away the lump in my throat, shovel down the rest of my oats before tossing my empty mason jar into the sink, and move out the door.

~

The doors to the machine shed, where we keep all our tractors and farm equipment, are already rolled up, and the tractor Dad needs to hoist up the pig is sitting out, ready to go. I frown. Why did Dad ask for my help if he already prepped the tractor? I hear rustling inside the shed.

"Dad?"

No reply. I take a timid step forward. A shadowy figure hovers over one of the workbenches.

"Jacob?"

Something metal falls to the ground, clanging on the concrete. My heart rate kicks up a notch.

"Just so you know," I call out, scratching at my elbows, "I'm a black belt in tae kwon do."

"A black belt from where?" a male voice calls back. "Walmart?"

Wait. I *know* that voice.

The man steps out of the shadows, holding a metal crowbar. "Sorry, Red. This fell."

"Tony?" I rush into his arms, and he hugs me with the classic double pat on the back before rubbing the top of my head. "Tony Baloney! What are you doing here?"

"Slaughter day. No way I'm gonna let your dad attempt this without me."

"But . . ."

"I know they can't pay me, Red. I owe 'em a few favors. It's all right. Your dad can't handle a saw right now. And who's gonna hoist up the hog?"

"Jacob?"

"Jacob weighs less than the pig!" Tony laughs so hard his belly shakes. "Listen, you go on and tend to your own chores." He winks at me. "I got it from here."

I step to the tractor, looking up at Tony as he settles in and twists the key into the ignition. I yell so he can hear me over the roar of the engine. "I wish you didn't have to leave us."

"Who says I'm leavin'?"

I frown. One time, I stumbled upon the W-2s for Tony's taxes. He makes sixty-five thousand a year working for us. I suppose it's not the hugest salary, but it's extra money Mom and Dad don't have lying around anymore. The price of everything farmers need has doubled— some of it's even tripled or quadrupled in the last year. Our friends the Shervingtons run a beef farm on the other side of the city. They sadly had to file for bankruptcy last month. The fact that the Morgan farm is staying afloat is nothing short of a miracle. "You know something I don't know, Tony? Did we win the lottery?"

"Ain't gotta win the lottery to trust the Universe, Red. Remember the 'ram in the bush' story?"

I do. From Sunday school when I was little. A man was in need of a miracle and got one, in the form of a ram tangled up in branches by his horns.

"There is always a ram somewhere, waiting to be found. You just gotta look for it." Tony pulls the door shut, and within a few seconds, he's driving across the field toward the hog barn.

"Problem is. We don't *have* rams on this farm." I press the button on the remote. The garage doors begin to slide shut.

"Please don't lock me in here!" a girl's voice cries out.

The heck?! I press the button on the remote again. The doors stop halfway down.

"Who's in there?"

It didn't sound like Loren. Besides, when I left the house, she was still in the shower.

I crouch low under the garage door and move back into the shed. Someone steps around our old combine. I can't make out exactly who she is, or if I know her. She's wearing black jeans, paired with a hoodie pulled low over her head and partially covering her face. She stands in the shadows.

"This is private property," I call out. "You can't be in here."

She steps forward again, into the light. "You must be the girl from the video."

She yanks off her hood, exposing a head full of wild red curls and a face *quite* similar to mine.

"Oh. My. Ga," I whisper in Loren fashion.

She extends her perfectly manicured hand, covered in intricate tattoos. "I'm Zay-Zay Waters."

FOUR

When I was seven years old, and Loren and Jaxson were three, Jaxson used to burst into my room every morning and call out, "Lo-Lo? Where Lo-Lo?" He would climb into Loren's toddler bed, and I thought it was the cutest thing. Twins reunited each morning. One day, I opened my eyes when I heard the door burst open, fully expecting to see Jax, dragging his blanky. But instead, I saw the beady eyes of a sharp-toothed *possum*.

I screamed.

Loren woke up screaming too.

A few seconds later, Dad burst into the room in his underwear, holding a hammer.

And Mom was right behind him with a bag of rock salt we used to deice the walkways in the winter.

I wasn't sure what they were gonna do. Dad was gonna hammer it to death? Mom was gonna throw salt in its eyes? Thankfully, the possum ran out the door, probably more scared than we were.

This moment, staring into the face of Zay-Zay Waters, is crazier than the possum, hammer, rock salt, *and* all of us screaming our heads off.

"I'm sorry." I finally find my voice. "But. Huh?"

She touches one of the wheels on the combine and looks up at it, as if she's trying to figure out what this machine is. "I know, right.

Random. I was in Chicago, rented a car, and came down. Iowa's what's up. I never really been."

She holds out her phone. On the screen is a picture from our website.

"I looked for you on social but didn't find anything. Then I found your pic on your farm's website, so I just put two and two and hoped I'd find you." She smiles at her phone. "Y'all are hella cute. Like the great American farm family. But Black. I'm wit' it."

Her Brooklyn accent is even stronger in person. And I'm still sorta not sure what to say here. "Are you trying to serve me with court papers?"

She frowns. "Say what?"

"Because I was pretending to be you last week?" My shoulders slump. "Is it defamation of character, what I did? In my defense, I was only playing around and—"

"Yo." She holds up a hand. "I'm not here 'cuz I wanna sue you. You know how many people pretend to be me? There is a drag queen in Vegas whose stage name is Zlay Zlay Riverwater. Like, really?" She rolls her eyes. "Whatever. Bye, Zlay Zlay!"

With her Brooklyn accent. When she says *whatever*, it sounds like she's saying *wha-ev-ah*.

She runs her hand across the combine's chipped green paint. "This looks like a murder machine."

"Um . . ." Zay-Zay Waters. Is in our machine shed! Talking to me! Like . . . there is a *celebrity* in our garage! *Ahhh!!* "It's a combine."

"Oh, word? What's it for?"

"It uh . . ." I study her hands. They seem soft and delicate. Her long pointy nails are painted pink, and she has tiny diamonds on the end of each one. I wonder if they're real. "We use it to harvest our oats." I'm trying my hardest not to gawk. It's not easy. Her teeth are super white. Her skin ridiculously *shiny*. She's like an anime come to life. "The . . . uh . . . machine separates the stem of the plant."

"Oats is a *plant?*" She laughs.

"That's funny." I wipe my sweaty palms on my jeans. Can she see *my* nails? No diamonds or fancy polish. Nope. My nails are all chipped and uneven. And dirty. I swear, no matter how much I wash, the dirt does not come out from under them. I wonder if Zay-Zay notices. Or can see that my skin *isn't* shiny. And that my teeth are . . . kinda dull.

"I guess I thought oats grew in boxes at the store," she says. "So then, what do y'all do with the oat . . . plant?"

I tug on my wrinkled She-Ra T-shirt and hope I don't ramble, the way I usually do when people ask me farm questions.

"Well, to start, what you're seeing in the front, that's a 915 grain head."

"Huh?"

Oh gosh. *Keep it short and sweet, Red!* "Basically that head separates the stem from the plant, and then we store the grain in our silos until it's ready to be processed. People come from all over to buy our oats. We only sell them locally." There. That was simple. Clear. A nonramble. "Would you like some? Oats, I mean. Much better than the stuff you'd get at a regular grocery store. Did you see our store? It's more like a . . . market. Like a country store. The Big Red Barn. Like a country store meets a farmers' market. Like . . ." I'm doing it. I'm rambling. "Sorry. My parents should've named me Ramble instead of Red."

"Your name is Red? Like your hair? Aw. That's *adorable.*" She kicks at the giant combine wheel. "Let me see if I was listenin'. This . . . murder machine picks up the plant. Takes off the stem. Then y'all store the grain in silos. Which, I used to have a friend named Silo."

"Oh?" I wonder if her friend knows they're named after grain-storage bins.

"And then after the silo, not my friend"—she grins—"you process it. Which I hope involves maple syrup. And raisins. Dang, now I'm hungry."

I laugh. Not a real laugh. A nervous, oh-my-gosh-I'm-having-a-conversation-with-Zay-Zay-Waters chuckle. Like a . . . snort. She probably thinks I'm over here choking on slobbers. "You could practically run that combine now."

She studies me. Is she trying to take me in? Thinking of all the ways we *don't* look alike? I stuff my hands into the pockets of my jeans so she can't see my fingernails.

"We really do look alike," she finally says.

"I mean, you're much shinier than me." Oy.

"Maybe we're related," she offers. "What's your mom and dad's name?"

"My mom? Her name is Gloria. My dad's name is Ellis. Ellis and Gloria Morgan."

"Never heard of 'em." She shrugs. "Guess it's a random glitch in the matrix. My name is Zenaria. Did you know that?"

Of *course* I knew that. I know pretty much all there is to know about Zay-Zay Waters! I even know she has celiac disease. Should I tell her our oats are gluten-free?

"Zenaria? Huh? I did not know that. Pretty." I scratch my elbows.

She runs a hand through the curls on her head. "I was in this movie, right. And we wanted a new look. So the director . . ."

"Director," in Zay-Zay's Brooklish = *Da-rek-tah.*

". . . and I'm like whatever, you know? I'm always down to try new stuff wit' my hair, you know what I mean?"

Her accent is a whole vibe. I'm decoding as she talks. When she says, "You know what I mean?" it sounds like . . . *Kna mean?*

". . . And he's like cool. I'm like cool. It's all good. You wit' me?"

"Yes." I scratch my elbow. "You have my undivided attention."

"So the shoot was only a few days, though. For my part. I was all set to put my extensions back in. You know the long black hair I wear? That's not actually my hair."

"*Really?*" More elbow scratching. "I would not have guessed that."

"Yeah, yeah. My hairdresser, his name is Randy. He's so dope. Everybody wants him, but he's mine. Not, like, *mine*, mine. He's gay. You'll meet him."

I'll . . . meet Randy?

"He makes all my wigs too. Anyway . . ." She looks at the combine again. "Can I climb in this?"

"Well, my dad just broke his arm falling off it, so—"

Aaaand she's climbing the ladder. Fast.

"This is lit!" She pulls open the door and scoots inside the glass-encased cabin. "Can regular people buy these?"

I'm not a hundred percent sure how to tell the world-famous Zay-Zay Waters to *get out of our combine!* But thankfully, I don't have to. Because she climbs down just as quickly.

"So, Red." She leans against the combine wheel and crosses her arms under her chest. "You wonderin' why I'm here?"

"I mean . . ." The thought *is* crossing my mind. "Perhaps. Yes."

"Yo, the way you talk."

Tawk.

"It's very, very proper. Like a news reporter."

My Brooklish is rusty, but I think she insulted me. "Is that a bad thing?"

"Everybody talks how they talk, you know?" She holds out her hands, in defense mode. "I hope that's not offensive. I mean, I grew up in East Flatbush, so we don't have girls that talk like you *there*. But it's cool. You won't never have to speak. 'Cuz that would be a dead giveaway."

"I won't have to speak?" What is happening here? "What do you mean?"

"What I mean." She inhales deeply, holds it, then exhales like she's in a yoga class. "I wanna hire you. To pretend to be me. You will live in my house, have a schedule of events, and, yeah, basically pretend to be me while I'm away on a private matter that I don't want anybody to know about, which is why I need you for exactly one week."

That was quite the run-on sentence. But, "No." The word rushes out of my mouth. "Yeah. No. Nope. There's no way." In fact, "You're joking, right?"

"Nah." She shakes her head, and the curls that look just like mine sway from side to side. "I'm being serious. I want *you* to pretend to be *me*. You'll have a schedule of events for one week."

I pull my hands out of the pockets of my jeans and hold them up. "You see these hands? No one would ever realistically believe that I was you, Zay-Zay. Your teeth alone are like five shades whiter than mine."

"Randy is a full glam squad," she tosses out. "When he gets through with you, we will practically be twins. I'm tellin' you. Plus, none of the events we have scheduled will require you to speak. Pictures only. No talking. *Definitely* no singing. Everything from a distance. We think it can work." She pauses. "Nobody is in here, right?"

I shake my head, and now *my* curls sway from side to side.

"Are you sure?" She places a hand on her hip.

The word *sure* has like four syllables in Brooklish.

"After all, *I* was hidin' behind y'all's concubine machine."

"Combine. And. No one's ever done that before," I say. "Unless you count Norman."

Her brow furrows the way Mom's does when she's sitting with our accountant during tax season. "How do we know Norman's not here now?"

"Norman's a dog," I explain.

She holds up her phone. "The dog in the pic on y'all's website? That's Norman?"

"Was Norman. Yeah." I smile at the memory. You'd almost think Norman knew he was being photographed by a professional. "He was *such* a good dog." The words are spilling out of my mouth before I know how to stop them. "Everybody says that about their dog, but Norman was, like, human. I swear. I'm convinced he didn't know he was a dog. He was born when I was four. Right before Lo and Jax. Can you believe that? My siblings. Twins. I have four. Siblings. Not twins. Sorry." Tears are forming. I get teary whenever I talk about Norman. "I'm getting rambly again."

"You wanna see something seriously crazy?"

Sari-us-lee.

She's scrolling through her phone, and finally lands on a pic of an American bulldog with a brown patch over his left eye. He's not as big as Norman was. But he's got the same gentle aura. "This is *my* dog."

It's not possible. I know everything about Zay-Zay Waters. "You do not have an American bulldog."

"He's new. His name is Tyrone."

I raise an eyebrow.

"It's a human name. I'm aware." She laughs. "He acts human! He's just a puppy, seven months, but I'm tellin' you, this dog has no clue that he's a dog. I know you get it."

Of course I get it. I smile.

"There is something kinda eerie here, Red." She speaks passionately as she pushes off the combine and takes a step closer to me. "Don't you see it?" She points to her forehead. "Remember the bump on my forehead? You had it too. In the *exact* same spot."

I touch my forehead, remembering our matching purple bruises. Certainly another one to be filed under "What are the odds?"

"Is the Universe talking to us here?" Zay-Zay asks. "It's gotta be."

"The Universe is definitely talking," I agree. "Not so sure it's making a whole lot of sense." I stare down at the concrete, contemplating her strange request. "You could hire anybody to dress up like you. You know that, right?"

"That's not true. Honestly, for a second, when I saw your video, I was like, 'Was I on a farm in Iowa and forgot?' We look alike, for *real*. And these paparazzi. They *wild*. Savages. They do anything and everything to get pictures they can sell. And don't get me started on phones. Even *kids* are photographers now, 'cuz the cameras on phones are, like, professional quality." She takes a deep breath. "Basically, my point: they'd be able to spot a fake. *Everybody* thinks the girl in your video is me."

"Not everybody."

"Most everybody. Even my own family. We *literally* look alike."

She steps directly into the sunlight beaming in from the lone sky-light above. For a second, I almost laugh. We're similar, sure. However, she could blend right in among a host of heavenly angels, the way her eyes are now lit up and the sunlight surrounds her like a halo.

"Please say yes." She reaches into her back pocket and takes out a folded sheet of paper, then hands it to me. "Here. It's like twelve events. That's easy, right? It might even end up being kinda fun."

I unfold the page. It's a typed itinerary.

1. Arrive at LAX, pass out golden ticket.
2. Red Carpet at Skybar in Hollywood with Koi.
3. Dinner at Sun and Sand with Koi.

Omigosh! I can't continue reading. "You said I wouldn't have to talk to anyone. Two and three sound like . . . *dates*. With your boyfriend?"

"I swear it's *just* posin' for pictures wit' him. No talkin' involved. I can't let you in on the particulars until you agree and sign an NDA."

"What's an NDA?"

"Nondisclosure agreement. Basically, it's a contract. You break it . . . I can sue you. But it's all good."

Sue me, but it's all good?! "I'm sorry." I toss the itinerary at her like it's on fire. The thought of her boyfriend, Koi Kalawai'a, gazing into my eyes and screaming *Impostor, impostor!* has my skin crawling with anxiety. "It all sounds like . . . too much. Besides, we had to fire our farm manager last week. With him gone, Mom and Dad are completely over-whelmed. Not to mention prepping for our annual Strawberry Festival."

"Is that where you pass out strawberries or somethin'?"

"It's like a carnival. Lasts for a few days. We have rides. Sell food, strawberries too. The whole city usually shows up. It's our big yearly moneymaker." I lean against one of the tractors and stare up at the metal rafters. "My dad's arm is broken. Our main clerk is officially on maternity leave. My little sister won't sleep. My other siblings won't . . . listen. I do a lot around this place." The realization of all I'm turning down is making me *slightly* sick to my stomach. Would there be limos? Fancy clothes for fancy parties? Maybe her glam guy, Randy, could figure out how to get the eternal dirt out from under my nails. That alone would be worth the trip. But still. "I'm really sorry, Zay-Zay. I can't do it."

Her face falls. "You're honestly turning me down?"

In Brooklish, you're = *ya*.

"Bright side," I say. "You got *here* ok without paparazzi trailing you. You could sneak off to where you wanna go. You don't *really* need me."

"Is that what you think?" She fiddles with her phone and shows it to me. I read the headline on the screen.

> Zay-Zay Waters and assistant rent car in Chicago. Is she
> set to revisit farm where she shot her viral promo video
> for *Oh, So You Think You Can Sing Live?*

Wait, what? "They know you're here?"

"I posted a video on the Gram before I came. To distract. It's the first thing I've posted in a week. The paps think I'm at the Sioux Gateway Airport getting ready for takeoff. That's where my plane is parked. But as far as bein' *here*. Nobody knows that. As you can see, though, they always on to me. Always. So, how much, Red?"

"How much?"

"Yeah." She shakes her head. "How much can I *pay* you."

Pay me? Oh. Wait a sec. *Ohhh.* Of course she wants to pay me! My stomach muscles tighten. Why didn't I consider this? With the right amount, Mom and Dad could hire Tony back! "Like, name my price?" I slowly cock my head to the side.

"Let's not go too crazy." She smacks her lips. "I'm not Elon Musk. How about this. Fifty thousand dollars. Cash. Half today. The rest at the end of the week when you finish. But you can't tell your family what you're doing."

Fifty thousand dollars?!!!

"Um . . . my mom and dad would *have* to know."

She sucks her teeth, staring up at the rafters. A few moments pass. "Fine. Tell them. But them *only*. Not the siblings. Your parents gonna have to sign NDAs, too, though. And if word ever gets out about this, through you or someone who knows you, I will sic my legal team on you, your farm . . . all of it. I will make it my personal business to make your lives miserable. Not to mention, that would void our contract, and you'll owe me all the money back."

"Sixty-five thousand," I blurt out, wishing I could be here when Mom and Dad break the news to Tony that he's rehired. "The first half deposited into Morgan Family Farms LLC today. You do that. I'm in."

She smiles. "I have an NDA and a car waitin' in your parkin' lot. After you sign, I'll go over more details. You don't even need to pack. Let's just go."

FIVE

H ey, Mom. You look pretty today."
Mom shakes out a white plastic trash bag. "I look like hell."
She's standing next to a metal bin right at the front door of
our store. "And I'm too tired to delegate. Go and do what you do. We
open in less than an hour."

"Right. Fun stuff. Can't wait. Hey—" I take the trash bag out of
her hands and stuff it quickly into the bin. "Any chance I could talk to
you in your office?"

"You can talk right now." Mom's eyes are so bloodshot she could
be starring in a horror movie. She moves off toward the two registers.

"We'd need privacy for this." I follow close behind, my eyes shifting
as I stake out the store like I'm casing the joint. There's Stan, our deli
guy, wiping down the glass on the seafood cases with soap and water.
And Loren, she's tossing out expired products at the refrigerated foods
section. Both are super focused on their work, but can they hear us?

Mom flips a switch under the register. The computer monitors spring
to life. "Fine, Red. This better be *quick*. We got a lot of work to do."

"It'll be quickish. Hopefully." I grab her gently by the elbow and
guide her around the register. When we move past Loren, we can see
she's eating sushi from one of the plastic boxes we sell.

Mom calls out to her. "Loren Margaret Morgan? Did you pay for that?"

"No, but—" Loren swallows. "It expired yesterday." She grabs another sushi roll, stuffs it in her mouth, and mumbles, "So we can't sell it anyway."

We push through swinging double doors at the back and move into the stockroom. As we near the door of the office, I turn to face Mom.

"Before we enter . . ." I slide my phone from the back pocket of my jeans and bring up the TikTok video Jax showed us. "This happened last week."

I bite my chipped nails, focusing on Mom's face while she watches. The clip ends. "I'm confused. People think you're . . . her?"

"Come. See the resemblance for yourself." I yank open the office door, and we both step inside. The office seems to be empty. Of course, I know better. I pull the door shut and lock it. "Zay-Zay Waters is here. In your office." I call out, "Zay-Zay. No need to hide anymore."

It's quiet. Hmm. Did she leave?

"All right, I see what's happening here." Mom brings her thumb and forefinger together in the universal OK symbol. "Is she standing in front of us, or flying over our heads?" Mom extends her hand, moving it up and down like she's shaking hands with the air in front of her. "Thanks for stopping by, Zay-Zay! Would you like to refill the toilet paper rolls in the bathroom, or should I do it?" Mom laughs like invisible Zay-Zay said something funny, and the real Zay-Zay climbs out from under the office desk. "No, Zay-Zay Waters," Mom says sweetly. "I'm not gonna kill her. She's my daughter."

Zay-Zay looks over at me, and I shrug.

"You must be Gloria," Zay-Zay calls out. "Can I call you Glo Worm? I always liked that nickname."

Mom freezes. She turns very, very slowly to face Zay-Zay.

Zay-Zay waves. "It's very nice to meet you. Your farm is lit."

I'm pretty sure I see Mom's knees wobble, and for a second I think she's about to faint. But thankfully she steadies herself, holding on to the filing cabinet.

"Hello there, Zay-Zay Waters," Mom whispers.

The whisper is actually super creepy. Zay-Zay doesn't seem bothered.

"Hope you don't mind me sneakin' onto y'all's property like this." She moves around the desk and comes to stand beside me. "Did Red fill you in on why I'm here?"

"Not quite the whole story," I say. Mom's left eye is twitching. Her hands are balled into fists, and she's standing on her tiptoes. Oh geez. "Mom? You ok?"

"Hmm?" Her eyes dart back and forth between me and Zay-Zay, like maybe she's not sure which one is her kid. "Sure. Here. Waters. Now. Office. Mm-hmm."

Aaaand now she's throwing out random words, like a caveman.

"Mom, you were right." She loves being right. I'm hoping it helps bring her back to normal. "Turns out I *do* resemble Zay-Zay. Like, a lot."

"Which is why I wanna hire her," Zay-Zay interjects. "To be my stand-in for a week."

Zay-Zay repeats the details. The paparazzi follow her around. She has no privacy. She needs my help. She wants to tend to a secret matter.

Mom raises her hand.

Zay-Zay pauses. "Do you have . . . a question?"

"I do. Sorry." Mom wrings her hands together and rolls back on the heels of her dirty sneakers. "What's the thing you need to tend to? Can we know?"

"Mom," I cut in. "It's obviously private." I turn to the international superstar standing in our cluttered stockroom office space that smells like old meat and metal. "You don't have to answer that."

"Nah, it's cool." Zay-Zay sits on the edge of Mom and Dad's desk. "I'm traveling to Brazil."

Brazil?! "Will you be in Rio?" I can almost see Zay-Zay blending in among all the wild colors of Carnival. Enjoying anonymity for the first time in a long time.

"Rio is wild." Zay-Zay shakes her head. "That would be the last place I'd wanna go. Where I'm going is near Santarém. There's a local shaman I wanna visit. He lives in the rain forest, and he's weird about celebrities visiting his home. 'Cuz it's not a real retreat place, and honestly, I think it's kinda low-key illegal. Like, he doesn't have business paperwork or a license or whatever." She crosses her legs and leans back on the desk. "Anyway. If I'm able to promise him no paparazzi—he hates celebrities—he'll let me come. And I *really* need this break. People who spend time with him. Their life is changed forever."

Ohhh. "Sorta like a wellness retreat center. For healing and stuff like that?" I've definitely heard of celebrities doing that. Regular people, too, sometimes.

"Exactly," Zay-Zay says. "Not much healing and wellness in the jungle, if the paparazzi munchin' on Lay's potato chips, hidin' in their Jeeps, watchin'. You feel me?"

How *noble*. She's trying to better herself.

"Mom, please let me go!" I shout. "I know it'll create a void while I'm gone. Especially with the Strawberry Festival approaching. But we've left out the best part of all of this. She's *paying* me. Enough to hire Tony back."

Mom's look of shock and awe is now replaced with disbelief. "Red, that's not possible. She can't pay you enough to bring back Tony."

"Is Tony the dude who was in y'all's garage?" Zay-Zay asks. "Ain't he already back?"

"Tony's *here*?" Mom raises an eyebrow.

"He came to help Dad with the slaughter this morning."

Mom places a hand over her heart. "That was so *sweet* of him."

I take a step closer to her and speak softly, though I'm aware Zay-Zay can still hear me. "While he's here, you guys can offer him his job back. Sixty-five thousand dollars. It's enough to pay Tony's salary for an entire *year*."

40

Mom shakes her head. "It's too much, Red."

"It's exactly enough. Please, Mom?"

She takes my hand into hers. They're rough, the calluses scratchy. These are the hands of a woman who has always put everyone else's needs ahead of her own.

"Of course I want you to do this." Mom's eyes are welling with tears now. "But do this for *yourself.* Not for us."

But everything I do for me . . . is for them. So suddenly the sun is shining. Birds are flying over my head. Except they're not regular birds. They're eagles. And they're *soaring*. With their seven-foot wingspans, their majestic presence and courage. With their magical ability to rise even above the storms.

"I am doing this for myself." I squeeze her hand. "You're taking the money. For you. Giving Tony his job back, for us. And giving Dad a big hug." Now *my* eyes are welling with tears. "From me."

"How did you become this way? Huh, kid?" Mom wraps her arms around me and holds me tight. The way I hold on to Daeshya at night when she can't sleep. Like maybe my warmth and love will calm her anxious soul and give her the respite she needs.

"Um." Zay-Zay clears her throat. "I hate to break up this, like, majorly touching family moment. But. We gotta go."

Zay gives Mom all the details of the nondisclosure agreement that will be coming from her lawyers. My mind drifts while she talks, wondering what awaits me. Fancy parties? Lavish meals? I look down at the dirt under my nails. It's been there for as long as I can remember. One time, in the seventh grade, a kid made up a song about me.

Red is covered in dust.
With her frizzy red curls.
She has no clothes to wear.
She's the dirty farm girl.

And everybody laughed. But the song never really bothered me. Being the dirty farm girl . . . kinda made me proud. Heck, one time I sang along.

"Red?"

Zay-Zay and Mom are staring at me now. How long have I been in a trance?

"Did I miss something?"

"Just that everything's settled," Mom explains. "I'll fill Dad in later, when he's finished delivering the hog. I'll try to record the moment when we let Tony know he's . . . *not* fired. Not anymore."

I lurch forward and hug Mom again.

"Spread your wings and fly, little butterfly," Mom whispers into my ear. "Or better yet, soar. Like an eagle."

I smile.

"You ready, Red?" Zay-Zay pulls the hood back over her head.

I'm about to live the life of Zay-Zay Waters. I mean, only for a week, but still. How could *anybody* be ready for a moment like this?

"I guess I'm as ready as I'll ever be."

Zay-Zay nods. "Dope. Let's go."

SIX

Boom. I knew it. Pay me, ma'am. Fifty bucks," a guy says as I slide open the door of an old Mercedes van.

I'd guess he's about nineteen years old. He has a shiny bald head and dark-brown skin, and wears cargo shorts and a plain white T-shirt. He's sitting in the seat closest to the window, staring up at me.

"Pay?" I repeat.

"Oh, not you, honey. Her." He points to someone in the driver's seat who seems to be about the same age as him.

"I owe you nothing of the sort." The girl has a head of thick jet-black hair that hangs right above her shoulders and speaks with a strong British accent.

I slide in and nervously pull the seat belt over my shoulder. The guy hands me two sheets of paper. The writing is so tiny I have to squint to read it.

"It's your NDA." He hands me a pen.

"What was y'all bettin' on?" Zay-Zay climbs in behind me.

"I told Aishwarya." The guy stuffs his hands into the pockets of his cargo shorts and stretches his legs. "I said, 'I bet you fifty bucks Zay will be convincing and most definitely return with the doppelgänger.' End quote."

The doppelgänger? They were betting on me?

"And Aish said, 'I bet not,'" the guy continues. "So *I* said, 'Ok, I guess we'll see.' And then she said, 'I suppose we will.'"

"First off," Aishwarya chimes in, "I was playing Wordle on my phone and hardly listening to Randy."

Oh, this is *Randy*?

"Girl, bye." Randy holds up his phone. "You owe me fifty bucks. I prefer Venmo or Cash App. Thank you."

"Don't hold your breath for that transfer, sir." Aishwarya looks closely at me now. "Wow. The resemblance is *uncanny*." She smiles. "You know, some folks say I bear a *slight* resemblance to my namesake, Aishwarya Rai Bachchan."

"Stop." Randy laughs. "Just because you're both Indian and named Aishwarya doesn't mean y'all look anything alike." He turns to me. "Sorry, can I touch you?" He grabs my hands and taps my nails. It makes a *click-click-click* sound. "We can fix these. And I have some stuff, it's called Better-Than-Henna. We will re-create Zay's tattoos. You can scrub at them in the shower. It still won't come off."

"You're doing the makeover on me?" I'm trying to use an even tone to hide the fact that I'm geeking out. I've always wanted a celebrity-style makeover!

"He will." Zay-Zay taps me on the shoulder. "But first, sign."

Oh! "Right." What do I have to lose? I scribble my signature on the bottom of the pages.

"Aish," Zay calls out. "Can you scan the contract on your phone and send it to the lawyers?"

"Copy that, boss." Aish reaches back and takes the papers from my hands.

Randy gently turns me to face him. "Hello, pores. We'll need a HydraFacial. Hair needs a *deep* condition. I'll do a protein treatment on the plane. Do you have allergies?"

"Oh, uh . . ." I think for a second. "Just peanuts. It's a mild allergy. Not anaphylactic shock or anything." Over Randy's shoulder, out the window, our farm seems so far away, though we haven't left the parking lot yet. Did Lyndia wake up Dae? Is Mom overwhelmed opening the store without my help? Has Loren asked about me yet?

Randy unhooks his seat belt and scoots closer, sliding his finger over my eyebrows. "I meant, like, to products and stuff. We'll need to thread these eyebrows. What's your name?"

"Her name is Red. Like the color of her hair. Which is natural, not from a bottle, like mine." Zay-Zay squeezes Randy's shoulder. "Please give her some space." She calls out to Aish. "And Aish, if you finished scannin' the contract, give it back to Red so she can finish reading, and let's go."

Aishwarya hands me the papers, starts up the van, and backs out of the large dirt parking lot that borders our farm and grocery store. In about an hour, the lot will be packed with cars full of people here to shop at the Big Red Barn. I wonder if Mom will have a tough time lying to Lo, Jax, and Eli. We agreed on the story: I'm off to visit Aunt Tiny in Iberia, Missouri. Which is a town of about eight hundred people. A town my siblings act allergic to. This way they won't think I'm having the time of my life but rather helping our aunt on *her* farm. But what if Loren FaceTimes me? What if Daeshya asks for Wed? What if the boys oversleep?

"Red." Zay-Zay interrupts my thoughts. "Now that you've signed, I can tell you about the situation with Koi."

"Oh yikes." Randy grimaces. "You haven't told her about that?"

"I'm about to." Zay-Zay pauses, like she's trying to properly gather her thoughts about her long-term boyfriend that every girl in the observable universe wishes she could date too.

It gives me a second to properly gather my own thoughts about Koi Kalawai'a. I used to have him as the lock screen on my phone. His band, Koi Kalawai'a and the Six, is one of my favorites. Their eclectic new-world sound is seriously refreshing. Koi's got soul. And . . . dreamy green eyes. Silky strands of long black hair. Beautiful, sun-kissed light-brown skin . . .

"Red, are you listening to me?"

"Oh. Uh, yes." I scratch my left elbow. "But could you repeat . . . everything you said?"

"I didn't say much. Just that Koi's not my boyfriend."

Zay-Zay Waters and Koi Kalawai'a broke up? *Noooo!!!* It's like a punch in the chest. Zay and Koi are . . . Zoi. They're relationship goals. "You guys are so good together. Why'd you break up?"

"Technically we're still together," she explains. "Which probably sounds confusing."

It sounds very confusing! "I don't think I get it. I thought you said he's *not* your boyfriend."

"Me and Koi are fake dating. Always have been. Basically, we're a fake couple. We only 'date' for work-related purposes."

It's like a gender reveal gone wrong has exploded in my face, and I'm now choking on pink-and-blue dust particles. How is this possible? "You recorded a song together." I point this out like it might make her undo what she said. "'Together with You' is the greatest love song ever written. I watched you two perform it at the Grammys. The way he gazed into your eyes. That was—"

"Good acting," Aish cuts in.

"It was great acting." Zay yawns, like this conversation is seriously boring her. "All our dates are photo ops. We barely talk."

"What about when you record songs together?" I ask.

"I record my part in LA. He's always in New York." Zay-Zay scrolls through her phone. "Anyway, I'm over all the attention we get. So the fake boyfriend is about to get dumped."

"But—" I swivel around to fully face her. "He'll know I'm not you."

"Nah. He won't. I swear we hardly talk or look at each other. We pose for pictures. That's it. When I get back from Brazil, I'm droppin' the news that it's the end of the road for Zoi." Zay-Zay mocks throwing up. "I always hated that portmanteau. The plan is to not make the breakup a big deal. After your dinner at Sun and Sand, he gonna be on certain red carpets. You gonna be on others. People gonna wonder why. Then I'll drop the bomb that it's over."

The end of the road for *Zoi*? "That's, like, the end of an era," I say sadly. "You realize how devastated everyone is gonna be?"

"They'll get over it." Zay tosses this out like she's pretty much *already* over it. "I'm trying to redirect my career to be less TMZ, more . . . Academy. You feel me?"

Wait till Eileen and Melissa find out. Even Mom will be devastated. Heck, Dad might be too.

"Back to our current situation," Randy cuts in. "What's the plan for getting two Zay-Zays on the plane?"

"That's easy." Zay hands me a plush red sweatshirt from her bag. It has the word **SUPREME** stitched across the front. "*I'm* not getting on my plane. I'm flyin' in a rental. From somewhere close by. Put this on over your T-shirt, Red." She holds up a giant pair of sunglasses. "Put these on when y'all get to the airport." She hands the glasses to me. "And take off those jeans. We can switch. No offense, but nobody gonna believe I would wear those."

Randy covers his eyes to give me privacy, and I unhook my seat belt, kick off my boots, and slide out of my jeans. I pull my She-Ra T-shirt over my butt so none of them will see the striped granny panties I got from the Dollar General. Zay passes me her sleek black jeans, and I quickly pull them on. *Whoa.* Are these lined with butter? My jeans are like construction paper compared to designer duds!

"Can I come out now?" Randy asks, his hand still over his eyes.

Zay bops him on the head. "Boy, you been out since, what, 2003?"

He laughs. "Way before that." He tugs on my sweatshirt and whistles. "Can I call you Little Red now? 'Cuz the hood is super on brand."

"Aish." Zay-Zay shimmies into a pair of stylish sweatpants from her bag. "Type 'Ed's Tire and Lube' into the GPS. That's where we're going first. There's a car waiting for me there. Zack is driving me to a private airstrip where the rental plane is parked."

"Copy that." Aish maneuvers the steering wheel with one hand while the other attempts to fiddle with her phone. Randy quickly snatches it away.

"No texting and driving *please*." He finishes typing out the address into Aish's phone. "We'd prefer to make it to Los Angeles *alive*."

Los Angeles? I guess with all the commotion, I forgot to let it sink in that I'm flying to Los Angeles! I've always wanted to visit California! Will I get to go to Disneyland? See the ocean for the first time? Walk Hollywood Boulevard?

A hand rests on my shoulder. It's Zay-Zay's. She's leaning over the seat. She smells like a basket of flowers.

"Red, you ready for this?"

Zay-Zay Waters should not be trusting me so soon. To *be* her. "Don't I need, like, practice?"

"It's a four-hour flight." Zay-Zay stuffs her hair into an oversize beanie. "You got time to practice."

This is all happening so fast. This is all *happening*. Even getting onto a plane seems like the most daunting task. What if there's a fan? What if they ask for my autograph? Should I ignore them? Wouldn't that be rude? A hand tugs at my hair. It's Randy.

"When's the last time you had a trim?" he asks. "I think you need one."

A trim? I shake my head in horror. "Never." I've never been to a hair salon. "I'm letting it grow as long as Rapunzel. It's my signature. Red is long hair and . . . red. You know?"

He pulls one of my curls, and it extends far past my shoulders, almost to the middle of my back. "Oh wow, your hair *is* long." He lets it go, and it springs back in place. "And bouncy."

"Stop bothering her." Zay-Zay slaps Randy's hand away. "Sorry, Red. Randy doesn't get that nobody wants him that close."

We ride for the next few minutes in silence. I stare out the window, studying the different hues of green on the oak and hickory trees as we whiz by. The last time we made the drive down this stretch of highway toward Sioux Gateway Airport, we were all headed to Meramec Caverns in Sullivan, Missouri. Jax and Loren were only seven and so enthralled with every detail about traveling that their never-ending questions drove me to bang my head against the car window. Eli was four and cried when we boarded the plane because he thought we were inside of a bird. He kept asking what would happen if the bird "throw'd us up."

"Did you get the messages from Susan?" Aish asks Zay-Zay. "She's unhappy about you passing on the movie. Wants you to reconsider."

"I don't care what she wants. I wanna be in movies, but not that one." Zay-Zay's hunched over her phone. "Why are they still makin' these movies? What is it now, *The Fast and the Furious Forty-Five*? Plus, I don't even like cars. Or Dubai. Which is where they're shootin'."

"I *love* those movies." I cover my mouth. "Oops. Sorry. I didn't mean to interrupt. But you could be in the next *Fast and the Furious*? That's so cool!"

"See there? The common folk love them," Aish calls out.

I twist around to face Zay-Zay. "Why don't you wanna do the movie? They're all so good."

"*Good* is relative, doll." She smirks. "I wanna be like Jennifer Hudson and do movies where I can win an Academy Award."

My eyes shift to the screen of her phone. She has 587 unread text messages. *Whoa.*

"What she say about the *other* film?" Zay-Zay scrolls through, deleting texts. "With Lee Taylor Thompson. I *love* him. I gotta work with him someday, for real."

I'm pretty sure she means Taylor Thompson Lee. And *everybody* loves him.

"It's Taylor Thompson Lee." Randy laughs. "If you love him so much, girl, learn the man's name."

Zay playfully punches Randy on the shoulder. "Whatever. It was close enough."

"Isn't your pretend boyfriend friends with Taylor Thompson Lee?" Randy asks.

My stomach sours at the thought of Koi Kalawai'a and our upcoming fake dates. Like those moments when the roller coaster is finally lurching into movement and the person running the machine is waving at you and you swear they're mouthing the words "So long, sucker!"

"Have *him* set up a meeting with Taylor," Randy suggests.

"I don't need a handout from *Koi*." Zay makes a face. "My agents gotta keep trying."

"Actually . . . ," Aish calls out sadly. "Taylor Thompson Lee cast the girl who played Shadow Weaver in the She-Ra film. They announced it on Deadline this morning. Sorry, Zay."

"Boo. I hate her." Zay-Zay smacks her lips. "And, she already *has* an Academy Award."

"Quite possibly the reason they cast her," Aish adds.

"That girl who played Shadow Weaver." I have no idea why I *continue* to butt into this conversation. "I'm not a fan. She overacts. You're way better than her." I mean, technically I've never seen Zay-Zay in a movie. But I've seen *all* her videos. She's so effortlessly *expressive*. Her song "Believe"—it makes me wanna cry just thinking about it.

Zay-Zay doesn't really reply to what I said. She only nods. Like my compliment means about as much to her as all the texts she's deleting. Her phone rings.

"What about you?" Randy asks softly so he doesn't disturb Zay-Zay, who is now on a call, chatting. "You can *sing*. You wanna be in movies? Perform on tour? What's your goals?"

"I'm a farmer," I declare proudly. "My parents are farmers. My grandparents too. My *great*-grandparents grew sugarcane in Louisiana." I tug at my hair. "That's where I got the red hair from."

"From sugarcane?" Randy blinks.

"No." I smile. "From my great-grandma. She's Creole. *Her* dad, my great-great, was from Haiti. A farmer too. I'm named after my great-grandma. Her name was Florence. So I'm Red Florence Morgan. And the fact that I'm Creole and have distant cousins in Louisiana and never visited . . . that's sad, huh?"

Randy blinks a few more times, like he's trying to make sense of all that. "So you speak Creole?"

"Haitian Creole. Little bit." I nod. *"Kisa ou ta renmen fe?"*

"Oh, the accent is *flawless.*" Randy claps his hands together like a kid sitting over a giant slice of birthday cake and turns to Zay-Zay, who's still on the phone. He whispers, "Love, she speaks *Creole.*"

Zay-Zay gives him an annoyed wave like, *Please stop talking.*

"I said that wrong," I add. "I meant to say, *What do you want me to say?* I said, *What do you want to do?*" I knock on my forehead with my knuckles. "My dad's fluent. Me and my siblings, not so much."

"All sounds the same to me." Randy stares at me like I'm a work of art instead of dusty, dirty, and fresh off a farm. Maybe he knows his work is cut out for him. It's gonna take more than a HydraFacial to make my skin as shiny as Zay-Zay's.

"What?" I touch my cheeks. "Do I have something on my face?"

"Face? No. But you do overenunciate. It intrigues me."

"I do?" Nobody has ever told me that before.

"She does not!" Aish looks over her shoulder. "Ignore him, Red. I fancy the way you speak. It's proper. Most Americans speak as if they're starring in a gangster movie."

"Red sounds like a newscaster." Randy crosses his legs. "I know you can do accents. Do Zay, like you did on the video."

"Oh no." I shake my head. "No way."

"Please?" Aish adjusts the rearview mirror so she can see me. "You did a perfect impersonation."

Impersonate Zay-Zay Waters *with* Zay-Zay Waters sitting right behind me? "No. I can't. I don't want to be offensive."

"It won't offend me." Zay-Zay is off the phone now. "And you do sound like a newscaster. Thankfully you won't ever have to talk this week. Let's hear it anyway."

"Um . . ." I have three sets of eyes staring at me. Waiting. I don't want to disappoint, but I'm not an actor. Although . . . being an actor sure would be cool. "Uh . . ." I clear my throat and put on my best Brooklish. "Aight bet. It's like, whateva, you feel me? Y'all not hearin' me. We 'bought to do dis. That's on everything."

Awn air-ee-thang.

It's silent for a moment in the van. Then Randy starts clapping, and Aish cheers.

"Oh my gosh!!" Randy bounces up and down in his seat, slightly shaking me in the process. "You sound *just* like Zay!"

"Agreed." Aish nods. "Brilliant. Spot on."

I could be imagining it, but when I look to Zay-Zay for *her* approval, her face falls flat. She seems unimpressed, maybe a bit . . . annoyed. But the moment passes.

She gives me a curt smile and mumbles, "It was aight." She turns her attention back to her buzzing phone.

Did I offend her? Should I apologize? I seriously could kick myself for doing my best Zay-Zay. What was I thinking?! Rambling to Randy about my grandparents? And then I brought up my *great*-grandparents? Who does that?! Am I striking out here? I tap Randy on the shoulder.

"Hmm?" He turns to me.

I whisper, "Sorry about all the rambling about my family history and stuff. I didn't mean to bore you."

"It's *fascinating*." He smiles genuinely. "Tell me more. I wanna know everything about you."

"Randy, are you gonna miss me?" Zay-Zay's now hanging off the van seat, so she's sort of between me and Randy now.

"Are you kidding?" Randy frowns. "I won't be able to text you, 'cuz you'll be in the *jungle*. What I'm s'pose ta' do? Hmm?"

As the two chat it up, and the van speeds across the freeway, I get a text from Loren.

Can't believe you're stuck helping Aunt Tiny for a week. And why didn't you say bye? 😕 Remind her I'm still the reigning Skipbo champion! Call me every day!

I stare at the text and scratch at my elbows. Lying to Loren is not going to be easy. Another text comes in from her.

Also. Why does Daeshya hate me? What am I doing wrong? 😕 Miss you already.

Zay-Zay's hand reaches over my shoulder and snatches my phone. I spin around.

"You can't have your phone," she explains. "It's in the NDA."

I can't have my phone? "You mean the NDA that I haven't had a chance to read?"

Zay-Zay zips up her hoodie. "You should read it now."

I do a quick scan of the contract. Most of it is language I can't understand.

Unauthorized disclosure . . .

Inadequate or difficult to ascertain . . .

Obtaining an injunction?

But when I flip to the second page, a list of things I'm not allowed to do is in bold and spelled out in simple language:

During time representing Zay-Zay Waters, I give up the right to speak on her behalf, sing on her behalf, or communicate with a private cell phone to friends and family members.

"Zay-Zay, this is unreasonable."

"How so?" She narrows her eyes like I'm really starting to get on her nerves.

Maybe Jax and Elijah would be ok not hearing from me. Melissa and Eileen . . . perhaps. But . . . "I can't *not* speak to my parents and sister for a week."

"FaceTimin' people and stuff like that? Nah. It would be a huge violation of my privacy. No offense. You seem nice and all. But real talk." She leans back in the van seat. "I barely know you. I'm takin' a huge gamble havin' a total stranger in one of my homes. And with a phone? C'mon. Be for real."

Ok, maybe she has a point. Most people probably would live stream and blab all this to the world. But, "I'm not most people. You can trust me."

"That remains to be seen," she says.

The van exits the highway. I hear the robotic voice of Aish's GPS: *"In two hundred feet, turn right. Then, the destination will be on your right. Ed's Tire and Lube."*

"I won't FaceTime. That's fine." There is a desperation in my voice that feels foreign. I mean, maybe sometimes I plead to Mom and Dad about this, that, or the other. Let me stay out past my curfew. Let me stay up late. But this feels like life or death. Not able to really and truly communicate with my family? Loren has nightmares sometimes. Mom gets stressed. Dad . . . depressed. They need me! "You know what? Take me back home. Now."

The van slows to a stop in front of an out-of-commission car shop. The windows and doors are boarded up. In the parking lot is a lone dusty black Ford Explorer with tinted windows.

"Ma, you playin' wit' me." Zay-Zay sits up tall, glaring. "You not bein' for real."

I'm not. But she doesn't know that. I lean my head back and sigh. I imagine Tony's face right now, back at work, doing the job he does so well. Dad, giddy from having the help he needs. My throat is closing on me. I can't get a good breath. I know so much is at stake.

"I'm for real," I lie. "I really want to help you out. But I can't be cut off from my family for a week." I pick up the NDA with shaking hands and hand it to Zay-Zay. My heart is beating so fast, like I took a drop on Pirate's Plunge at Wacky Waters. Can I speak ever again? Have I lost my voice forever? Did I really challenge Zay-Zay Waters? "Thank you for the opportunity. Take me home."

Randy and Aish sit quietly, staring with wide eyes, probably wondering how loud Zay-Zay is about to scream. When she finally does speak, she's cool, calm, and quite collected.

"Every evening you can exchange texts and calls with your family only. No video calls, period. Aish or Randy will monitor. Like, literally sit beside you. Your phone will be locked in my safe when you not usin' it. Here." She extends my phone to me. "Let your family know the deal. *If* we have a deal. Do we?"

I take the phone. Loren's text sits so heavy on my heart. I type out a quick reply.

I'll help you with Dae, promise. I miss you too. Will be away from my phone 'til this evening. Text you guys then. Love you so much sissy.

"We have a deal. And I promise . . ." I hold up the phone for Zay-Zay to read the text. "You can trust me." I place my cell into Randy's outstretched hand and watch him power it off.

Zay exhales. "Aish, pull up. It's Zack, so you don't gotta worry."

Aish pulls into the lot and parks beside the Explorer. Zay-Zay puts on a pair of oversize sunglasses and slides her bag over her shoulder.

"Please text me when you land." Randy's wringing his hands together nervously.

"Relax, Randy. I'mma be cool. You focus on Red." She leans forward and hugs him. "Aish," she calls out. "Stay British."

"As if I have *any* choice in that matter," Aish replies.

"And you," Zay-Zay says to me. For the first time since I met her a few hours ago, she seems a bit . . . uncertain. "Thank you. For givin'

me a chance to do better for myself. To . . . find myself. It means a lot."
She slides open the van door. "Also. Make me look good."

Make Zay-Zay Waters look good? That's a tall order.

"I'll do my best." I hope I sound convincing.

She climbs down onto the pavement and pulls the van door closed, yanks open the back door to the Explorer, and quickly hops in. Within a few seconds, the SUV is driving out of the parking lot, and Zay-Zay Waters is officially off to destinations unknown.

SEVEN

Sioux Gateway Airport seems like business as usual. A security guard drinks a Red Bull in his booth. A few people drag luggage toward the entrance. Cars search for open spaces in the parking lot. No one would ever guess there are paparazzi lurking in the shadows here. Are there? Aish lowers the window as we pull up beside the security booth.

"Hello." She puts the van into park and unhooks her seat belt. "We're not boarding commercial. Could you point us to the private hangar?"

"Private hangar?" The security guard tries to peek inside.

I yank my hood on.

"FBO," Aish says. "Fixed-base operator? You're aware that private jets fly out of this airport, are you not? The airport has ramp access."

"Ramp what?" The security guard lifts his drink and takes a long swig before scratching his head. "Just park your car, check in like everybody else."

I hear Aish mumble "Incompetent" under her breath. "Thanks so much for all your help." The window rises, and as she pulls off, she mutters, "By *thanks for your help*, I rather mean thanks for nothing."

She maneuvers the van into a parking space.

"How can airport security not know if they have ramp access?" Randy asks.

"These security guards are mostly decoration." Aish turns off the ignition. "I suppose we'll do an old-fashioned check-in, since these small-town *imbeciles* won't let us drive onto the tarmac."

"Aish gets systems rage when businesses don't act right," Randy whispers as Aish, frustrated, grabs her things from the passenger seat. "It's like road rage but with*out* screams. You'll see."

"Red, speak to no one. I mean that. Keep your head down as much as you can." Aish pulls a leather backpack over her shoulder. "Randy . . ."

"Girl, you know I know what to do." Randy scoots around me and slides open the van door.

He extends a hand, helping me onto the pavement. I quickly realize Iowa's humid summers are not meant for thick sweatshirts with hoods. Sweat is already dripping down my back. And my arms. Is this an airport parking lot or a sauna? Plus, my nose is starting to run, since I've been staring down at the concrete, and my neck already hurts from hunching over.

"You ok, boo?" Randy whispers as we walk behind Aish.

So far, so miserable. "I'm ok."

I wipe my nose with the back of my sleeve—well—Zay-Zay's sleeve. Randy places a hand on my shoulder, and I swear he feels like a giant *oak* of comfort. May he never leave my side.

Click-clack, click-clack. My boots sound like tiny firecracker explosions against the walkway as Randy and I almost run to keep up with Aish. Maybe Zay-Zay and I should have exchanged shoes too. Would she wear these old things? Are paparazzi taking pictures right now?

We make our way to the double doors of the terminal. They slide open. Thank goodness no one really pays much attention to us as we maneuver through the quiet airport and approach one of the open counters. I listen as Aish explains our details to a young attendant.

"Whoa." The attendant holds up her hands. "Let's start with your IDs." She must be referring to me when she adds, "Remember to remove your glasses and take off your hood before going through TSA."

IDs? TSA! I grabbed nothing when I left. How am I supposed to get on a plane without an ID? I tug on Aish's shirt.

"Yes?" She turns to face me.

"My ID," I whisper. "It's at home."

"No, silly goose. It's with me."

Huh? Did my mom give my license to Zay-Zay and not tell me?

Aish turns back to the attendant. "We're exempt from TSA." She reaches into her bag and places three IDs on the counter. I peek over her shoulder. Zay-Zay's ID? Wait, I'm using Zay-Zay's ID? Wouldn't that be . . . illegal?!

"Everyone here goes through TSA," the attendant explains. "Sorry."

"Have you not recently boarded individuals onto a private jet?" Aish sounds very irritated. "Please check our IDs before you answer that."

It's silent for a moment. The attendant stares down at our IDs. Her head shoots up, and she looks right into my eyes. My . . . sunglasses.

"Zay-Zay Waters?" she whispers. "No *way*."

It's suddenly very hot in here. I tug on my sweatshirt to blow air around.

"Yes, way," Aish replies. "Obviously you can't expect her to be patted down by TSA while they sneak selfies with their smartphones."

"They wouldn't do that. I'll have to ask about this." She calls to another attendant. "Um . . . Jenny?"

"Yeah?" The other attendant looks up from her station. "You need help?"

"We're fine, Jenny." Aish waves. "You're killing it over there. Keep up the good work."

Jenny seems confused, but she returns to whatever she was doing.

"Jenny won't be helping us today. You will," Aish says to the first attendant, barely above a whisper. "Are you aware of the McBrane Lend

Act? Instated by the United States Supreme Court in 1997? Or are subordinate airport employees not properly trained in Iowa?"

The attendant shakes her head. "I don't understand . . . what you asked me."

"Oh, well then, let me *help* you understand." Aish speaks with an eerie authority. This must be the *systems rage* Randy told me about. "And trust that I know what I'm talking about, because I'm studying for my citizenship test and probably know more about United States laws than you do."

"Uh." The attendant blinks. "O . . . k?"

"The McBrane Lend Act established the right of anonymity in regard to information spread by individuals, public or private, *and* unauthorized disclosures in regard to autonomies regarding travel." She leans forward. "Zenaria Waters is to be granted special privacies not simply by McBrane Lend but under HGIT, Federal PTI, and any other applicable laws that specify privacy, security, and security *breach*. Would you like a mob of starstruck travelers descending upon us? Would that give you *pleasure*? It would be a shame to see your job on the line, should any of these laws be violated, wouldn't it? Shall I email your super once we're boarded? I hope it isn't *Jenny!*"

The attendant blinks, looking like a deer in headlights. "Super?"

"Your boss," Randy cuts in. "Sorry, she's British."

"No." The attendant begins typing furiously. "She'll write me up again. I can handle this."

"*Brilliant.*" Aish drops the keys to the van on the counter. "And if you could handle the return of our rental, too, that would be lovely."

The attendant taps a few additional buttons on her keyboard, then slides the IDs back across the counter before snatching up the rental keys. "I'll just say she's a foreign dignitary." A final tap on her keyboard, followed by a look over both shoulders. "You don't need help with luggage?"

Aish holds up an empty hand. "Already on the plane."

"Right, ok." The attendant lifts a section on the counter, which allows us to move through to where she's standing. Her eyes rest on me when she says, "This way."

She pulls open a door with the words AIRPORT EMPLOYEES ONLY, and we follow her to the other side, travel down a narrow hallway and around a corner, and push through another door. Where we land is your average check-in gate. Except we're the only ones here. To our right, through the glass wall, we can see a beautiful white private jet out on the tarmac. This must be Zay-Zay's plane. It looks so sleek and shiny. Like someone hand polished it.

"After you, Ms. Waters." Aish pushes open the door.

Ms. Waters? Oh! That's me.

I move toward Aish, but the attendant whispers, even though no one is around. "Zay-Zay?"

I turn to face her, my head still angled toward the floor. Oh gosh. My stomach tightens. She's *talking* to me! What do I do?!

"Could I at least shake your hand? I'm such a fan. Your song 'Believe' helped me during a really rough time in my life. It was like you understood my story."

I know the song. Who doesn't know "Believe"? Zay-Zay wrote it for a movie about a little girl battling an incurable disease. *That* song is *this* girl's story? Tears slide down the attendant's cheeks. She wipes at them.

"Please shake my hand. Please . . . talk to me?"

I'm not allowed to talk! And if she shakes my hand, she'll see the dirt and chipped nails. Feel the rough farmer hands of Red Morgan. Not the soft celebrity hands of Zay-Zay Waters.

But . . .

Zay-Zay also told me to make her look good. What better way to do that than acknowledging the request of a fan who has boldly declared that a song about fighting to live another day is her song too. Zay-Zay would *not* want to let this girl down. I pull my sleeves over my farmer hands, lurch forward, and hug her.

"It's nice meetin' you. For real." I say it softly, in my best Brooklish, before turning and rushing out the door.

I'm hurrying across the tarmac toward the plane when Randy comes up behind me.

"Omigosh, *girl*." He grabs me by the arm to slow me down.

"I know, I know," I mumble. "I wasn't supposed to do that."

"You actually *convinced* her, though," Randy says in amazement. "She was crying so hard."

Now Aish has caught up to us.

"You were instructed not to speak," she whispers.

"I know, but—"

"It's quite all right." She squeezes my shoulder. "This is working. It's *working*. So impressed by you."

I grin as we walk together. Aish is not upset with me. Yay! "I'm impressed by *you*. How did you know about all those laws?"

"Oh, I made that stuff up. Barely remember half of what I said to her."

"Aish is queen when it comes to rambling out randomness that means nothing but scares people." Randy laughs. "She could probably get us into the Pentagon. And it's crazy, 'cuz the girl don't really wanna be a personal assistant."

"That's right. I hope to be a publicist someday. That's the real dream." Aish stops at the base of the jet's stairs. "You're about to meet Diamond, Zay's aunt and manager. She seems terrifying. I mean . . . she actually *is* quite terrifying."

Aish leaves me with that, climbs the stairs, and steps onto the plane.

I marvel at the jetliner for a moment. It's almost glimmering, like there are crushed diamonds in the white paint. Would it be weird if I reached out and touched it? I've never been this close to a private jet before.

"Girl," Randy whispers. I turn to face him. "There are *always* cameras. Zay-Zay does not gaze at her plane. Just get on."

Oh shoot. Right. "Copy that."

I rush up the stairs and step through the archway, pausing to catch my breath. Of course I've never been *inside* a private jet before either. It's like all things rich and famous threw up in here.

The seats aren't arranged in rows like on a regular plane but rather are facing each other. And they're movie-theater-style seats. Leather and cushy. There are tables, too, and a lounge area featuring a giant flat-screen TV that somehow seems embedded into the wall of the plane. A door to a bathroom is open, and I can see inside—there's a sink, a shampoo bowl, a *shower*? People shower on airplanes?

"Whoa." I stand in awe for a moment. Taking in the unbelievable *decadence*. "A person could live on this thing."

"That's Diamond over there," Aish says in a hushed tone. "She's your manager and aunt. There are pilots in the cockpit, so pretend you know her. Also, stop acting so gobsmacked."

I don't know what *gobsmacked* means, so I just close my mouth. Seated on one of the leather couches is a woman talking on her cell. Probably the same age as my mom, though they couldn't be more different. Mom wears sneakers, jeans, and grocery-store aprons, and she keeps her hair braided so she won't have to deal with it. This lady wears a skintight pencil skirt that hangs just over the knee and sleek black shoes with heels so long and pointy they could double as weapons, paired with a meticulously tailored button-up silk shirt. All she needs is a leather jacket and she's one of the cast members from *The Matrix*.

I wave. "Hi. Nice to . . ." Oh wait. I already know her. "See you. Again. Auntie?"

If this lady was on our farm or at our store, I'd think she was *lost*. Nobody who dresses like her comes anywhere near us.

"Let me call you back." She ends her call and speaks directly to Aish. "Her nails."

"Oh, don't worry," Randy cuts in. "I'm on it."

"And the hair?" Diamond stands. "The frizz?"

"Deep condition and protein treatment." Randy steps around me. "By the time we land, she will look like a million bucks."

Diamond inhales deeply before making a disgusted face. "And the smell."

Oh no she didn't! It's true I didn't take a shower this morning, and yes, I'm fresh off a farm. And ok, I live next to a hog barn! But do I smell?

Randy places a comforting hand on my shoulder. "C'mon, doll. Let's get started on those tattoos. There's a shower on the plane. Maybe a good idea before we ink you up."

I want to say, *It was nice to meet you, too, Diamond*, though it was actually quite frightening. But she's supposed to be my aunt and manager. So I say, "Happy to be here."

She nods.

~

"Let me know if the water's too hot." Randy massages the conditioner out of my hair. He's been hard at work since before we took off. Nails. Fake tattoos. Facial. I'm leaning back in the shampoo bowl. The hot water is relaxing on my scalp, and the conditioner smells like sage, tea tree oil, and . . . oranges.

Aish steps around me to hand Randy a plush purple towel. "Got a text from Zay." She speaks softly, even though the two pilots are in the cockpit and only peeked out to introduce themselves briefly before we took off. "Made it to the rental plane. She's en route."

"I hope this trip is worth all the trouble." Randy wraps the towel tightly around my head. "That shaman better be able to do amazing things."

Speaking of people doing amazing things, I stare down at my hands. The tattoos Randy drew are *identical* to Zay-Zay's. "Randy, you're an artist. I'm so impressed."

"Thank you, doll. Better-Than-Henna is my own creation. I got the formula patented and am in negotiations for a deal with NYX Professional Makeup."

NYX? Wow. I see those products everywhere in Orange City. "Pretty cool."

"Yeah." He shrugs. "I don't know if it's gonna happen. I'm hopeful, though. You can shower, scrub at them. They won't come off unless you use my special solution." Randy taps my back. "Let's move out to the styling chair. And you can take off those whitening strips."

I peel them off, toss them into the trash, and follow Randy to the far corner of the plane, where I sit in a styling chair set in front of vanity mirrors. When he pulls the towel off my head, my curls fall onto my shoulders. I barely recognize them.

"*Shiny.* Wow." I reach to touch my hair, but Randy softly slaps my hand away.

"Only the artist can touch right now." He moves his hands through my hair so my head sort of rocks back and forth and sprays the ends with something in a blue bottle that smells like cherries. I gaze into the mirror. I really am becoming Zay-Zay!

The plane shakes from slight turbulence as Randy reaches under a cabinet, pulls out a blow-dryer, and twists on an attachment with tiny knobs on the end. I know these are called diffusers, though I've never used one before. I watch in the mirror as he sets the ends of my wet hair on top of the diffuser knobs. The sleek blow-dryer barely makes a sound.

"Randy?" I call out over the soft whir.

"Hmm?" he replies.

"How come you guys don't seem nervous? This might not work."

"You're a real-life look-alike. How could it go wrong?"

I could give Randy about 267 ways it could go wrong! Or maybe just one. "What if Koi can see I'm not . . . her?"

Randy laughs. "Koi Kalawai'a has one thing on his mind: Koi Kalawai'a. Trust me. He and Zay-Zay barely speak to one another. Ignore him. That's what Zay does."

On the other side of the plane, Aish and Diamond sit talking at a table. I accidentally make eye contact with Diamond. I swear she's like a superhero with the power to send messages of hate with her evil glare.

"What about Diamond?" I whisper. "I don't think she likes me."

He leans, speaking softly. "Honey, that woman really only likes a few people. And none of them are on this plane."

"Can't she at least be nice? It's not like I asked to be here."

"Underneath all that ice is a heart. She might not show it. But she appreciates you for helping. A lot of celebrities go to the dark side. We don't want that for Zay." Randy sets another chunk of my hair onto the diffuser. "You're our hero. Diamond knows everything. Trust and believe she knows that too."

A hero? Nobody has ever called me that before. Unless you count the time two of our chickens escaped and I led the family search with a flashlight in the backwoods that border our property. When I found them roosting on a low branch, Mom called me a hero. It *was* after midnight, though, and she seemed kinda delirious, to be honest.

"May I see your hands, Red?"

Diamond is standing at my side. It's the first sentence she's spoken to me during these hours flying to LA.

I present my newly manicured hands. They're foreign to me. Would I be able to clean the coop with these things attached to my fingers? The tips of the nails are so pointy, I might accidentally *stab* one of the chickens.

"Excellent work, Randy." She slides on a pair of glasses that hangs around her neck and takes my hands into hers, studying the tattoos like she's not Diamond Waters but a diamond *dealer* and I'm a rare new find. For the first time in . . . ever, I don't worry that someone is feeling my calluses. Randy spent an hour basically shaving them off.

"I went for simple elegance. It'll match her look for Skybar." Randy flips off the diffuser and leans over my shoulder. "It's an acrylic overlay. Classic French with rhinestone accents. Stiletto tips, but I went shorter 'cuz she's never had fake nails before."

"Simple, but elegant. Very Zay," Diamond replies. "Major improvement."

"And the tattoos? Sick, right?" Randy's beaming. "I took so many pictures so I could get them just right."

"You never fail to amaze me, Randy." Diamond studies my hair now. "She has nice hair."

She says *she* like I'm a species and not a girl with a name sitting right in front of her.

"She don't even know it." Randy flips the diffuser back on. It whirs softly. "I worked for hours to make Zay's hair like this, and Red's is the same straight out the bowl. It's amazing."

"I like *your* hair," I say to Diamond, hoping to get on her good side somehow. I'm not entirely blowing smoke. I do like her hair. Her curls are super defined, feminine and classy. "Also, I took a shower. Hope the farm smell is gone. I blame the hogs." I laugh so she'll think there are no hard feelings. And really, how can I have hard feelings? They set everything up for me. All the toiletries I could ever need, including a bottle of shower gel that smelled like pineapples and mangos and made me feel like I was on an island instead of navigating turbulence while stuffed inside a tiny shower. They also had comfy shoes for me to wear, with **FENDI** written across the tips. Plus, I'm currently rocking leggings with **LULU** on the right leg. Not sure who that is, but the black T-shirt I'm wearing feels like silk. Though I'm pretty sure it's cotton. Since Diamond is also wearing all black, I add, "We match now. We're the All Blacks."

She blinks.

"You know. The rugby team in New Zealand?"

Her eyes shift to Randy. "We should go over details. Especially for the first red carpet."

"So cool I'm gonna be on red carpets! I mean, oops." I look over at the closed cockpit door. It's not like the pilots can hear me. I switch over to my fake Brooklish accent anyway. "I mean, red carpets? It's what I do, son! Kna mean?"

"Talk less," Diamond replies. "Please."

Ugh. I'm totally striking out with her. I pretend to zip my lips shut.

She turns her attention back to Randy. "Who is she wearing at Skybar?"

"The asymmetrical Prabal Gurung," Randy replies. "It's perfect for poolside. Flowy and summery."

Diamond nods. "I'll text Shannon about the dinner with Koi."

Dinner?! I mime unzipping my lips and raise my hand. "Hi. Sorry, I know I'm supposed to be talking less. But. Dinner? I thought they were all photo ops."

"It is a photo op," Diamond explains. "You won't actually be eating."

"Oh." I exhale. "Ok, cool." I mime zipping my lips again.

Diamond seems to be studying me now. "Red?"

She's talking to me again? I unzip my lips. "Yes?"

"Please stop doing that." She sighs. "When you're finished with Randy, let's you and I have a little chat. How does that sound?"

Um . . . scary? "Sounds perfect." I toss her a thumbs-up. "Can't wait!"

She moves to her seat on the other side of the plane. I look in the mirror and mouth to Randy, "Help me."

He covers his mouth to stifle a laugh as he leans to whisper in my ear. "When it comes to Diamond Waters, she's all bark. No bite. Unless you mess with Zay. Then she'll come for you. Keep doing what you're doing. You'll be fine."

I exhale.

~

Diamond's sitting across from me. Holding a tablet computer. Scrolling. Not speaking. I flip the tab on a can of vanilla cream soda. When I bring the can to my lips, a bump of turbulence sends the soda down my shirt instead of into my mouth.

"Oops."

"Do you need a paper towel?" Diamond asks.

I dab at my shirt. "I'm good."

She's quiet again. Scrolling. On the other side of the plane, Aish and Randy laugh and chat together like they're the best of friends, which, I imagine, they are.

"So . . ." I take another sip of soda. Thankfully, the can finds my mouth this time. "Are we talking about my schedule? Clothes? Red carpets? I was practicing posing in the bathroom. It's funny because just yesterday, which is super random, I was watching a video on *smizing*. You know, smiling with your eyes." I demonstrate for her, stretching out my eyes. "Do my eyes appear happy?"

She flips the tablet around and shows me a collage of pictures.

Whoa. I stop midsmize and sit up. "That's our farm."

"Yes. It is." She scrolls through more pics. Our store. Our machine shed. "Did you know your parents refinanced the home on your farmland last year?"

They did? "Are you sure about that? They never told me."

"You'll learn someday—we don't always tell our children the things we do. It was a cash-out refi. They used the extra money to build the machine shed on the property and make repairs on your greenhouses."

"Ok." I remember the repairs. The machine shed build too. "I guess I'm confused. Why are you telling me this? How do you know this?"

"The refinance left them upside down on their loan." She leans back coolly in her chair. "Do you know what that means, Red?"

"Not really. No."

"It means they owe more than the home is worth."

Oh. "That doesn't sound good."

"It's not. And I haven't even gotten to the financial woes of the farm, the store—"

"Hold on a sec." I'm hot again. Did somebody crank up the heat on this plane? "Did you send people to snoop into my parent's finances? With respect, that's a terrible invasion of our privacy."

"I couldn't agree more. It is a gross invasion."

"Ok?" I ball my hands into fists. Something I do to redirect tension. "Why do it, then?"

"To prove a point. This is what the mainstream media does to my niece. They dig into her personal affairs. In their case, they take that information and spread it across the news for people's entertainment. How do you think that makes Zay-Zay feel? Hmm? How do *you* feel right now, with me having the capability to do something similar?"

Something similar? "So." I take another sip from my can of soda to wet my throat, which now feels as dry as hot sand. "What are you planning to do with the information about my parents and their farm?"

"Considering your family has a possible deal with a distributor for their oats—"

"Wait, *what*?" A distributor? My eyebrows rise. "Like, our oats will be in other stores . . . besides ours?"

"With a fancy logo on the box and everything. Should it succeed, it could quite literally save your farm. But trust me when I say this: no one wants to do business with a sinking ship." She speaks pointedly. "Should you violate the NDA and purposely harm my niece's reputation, I will spread this information and get your family's farm quickly canceled."

I feel the plane begin to descend, ever so slightly. The movement makes my stomach drop a bit. Or maybe the sinking feeling is due to the unbelievable *threat* tossed my way.

"With the exception of my husband and my son, Zack," Diamond continues, speaking so softly I have to lean forward to hear, "and the lawyers, of course, there are only a few people in on this switch. They are within your eyesight. Do whatever you must do to keep distance between you and anyone not on this plane."

"Here's the thing . . ." I pause to pull at one of my curls. It's as soft as a freaking *feather*. Geez! What did Randy put in my hair? "You guys have events set up for me. What if people want to talk to me? Or, I mean, talk to Zay-Zay? It already happened just trying to get on this plane."

"If a friend, or foe, or publicist, or . . . fan, accidentally gets close—make it short and sweet. Toss out a hello. Get away as quickly as possible. Fake a cold, say you're contagious, your stomach hurts. Do whatever you must do. Are we understood?"

"We're landing soon." Aish plops onto the seat beside me, oblivious to the tension between me and Diamond. She cracks open a LaCroix she must've gotten from the fridge. "It's straightaway to Skybar after LAX. I got a text from Koi's publicist. He landed a few minutes ago and is already en route."

Omigosh. I ball my hands into fists again. It'll be fine. It's all good. He won't notice. He won't scream *Impostor, impostor!* and call for security.

Diamond presses a button to lock the screen on her tablet. It makes a loud clicking sound. "You and Red should go over what she should expect after landing, and how we expect her to handle it. Get her dressed. I have a few phone calls to make."

Diamond makes her way to the opposite side of the plane.

"Whoa. You all right, love? You're positively pale."

"Just nervous, that's all." I force a smile. Diamond Waters . . . *threatened* me.

"As far as LAX, it will be a *nightmare*," Aish explains. "Mostly because Zay-Zay tweeted about landing there to ward off paparazzi from *your* farm. Also, do not sign *any* autographs. Act like you didn't hear the request. Zay-Zay only signs at scheduled events for people who have paid ahead of time."

Fans pay for autographs now? "Are you sure? I have a T-shirt with Zay-Zay's signature printed on it. I could imitate it perfectly."

"Don't do anything Zay-Zay wouldn't do. She's been doing this long enough to know she has to put the oxygen mask on first."

I scratch my head. Not sure I understand that one.

"You'll need to hand out a golden ticket. A lucky fan is winning entrance to the party. Remember . . ."

I don't mean to tune out what Aish is saying, but my thoughts are on Mom and Dad. If they're getting loans and searching out ways to save our farm, and decided *not* to tell me about any of it, they probably had good reason. Diamond Waters really had no right to go snooping into their personal affairs. I heave a sigh. No one has *any* right to go snooping into people's personal affairs. No wonder Zay-Zay wanted to get away. This celebrity life has perks, but it's not without its complications.

"Oh, and maybe toss out a wave here and there." Aish demonstrates, as if I don't know how to wave. "Care to practice some red-carpet poses?"

"Sure, sounds great. Hey, Aish." I honestly wish I had the NDA so I could sign it again. I'll sign it in all caps. I'll sign it with my right *and* my left hand. Anything to prove to Diamond that not everyone is out for their own personal gain. Only I can't double-sign an NDA. I'll have to *prove* I'm worthy. With my actions. I told Zay-Zay she could trust me. I meant it. "Whatever you guys need. I'm here. Ok? Really happy to help. Helping is the least I can do."

"We're glad for it." Aish squeezes my shoulder.

EIGHT

Z *ay-Zay!*
Zay-Zay, over here!
Zay, I'm with TMZ, can we get an interview?
Zay, how long are you gonna rock the red hair?
Zay! Who gets the golden ticket?
Look at me, Zay-Zay!
Choose me, Zay-Zay!

If I were actually Zay-Zay, maybe I could tolerate this extreme display of adoration with a dozen paparazzi rushing beside me, snapping pictures as we step out of the sliding doors of the LAX airport terminal. Heck, it might even feel remarkable. But as it stands, with me *not* being Zay-Zay, it all feels like tiny tornadoes barreling across our oat fields, blowing over and destroying everything in their paths. Including Mom and Dad's secret distribution deal! My stomach is tight, my hands balled into fists at my side, my legs a bit wobbly. Thank goodness I'm wearing sunglasses, because I cannot stop with all the blinking!

In addition to paparazzi, there are fans holding up their phones, yelling, crying, shouting out their general love for Zay-Zay or random info like their social media handles. Not to mention the older folks who clearly don't know what's going on, but they stop and stare too. Walkers, wheelchairs, baby strollers. I have no idea how we're pushing through all of it. I just keep my blinking eyes toward the concrete, hoping no one shoves me so I tip over in these platform heels and mess up my new dress—the asymmetrical . . . Babal Bagung? No, that was not the name of the designer. Oh gosh, please nobody ask me who I'm wearing! The dress is a vast array of colors blending into one another, and it kinda makes me feel like I'm Joseph—the one who's dad gifted him an exclusive, one-of-a-kind Technicolor dreamcoat. So I'm, like, looking around for eleven jealous brothers to knock me over the head and steal it off me.

Zay-Zay, can I have the ticket?

Zay! I deserve it!

I want the golden ticket!

I should pick someone. I'm holding a copy of the ticket from the Willy Wonka story, printed onto a thin piece of gold foil-like paper. Instead of welcoming them to the factory, it welcomes someone to a pool party at Skybar in West Hollywood. Aish told me to choose a very specific type of fan. Older, obviously, since you need to be twenty-one to get into Skybar, unless you're famous and nobody cares how old you are, like Zay-Zay. Aish also told me to choose a girl. Preferably someone very pretty and classy, who won't make the other celebs at the event nervous.

Worth mentioning, there is a new addition to the entourage of Zay-Zay Waters. His name is Frank. He's six feet six, 245 pounds, and looks like he eats whole cows for breakfast.

"Back up!" he shouts at a girl who is trying her hardest to reach around Randy and grab at me as we stop near the curb.

"You back up!" the girl barks.

There are so many people pointing cameras and phones in our direction, I'm sure I'm going cross-eyed behind these glasses. I also need to pick a golden ticket winner before we get into our car.

"Zay-Zay, I love you!" the girl who yelled at Frank cries hysterically.

Beside her is a pretty brunette. She's older, college age—maybe twenty-one. She's wearing a chic summer dress with strappy sandals and is quiet among all the other ragers. She seems to fit all Aish's parameters. I don't *think* celebrities would be afraid of her.

I tap Frank on the back. When he turns to me, I lift the golden ticket and point to the girl with the flowy dress. He walks me toward her.

"No way. *Me?*" She covers her mouth with both hands as we approach.

I smile, though I could use about ten more white-strip sessions before my smile is as bright as Zay-Zay's. I hand the girl the golden ticket, remembering exactly what I'm supposed to say . . . nothing.

"Omigosh, I *love* you, Zay-Zay Waters. Thank you!" She wipes at her eyes, which are brimming over with tears, as dozens of cameras now turn to point at *her.*

"Man, you know you can't get that close." Frank extends his arm to block someone attempting to get right in my face with a very expensive-looking camera.

The guy dramatically stumbles and falls into the street. "Hey!" He cradles his camera like it almost broke. "You pushed me!" Another of the paparazzi rushes to help the man to his feet. "Did you see what he did?"

I certainly saw it. Frank didn't *touch* that guy. What a lying jerk!

Frank rolls his eyes, like he's used to lying jerks but so over them. He pulls open the back door of a Suburban parked on the street and offers his hand. I climb in. The door slams shut, and in a few seconds, we're all speeding away, the roar of the chaos behind us fading like the subtle diminuendo of a beautiful but terrifying symphony.

I don't realize I'm breathing fast until someone taps my shoulder. It's Aish. She's sitting right beside me. She hands me her phone. Typed out in her Notes app is a message.

You alright? You're breathing really hard.

My hands are shaking. My thumbs manage a quick reply.

Will it be like that at Skybar too?

Aish types back.

It's always like that.

Right. Of course it is. I mean, I can handle. I can deal. I got through that one ok. Or did I? I type another message onto her phone.

Did I seem convincing?

"You're a natural," she whispers. "Quite amazing to witness."

I adjust my sunglasses and decide to believe she's being honest. I, Red Morgan, am quite amazing to witness. But the truth is . . . *that* was amazing to witness. I know the adoration wasn't meant for me, but it still fuels me like a sixteen-ounce can of Red Bull. I see that Frank is in the front passenger seat beside the driver. Randy and Diamond? I twist around. They're seated behind me, hunched over their cell phones.

"You want us to stop at your favorite spot for a quick shot before we head to Hollywood?" the driver calls out. He's got white hair and wears glasses similar to the kind Loren wears. His voice is raspy, gentle, and kind.

A shot? Of espresso? I think I might blast off to space if I actually added caffeine to my already high level of adrenaline. "Um . . ." I look to Aish and mouth, "Help?"

"We'll pass on the wheatgrass for now, Aaron," Aish replies.

Zay-Zay drinks *wheatgrass*? Yikes. I place a hand over my stomach and push away the thought.

"No worries, miss," Aaron replies. "And how was your flight?"

This not-speaking thing might get tricky. Thankfully, it's Aish to the rescue. She leans forward and answers for me.

"Stupid paps still tracking the flights and calling Zay an environment destroyer on social. What else is new?"

Aaron shakes his head. "Not like you can fly commercial. What do they expect?"

"Precisely," Aish says.

Aaron seems perfectly content to be having a conversation with Zay-Zay . . . *without* Zay-Zay. Maybe this won't be as tricky as I thought.

I rest my head against the seat and attempt to relax as the SUV merges onto a freeway. A freeway that looks a lot like a parking lot. Bumper-to-bumper traffic as far as the eye can see. It's gonna take some time for us to get to where we're going. Since I'm not exactly in a rush to meet up with another screaming mob, I take this moment of peace to slide off my sunglasses, scope out the city, and simply let it all soak in. Everything is so bright, colorful, and vivid. And *loud*. I lower the window to take in the sounds. Giant truck horns blare; motorcycles with roaring engines weave around the slow-moving cars and trucks. A city bus pulls up beside us in the next lane. I take a deep breath, trying my hardest to inhale it all and savor the moment . . . though maybe I inhaled a bit too deeply, 'cuz I start coughing.

"Are you all right?" Aish asks me.

I nod. I might want to find another way to savor the moment. The LA air obviously isn't the same as in Orange City. Speaking of my hometown, a few hours ago, I was there, on our quiet farm. Heck, last week I was knee deep in manure. Now I'm fresh off a private jet, dressed in designer duds, and being whisked off to a fancy red-carpet event to meet up with my fake boyfriend. Who knew the Universe had *this* in store? Coulda sworn I said *nothing too crazy*.

"Hey, Aish," I whisper as Aaron switches lanes.

"Hmm?" She's scrolling on her phone. I take it gently out of her hand and bring up the memo app.

Maybe I could text my family now instead of later? Let them
know I arrived safely?

"Oh, right." She reaches into her bag and removes my phone.
Hands it off to me with a gentle reminder. "Only texts for now, yeah?"

It feels like a lifeline. Like a connection to a portal of common sense
and decency. I text Mom first.

Landed. Safe. This is like a dream. Miss me yet?

I wait for a few seconds. No reply. Hmm. Perhaps Dad's free after
finishing with the hog?

I'm in LA, Dad. Was Tony excited when you rehired him?

I wait for a bit. Nothing. Ok, weird. Dad usually has his phone on
hand. I *know* Loren's available. When doesn't she have her phone? She's
probably hiding out in the greenhouses, watching YouTube clips of *Oh,
So You Think You Can Sing Live?*

Sis! I have an idea for Daeshya. She really likes those Lara bars.
Get the cherry one and secretly let her have it before bed. She
will be so happy after that. Also . . . miss you.

I wait. And wait. And wait. We inch along in traffic. Sunlight
reflects off a pair of tall buildings that seem entirely made of glass, like
thick panes of black ice off in the distance.

Why is no one texting me back?!

"We should go over a few things, yeah?" Aish whispers. "Mind
powering that down for now?"

"But . . ." Power down my phone? When I haven't had a chance
to connect with anyone yet? Then again, there really is no telling when

the family will get back to me. Without me around to help, they're probably busier than ever. I should stay focused. I hand her the phone. "Here you go."

"Perfect." She clicks the side button to black out the screen before stuffing it into her bag.

~

Sunset Boulevard. I've heard of it before. Listened to songs about it. Once saw a play with the same title, about a washed-up actress trying to make a comeback. But nothing can prepare you for seeing Sunset Boulevard live, in person. Saying it's cool would be a huge understatement. Landmark buildings like the giant Sunset Tower Hotel; high-end fashion displayed in store windows; sprawling billboards with chic, scantily clad models; lines of skinny palm trees that stretch high into the sky; and *throngs* of LA locals. Many in heels and party dresses, holding drinks, laughing and happily chatting like it's perfectly normal to party in the afternoon. Why are all these people out on the streets? Shouldn't they be at work?

"That's *ridiculous*," Aish growls into the phone. "Clearly not! Are you mental?" She pauses for a moment, listening. "A legal agreement between two parties . . . I believe that's the precise definition of a contract. File a countercomplaint!"

Uh-oh. Aish is entering into systems rage again. I turn back to the window. The event is coming into clear view. Tons of studio lights are set up on tripods, reporters talk into microphones in front of camerapeople, and a host of very well-dressed Californians exit cars after pulling up to the curb. This *must* be Skybar! My stomach tightens; my hands ball into fists again. But before I have a proper panic attack, Aish cries out.

"Why are humans evil?" She drops her phone onto her lap. Up front, Frank and Aaron are in conversation, oblivious to Aish's systems rage. Or maybe . . . used to it.

"What's happened?" Diamond asks calmly.

"Slight change of plans. Zay-Zay won't be going into Skybar right now."

"Oh. Ok." I definitely don't mind waiting in the car. More time to work out the nervous jitters. I'm sure Zay-Zay's knees don't typically knock together when she's on the carpet. I glance out the window again. As we get closer to the commotion . . . I see him. Stepping out of a black SUV, similar to the one we're in, is Koi Kalawai'a!

His long black hair is pulled into a messy bun on top of his head. The kind of messy bun that probably took half an hour to put together. His eyes are covered with green-tinted sunglasses, and his tall, lean frame is dressed simply in black pants, black T-shirt and jacket, and bright-blue sneakers, the same color as the sky. And his watch. *Whoa.* It looks encrusted with about a hundred diamonds. I have to squint to take it all in!

"Zay-Zay."

Hmm? I turn to Aish, lean forward, and whisper, "Are you talking to me?"

"Yes." Aish smiles sweetly. "Since . . . Zay-Zay is your name."

Zay-Zay? Oh right!

"I'll repeat what I said. Someone anonymously filed a report with the Alcohol Beverage Control Board. Which, I didn't know that was a thing."

Alcohol Beverage Control Board? "Neither did I."

"They reported Skybar for serving alcohol to minors." She holds up her phone. "That was Skybar's general manager. They know they're being watched now. If they let anyone under twenty-one in, they could lose their liquor license. They can't take the risk. Not even for . . . you." Aish pulls at thick strands of her black hair. "This infuriates me."

Diamond unhooks her seat belt. "It's fine. Better actually." She speaks directly to me. "You'll still walk the carpet. That's what's most important, anyway. Red-carpet pictures to prove you're . . . here. Those will be quick and easy." She grabs her purse. "I'm heading out to find Shannon." She calls out to the front. "Aaron, I'll get out here."

Diamond climbs out of the SUV. The door closes, and I watch her rush across the street.

She said walking the red carpet would be quick and easy. That madness out there seems worse than LAX! At least at the airport, I was surrounded by paparazzi and regular people like me. These people are *fancy*. This is actual press. There are signs for NBC, CBS, FOX, E! Entertainment, and more. Will they be able to tell I'm fresh off a farm? What if they sense there's something going on here? 'Cuz let's be honest—there is definitely something going on here!

"Don't worry," Aish says as if reading my mind. "You're quite lovely. The outfit is stellar." She whispers softly into my ear. "And these people are so focused on themselves, they barely look you in the eye anyway." She gathers her bag and phone and reaches to squeeze my shoulder. "Randy and I are about to switch places so he can do touch-ups. Oh, and one final thing." Her whisper grows softer. "Your name is Zay-Zay Waters. Answer when people call you that, yeah?"

Aish and Randy do a quick switch, which requires Randy to climb over the seat. I'm not quite sure how he does it without falling over, but he does. He fiddles with my hair.

"Everything's holding up nicely. Turn and face me?"

I click off my seat belt, turn to face Randy, and slide off my sunglasses. He's got a neatly organized black bag filled with makeup and brushes slung over his shoulder.

"Close," he says.

I feel a brush dusting gently over my closed eyes. "I'm going to be wearing sunglasses."

"Of course. But what if your glasses fall off?"

The sunglasses are like a cloaking device. If I wear them, I *really* look like Zay-Zay. But without them . . . will they see? Can they tell?

Aren't eyes the windows to the soul? Besides, Koi Kalawaiʻa had his sunglasses on too. We'll match. Wait. Do we want to?

My eyes pop open. "Randy?"

"Hmm?" Randy is sharpening an eyeliner pencil. "Look up for me?"

I do, and he adds more liner to my bottom lids. I don't think I've ever had a person write on my eyelids. It tickles a bit and makes me blink like crazy.

"Honey, stop with all the blinking."

"I saw Koi Kalawaiʻa," I whisper.

"Right." Randy finishes with the eyeliner and puts it away. "He's scheduled to be here with you, remember? A few pics and you're done until Sun and Sand this evening." He removes a long-handled brush from his bag and dips it into a small container of fine powder the same color as my skin.

"What do I do if he tries to talk to me?" I whisper.

"The most he'll probably say is hi." Randy applies pink blush to my cheeks. "Say hi back. Then be done."

Hi. Ok. I can manage that.

"Warning," Randy whispers. "Your publicist is approaching the car. Shannon Miller. She's a *lot*."

The door yanks open.

"Why aren't you answering my calls?"

I twist around to see a lady with extravagant ultrablonde extensions that look so dry and flat ironed I can almost smell the burning hair. She's wearing a black pantsuit and a lot of thick makeup. And maybe I'm imagining it, but her cheeks seem . . . frozen in place. Seriously, no part of her face is moving, even though she's smiling.

She climbs into the car, so I have to scoot over to make room.

"Seriously, hon, all my calls are going straight to voice mail. What is wrong with your phone?" She pulls the door shut.

I squirm in my seat. Shannon Miller is so close to me! They said no one would be close. Surely she'll be able to tell I'm not Zay-Zay.

"Why do you look different?" she asks.

Oh no! She *can* tell!! I hold my breath, as if that can somehow help this awkward moment of reveal. Do we have to let her in on it too? Should we call for Diamond? Push Shannon out of the car and run for cover? Oh shoot, I need oxygen!

She snaps her fingers. "It's the *hair*."

I exhale. Happy to breathe.

"It's growing on me." Shannon nods. "I'm loving it on you. Makes you seem fresher, happier, brighter. Like you just got back from two weeks in the jungle and discovered the meaning of life. You're no longer you."

"Ha." Randy covers his mouth. "Oops. My bad."

She tugs on the skirt of my dress. "Who is this? Love the asymmetry. It's stunning."

Probable Grunge? No, wait. I give Randy "Help me" eyes.

"Prabal Gurung," he answers.

"Oooh. Gurung's *perfect* for today." Shannon says. "I could eat you with a fork and steak knife."

That sounds . . . weird. I give her a close-mouthed smile so she can't see that my teeth aren't as white as they should be.

"I'm serious, you young kids have no idea how lucky you are. When you get to be my age, you'll need a steady stream of Botox coursing through your veins to look as good as you do now. Driver?" Shannon leans forward to tap on Aaron's seat. "Driver?"

"Oh, that's Aaron." I cover my mouth. Oops.

Shannon rolls her eyes like she couldn't care if the driver's name was Alexander Hamilton. "*Driver.* Could you pull up?"

Aaron calls back, "Actually, the police officers are waving at me to move around. I don't think I *can* pull up."

Shannon reaches into her purse and removes plastic passes. She hands them to Aaron. "Hang these on the mirror and then pull *up*, like I asked you to."

Yikes. Randy mouths, "A lot."

Aaron does as he's told, hanging the passes on the rearview mirror, and the officer finally waves him through. The car inches forward.

"You ready, Zay?" Shannon has a hand on the door.

I feel like saying, *Nooooooo*. Instead, I nod and pray I don't throw up all over the carpet.

"Great," she replies. "And ignore these paparazzi mosquitos. The real press starts on the carpet. You know that. There's so many news outlets here to talk to you, including E!, CNN, Facebook, FOX, Yahoo, Huffington. Whatever. You get it."

I do not get it. I thought it was just pictures! My hands ball into fists again.

"Quick reminder. No live press today," Aish calls out from the back. "Diamond said no."

Shannon laughs. "Doll, let Randy do Zay's hair and makeup, you . . . fill out the calendar app on Zay's phone, and let me do Zay's PR. That's why they called me her *publicist*, 'kay?" She turns to me. "You're doing interviews. It would be insane not to. You didn't come here just to pose for pictures."

Actually, that's exactly what I came here to do.

Shannon's phone rings. She taps the screen and holds the phone to her ear. "Yes. We're coming right now . . . well, I never ok'd that . . ."

I turn to Aish and whisper, "What do I do? I can't do live press!"

"I'll talk to Diamond. She'll handle Shannon."

"Like I said," Randy adds softly. "A *lot*."

The car crawls to a stop at the curb. Shannon ends her call and turns to me. "Ready?"

I slowly unclench my hands and nod, though I'm literally shaking. How do I make it stop? How can I calm my body?

When Shannon pushes open the door and steps onto the pavement, the calls are so loud I almost pause to cover my ears before I remember Zay-Zay probably wouldn't do that. Thankfully all 245 pounds of Frank appears at my side. He offers a hand, and I step down out of the SUV. Shannon leads us around the *chaos* of paparazzi.

Zay-Zay, are you allowed to enter into Skybar?

Geez. How do they already know about that?

Zay-Zay, why do you need a security guard? Is that a wise use of your money?

Huh? People literally chase Zay down the street!

Zay-Zay, PETA wants to know why you wear fur!

Fur? It's June!

Zay-Zay, are you aware your jet is polluting our city?!

And other jets aren't?

The questions continue. Rapid fire. One after another. Aish explained the difference between paparazzi and actual photography press when we were in the car. Apparently paparazzi are freelance photographers who sell their pics and stories to the highest bidder. She said they cheat, steal, lie, and ultimately destroy without conscience. They'll cause car accidents and snap pictures of the mess *they* caused without an apology. Mostly because they're not sorry. Photography press, on the other hand, are hired by networks, follow protocols, and work within a specific set of parameters and boundaries.

"Celebrities are contractually obligated to press," Aish said to me in the car. "And dejectedly bound to paparazzi."

Now I get what she means. What I don't get is how any of this could ever seem normal. How does Zay-Zay live this way? So much commotion, so much shouting, so many flashing lights; it's like I'm in the center of an apocalyptic attack. Aliens are chasing me, but there is nowhere to run.

I keep my eyes planted firmly on Shannon's back and pretend I don't hear or see anything. It's all deafening, my ears are ringing, and my heart has jumped into my throat. We make it safely past the mob of paps, and fresh air rushes in. I gulp it up like ice cream on a sweltering-hot day. Shannon marches on, and I follow close behind, toward a different type of melee. Now it's a cluster of important-looking people who seem to be waiting in line. It's an interesting assortment of strange fashion. From jeans with so many holes they're like hanging threads of denim to barely there shorts and tube tops, plastic ponchos, and on one person, a black cloth mask covering their entire head and face. I wonder—if I wore a feeder bag over my head, would that be considered fashionable too?

I want to look past these interesting outfits to see who I'm cutting in front of. To at least apologize. Cutting in line gives me flashbacks of preschool roundup. No rational person over the age of six cuts in front of people. But Shannon clearly isn't the rational sort. She's moving like a woman on a mission, and I follow like I know I'm supposed to, until the red carpet comes into clear view.

It's not as big as I thought it would be. If I ran, I could probably be done in ten seconds. Behind the carpet stretches a silver backdrop with giant Steaz logos printed across it. Which, I know Steaz! We sell their ice teas in our store. Lining the whole carpet are those theater safety barriers, with red velvet ropes connecting metal poles. I find it funny they're called barriers, since Daeshya could easily knock one over. Anyway, the throngs of reporters are safe behind the "barriers," waiting for the next celebrity to walk so they can take photographs with their big fancy cameras.

"As if this one needs an introduction!" one of the reporters calls out.

I quickly realize that's my cue when the shouts of Zay-Zay's name start to ring in my ears. Hands guide me forward. I think they're Shannon's. I hope so, anyway. I take timid steps and boldly go where no Morgan has gone before . . .

Zay-Zay Waters, this way please!

Zay-Zay, right here!!

Zay-Zay, can we get a wave?

Lights flash. The calls are thunderous. It's as if I've stepped into an alternate dimension where I am the most important person in the entire *world*. A girl could get used to this. I smile.

Zay-Zay, you're stunning!
Zay, who are you wearing?
Oh! I'm allowed to answer this.

"Prabal Gurung," I call out before spinning around so the Technicolor asymmetrical dreamcoat dress flares out in an explosion of color.

Click-click-click. The cameras go into *overdrive.*

I can hardly see for all the flashing lights. And honestly, I don't know what's come over me. Have I been possessed with the spirit of Zay? Or maybe I've watched way too much of her on red carpets. 'Cuz this feels *natural.* I jut out my leg and pose with a hand on my hip. I wave. I blow a kiss. I smize. Oh yes, Diamond Waters! You scoffed when I mentioned smizing practice, and here it's coming in handy. I am smizing my *face* off. I continue down the carpet, where more photographers are lined up. More smizing. More waving. More posing. I flip my soft feathery curls over my shoulder, and the cameras go *click-click-click.*

I move another ten yards down the carpet.

Click-click-click.

I blow another kiss.

Zay-Zay, over here!

Zay-Zay, can we get one without the sunglasses?

No, thank you. They're my cloaking device. Without them, they'll know I'm just Clark Kent. Not Superman. I ignore the request and toss out a peace sign with two fingers. I walk another five yards down the carpet.

Zay-Zay, right this way!

Zay-Zay, can we get a smile?!

Zay-Zay, can we get one without the glasses?

Ugh. Another request for Zay sans glasses?

I guess I can take them off. Randy *did* spend an extra five minutes writing on my eyelids. What for, if not to display his artwork? Ok. Deep breath. You got this, Red. I'm reaching now. But a hand grabs mine.

The hand is warm, *super* soft, comforting. It squeezes as if to say *Hey, I'm here for you.* I turn and look up into the face of Koi Kalawai'a. *His* sunglasses are off now, so his pale-green eyes seem ever so bright in the Los Angeles sunshine.

"Koi Kalawai'a?" I hardly recognize the sound of my own voice.

"Zay-Zay Waters." He nods. "Hi."

NINE

With Koi at my side, the reporters seem to have forgotten about my sunglasses. And that is just fine with me.

Zay-Zay and Koi! Over here!

Zay-Zay Waters and Koi Kalawai'a, this way!

Zay-Zay! Koi!

Koi and I pose for pictures, and like Randy, Aish, and Zay-Zay discussed . . . he does not actually speak to me. Or look in my direction. He's posing and smiling and waving and holding my hand like he's contractually obligated. Sort of the way a five-year-old holds your hand when you help them cross the street. As if they can't wait to let it go so they can run toward the slides at the park.

Even though he's not looking at me, I can't help but bend my neck back to look up at him. How tall is he? Oh, I remember from his "How Tall Are You" TikTok challenge—six feet three. My knees want to give way, and my legs feel like they're strands of spaghetti, but "Zay-Zay Waters Faints on Red Carpet" would not be a great headline.

Oh, but his eyes. They're like portals to the seaside town of Lahaina, Hawaii, where he was born and raised. I can see ocean waves in those eyes. I swear I can.

Uh-oh. He catches me gazing at him like a superfan stalker.

"What?" he whispers.

Oh gosh, he's talking to me. Dang my stupid knees. They buckle again. I regain my footing and plant my feet firmly on the carpet. I have *got* to push all fangirl stuff to the side. Sure, I used to tell Koi Kalawaiʻa's picture good night, since it was hung on my and Loren's closet door. And . . . ok, I've binged his Netflix series, *Koi Kalawaiʻa— Unplugged.* Twice. Memorized lyrics to the songs he sings with his band. Contemplated appropriate portmanteaus for us and settled on Ked. But right now, he and I are on the same level. Actually, strike that. We're not on the same level. As Zay-Zay Waters, I'm a mountain, and he's a . . . plateau . . . sitting peacefully in my shadow. I straighten out my shoulders and unspaghetti my legs as more camerapeople call out to us.

Zay-Zay Waters, this way!

Zay-Zay and Koi, could we get a kiss on the carpet?

Before I have a moment to contemplate all the ways we can deny that request, Koi wraps an arm around my waist so that I stumble into him. He leans forward and presses his lips to mine. The *click-click-click-click* of the cameras go silent in my ears as the feeling of his lips pressed against mine makes me gasp ever so slightly. My legs return to their previous, spaghettilike state. He strengthens his grip around my waist, pulls his lips away from mine, and whispers again, tickling my ear.

"Are you sure you're ok, Zay? You seem . . . wobbly."

I *am* wobbly! Koi Kalawaiʻa *kissed* me! He smells like a mixture of so many good things. Sandalwood. Cinnamon. Vanilla. And how can a person's lips be so soft? Ahhhhh!! If there weren't three dozen cameras taking pictures of me right now, I would be jumping up and down and squealing like one of our pigs.

"Zay-Zay and Koi!" a female reporter calls out. "It's Sophia Ruiz. Can I ask you two kids a few questions?"

An interview?! Oh gosh. Before I have a chance to toss out a proper *Heck no*, Koi is gently pulling my arm toward the end of the carpet, where some reporters are holding microphones and interviewing people before they enter Skybar.

I pull my arm away. "I . . . can't. I'm good."

"You have to do press. Stop being weird." He gently grabs my arm again. Where the heck is Shannon? Diamond? Aish . . . Randy? Heck, I don't even see Frank!

"KK and Zay-Zay. My favorite alliterations!" Sophia calls out. "Come here, you beautiful humans!"

I *remember* her. Oh wow. It's the same girl who did a story on *Entertainment Now* about Zay-Zay at a restaurant in Chicago. She reminds me of a young Shannon. Enough makeup to look like a second skin. Long flat-ironed extensions. Dramatic, maybe-fake eyelashes and a frozen face that doesn't move when she smiles. Koi approaches her, dragging me along. I try to pull my hand away, but he's got a tight grip, and I don't want to draw too much attention anyway. "Zay-Zay Waters Attempts Escape from Koi Kalawai'a" would also not be the greatest headline.

"What a privilege to be chatting with you two," she says excitedly. "You're hot. So hot *together*. I love it. We've been hearing rumors about you two breaking up. It's obviously not true. You're both beaming bright."

I feel like a deer in the oncoming headlights of a semi. Is this live? Could my family be watching? Friends from home? Would Zay-Zay approve of this?

Koi completely ignores Sophia's question and instead starts talking about "Together with You" and how strange it was working on his first music project without his band, the Six. While he's talking, I search for Shannon. How could she have disappeared like this? I still don't see her! I do see an actress I love, Elle Milian, standing in the same spot I was standing in a few minutes ago. She's stunning. Posing. Waving. Reporters shouting her name as if they've forgotten that Zay-Zay just slayed that carpet. I frown. Have they forgotten?

"What do you think, Zay-Zay?"

Hmm? Oh shoot, Sophia's talking to me. I spin back around. Sophia is holding the microphone in my direction.

"I'm . . . torn?"

"Exactly," Sophia replies. "I'm torn too!"

Whew. That was close.

I decide to keep my focus on the reporter from *Entertainment Now*. Besides, I do a great Zay-Zay. And I can't exactly get in trouble for this. They're the ones who deserted me on the carpet. Worth mentioning, there is something about Sophia. I can't quite put my finger on it. Her eyes are sort of glazed over. In fact, she's not looking Koi in the eye as he rambles on and on about why he's *not* torn. Instead, she's sneaking peeks over my shoulder to see who else is on the carpet.

"I'm so for it. Fabulous. Love it, Koi. You're *amazing.*" She's talking like she's reading a script. Like she's a Hollywood AI, programmed with a peppy personality, and her creator typed in her dialogue. Is there a teleprompter somewhere around here?

Amazing.

Fabulous.

So for it.

When she turns to me, she's smiling and making eye contact, but I have to resist the urge to wave my hand in front of her face and say *Helloooo.*

"Let's switch topics. Zay-Zay, 'Believe' was nominated for a Golden Globe *and* an Academy Award for Best Original Song. You didn't manage to nab a trophy for either. How do you move forward and persevere when faced with disappointment in your career?"

What the *heck*?! First of all, Zay-Zay got robbed at the Academy Awards. "The fact that a song from a movie about talking gophers won . . . it's a crime against humanity."

Oh no! Did I really say that out loud?! I have *got* to stop speaking my thoughts!! Sophia pauses for a moment before she and her camera guy both burst into laughter. Oh good. I can pretend it was a joke.

"Obviously, I'm playin'." Whew, that was close. I laugh too. "You win some, you lose way more. That's what my mom used to say." At least that's true. Mom did used to say that. "And 'Believe,' it's about redefining what it means to win and lose, anyway. So, I pretty much feel like a winner all the time. Why? 'Cuz real winners wake up in the mornin' and do what they gotta do. Period. That makes you a winner, too, Sophia."

Oh wow. That sounded pretty dang good!

"Zay, I *love* that message." Sophia smiles. "So powerful. Thank you. And you're such a breath of fresh air. Breathtaking today. Who are you wearing?"

"Probable Grunge," I say. Then quickly realize my mistake. Crap! "Except he gets mad when I call him that."

More laughter from Sophia. I glance around again. There are so many people clumped together, on and off the carpet, and so many of them identical to Shannon. Why do they all wear black pantsuits? I turn back to face Sophia.

"Prabal Gurung is great on you, Zay-Zay." Sophia switches her mic from one hand to the other. "Now. Are we gonna see more collabs with you two kids?"

Hmm, the fact that Zoi is scheduled for a fake breakup tells me they are definitely *not* planning any more collabs. I'm about to say, *Nope, sorry about that,* when Koi speaks up.

"Of course." He wraps an arm around my shoulder. "You up for it, babe?"

"Sorry, we have to cut this short." Shannon has appeared at my side.

Oh, sweet Universe of goodness and *life*! I feel like screeching *Where the heck have you been?* I sigh with relief instead. Shannon grabs my arm and drags me away from the interview before Sophia and Koi can react.

"What the hell is wrong with your aunt?" Shannon guides me off the carpet. "I got *screamed* at for letting you speak to *Entertainment*

Now. Like, top-of-your-lungs, two-year-old-tantrum scream. Can somebody tell me what's going on? Since when do you opt out of press?"

I feign surprise. "What? Why? Yeah. So weird."

"I know!" Shannon exclaims. "You're almost twenty! Stand up to her. I swear your aunt is a freaking *tyrant.* Fire her before she ruins your life."

I try to match Shannon's confusion and shake my head. "I don't get the woman. She's wack." Shannon gives me a weird look. "What? Do people not say *wack* anymore?"

"Anyway. Head back to the car, I guess." She sighs. "This whole thing's been a total nightmare. At least we showed up, right? And you honestly have never shined brighter. These pics will go far."

Zay-Zay has never shined brighter? Surely Shannon's blowing smoke. She probably says that to Zay-Zay every time she sees her.

"Are you ready, Zay? I can walk you back." Frank is at my side again. And Shannon is moving off, ranting into her phone.

"Yeah. I'm ready."

I follow Frank down a side walkway, where a few security folks mingle.

"Zay-Zay, I love you!" one of them calls out.

I toss them a wave, and the group hollers and cheers as we pass by.

"Can we get a picture?" Four teenage girls approach as we make it back to the street, where there's a long line of waiting SUVs, cars, and limos. Police and security guards sort of meander close by. A group of paparazzi hovers near the curb. Of course they start snapping photographs as soon as they see me. It *seems* safe enough to pose with the girls. I've already broken so many rules tonight. One more won't hurt.

"Uh, sure," I say. "No doubt."

I stand next to them, and one of the girls holds out her phone. I pose with my best half smile and smize. They seem *thrilled.* I have no idea why, but it thrills me as well. Making someone's dreams come true is like walking on sunshine that doesn't burn your feet.

"We love you!" they say in unison.

Aww. "I love y'all too!" Good deed accomplished. Step right up, folks. What else can I do to make people happy?

"Can you sign this?" One of the girls thrusts out a notebook and pen, as if in response to my silent question.

Hmm. Aish said Zay-Zay only signs at events where people have paid. This might be the end of my day of good deeds.

"Pleeeease, Zay-Zay," the girl begs.

Zay-Zay told me to make her look good. That trumps all other rules. I think.

"Sure." What could it hurt? "Of course."

I take the notebook and pen. Big *Z* . . . scribble, scribble. Another big *Z* . . . scribble, scribble. *XO.* And a giant heart. Boom. Perfectly matches the signature on the T-shirt I have at home.

"There you go." I hand her back the notebook.

Now another girl in the group steps forward and holds out her arm.

"Can you sign my arm?" She hands me a Sharpie. "I will *never* wash it."

I laugh. "You gotta wash it someday." I scribble out the signature again. Which . . . writing on skin isn't easy. I do finally figure it out, but by the time I look up, a whole line has formed behind the girls.

Whoa. Where did all these people come from? Before I know what's happening, I'm posing for selfie after selfie. Leaning my head in, smiling, smizing, posing, and fake laughing with person after person after *person.* Why won't anybody save me?

"Zay-Zay." Fan number twenty-one steps forward. "Can I tell you how much I love your song 'Believe'? It was like this anthem for . . ."

The young guy keeps talking. And talking. And talking. I literally can't follow.

"Does that make sense?" he asks.

I nod. "Hundred percent."

Someone behind him yells, "Hey, hurry up! We all want a turn!"

"Oh. Sorry." The boy holds up his phone. "Pic, please?"

I think I feel the earth move under my feet. Either I'm experiencing my first California earthquake or I'm dizzy and need water. I pose for another picture. More autographs. More pics. Finally, it hits me— signing autographs was a bad idea. My arm feels numb. My fingers burn. My nose does, too, from all the different smells of all these different people. That last guy had garlic breath that made my eyes water.

"Frank?" I call out weakly as a shirtless kid steps forward with a Sharpie.

Frank slides off his glasses. I motion for him to come closer. When he does, I whisper, "Help?"

Frank steps in front of me and barks. "Everybody back!"

He sounds thunderous and mighty, like he could turn green at any moment and rip an evil villain's head off. The people in the front of the line step back, but I do hear a few of them groan, and one person from the end of the line shouts, "Zay-Zay, please! You would make my life. *Please* talk to me!"

I wanna make his life. I really do. I mean, walking on cold sunshine is pretty cool. But if I pass out, it wouldn't be a good look. Oxygen mask for me first. Frank helps me climb inside the SUV to the sound of groans, moans, and, yep, some boos. Still, the line's not dispersing! They continue calling for Zay-Zay. More requests for pictures. More begging for a turn, a wave, a shout-out. One guy pulls off his shirt and has ZAY-ZAY MARRY ME written in black Sharpie across his chest and stomach. I'm letting him down. I'm letting them all down.

I sigh heavily and stare at the ceiling of the car. "Ok, Universe. Show me something good. And remember . . ." I rest my head on the seat and close my eyes. "Nothing too crazy."

"Which car is ours?" I hear Aish outside. She must be speaking to Frank.

A few seconds later, the car door on the other side opens.

"Am I in trouble?" I exhale. "That kiss was not my idea."

"You seemed into it, though."

My eyes pop open, and I turn to see none other than Koi Kalawaiʻa. He smiles the most perfect smile I've ever seen and slides onto the leather seat beside me.

Omigosh. I sit up, straighten out my dress, and pull at my curls so they're not flat in the back. "What . . . are you doin' in my car?"

"Funny." He yanks the door shut, drowning out the chaos of the screaming fans. "I was about to ask you the same thing."

I glance outside, where Frank still stands, his arms folded across his chest as he chats with Aish. I turn to Koi. "This *is* my car."

"Then why does it have my name. Right there. On that little sign?" He points.

Sure enough, on the dash is a sign with KOI KALAWAIʻA printed on it. I slap my palm against my forehead. "My bad."

He leans back, stretching out his arms so they're almost touching me. I squirm a bit in my seat, pressing my shoulder against the door to get as much space between us as possible, wondering if I'm the only one who felt the temperature rise substantially in here.

"I actually wish they'd stop putting our names on these cards." He rolls his eyes. "Are they *trying* to make life easier for stalkers and serial killers? Where's Koi Kalawaiʻa? Right here. In this car with his *name* on it."

His voice is like a melody. The anxiety crawling up my spine, making my chest feel like it's about to cave in on me, seems instantly soothed. Is he a skilled hypnotist?

"Is it warm in here?" I fan my face with my hands, which doesn't cool things down in any way.

"No." He looks at me. "How are you, by the way?"

How am I? I thought these two never talked!

"I'm . . . cool," I say softly.

"Really? I thought you said you were warm." He laughs.

I laugh too. But now I'm wondering if Zay-Zay would laugh like I just did. Probably not. I reach for the door handle. "Anyway, see you—"

"Wait." He rests a hand on my knee. "Why were you acting so *weird* on the carpet?"

I shift a bit to free my knee from his grip, which feels as hot as a flame. "I wasn't."

"Zay, you were acting like you ate a bag of sugar. I thought you were gonna faint for a second. And *Probable Grunge?*" He raises an eyebrow. "Not to mention, the way you kissed me. *Really* weird."

Should I be offended? "What's that supposed to mean?"

"I dunno." He winks. "Seemed like you were into it. Were you?"

I force a laugh. I definitely was. "I was not."

"Liar." He smiles.

First of all, I think, *I didn't kiss you. You kissed me.* "I wasn't expectin' you to do that. Tha's all."

"We kiss all the time. I'm contractually *obligated* to kiss you."

"Ok. Well. Our breakup can't come soon enough." No wonder Zay never talks to him! I grab the door handle again.

"Breakup?"

I twist around to face him. His brow is furrowed, pretty green eyes narrowed. "Yeah. You know. Our . . . breakup?"

He crosses his arms under his chest. "Who decided we're breaking up?"

Omigosh. He doesn't know? I'm frozen in place, like somebody glued me to this seat, even though my instinct is screaming at me to run. "Um . . ." *Crap!* "I was kiddin'. Anyway, bye."

He grabs me gently by the arm. "Is *that* why all these rumors have been flying around? You're planning on breaking up with me? You know the band's trying to get the replacement gig. We can't end things now. C'mon, Zay. You're being selfish. For some reason, you and me . . . create something."

Ok, woooow. Hulu, Netflix, Starz, Amazon Prime—I got subscriptions to all of them. But I have to say, "Not sure I've heard a better '*Hey, let's fake stay together*' line. That's up there with some serious top-notch Hollywood writing."

He frowns. "I'm being serious."

"Right." I fan my hands in front of my face again, which still does nothing to cool me down. I wonder if anyone has ever spontaneously combusted around Koi before. My temperature continues to rise. And not *just* because Koi looks like Aquaman's skinny younger green-eyed brother. Being more attractive than 99.9 percent of the entire world population probably has its downsides. Like, people stare at you. I'm more concerned with the fact that I just let the breakup cat out of the bag. How do I fix this? "I was only kiddin'. About the breakup stuff. Gotcha."

"You never kid." He frowns. "Something's weird about you, Zay."

Oh gosh. I'm failing at this! He knows I'm not her! It's officially time to exit this car. I will break the windows to get out of here. But before I have a chance to bolt, Koi extends his hand and snatches off my sunglasses.

Oh.

My.

Ga.

We sort of stare at one another for a few seconds, until the door opens and the sounds of screams are amplified. I turn to see Aish with a hand on her hip.

"You do realize you're in the wrong car? Let's get a move on, yeah?" She waves. "Koi, we'll see you at Sun and Sand."

I quickly take the glasses out of Koi's hands, slide them back onto my face, and am out the door before he can say another word.

"What was that all about?" Aish has to shout in my ear over the fans and paparazzi screaming for Zay. As we move past the line of parked vehicles, Frank follows close behind us. "Trapped in a car with Koi Kalawai'a? Diamond's going to kill you. You're supposed to be keeping *distance*."

"It was nothing."

We climb into the right SUV. The doors slam shut. Aish and I are alone, so I talk fast.

"I got into the wrong car. He got in a few minutes later. We barely said a word to one another."

"That was all?"

"That's it." I mean, obviously that's not it. I'm leaving out 92 percent of what actually happened. There is no way I can risk telling her the whole story.

"I heard you did a bit of an interview with *Entertainment Now*?"

"Aish, I was forced to. It wasn't my fault."

"Relax." She places a hand on my shoulder. "You're not in trouble. Diamond's blaming Shannon." She makes the nervous emoji face. "Shall we watch the clip?"

"No!" I shake my head.

"C'mon. We *have* to. Diamond said you were a natural." She whips out her phone, and in a few seconds, the interview is playing. I watch over her shoulder. It's amazing. I really do look and sound like Zay-Zay. Another amazing thing . . . Koi and I have some serious *chemistry*.

"Oh dear." Aish frowns. "You and Koi have *chemistry*."

"I was literally just thinking that."

"It's not good. They're going to be breaking up. Act more distant. Aloof. Irritated. Do you think you can do that?"

Ha! "I'll . . . try."

"Do or do not. There is no try." She turns her full attention back to her phone.

"Oh, hey, Aish. Quick question."

"What?" Now she's typing out a long text.

"Koi doesn't . . . know about the upcoming breakup?"

"Of *course* not." She gives me wide, terrified eyes. "Everything was stated very clearly in the contract. He doesn't know. He *can't* know."

"Oh, yeah. I . . . know," I lie.

She exhales. "Good."

I wish there was a way to literally kick myself for not reading every word on those stupid papers. Why *didn't* Zay tell me Koi wasn't in the know? Seems like pretty important info! "What would happen if he found out? Just curious. Randomly . . . curious."

"It would be a *disaster*. Koi is not like Zay-Zay. He *wants* to be the top trending story on TMZ. Who knows what he'd do to keep things going?" Her phone rings. "Sorry. I should take this." She taps her screen. "Hi, yes, it's Aish . . ."

I tune out Aish's phone call, grabbing at my hair, not caring if I frizz up all of Randy's hard work. It's day one, and I've possibly made a mess of things! I'll fix it. I know I can. I'm Red Morgan, of the clan Morgan. If there's one thing we Morgans do well, it's fix messes. The short encounter with Koi *will* get fixed.

I lean my head back against the seat and sigh.

I'll make sure of it.

TEN

We're pulling in to Zay's house. A few paparazzi are camped across the street. An armed security guard stands at a guard post, waving as he bends to peek inside the car. Frank, Aish, Diamond, and Randy have their noses buried in their cell phones, leaving me alone with my thoughts. Actually, just one thought: Koi might be onto me. Tonight . . . I *will* turn this thing around. It will be my greatest performance as Zay-Zay yet.

The sleek gates open slowly to reveal a private entrance into . . . an exclusive country club? That's what it seems like. Tall palm trees stretch high into the sky, and the grounds are meticulously manicured, like someone hand cut the bushes and painted the grass. Three different black paved roads lead deeper into the estate. At the beginning of each road is one of those reflectorized street-name signs on a long metal pole. The car turns left, onto Summerland Drive.

As we head down the winding road, I forget my dilemma for a moment, staring in awe as we move past lush gardens with peonies and poppies in all the colors of the rainbow. Summerland Drive is like Wonderland, everything beautifully and magically landscaped. I turn to Aish and tap her on the knee.

She doesn't look up. "Hmm?"

I lean and whisper, "This is all Zay's?"

She shakes her head. Fiddles with her cell phone and shows it to me. I read the memo app.

It's a gated community. There are other houses on the property.

Wow. I return my attention to the spectacle outside. We pass a full-size tennis court. Does Zay play tennis? I never have, but I'm certainly willing to try. The tennis court is surrounded by more peonies, poppies, sunflowers, and trees too. Palm, oak . . . pretty sure that's a eucalyptus tree. The glossy, slender leaves hang downward and narrow to a point. Dad was gifted a eucalyptus plant once for his birthday. He tried to tend to it in our nursery, but it died after the first freeze of winter.

The Suburban moves up a hill. Past more meticulously curated grounds. Grass so shiny it looks plastic. Trees with leaves that rustle like metal chimes in the wind. Finally the hill levels out, and the road opens to a sprawling driveway. And there it sits—Zay-Zay's house. No, sorry. It's not a house. It's a manor, a villa, heaven's waiting room. This place is *paradise*. We slow to a stop, and I push open the door, step out of the car, and stare.

Rolling hills are covered with trees and bushes, and little hiking paths wind into destinations unknown. To the right, the purples, reds, and oranges of the evening sky . . . meet the ocean. Endless *ocean*. I gaze upon the sparkling waters. I always imagined my family would be by my side when I saw the Pacific Ocean for the first time. Mom would be crying right now. Jax and Eli would jump up and down with glee. Loren would be taking TikTok videos with the ocean in view behind her, and Dad . . . he'd probably be declaring, "I'll be!" Heck, Daeshya might be cured of her overwhelming desire to throw things at people. The ocean is that magical. It *cures*. I am renewed. Exhilarated. Enthralled. Zay-Zay wakes up to this? People *live* like this?

Aish steps beside me. "Would you like to see the inside of your house for the week?"

"Of course I would. But wait. One sec." I rush to the other side of the car, where Aaron sits. "Bye, Aaron. Thanks for the ride." I wave, and he lowers the window. "And bye, Frank. Will I see y'all again?"

Aaron smiles warmly. "I certainly hope so. I'll be taking you to Sun and Sand in about an hour."

Frank nods. "I'm always here. You know that. I'll wait in the club-house while you get ready."

Oh. "Tha's right. My bad." I slap my palm against my forehead. "See y'all soon, then."

"Zay." Diamond pushes her door shut and steps over to me. She places a hand on my back and guides me along the patterned driveway. "Aaron's driving me home before he takes you to Sun and Sand. There's a matter I need to tend to with my son, Zack. I'll return tomorrow."

"Oh," I whisper. "I dunno why I thought you lived with Zay. It certainly looks like there's room for you."

She smirks. "Thankfully, at the ripe old age of forty-seven, I have my own home. With lots of room for me." She pauses for a second, as if gathering her thoughts. "Also, I want to thank you."

My eyes widen, then narrow. "You do?"

"You handled yourself beautifully on the carpet. I'll admit, I was impressed. You seemed quite comfortable."

"I *was* comfortable! Which surprised me." The Malibu breeze moves through my hair and tickles my skin. "Posing for pictures was fun."

"I'm glad you enjoyed it. Keep up the professionalism. But when it comes to Koi . . ." She lowers her voice to almost a whisper. "Do not let him kiss you again."

I should be disappointed at being ordered to *not* kiss Koi Kalawai'a. But relief rushes up my spine like the cool breeze. "That shouldn't be a problem. What do I do if he tries again?"

"Tell him you have a cold. He's terrified of germs. That should do the trick."

"And dinner won't actually be dinner." Aish has appeared at my side. "You'll sit. Order drinks. Act bored. Focus on your phones. Aaron will stay parked outside the restaurant. Fifteen minutes, max."

"Yes," Diamond replies. "These little outings with Koi don't typically last much longer. Also . . ." She crosses her arms under her chest. "Talk less. Zay does not thank her driver for driving her."

Once again I slap my palm against my forehead. "Sorry, sorry. Natural instinct to say thanks. Won't happen again."

"Good." Diamond seems pleased with my apology. "If you're going to stand in for Zay, act like her."

But I don't know how she acts! "Copy that. I'll . . . keep the thank-yous to myself. Except." I scratch my head. "Thank *you*, Diamond. Today's been super cool. And you, too, Aish."

Aish smiles.

"Ok, sorry. No more thank-yous!" I say. "Starting now."

Diamond walks back to the SUV and climbs inside. I watch Aaron back out of the driveway with Frank in the front seat. Waving would be so natural for me, but I keep my hands at my side. Gotta remember, Diamond said to act like Zay. Zay's so cool. She doesn't wave.

Randy grabs me by the arm. "C'mon. Let's tour the manz, then get you changed for your fake date."

I turn my full attention to the beauty and splendor of Zay's seaside mansion with all its glass panels and ultramodern style. I remember when she bought it. It was on TMZ. Every picture of every room. I marveled that rich people had movie theaters in their homes. Is it normal that I know she's the youngest millionaire to buy property in the Malibu Hills? Now that I'm literally walking in her shoes, it's weird to have had so much access to the details of her private life.

We step under a covered entry, Aish types a code onto a keypad on the wall, and the thick pane of glass that is Zay-Zay's elaborate front door opens automatically. We step in.

"Lights on," Aish calls out.

The lights flip on, casting a luminescent glow. Through floor-to-ceiling windows, the view of the sun setting over the Pacific takes my breath away. White marble flooring glimmers. Panoramic views of the landscape reveal palm trees swaying and gentle ocean waves. I follow Aish and Randy past a set of floating stairs that lead to the next floor, into the grand living room.

"Doors open," Aish calls out.

Accordion-style sliding doors slowly open to the back patio. It's like the outside has become one with the inside of the house.

"This is unbelievable," I declare.

"Staying here on workdays is definitely one of the perks of the job," Randy says.

All the furniture in the living room is white, but it doesn't feel sterile or uncomfortable. It looks like clouds. I could jump on these cushions and float off into the sky.

I pause. Either I hear a dog barking, or the ghost of Norman has found me at last.

"The dog walker must've left Tyrone out of his crate." Aish drops her bags onto one of the couches. "Tyrone's a wild one. Brace yourself."

An American bulldog comes racing around the corner, past Aish and Randy, and directly into my arms, knocking me to the floor.

"Hi, boy!" I scratch his belly and under his ears as he licks my face. "Hi! Omigosh, you're so cute!" I don't realize my eyes are filled with tears until they start sliding down my cheeks. I wipe them away as Tyrone jumps and spins in circles.

"Fascinating," Aish says. "He believes you're Zay."

Whoever said love at first sight is not a thing . . . is a moron. I'm already trying to think of ways I can stuff him into a bag and get him back to our farm. My mom has to be sensible. We cannot be a proper farm family until we get another dog. Norman would want it so. I know he would. Aish and Randy are staring at me as I wipe tears.

"We had one just like him. Norman." I pause to scratch Tyrone's belly again. "Fourteen years old when he died." I pull myself off the floor, not wanting to harm Zay's dress. "Best dog ever."

Aish looks like she might start crying too. "Aww. Really sorry for your loss, Red."

Tyrone barks.

"But not better than you, Tyrone." I laugh and wipe more tears. "I'm sorry, little buddy. You're the best dog, too, I'm sure."

He starts with the zoomies again, running around in circles at my feet.

"He does that all day. It's why we keep him in his crate so much." Aish sighs. "It's maddening."

Keep him in his crate? Yikes. "It's zoomies," I explain. "These kinds of dogs prefer to be outside is all. They're farm dogs. The crate is the worst place for them."

"Zay *used* to let him roam free," Aish explains. "Until he got into a fight with a rattlesnake up on the hill, which sent him straight to the veterinarian for emergency treatment. Now she's afraid to let him past the driveway."

Tyrone jumps, resting his paws on my belly. I stumble back.

"Tyrone, get down!" Randy snaps at the dog. "That dress cost two thousand dollars."

Tyrone sits, his ears roll back, and he whimpers.

"Aww." I pat him on the head. "Don't cry, little buddy."

Randy motions to the patio. "Red, you wanna see the pool?"

"It's an energy-efficient smart house," Aish explains as we move toward the patio. "You can talk to everything from the blinds to the pool, even the fridge. You'll get used to it."

"Sometimes stuff talks back," Randy adds.

"If our fridge at home could talk, it would say, *Clean me, I smell like rotten eggs.* Holy moly." We step out onto the patio. "This is insane." There's a full outdoor kitchen, two bars, lounge chairs situated around a firepit, and a covered gazebo. The pool seems to blend with the horizon . . . it's beyond words. I could stay here forever. "What would life be like if we could all live this way?"

"Perhaps that's what heaven is like." Aish inhales deeply, absorbing this Malibu vibe. "A Malibu mansion for everyone."

"I like the sound of that!" I kick off my shoes, march right over to the pool, sit on the edge, pull up the dress a bit, and let my feet dangle in the water. It's so *warm*. The walls of the pool are covered with mosaic tiles; the light from the setting sun makes them shimmer like twinkling stars. Tyrone snuggles up beside me. I exhale.

"When you're out here, watch for the drones." Aish sits on the other side of Tyrone and pats him on the head.

"Drones?" I repeat.

"Paparazzi drones," Randy chimes in. "We used to get them more, but Frank started to shoot them out of the air with a slingshot. That stopped the madness for a while. They still take their chances sometimes."

"Can you believe one photographer tried to sue Zay when his ten-thousand-dollar drone got destroyed on her property?" Aish shakes her head. "They went to court and everything. Thank goodness he lost. It would have set a terrible precedent for the others."

"Wow." I frown, looking into the sky. I don't *think* I see any drones.

"Thanks to shoddy news networks that use unethical measures to get their stories and pictures," Aish explains, "whenever celebrities purchase homes, it's national news. So everyone pretty much knows precisely where they live. It's uncanny. Privacy is a thing of the past."

"Even *I* knew where she lived," I reply. "I saw pictures of this house online and everything. Scrolled through each room."

"Don't do that anymore. People need to stop clicking." Aish's bag vibrates. She reaches in and takes out my phone. "It says 'Mom' calling. Would you like to talk now?"

Would I *ever*? She hands me the phone, and I grip it tightly. It feels like my arm's been reattached.

"Let's head inside, though, yeah?" Aish stands. "Sometimes the drones have microphones."

Dana L. Davis

~

"Mom! I miss you *so* much!"

"Oh, hon, I miss you more." Mom's whispering. "We saw you on TV, Red. I couldn't believe it was you. I hardly recognized you. Are those tattoos real? And that dress? Oh, kiddo, you had superstar vibes. I mean, I always thought you two resembled one another, but you're her twin now. And Koi Kalawai'a? Tell me *everything*."

"I'm not actually allowed to talk about . . . anything. It's in the NDA. I'm sorry." I'm sitting in Zay's kitchen, on a barstool at her giant white marble-top island. This kitchen looks more like a set on a Food Network show than a place where normal people make food. I can almost see Bobby Flay in the corner prepping shrimp and roasted garlic tamales on the indoor grill.

"Oh, that's ok, hon," Mom says with a sigh. "I understand."

"Is that Red?" I can hear Loren now. "Did you tell her Dad sold another pig?"

"We sold another pig!" I say excitedly. "That's so awesome."

"And that the Ferris wheel arrived for the Strawberry Fest!"

"Loren, I was getting to all that," Mom says. "Loren, no . . . because *I* wanna talk to Red. Come back in five minutes. Go play."

"Mom, I'm fourteen. Go play where? Just give me the phone." I hear rustling and then Loren's voice. "Red?"

She sounds thousands of miles away. It makes my heart ache.

"Hi, Lo! It's amazing where I am. I wish you could be here."

"Amazing in Iberia, *Missouri*?" She laughs. "That one-horse town? Nice try. We all know you're suffering for your good deed."

Oh geez. That's *right*. For a split second, I almost forgot. I look over to see Aish messing around with the fridge, scrolling through a massive touch screen on the door. There's a button that shows you what's inside. If we had that fridge, Mom would never have to yell at us for holding the door open while we search for food.

"Red, Dad sold another pig. Daeshya walked from her playpen to the couch. And the Ferris wheel is halfway up! It's so cool," Loren exclaims. "I can't believe you're gonna miss the Strawberry Fest."

"Wait. *What?* Dae's *walking?*" I cover my mouth in disbelief.

"Yeah, yeah. Can you believe?"

I mean, I've only been gone for a few hours! "How could this happen without me?"

"Oh, here comes Dad," Loren says. "He wants to talk to you."

A few seconds later, I hear Dad's deep, resonating voice. "Red?"

"Dad!" Gosh, I can't believe how much I miss Dad already. He sounds relaxed and happy. "Was Tony excited when you rehired him?"

"We can't get rid of him!" He laughs. "He stayed for dinner and is now playing Xbox with the boys. I'm trying to kick him out so we can all go to bed."

"Sounds like a family party." I scratch at my elbows. "Glad you guys are having fun."

"Nah, Tony," Dad calls out. "Give it up!"

I hear Tony's muffled voice, though I can't make out his reply.

"Exactly!" Dad laughs heartily again. "You know you can't hang with them boys!"

"Dad?"

"Oh, sorry, hon. It's not the same without you here. We miss you so much."

I exhale. "I miss you guys too."

"Hold on a sec, Red. Let me try to find some privacy. I wanna hear about . . . you know. *Stuff.*" I hear more rustling; then it turns very quiet. "Can you hear me? I'm in the closet."

"I can hear you." I smile at the thought of Dad hiding in our messy hallway closet.

"I'm still in shock this all happened. Your mom showed me a video of you from *Entertainment Now.* Couldn't believe my eyes. That was *my* daughter."

My phone beeps. I look at the screen. Two percent. Dang it. "Hold on, Dad, my phone's about to die. Let me grab a charger."

"No problem, kiddo. But you're safe, right? You're good. You feel good?"

"I'm *so* safe, Dad." I'm sure they won't mind me sharing *that*. "Seriously, they have a gate and guards and everything. They're being great to me." I call out to Aish, "Hey, Aish, do you guys—" My phone screen goes black. Ugh! "Great. My phone died."

"Oh no." Aish turns to face me. "I'll grab you a charger. USB-C or Lightning? What sort of phone is that?"

"It's an Android."

She makes a face. "Everything here is Apple. May I see your phone?"

I hand it to her, and she checks the charger input. "Oh, bum. Pretty confident we don't have a charger for this."

Dad's probably still sitting in the closet, patiently waiting for me to call back. "So, what do I do?"

"No worries. I'll run right quick to a market while you're out with Koi. Your phone will be charged and ready upon your return."

Home is two hours ahead. They'll all be asleep by then. "Uh. Ok. Thanks, Aish."

"Your family sounds awfully fun. This house must seem quiet compared." The disappointment must be reading pretty loud on my face, because Aish adds, "Don't worry. We're fun too. Sometimes."

Randy peeks his head into the kitchen. "You ready to change for your dinner date?"

I glance out the window that overlooks the outdoor dining area. The sun has set, and with the twinkling outdoor string lights, the infinity pool glowing from underneath, and the acoustic-guitar music playing softly from overhead speakers I can't see, it feels like I'm in the castle of a magical kingdom. Anyone would be thrilled to be in my position. So why do I feel such a longing in my heart?

I hear whining and look down to see Tyrone's big brown eyes staring up at me. Norman didn't have the patch over his left eye, like

Tyrone, but otherwise, *they* might be doppelgängers. I bend to rub Tyrone's belly.

"Earth to Red?" Randy says. "You ready?"

I push away the feeling of longing. I don't even know what I'm longing for. My family is fine. I've got a job to do.

"Copy that. I'm ready."

ELEVEN

Riding in the back seat, cruising down the road, the entire Pacific Ocean to my right, headed to see my childhood music inspiration, and all I can do is silently pray that the Universe makes Koi Kalawai'a . . . disappear? Ok, too dramatic. Maybe he can just cancel at the last minute.

"Here you go. It's one of mine." Aish reaches over my shoulder to hand me a phone. "Focus on it, instead of Koi. Remember, he's a boring boy that Zay's sick of. Not the eighth wonder of the world."

I tuck the phone into my borrowed purse. Randy's beside me, fiddling with my hair. He reaches into his makeup bag and removes a small spray bottle. "Close your eyes." I close, and Randy sprays something onto my face that smells like grapefruit. "Ok. You can open."

When I open, I see the restaurant up ahead. At least, I think it's the restaurant, since a giant SUN AND SAND sign is right beside it. Aaron pulls off the main road and drives to the valet stand. Two men dressed in black pants and yellow polos stand beside a wooden podium. Under nonstressful circumstances, I'd really be looking forward to this. But something about an outing with Zay's fake boyfriend, who she's planning on dumping against his will, has disaster written all over it.

"You sure this outfit is ok?" I whisper to Randy.

"Honey, you're the blueprint," Randy replies. "The main character for sure."

Which means good, I think. I'm dressed much more casually now. Randy called it *natural chic*. A pair of ripped distressed jeans, a sheer black top, and a long gray cardigan. Matched with a pair of black heels. I feel like I'm wearing a Halloween costume. I have never been so stylish.

"We'll be waiting here in the car," Aish adds. "Order coffee. Paparazzi will take pics, and then we can head back."

As Frank hops out and rushes to pull open my door, I see them. Men and women holding professional-looking cameras in the parking lot, a.k.a. paparazzi. Not as many as there were at the airport or Skybar. But enough to make me wanna drop my jaw and say *Woooooow*. I slide on my sunglasses as the door opens. Frank offers me a hand. I take it and carefully step down onto the pavement.

Zay-Zay!

Zay-Zay Waters!

Zay, can we ask you a few questions?

Zay, I'm from TMZ. Give us an interview.

I think I'm doing a good job of ignoring the paps as Frank guides me past the valet stand and across a cute paved pathway to the front door of the restaurant. When we step inside, the glass doors shut behind us. It's a comfortable retro-style beach restaurant with flowered couches and classy wicker tables and chairs. It seems cozy and homey. And the *views*. Though it's evening, the views of the Pacific are pretty breathtaking. Outside, the waves crash peacefully onto the sands.

"Welcome to Sun and Sand," a friendly hostess greets me.

She's standing beside a sign that says NO CAMERAS / NO AUTOGRAPHS / PLEASE RESPECT OUR GUESTS.

I can see she's trying her hardest to dial down the fan screams. Her hands are clenched into fists at her side, the way mine are when I'm feeling anxious, and she's biting her bottom lip and going up and down on her tiptoes.

"Miss Waters." She points toward the patio. "We have a special private table on our heated patio for you."

I follow her through the quiet restaurant. A few heads turn as we move by. I hear a lady say, "Omigosh, is that Zay-Zay Waters?"

The guys she's sitting with replies, "Holy heck, I think it is."

We move through a back door and out onto a massive seaside deck decorated with little tiki torches and plants. The nighttime waters of the Pacific Ocean seem as though they have life. Like a mythical water monster you don't want to get angry. You know it's capable of anything, but for now, it's just gentle waters moved by gentle winds. My anxiety melts away. I exhale.

The hostess, who wears the same black pants and yellow polo as the valet boys from outside, places the menus on a table that's pushed into a far corner, away from the other guests.

"I think you're so talented," she blurts. "Sorry. We're not supposed to say things to celebrities. But you're my favorite singer. I know you live in Malibu, and I've always hoped you'd stop by here."

I smile weakly. These people think they're meeting their idol. "That's . . . what's up."

She seats Frank at another table before heading back inside. Thankfully his table is far enough away for privacy but close enough that he could leap and take down a crazed fan.

I study the menu. In spite of the nervous jitters and slight feeling of impending doom, I see food for sale. I wish I could order some. Can I? They have a cute "Breakfast for Dinner" menu. Apple cinnamon pan-cakes. Blueberry too? Oh wait, and bananas Foster french toast? I don't know what that is, but it sounds *delicious*. And fried potatoes. Yum.

"Hello, Zay-Zay."

Koi Kalawai'a is standing in front of me. He's changed clothes, too, now dressed in flip-flops, board shorts, and a plain black T-shirt. He still looks like a billion bucks.

He walks over to Frank first. "Frank. My man." They bump fists.

Down below on the beach, paparazzi aim their cameras toward us. Koi seems to know it. He takes forever to sit down. Stretching out his arms. Slowly taking off his sunglasses and setting them on the table. He seems to be soaking up the attention like a sunbather soaks up the sun.

"So." He finally pulls out his chair and takes a seat across from me, his green eyes glistening under the hanging lights. "I was thinking about our conversation earlier."

"Let me explain." I swallow nervously, still making sure to speak in Brooklish. "About earlier, I mean."

Our waiter arrives holding a silver pitcher. I can hear the ice sloshing around as he pours water into our glasses.

"Good evening. My name is Miguel. Would you two like coffee? Tonight's is an Ethiopian organic blend. Slightly floral. Quite fruity. One of my favorites. And our special, from the 'Breakfast for Dinner' menu, is the quiche lorraine."

"Coffee, sure." Koi stares down at the menu. "With sugar. And milk."

"Miss?" Miguel speaks to me. "Do you prefer oat, almond, rice, or cow's milk?"

Oh gosh. *I* prefer cow's. But would Zay? No stress. Aish and Randy say Koi and Zay are practically strangers. But to be safe, I hear these Hollywood types love their nut milks. "Almond."

Koi speaks up. "Almond milk for me too."

Whew. Ok. I ordered the right nut milk. All is well.

"I'll return shortly." Miguel turns and leaves.

Over the railing, the photographers are snapping photos like crazy. I lean back and try to act bored. Except I'm wearing sunglasses at night, and I don't really know how you can be bored sitting at such a fancy and amazing place.

"They are not supposed to be down there." Koi peeks over the railing. "Twenty bucks says the manager comes out and asks them to leave in a few minutes."

"Listen." I take a sip of my water. "I wanted to say sorry for sayin' that stupid breakup stuff. We're not breakin' up. We good. I was only messin' with you."

"You scared me." He pushes a loose strand of hair behind his ear. "Not gonna lie. It had me seriously stressing. I almost started to freak out, you know. I thought, How can I get on top of the press before this explodes in my face?"

I grimace. That's exactly what Aish said he would do.

"I figured I'd wait until tonight, to see what the real deal was." I force a pained-looking smile. "Bad joke. Sorry."

"Very bad joke." He takes another sip of water. "I need you right now. I need . . . us." There he goes with the Hollywood screenwriter lines. He leans forward and adds, "A band backed out of Lollapalooza at the last second. No one knows about it yet. Koi and the Six are on the short list to replace them, miraculously. Us breaking up would not be good for our chances. Us together? We're in."

He's not even trying to pretend. He's using Zay-Zay and not ashamed at all.

"I'm sure you think that makes me a common opportunist." He shrugs. "It's not like you haven't done something similar. After all, you're the mastermind behind 'us' in the first place."

Really? Zay-Zay was the mastermind behind Zoi? I have questions. But we're not supposed to be talking. I nod and pretend to study the menu.

"Hey, Zay?"

Gosh, why does he keep talking to me?!

"Would you mind if we actually ordered food this time? I'm kinda starving. I was so stressed earlier I forgot to eat."

Food? I can't help it, but a huge smile erupts onto my face. "Let me check and see if it's aight. Aish and Randy waitin' in the car."

"Since when did you start caring what Aish and Randy think?"

Duh, Red! Zay-Zay wouldn't ask *permission* to do something. "I just, you know, don't wanna be rude."

"Serious?" He laughs. "You once made Aish and Randy wait for four hours in the car, during freezing rain in New York, while you shopped for shoes. They're used to you by now."

Geez. Shoe shopping in freezing rain? "People change, I guess." I quickly type out a message to Aish.

We're ordering food. Is that ok?!!!!

"So. How have you been, Zay?"

Why oh why is he *still* talking to me?

"Coo. Yup." I sit back. Attempting to relax, while simultaneously sighing with pretend boredom. Aish texts back.

It's fine. We're gonna make a quick run to the market down the street for snacks. And your charger cord. Brb.

Oh good. "They don't mind. We can order."

He rolls his eyes. "Glad your assistant and *hair*dresser approve."

How can I turn around this conversation we're not supposed to be having? Aish did say he likes to talk about himself. "I saw you in *People*. One of the world's sexiest men? Congrats."

"Yeah, it's all politics. You know that. I wanted the cover. I would have been the youngest sexiest man ever. But nope."

"You looked good in the pics, though." And boy, did he. Shirtless in jeans, coming out of a hot spring. Really artistic. I bought two copies. "And the dude who was on the cover? That astronaut guy? No way he's the sexiest man alive! He's like sixty-two."

"I think they're trying to be inclusive to old people." He takes another sip of water. "Hey, how come your phone is going to voice mail?"

Oh. Uh. "I dropped it in . . . the toilet. So it's . . . flushed."

"You flushed it down the *toilet*? Is that possible?"

Definitely not possible. "With these newfangled wide . . . holed toilets. Boy, I could flush you down the toilets in my house."

He motions toward the phone on the table. "Is that a loaner?"

I hold it up. "Nah. It's just my . . . other phone."

He squints. "Have you fallen in love with your assistant?"

"Huh?"

"Her picture is your lock screen."

I flip the phone around and—oh wow. Giant selfie of Aish. "Ok, it's one of *her* phones. Obviously. She lettin' me use it until I replace the flushed one."

"Zay, you made seventy-eight million dollars last year. Get a new phone."

Zay made $78 million? In a year!

The waiter returns and sets down two coffees with foam hearts on top, which, I can't help but wonder how they did that. There is also a small saucer decorated with an assortment of tea biscuits. I wanna grab one, but I don't want Koi to think I'm greedy. I'll wait for the meal.

"Are you two ready to order? Miss Waters, could we start with you?"

Yaaas. Omigosh, food. "Mos def." I read from the menu. "I'll take the bananas Foster french toast, a side order of the . . ." I pause. "Wait. Which is better? The blueberry pancakes, or the apple cinnamon?"

"The blueberry are less sweet but do come with a maple-blueberry compote that's simply out of this world." He kisses the tips of his fingers. "The apple cinnamon tastes more like a pastry. They have a cream cheese filling and don't really need syrup."

"They both sound super lit." I have never been this excited about food. I drum my long nails on the table. "I'mma go with the blueberry ones. Extra compote. Some fried potatoes too. You know what, add the side salad from the other dinner menu. 'Cuz I gotta have my greens, right? With croutons." I hand the menu off to Miguel.

"All excellent choices, miss." He turns to Koi. "And you, sir?"

Koi stares at me for a few seconds before turning his attention back to Miguel. "I'll . . . uh, have the fruit plate."

"Very good." Miguel takes both of our menus and disappears back inside.

Koi is giving me the strangest stare. Maybe I shouldn't have ordered so much food? Especially with him eating like a bird. "What?"

"You seem . . . cured," he says.

"What do you mean?"

"I mean. You ordered pancakes *and* french toast. And croutons."

"So? What's the big deal?"

"The big deal, *Zay*"—he's speaking very, very softly now—"is that you have celiac disease. You'd be hospitalized if you ate all that. Or did you forget?"

Oh.

My.

Ga.

"I can't believe it." He quickly reaches across the table and snatches off my glasses. "You're not Zay-Zay."

TWELVE

I'm looking down at the table, a hand placed over my eyes, pretending I'm studying Aish's phone. The photographers below continue to take photos. I don't want them to see me without my glasses.

"Give me the glasses back, and I can explain. Please. They'll know I'm not her."

"Will they?" He folds the glasses and places them on his lap. "*I* can hardly tell, and I'm sitting right across from you." He stares at me again. "Why do you look so much like her? Are you some crazed fan who got plastic surgery or something?"

"*No,*" I whisper. "I'm just a girl from a farm who fell into a pile of manure while my sister was recording it."

"Wait." His eyes light up. "That was you?"

I nod.

"And she . . . tracked you down?"

"I guess you could say that." I twist around to make sure Frank isn't listening. He doesn't seem to be, but I lower my voice anyway. "She saw the video, obviously, and found me. It was a strange twist of fate that she changed her hair a few days before. It's been a whirlwind. A few days ago, I was on my farm in Iowa. Today, I'm sitting across from . . . you."

"Unbelievable." He shakes his head in disbelief. "You know, she told me once that it would be a dream of hers to find a look-alike.

I gotta say. The girl has some serious manifestation powers. Where is she?"

"I mean . . ." I twist my water glass around in my hands. It makes the tips of my fingers wet and burn from the cold. "I'm contractually obligated not to answer that."

"C'mon. I won't tell anyone you told me."

"I don't know if I can trust that." I tap my long nails on the water glass. They make a sound like the *ding, ding, ding* of a tiny bell. "If I mess things up, her aunt Diamond will ruin my life. There's a lot riding on this."

"Crap." He leans forward, taking my hands into his so that our fingers intertwine. A chill moves through my entire body. Why is he touching me right now?

"W-what are you doing?"

"Shhh." He speaks softly, barely moving his mouth. "The table to the far right of Frank. They're *recording* us. I don't want them to think we're arguing or anything."

I take back one of my hands and pretend I'm scratching my shoulder. Yep, sure enough, a girl at the table has her phone set against a saltshaker and is secretly recording us!

"Do you think the mic can pick up what we're saying?" I'm whispering, my face pointed away from her camera.

"Probably not. But these people lip-read." He stands and acts like he's yawning, then moves over to Frank, leaning to speak into his ear.

Frank marches over to the table and snatches the phone.

"Hey!" the girl yells.

"Delete." Frank taps the screen. "Delete. Aaaand delete forever." He clicks the side button on the phone, and the screen goes black. "Do it again, and I'll have you kicked out of here."

"Whatever." She snatches it from his hands. "We were about to leave anyway."

"Oh good. Byeee." Frank returns to his seat and assumes his position, as if nothing happened.

I should get the heck out of here. Run. But where would I go? Aish and Randy left to get snacks! Maybe things aren't as bad as I'm thinking. Koi did go through the trouble to make sure we weren't being recorded. Not to mention he hasn't stood and screamed *Impostor, impostor!* Yet. So, he can't be all bad.

"What does all of this mean? She hired you to . . . break up with me?"

"Why would she do that?" I wrap my hands around my coffee cup. It's warm and makes my hands feel like they're covered in soft, fuzzy gloves. "You two aren't even together." I'm making sure to barely move my mouth, since Koi said people can read lips. At this point, privacy seems like an illusion. "She hired me because she needed a break." I lift the cup to sample my coffee.

"Just so you know. Zay's more of a tea kind of girl."

I frown. "Is she allergic to coffee?"

He shakes his head no.

"Then I'm drinking it." I take a sip. *Wow.* This is nothing like the stuff we sell at our grocery store. The hot liquid instantly warms my insides. It's suddenly like the morning of my favorite holiday, with fresh food cooking in the oven making the house smell divine. "This tastes amazing . . ." I pause to lick the foam off my lips. "I've never tasted something so good."

Koi takes a sip of his own. "It's not bad. Coffee at home is better. My hometown is known for good coffee."

"You're from Lahaina, right?"

"Oh, you know things about me?" He raises a bemused eyebrow. "Google? Wiki? *Page Six*? Where you getting your info from, stalker?"

"Don't flatter yourself." I drink more of my delicious coffee. "I heard. From my sister. And . . . friends. I don't google. Especially about you."

He tosses me one of those "Yeah right" smirks. "Even *I* google, Brown Eyes. But since you've been misled, I'm not from Lahaina. Technically speaking, anyway."

He's not? "Where are you from?"

"Not that it's any of your business, complete stranger, but"—he pauses to take another gulp of coffee, licking the foam off his lips—"I'm *originally* from a very small town, Hanapepe. That's Kauai, in case you didn't pay attention in geography class."

Kauai? From what I know about Koi, and I know a lot, he grew up in Lahaina. I sit back in my chair. "You lived there with your mom and stepdad, right?"

"Obviously there's more to my story, and way too much to unpack with the truth. Plus, it's nobody's business that my mom and stepdad are self-involved losers who didn't actually raise me. Who cares, right?"

I specifically remember an interview with Koi and his mom. Clearly where he got his sparkling green eyes and good looks from. She was as gorgeous as a Miss Universe contestant, with light-brown skin and long waves of dark hair. They seemed so in sync, and she absolutely talked about being a single parent and raising Koi. He's saying that's not true? "So your mom didn't raise you?"

He shakes his head from side to side. "I strategically skip over all the sad stuff in interviews. Besides, I sing. I write music. I travel with my band. I entertain people. It makes me happy. What's my childhood got to do with it? I hate when reporters ask invasive questions. One of these days, I'm gonna flip the script and be like, 'Tell me, reporter person, since we're tossing around useless information, what kind of toilet paper do you use?'"

I play along, pretending to be Sophia from *Entertainment Now*. "Oh, Koi, that's a *fabulous* question. I absolutely love Charmin. Charmin's, like, *so* hot right now. What about you? Yeah. Tell me all about it."

He laughs. "You get it. They're all full of it." His brow furrows as he studies me. "Don't let this go to your head, but I can see why Zay decided to trust you. You don't seem so bad, complete stranger."

"Don't call me *complete stranger*. It's weird."

"That's what you are."

A seagull lands on the railing beside us. I notice it's missing a foot. "Aww. Look at that." I say. "He's *injured*."

"Poor dude." Koi breaks off a piece of one of the tea biscuits and places it on the railing. The seagull snatches it and flies away.

"So she's breaking up with me? And you accidentally let it slip?" Koi sighs. "Tell me, so I can know. I need to prepare for this."

"I mean . . ." I drum my nails against the coffee cup. "I'm not . . ." I pull at my hair. "I don't . . ." *Ugh.* How can I get out of answering this?!

"It's ok. I get it. She's probably off with her real boyfriend while you're tending to the fake one. She's the worst."

"That's not true," I say in her defense. If he only knew. Zay-Zay is in the Brazilian jungle, trying her hardest to *better* herself. "You wouldn't understand."

"If there is one thing I understand, it's Zay-Zay Waters. She is president and CEO of the master-schemer club. But guess what? Joke's on her."

My shoulders tense. "What do you mean?"

"I've literally, just this second, come up with a plan of my own, complete stranger."

"What if someone hears you?" I lean forward and whisper, "Stop calling me that!"

"What if I called you *fiancée?*" He stands. "'Cuz I *really* like the sound of that."

"Fiancée?" My stomach muscles turn hard as rocks as he skirts around the table and moves toward me. What is he doing? "W-what are you doing?"

"Two can play at the scheming game." He gets down on one knee right in front of me and takes my left hand into his.

"Koi Kalawai'a!" I whisper-scream, looking at him in horror. "Have you any sense at all?"

"Careful, now. People *are* taking pictures. You don't wanna make Zay look bad, do you?"

I turn to my left. Below, the photographers have cameras pointed in our direction. The *click-click-click* is louder than normal. I shift to my right. The diners on the patio are focused on us now, too, phone cameras aimed, locked, and loaded. I guess **Do Not Film the Celebrities** signs matter not when a proposal is happening. Albeit a very, very fake one!

"Get up!" I whisper. "We're supposed to be disengaged so the breakup isn't a shock when it happens." Doh! I slap my palm against my forehead. "You didn't hear me say that."

"FYI." He grabs at his hair and literally pulls a strand out. He holds it up for me to see. "I'm gonna tie this around your finger as a mock ring." He takes my hand. "Act touched."

"How weird is that?" I attempt to pull my hand back. "You can't do this."

He yanks on my hand and whispers, "Zay-Zay resisting my proposal? Not gonna be good."

He's right. Reluctantly, I give in, allowing him to tie his stupid strand of hair around my finger.

"There." He winks. "Pretend I asked you to marry me. You should cry or something."

"Oh, I feel like crying, all right."

"*Fine.* I'll be the only one crying." He wipes at his eyes as if wiping away tears. "You've made me so happy, fake Zay." He stands and calls out to the restaurant. "She said yes, everyone!"

The patio erupts into cheers, whistles, and foot stomps.

Koi pulls me up. He places his hand under my chin and stares lovingly into my eyes as the cheers and whistles continue. I hear shouts.

Congrats!

Mazel tov!

Such a beautiful couple!

Omigosh, they're perfect.

"In a few minutes . . ." He brushes his thumb down the side of my cheek. "Our 'engagement' will be the top trending story on TMZ. Break up with me now, Zay. I dare ya. Should we kiss to seal the deal?"

"If you kiss me again," I whisper back. "I will karate chop you in the throat."

"How 'bout I hug you?"

He wraps his arms around me as the cheers continue, pulling me so close I feel the warmth of pretty much all of him. It might even be a charming moment, if I didn't have the very strong desire to push him off this deck. He pulls away. "Oh good. Here comes all the food you ordered that you can't eat."

"Congratulations to the newly engaged couple." Miguel has a tray loaded with quite a few plates. "How old are you two?"

"I'm nineteen." Koi returns to his seat. "So is my soon-to-be bride."

I need to talk to Aish and Randy. We have to figure out what to do. How to fix what Koi . . . did! Zay-Zay is currently connecting to the Universe in a Brazilian jungle with a shaman and has no idea that she is now fake engaged to the fake boyfriend she's planning to get rid of!

"Bon appétit." Miguel sets the steaming plates of food in front of me.

"Actually." Koi slides the plates across the table so they're now in front of him. "My beautiful fiancée here, that I love with all my heart, forgot that she's allergic to . . . everything on your menu. Celiac. So, I'll take all of *her* food, and she will take my cute little fruit plate."

"I apologize, miss." Miguel seems horrified as he sets the fruit plate down in front of me. It's a nice assortment. Decoratively cut slices of pineapple, apples, pears, strawberries, grapes, and melons. In the center, a small bowl of something purple. Like a slushie with . . . white cheese?

"It's fine," I say to Miguel. "What's the stuff in the center?"

"It's an acai bowl," he replies. "Shredded coconut on top."

Oh, *coconut*. It's no pancakes with syrup, but ok. "Got it."

"When's the wedding?" Miguel sets the steaming potatoes and side salad in front of Koi.

"I'd marry this girl tonight if I could." Koi winks at me and reaches across the table to take my hand.

"Love is such a beautiful thing," Miguel says before disappearing back inside the restaurant.

I squeeze Koi's hand. Tight. Hoping it hurts. "You're laying it on pretty thick, dude." I pull my hand back and decide to text Aish. "Zay-Zay is going to kill you."

Slight . . . thing happened. Not sure what I should do? Please call and advise?

I click send. The restaurant patrons on the patio seem to have returned to their meals. The table where the girl was recording me is empty now, and a busboy is clearing off their plates. That could've easily been Loren. Secretly recording a celebrity, not quite understanding why it might not be ok. I twist back around to face Koi.

"Zay might fire me now," I declare angrily. "My family needs the money. Zay's paying me. The money is for our farm."

"You're trying to save your *farm*?" He cocks his head to the side. "That's adorable. Cute little farm girl, here to save her farm. I swear you get more and more interesting with each passing second."

I think of those cartoons where smoke comes out of a red-faced anime character's head and wonder if that's what's happening to me right now. "I'm giving the money to my family so we can hire back our farm manager. Once Zay finds out about this, I'll be fired for sure."

"Seriously. You should calm down." He holds up his phone and shows me Zay-Zay's name before tapping it. I hear her voice through his speakers. *"You've almost reached me. Leave a message."*

He ends the call. "Wherever Zay-Zay is, her phone is off. She's disconnected. She has no idea what's going on. You're fine."

"What about Aish? And Randy? They'll be mad at me."

He picks up his fork and laughs. "Her hairdresser and assistant?"

"They're more than that. She said Aish was her left hand. That she can't do anything without her."

"Zay said that about her last assistant, Chanie. Chanie got fired in a text message on Rosh Hashanah, the Jewish New Year. And Chanie's

Jewish! She didn't see the text for two days. Happy New Year. Now I have no job. When Zay is ready to move on, she just . . . does. Obviously."

"But Diamond." I shake my head. "She's going to be so upset."

"Aunt Diamond?" He grabs the cup of blueberry compote off the table and pours it over the pancakes. "She *loves* me. She'll be thrilled we've taken our fake relationship to the next fake level."

Would she be? "But . . ."

"Look, stranger." He takes a giant bite of the pancakes and talks with his mouth full. "You know what Lollapalooza is, don't you?"

"I live on a farm, not under a rock." Of *course* I know one of the biggest music festivals in the world.

"Well, just like you're taking care of your cute little family farm, I'm taking care of mine. The Six. They're my brothers. Not by blood. Just by"— he bangs his hand on his chest—"heart. 'Ohana. And nothing is guaranteed in this business. Zay made seventy-eight million last year. I made . . . two."

"Two dollars?" I grimace. "No wonder you're acting like a moron. You've got serious financial problems."

He laughs. "You're *cute*. Anyway, two million might seem like a small fortune, but . . . divided by seven. 'Cuz I split everything with my brothers. Plus agents and lawyers and blah, blah, blah. Lollapalooza will ensure a lot of things for us. We need it. Don't judge me, and I won't judge you for walking around in Zay's clothes and pretending to be her." He takes another bite of food and mumbles, "If you're gonna cross a river, you need stepping stones, right?"

"You need a boat."

"Zay-Zay is a boat. Hey, how much does it cost to hire a real-life Designer Imposter anyway?"

"I can't say." I specifically remember reading that part in the NDA. "But again, I didn't keep the money. I gave it to my parents. They needed it more than me."

"You're a saint."

"Says the boy who lets his mom pretend she raised him so the world won't judge her. And splits all his money with his six nonbrother 'brothers'? You got a *little* saint in your blood, Koi Kalawai'a. Even if you are extremely annoying."

He smiles. It's a soft smile. A genuine smile. The two of us sit in silence. Maybe he's right. Maybe Diamond will be ok with this. Not the original plan, but I could tell her he was joking. Teenagers getting engaged with a lock of hair isn't really a thing.

I hear arguing down below and stretch my neck out over the railing. A man, possibly the restaurant manager, dressed in black slacks and a yellow polo, is yelling at the photographers on the beach, pointing to signs that say PRIVATE BEACH and NO PHOTOGRAPHERS ALLOWED.

"If celebrities don't wanna be photographed, why come here? I can guarantee there are no paparazzi hanging around at IHOP or Waffle House."

"Obviously there's a lot of 'I actually do want to be photographed' going on."

I reach for one of the tea biscuits.

"You can't eat that," Koi says quickly.

Oh geez. I toss it back onto the plate.

"Can I ask you a personal question?"

"Yes, obviously I've googled you before. No, I didn't have a poster of you on my wall. It was on my closet door, thank you very much."

"What's your name?"

Aww. What a nice question. "It's Red."

"Little Red? Are you off to Grandmother's house after Zay's?"

"If I'm Little Red"—I pick up my fork—"does that make you the Big Bad Wolf? 'Cuz you seem too wimpy to be a bad guy."

"My ancestors threw javelins and lifted stones with their bare hands. Put me in the forest and people might mistake me for a Sasquatch."

"Sure. Yeah. All . . . one hundred and twenty-two pounds of you."

"I'm six three, a hundred and forty pounds. I'm rugged. I'm strong."

"Oh, my bad. You're practically the Hulk." I dig into the purple slushie with a spoon. It's pretty good.

He grabs his fork and cuts into the stack of french toast.

I frown. "Stop eating all my food. I was gonna get some of it to go."

"You've got food." He points to my tray. "How is it, by the way? Cold? Mushy?"

I stab a grape with my fork and pop it into my mouth. "Grape-y."

He laughs. "You look like Zay, but you're different. It's intriguing. *You're* intriguing."

"Thank you. When you're not scheming and fake proposing to me, you seem kinda nice."

He takes another bite of french toast, then talks with his mouth full. "When the drones started showing up at Zay's house, I figured our days were numbered." He downs a gulp of coffee. "Hey, what else is on your schedule? I can give you some tips on how to get through it."

I think back to the schedule. "Red carpet at this one place. Red carpet at somewhere. Another red carpet at somewhere else. Oh, I remember a ribbon cutting at a concert hall. Unless I'm fired because of you."

He makes a disgusted face. "Sounds like they have you in useless-event hell. Celebrity life at its finest."

"Honestly, I'd be happy to hang out at Zay's mansion and wave at paparazzi drones."

"That's all you want out of this? You gotta dream bigger. You're on a boat, crossing a river."

Am I?

"C'mon. I'm pushing for Lollapalooza. Zay's using you to get away. Play the game. It's not give and give. It's give and *take*. What do *you* want?"

Hmm. Nobody's ever asked me what I want.

"I'm not getting any younger here." Koi moves a hand through his hair. "More ruggedly handsome?" He smiles. "Perhaps."

Ok. He's not asking my life's ambition. He simply wants to know what I want out of *this* experience. That I can answer. In fact, I can keep it simple too. Private jets are amazing. Red-carpet events are . . . fun. Zay's house is extremely cool. But Aunt Diamond's not exactly loads of fun to be around. Aish and Randy are technically working, and I'm their project. I'd rather be on vacation. "I've never been to LA before," I finally say. "I'd like to see some of it without Zay's entourage. Like this, with you. I mean, there have been moments when I've wanted to push you off this deck. Still, hanging out at Sun and Sand, this is nice. Is that a lame want? Should I wish for something bigger. Ok, I change my mind. I want seventy-eight million dollars a year."

The loaner phone rings. I look down at it.

"You might wanna answer that," Koi mumbles, mouth full of food. "It could be Aishwarya wondering why Zay's trending on social." He snaps his fingers. "Wait a second. I think I might be able to assist the Universe to make this want of yours a reality." He reaches across the table and snatches the phone out of my hands.

"Hey," I say as loudly as I can without making much sound at all. "Give it *back*."

He taps the phone and holds it to his ear. "Hello? Hi, Aishwarya, I was hoping it was you." He pauses. "I know. I'm so sorry I'm answering her phone, but she went to the bathroom."

Omigosh! "Koi, seriously. You'll get me in trouble."

He taps the mute button. "I have a plan. Do you trust me?"

No. But when in Rome . . . gamble, I guess? "Ok, fine. This better be good, though."

He taps the mute button again. "Aish? Yeah, I know. And I'm sorry about that. It was only a joke. I'll fix it for sure. I've actually been acting like a total douche tonight. Been on the phone closing a deal with my agent. I'm gonna be in a . . . Popeyes chicken commercial." He smiles at me and rolls his eyes. "Why, thank you, love. It is awfully exciting, isn't it?" He imitates her British accent with that last sentence. I'm sure she's far from amused. "They're paying me a boatload of money to pretend I eat that crap."

I sit back in my seat. What's he up to?

"Anyway, Aish, I've barely spoken a word to Zay since I proposed to her," Koi continues. "I'm going to the Getty with my best friend and his girlfriend in a few days. There's a band performing that evening. My friend's been in France for a year, filming." He gives me a thumbs-up. "Yeah, yeah. Taylor. Still my bestie. Yep . . . Aish, are you sure? What if she says no? . . . Tell her she's not allowed to say no?" He winks at me. "She's coming back from the bathroom now. You can tell her yourself." He taps mute. "You're coming with me to the Getty in a few days. There's a concert too. No entourage allowed. Plus, you're off the hook for being my fake fiancée. Thank me later." He hands me the phone.

I quickly tap the unmute button. "Hello?"

"Oh my *word*. Can he hear you?" Aish has a strange excitement to her voice. "Could you step away from him for a moment?"

"Um. Yeah. I'm walking away right now." I lean back in my seat. "Ok, he can't hear me." I scratch at my elbow.

"Red, I swear you've got some sort of kismet. I know he's insufferable, but he's headed to the Getty in a few days with Taylor Thompson Lee and wants you to tag along. You simply *must*."

Taylor Thompson Lee?!

"Diamond will freak when she hears this. This is the director Zay has been dying to connect with. Plus, the actress starring in his new movie just pulled out for whatever reason. He wants to cast a real singer. Charm him with your rambles. You can be quite charming, Red. You know that?"

I really do not know that. Not to mention "Charm him with your rambles" sounds downright scary.

"This could be huge for Zay. Anyway. See you soon."

"Wait," I whisper. "What do I do about the . . . fake proposal?"

"Not your concern. Diamond adores Koi and wishes he and Zay were *actually* together. She'll be thrilled. As for Zay? Let her deal with it when she gets back. You get her an audition with Taylor Thompson Lee . . . I don't think Zay will care either way."

She ends the call. I set the phone on the table.

"See?" He pours maple syrup all over the french toast and takes another giant bite. "It's fun to play the game of life. Place your order, ladies and gents," he calls out like a circus ringmaster. "See what the Universe has in store."

"Is Taylor Thompson Lee really your best friend?"

"Yup." He swallows. "You know me and my band's song 'Still in Love with You'?"

Know it? I want it to be played at my wedding. I know every lyric. "I might have heard it. Maybe."

"Well, the video. He directed it. He's so much fun. Cracks me up. We kept in touch after the shoot and became friends after that. He's a total weirdo. Not as weird as you, farm girl." He grins. "Weird just the same." He checks the time on his phone. "I gotta run." He wipes his mouth with the napkin and chugs the rest of his coffee.

I'm pretty sure Koi lives in Brooklyn and must be staying at a hotel here in LA. He's doing me a favor. Should I do him one too?

"Where are you staying?" I ask. "Do you . . . I dunno . . . wanna stay at Zay's place instead of a hotel? I could ask them. She has a pool house."

"Gross. No. I'm staying at the Chateau Marmont on Sunset. Malibu is like a retirement village. I hate it there. Zay does too. She's trying to sell that house. Did she tell you?"

Huh? "She lives on a cliff overlooking the beach, and she has a theater in her house and an upstairs in her *room.* It's practically perfect. Why on earth would she be selling that dream home?"

"You'll soon see, all that glitters ain't gold." He tosses his napkin on the table. "Are you excited to see some of LA and hang with normal people later this week? Like me?"

"There's a guy named Doug Meyers who inseminates the pigs on our farm. He's normal. You are not."

"You're not normal either." He stands. "You wouldn't be here if you were."

Red Morgan? Not normal?

"Enjoy all your boring events until you see me again," he says. "You'll love Taylor. He's a hoot."

Taylor Thompson Lee? One of the most famous directors in the world? At twenty-five, he's the youngest director to win an Academy Award. And I, Red Morgan, from Orange City, Iowa, will be hanging out with him.

"Can I hug you goodbye? After all, you're wearing a strand of my hair around your finger."

He doesn't wait for an answer. He steps toward me, grabs my hand, pulls me up, and wraps his arms around my waist. He might be thin, but the boy *is* strong. His arms feel so supportive. The warmth of him blocks out the Malibu breeze. If somebody would've told me last week I'd be standing on a patio in Malibu with Koi Kalawai'a's arms wrapped around me, I would have patted them on the shoulders and said, "Yeeeeah, suuuure." And yet. Here I am. He rests his chin on my head. I lean into him and exhale.

"It was very nice to meet you, Little Red. This is one of the most interesting dates I've ever had."

This is *the* most interesting date I've ever had. I hope it's a memory that stays fresh in my mind forever.

He grabs my hand. "Ready?"

Together we move across the deck and back into the quiet restaurant. Heads turn as we pass. Whispers. Points. Stares. I decide to take notes from Koi, mimicking the confidence in his walk. Shoulders back, head high.

"Thank you for coming to Sun and Sand." The hostess speaks to Koi like he is all her dreams come true. When she turns her attention to me, she's back to bouncing on her toes. "Bye, Zay-Zay Waters. I seriously love you."

I wave. "Love you too."

Once we're out the front door, we're greeted by the flashing lights of dozens and *dozens* of paparazzi. It's like Skybar all over again.

Zay-Zay and Koi!

Koi! Zay-Zay! This way!

Are you guys really engaged?!
Koi Kalawai'a and Zay-Zay Waters!

A cameraman tries to step in front of us, but Frank is there to block. "Back up, man!" he shouts.

The cameraman stumbles back but calls out, "Can we get an interview? Please?"

Zay's SUV is parked at the valet stand. Koi's is there as well.

Zay-Zay!
Koi!
This way!
Right here!

So many lights flashing, so many screams and shouts. I should be overwhelmed. I could even be . . . afraid. Only it's like I'm somehow back on the red carpet at Skybar. Stepping into unknown waters and swimming just fine. The energy of the madness has my body buzzing. Or maybe it's the organic Ethiopian coffee. I'm like the roaring engine of a race car, ready to take my mark and go.

We reach the doors of our cars. Koi kisses me sweetly on the cheek.

"Welcome to the game of life," he says softly. "To play, all you gotta do is place an order. Place a few, if you want."

This sounds like it could be a *really* fun game.

"And expect a package from me," he adds. "You have to have it before the Getty. For things to be proper. Front door delivery to the manz. Just for you. Promise."

I watch him disappear into his SUV. My mind races with thoughts I've never . . . thought before. I've always asked the Universe to show me something good. Have I been going about this all wrong? I should be telling the Universe what *I* want to see?

C'mon, Universe, I think. *Let's . . . do this?* Nah, I can come up with something better than that.

I'll work on it.

THIRTEEN

I don't hear from Koi the next day. Or the day after. He promised his mystery gift would be left at Zay's front door. So far . . . nothing. Now the sun is setting on another red carpet, this time at the Los Angeles Zoo. I immediately kick off my high heels as Aaron pulls out of the parking lot. The deafening screams for Zay from the fans behind crowd-control gates are muffled now that I'm back inside the car.

"Randy, these *shoes*," I groan as I click on my seat belt.

"They're cute, right?" Randy declares proudly.

I grab one of them, hold it up, and knock on the thick heel with my knuckles. "They're *wooden*. They hurt. I think my toes are bleeding. If it wasn't for Frank, I woulda fell over."

"No pain, no gain." He smacks his lips. "They're Bergdorf Goodman. Get over it."

"Slight change of plans." Aish taps my shoulder. I turn to face her. "Getty's been moved to tomorrow. Just got a text from Diamond confirming. Hope you don't mind."

Mind? I bite my lip to stop from grinning like a fool. It's an outing with Taylor Thompson Lee! Play it cool, Red. You're standing in for Zay-Zay. Play it cool. "Oh?" I shrug. "All right."

A few moments pass. Aaron and Frank chat casually up front as we merge onto the freeway.

"Hey, uh, Aish?" I whisper.

"Hmm?" She types out a text on her phone.

"Did a package come from Koi? He said it would come *before* we went to the Getty. You think he forgot?"

"What? Like flowers?" She rolls her eyes, as if the thought of fresh flowers fails to impress her.

"He didn't say. Only that I should absolutely expect it before. He said I would need it for a proper outing."

"Maybe he forgot." She seems uninterested. "Oh, check this out." I peek at her phone. It's a story on TMZ. Zay-Zay . . . well . . . me as Zay-Zay is posing with a little boy at the zoo with a headline: Something is Different About Zay-Zay Waters.

My heart rate kicks up a notch. Are they on to us?

"Don't worry." Aish laughs, reading my horrified expression. "The article only says you're acting relatable and kind and being really attentive to your fans. That's all. It's good stuff. Keep it up."

"Oh." I exhale, relieved.

~

When we make it back to Malibu, a black armored truck is waiting in Zay's massive driveway. Standing in front of the truck, a guard wears a bulletproof vest. *Whoa.* He has a gun in a holster on his waist. I sit up in my seat.

"What's happening here?" I've seen armored trucks in Orange City. They usually arrive to empty or refill the ATM machines with cash. I lean toward Randy and speak softly. "Is this how Zay gets paid?"

"No, silly. It's a delivery." He winks at me. "*You* get them all the time." Delivery?

Randy and Aish push open their doors and step onto the driveway. Wait a second. I cover my mouth. A *delivery*! I jump out of the car.

"It's for you," Diamond says as she signs on an electronic device. "From Koi."

I'm beaming as bright as the Malibu afternoon sun. It's here!

"If it was sent by armored truck, it's most likely worth a small fortune," Aish adds.

"You all have a good evening." The guard hands Diamond a light-blue bag before moving back to his truck and pulling quickly out of the driveway.

"I wanna see!" Randy calls out. "Gimme."

"Me first!" Aish pushes Randy and reaches for the bag.

Diamond laughs, holding it high above her head. "Let's reveal the mystery gift upstairs. Zay's room." She moves toward the front door and disappears inside. Aish and Randy follow. I know I'm not supposed to—I can't help myself. I wave to get Aaron's attention as he slowly backs out of the driveway with Frank in the front passenger seat. Aaron puts the car into park and lowers the window.

"Yes, Miss Waters?"

I rush back toward the car. "Thanks for today. See y'all tomorrow?"

Frank waves. "See you, Zay."

"I see such a change in you. It's very refreshing." Aaron smiles so genuinely. "And yes. See you tomorrow."

～

We're upstairs in Zay-Zay's *massive* two-story bedroom suite, in her custom walk-in closet. There are floor-to-ceiling mirrors, comfy chairs, and a small round platform for when Zay gets measured and has fittings. Down below, accordion-style doors open to a wraparound balcony. The nighttime breeze pours into the room.

"Well." Diamond sets the bag on the table. "Would you like to do the honors?"

"Me?" I reach to pat Tyrone on the belly. He's whining the way dogs do when they want to go outside.

"Girl, if you don't see what's in that bag, I will." Randy reaches over my shoulder.

"Hey." I playfully slap his hand away. "I got this." I stretch my hands to stop them from shaking and reach inside, finding a sleek velvet ring box with a card. I set both on the table.

"Read the card first," Aish suggests.

I pry the card open and read out loud: "Dear Zay-Zay. I can't have a proper fiancée without a proper ring. Got this one on loan. Hope it fits, and see you soon. XO, Koi."

The velvet box makes a squeaky sound as I pry it open. I swear I'm temporarily blinded by what's inside.

"Holy—"

"Randy." Diamond cuts him off.

"What?" Randy says. "I was gonna say holy moly."

"*Holy moly* is a grand understatement." Aish whistles. "That thing is huge."

A diamond ring. "Koi sent me . . . a diamond ring?"

"The least he could do after his little proposal stunt." Aish is reading a sheet of paper that was inside the bag as well. "It's an eight-carat emerald-cut Blue Nile." She folds the page in half and sets it on the table. "These rings retail at half a million dollars. Sometimes more. It's the perfect engagement ring for Zay. Not too flashy. Sweet. Simple."

Since when is a $500,000 ring sweet and simple?!

"Ever worn half a million dollars on your hand before?" Diamond carefully removes the ring from the box.

"That would be a hard no." I scoot back in my chair. "I can't wear that thing. What if I lose it?"

"Oh, it's fine. It's insured," Randy explains casually. "Just don't take it off and you'll be good."

"What if someone . . . I dunno . . . clunks me over the head and steals it off me?"

"At the Getty?" Diamond motions for my hand. "Stop being silly. You're wearing this. Let's see if it fits."

I reluctantly place my manicured and heavily tattooed hand on the table. Diamond slides the diamond onto my left ring finger. The platinum band seems like it would be cold, hard, and uncomfortable, but the metal connects to me in a way that's as gentle as the breeze pouring into the room. Like me and this ring were meant to be together. Like it really is mine. Or . . . it's supposed to be. I lift my hand to study the sparkle. It's a perfect fit.

"Stunning." Aish claps. "Love it."

"Congratulations, fiancée," Randy says. "Too bad you can't keep it. That ring looks like it was made for you."

I know, right? "I think I'm gonna call her . . . Starshine. Yeah. I like that name for her. Hey, what does it mean to get a ring on loan?" I never thought much about jewelry before, but there *is* something mesmerizing about the sparkle and shine of a rare diamond.

"Jewelry dealers loan pieces to celebrities," Aish explains. "Take this, for example. Consumers see it on Zay-Zay, search out where it comes from, and suddenly *everyone* wants to buy it. Or something like it."

"Right," Diamond agrees. "It's no longer just a ring, but a ring worn by Zay-Zay Waters. She's their living billboard."

Ohhh. "I get it." Celebrities get free jewelry, so long as they understand they're walking billboards. And also that they have to give it back. Like Koi said, give and take. I'm starting to understand this Hollywood stuff more and more.

I hold out my hand. "What do *you* think, Tyrone?"

He barks and playfully bites at my feet.

"I think Tyrone's bored." I carefully take the ring off, instantly missing the weight of it. I hand it back to Diamond. "He wants to go outside."

"It's too late. He's fine." Diamond places the ring back inside the box.

"It's not too late. Please? I can take him."

"Oh no. You have work to do. Aish can take care of Tyrone."

"I call *not it* on dog duty." Aish frowns. "I have work to do as well."

"Make it a quick walk," Diamond says. "Then put him in his crate so you can get your work done. Everyone's happy."

Quick walk? *Crate?*

"He won't be happy with a quick walk." I stand. "He's super bouncy and fidgety. That means he wants to go outside and *play*. A quick walk won't be enough. Trust me, I grew up with an American bulldog. Let me spend some time with him. I don't mind."

"You didn't come here to be a dog walker." Diamond snaps her fingers and calls out, "Tyrone. Go with Aish."

"Yeah. C'mon, boy." Aish claps her hands together. "And Red, I'll bring your phone back in a bit. So you can ring your family."

Tyrone's ears roll back. He whines, like he's fully aware of Aish's plan to stuff him in a crate so she can work. He slowly follows her as she moves down the staircase, and the two of them exit the room.

"Now." Diamond sets her phone on the table between us. On the screen is a photograph of Taylor Thompson Lee. I know he's twenty-five, but you'd guess he was my age, standing on the red carpet in a yellow-and-green-striped leather jacket, purple hat, and linen shawl around his shoulders. "This is Taylor Thompson Lee."

Should I say *Duh*? I decide to stick to politeness. "Ah, yes. I'm aware of who he is."

"Still, I want you to spend some time researching him. This is your evening homework. If he's like most Hollywood types, which I imagine he is, you should keep the conversation focused on him. Stroke his ego. A lot."

Taylor Thompson Lee has won an Academy Award at twenty-five. He just spent a year in France filming a DreamWorks *trilogy*. I shake my head and think, "If he needs his ego stroked by *Zay-Zay*, something is seriously wrong with him." Except. Oops. I said it. There I go, speaking my thoughts again! "Sorry. I'll do all that. Research. Stroke ego. Consider it done."

"There's a computer in Zay's office." Diamond stands. "You have my permission to use it. Google him. Watch YouTube interviews. Get familiar. A lot is riding on this."

"Office. Study. Google. Got you." I snap my fingers and point at her. "I mean, I got . . . it."

"Also . . ." She fiddles with her phone. On the screen now are pictures of Koi and me at Sun and Sand. These pictures seem a hundred percent authentic. I'm pulling this off. I really am! The pictures of the proposal look sweet. You'd never guess I was quietly yelling at him and threatening to karate chop him in the throat.

"Since my niece is not available for counsel regarding the fake engagement, I have to do what *I* feel is best. Koi's gone through the trouble of getting you a proper ring. You should play up the fake engagement."

"But . . ." I wring my hands together nervously. "Zay's breaking up with him when she returns. Won't she be mad at me?"

"Zay understands you do what you're told. I'm telling you. Act in love."

Act . . . in love? "I've never been in love."

"Being in love is *so* fun." Randy places a hand over his heart. "At least in the beginning. Everything the person says is interesting and amazing. You touch them a lot. You wanna be close to them."

Hmm. I remember when Aish said don't stare at him like he's the eighth wonder of the world. I guess now I should.

"You guys are sure? Even though she's breaking up with him when she returns?"

"Breaking up with Koi now?" Diamond has a smug look of satisfaction on her face. "She wouldn't want the attention. I'm afraid Zay's stuck with him for a bit longer. She could do worse."

"And she has," Randy adds with a grimace. "Remember the rainbow-haired dude with the copper-plated teeth who was a guest judge with her on *Oh, So You Think You Can Sing Live?*"

"I love that show!" I blurt. "Sorry. But I do. It's like a secret dream to get the platinum buzzer and have it rain silver confetti on me."

Diamond places the box with the five-hundred-*thousand*-dollar ring back in the bag. "Randy, could I see the wigs you made for the commercial shoot for next week?"

"Oh yes. You gonna *love* them."

They move down the staircase, chatting about all things Zay. A moment later, their voices trail into the hallway, and I'm officially alone. I don't think I've been alone since I got here. I take a moment to day-dream that I *am* one of the contestants on *Oh, So You Think You Can Sing Live?* Would Zay-Zay be kind? Or give me her signature eye roll. *Nah. Not feelin' it, ma.* But the crowd rises to their feet in protest, the other judges disagree, and suddenly it's raining silver confetti. Of course, I'm crying. Platinum-buzzer winners always cry. I close my eyes and place a hand over my racing heart, the silly daydream giving me a strange rush of adrenaline.

"Can I clean here?"

My eyes pop open. A lady is standing at the top of the stairs. She has dark skin and wears simple jeans, an oversize T-shirt, and a pretty scarf tied around her head. She's also holding a bucket of cleaning supplies.

"Or I can come back," she adds. "You know, I don't usually work so late. Had lots to catch up on today."

She has an accent. It's actually one I recognize. Is she from Haiti? Hmm. Maybe New Orleans?

"Eske ou de New Orleans?"

Her jaw drops. "I *am* from New Orleans. And how you speakin' Haitian Creole? Amazin'."

Oh geez! Why do I keep speaking my thoughts? I should abort this conversation. Instead, I put my thumb and forefinger together and say, *"Wi, piti piti."* That means *a little.*

"Sezi kou berejèn!" she says excitedly.

Which literally means *I'm as surprised as an eggplant.* I think. My Creole is a bit rusty.

"I better get to work." I give her a wave. "Could you tell me where I can find a computer?" Oops. I force out a laugh before she can respond to that. "'Cuz that's how tired I am. Can't find one."

"You usually prefer your office. But not good to be so tired, when your office is in the pool house. Don't fall in the water. Ey?"

Whew. Pool house. Got it. Thank you. I toss her a thumbs-up. "Promise I ain't gonna fall in."

"Orevwa," she says.

"Orevwa." I head down the stairs.

FOURTEEN

There is a song playing softly through my speakers. I reach to grab my phone from under the pillow to switch off the alarm, except I don't feel my phone. Hmm. Maybe I left it on our nightstand? I yawn.

"Loren? You up?" I lift my hand to bang my fist on the slats of wood under the top bunk, but I don't feel anything above me. What the heck is going on? "Lo?"

"Are you playing charades? Talking to spirits? Who's Lo?"

My eyes pop open. Randy is standing at the foot of Zay-Zay's massive king-size bed, drinking something green from a plastic cup.

I sit up and rub my eyes, looking around the expansive two-story master suite like I'm seeing it for the first time.

"Hey, Randy." I slap my hand against my forehead. "I literally forgot where I was."

"You're in Malibu, California. How'd you sleep?" He drinks from the straw of his green cup. "You want some breakfast before your date?"

That's right. It's my date today. The one where I get to wear the half-a-million-dollar engagement ring, hang out with the Academy Award–winning Taylor Thompson Lee, and be paraded around town by Koi Kalawai'a. "You sure I'm awake? I swear this all feels like a dream."

"Want me to pinch you?"

"That's ok." I yawn. "I think I'll take you up on that breakfast. What's on the menu?"

"This." He holds up his other hand. Presenting a second cup of green juice.

That's my breakfast?

"Don't knock it till you try it. It's kale, spinach, lime, spirulina, some other stuff I can't pronounce. It's good."

He hands me my cup, and I take a sip from the metal straw. It tastes like grass mixed with lemon and lime . . . and dirt. Maybe a banana? Certainly not an acceptable breakfast by any stretch of the imagination.

"See? Good, right?"

"Uh, yeah. Yum." I place it on the end table beside the bed.

"Zay's chef is here preparing food for the week. Just FYI, his name is Caleb. He's the one that made the smoothie. Lovelie is here cleaning. I swear that lady never leaves."

Lovelie. She must be the lady from last night. The one who speaks Creole.

Randy sips from his straw again. "And Koi is here too."

What?! I yank the covers off and swing my legs out of bed. "What do you mean Koi is here? Why is he here so early?"

"Y'all supposed to be leavin' at eleven."

"What time is it now?"

"Ten forty-five."

Omigosh, I overslept! I jump off the bed. "Why didn't you guys wake me?"

"I was gonna. Except Aish said to let you sleep so your face wouldn't be puffy."

"Is my face puffy?" I grab at my cheeks. "I need to shower. My hair's a mess. What am I wearing?" I pace back and forth beside the bed. "Did you pick out a dress? Should *I* pick something out? Oh gosh, Randy. Please tell Koi I'm sorry."

Randy laughs. "Red, girl, calm *down*. You're unofficially 'officially' Zay. She is *always* late. Nothing new for Koi. He's used to waiting. I'll have you ready in no time."

~

Randy is true to his word, though I wouldn't call forty-five minutes *no time*. I'd call that almost an hour. As I move slowly down the floating stairs with Randy still picking at my curls, I playfully swat at his hands.

"Randy, I'm fine."

"I can't help it. It's what I do." He adjusts my necklace. It's silver, with a pretty infinity charm.

"Did Tyrone finally get to play this morning?" I ask.

"Oh, he's locked in the garage. I didn't want him climbing on you. Gettin' dog hair all over this outfit? No, ma'am."

I groan. From the crate to the garage. Poor Tyrone. But this outfit is pretty fancy. A tiered skirt; boho-style, off-the-shoulder blouse; and black-and-brown leather boots to match. Plus the necklace. Oh wait. "Randy, the ring?"

"Koi has it. He'll put it on ya."

We reach the bottom of the stairs. I can hear Koi's soothing, hypnotic voice.

"Yeah, yeah," Koi says. "*Zoiforever*'s been trending on social. It's wild."

Randy and I move into the living room. Koi is sitting on one of the cloud couches, chatting casually with Diamond. He's wearing a blue blazer over a white T-shirt with dark jeans and blue slip-on sneakers. Celebrity and superstar appeal sort of ooze off him. He stands when we enter.

"Ah, here's my niece." Diamond gives me a wink. For a second I wonder if she's been abducted by aliens and replaced by *her* look-alike. "You two crazy kids have fun."

Koi holds up the ring box and says casually, "Wanna wear this?"

Not the proposal of my dreams. But, "Sure."

He crosses to me and takes my hand into his. "You like it?"

I watch him slide Starshine onto my finger. She really does shine like a star plucked from the nighttime sky. "Yeah. It's . . . lit."

"Cool." He doesn't make eye contact with me when he says that. Instead, he grabs his phone and glances at the screen. "Sorry, gotta take this." He waves at Diamond. "Nice chatting with you." He squeezes my shoulder. "See you in the car." A moment later he's moved out the door.

"I have no idea why my niece doesn't *adore* him." Diamond pops off the couch with the brightest expression on her face. "Keep up the good work, Red. You're doing great. He honestly has *no* idea."

"Oh. Yeah. I'm . . . doing . . . yeah." I wonder if Diamond would lose this whole nice act if she knew what I know. That Koi has *every* idea.

"Are Frank and Aaron outside?" I ask.

Diamond shakes her head. "Koi promised you'd be taken care of. So Frank and Aaron got the day off."

No entourage? I smile. I also smell food cooking. Would they let me eat some?

Randy hands me one of Zay's purses. It's pink and has **DOONEY & BOURKE** written on the side. "It's got makeup for touch-ups and other things you might need. ChapStick. Gum. Stuff like that."

"Does it have food?" I grip the handles. "I'm starving."

Diamond motions toward the kitchen. "Grab a snack. Nothing too heavy." She pats her stomach. "You don't wanna bloat."

I make a beeline for sustenance. When I move into Zay's massive kitchen, an older man stands over the stove, tending to a steaming pan that smells divine. This must be Caleb, the chef Randy mentioned. He's maybe in his sixties, wearing a white chef's coat and hat. He also has the same white tassels hanging off his pants, like the little boy, Mendel, who shops in our store with his mom.

"Good morning, Miss Waters," he says kindly. "Preparing lovely things for you this week. You will enjoy."

Another beautiful accent. I wonder where he's originally from.

"Hey, Caleb. You got anything that travels well? I'm starvin'. I mean, the green juice was . . . lit. Still hungry, though."

"I have something you will enjoy." He uses a brightly colored mitt to pull open the oven, removing a hot tray that he sets on the counter. "Your favorite bars. Only four ingredients. Oatmeal. Eggs. Cinnamon. Agave syrup."

Yaaas. Oatmeal! Zay likes something I love. *This* is what I'm talking about. I watch as he cuts a bar and slides it into a paper bag.

"*Thank* you." I stuff the bag into my purse. "Hey, can I ask you somethin', Caleb?"

"Anything, Miss Waters." He turns his attention back to the stove, stirring the food in the skillet with a large wooden spoon.

"What's the little tassels hangin' from your pants." I have to stop myself from telling him about the family that shops at our store. So I add, "I know a little boy who always has them hanging from his pants too. Wondered what they are. Looks kinda cool."

Thankfully, Caleb seems happy to answer. "Tzitzit."

I try to repeat the word. "Tzitzit?"

"Yes." He rinses his hands, dries them with a paper towel, and grabs the tassels. "A daily reminder. A connection to"—he pauses, as if struggling to find the right way to explain—"my purpose in life. We all come here with a purpose. Don't we?" He points toward the ceiling and folds his hands in prayer.

We do come here with a purpose. I guess discovering that purpose is the great mystery. "That's what's up. Thanks for explainin' that to me."

"Thank you for asking. One day, you might come to my hometown. Tzfat, in Israel. You see tzitzit *everywhere*. It is a beautiful sight."

Israel? Who knew so many adventures could await? "Maybe someday I will."

~

Koi turns off Summerland Drive. He's still on a call, which has allowed me to sit quietly, taking tiny bites from Caleb's delicious oatmeal bar. It's enough to dial down the stomach growls, but I can't help but think these things would be a whole lot tastier with Morgan Family Farm oats.

"Ok, sure." Koi's cell is pressed to his ear. "We can talk about it when I get there. Yeah." He looks at me and mouths, "Sorry."

I hold up the remainder of my oatmeal bar, lick my lips, and say, "Nom, nom." Then pop a final piece into my mouth. He playfully rolls his eyes.

I focus on the paparazzi loitering in front as the gates slowly slide open. Koi tosses the security guards a wave, and we pull into the street. A few of the photographers shout to get our attention, but Koi speeds away so fast I tug on my seat belt to make sure it's locked in place.

"Fine. I'm going under a bridge. I might lose service. Hello? Can you hear me now?" He ends the call and exhales. "Why do people talk so much?" He comes to a stop at a sign before switching on his blinker and turning down a hill. "By the way, you look very Zay. Twinning for sure."

"I'm gonna pretend you said I look pretty."

"You think I have a doppelgänger out there?" He tugs on his blazer. "Like, a human who enjoys this level of handsome?"

"So modest." I pry open my purse. Randy packed quite a few items that could come in handy, including a tiny bottle of water. I twist off the cap and take a small sip.

"That was so nerve racking in there. Pretending I didn't know. Trying to act aloof. And having to put a *ring* on your finger. I was literally sweating."

"Well, it didn't show. You seemed totally relaxed."

He pretends to wipe sweat off his forehead. "And you like the ring? You sure?"

"Koi?" I stare down at the shimmering stone. *Half a million dollars.* "This ring . . ." Should I tell him that it feels like it belongs to me? That I don't like it—I love it? That I named her Starshine? Nah, I decide to keep it simple. Play it cool. "It's beautiful. Thank you."

"Glad you like it."

"Oh, I have good news and bad news. Which do you want first?"

"Bad news," he replies quickly.

"Really?" We're traveling fast down a road called Pacific Coast Highway. The wind feels like tiny kisses on my skin. The ocean is to my right. The sky is a picturesque azure blue, like I'm starring in a magical movie. "Most people want good news first."

"Clearly I'm not most people," Koi calls out over the loud sound of wind and traffic. "By the way, I can put the roof up if you want."

"No, I love it!" I lay my head back and attempt to absorb *all* the California sun.

"So what's the bad news?"

"Aunt Diamond wants us to play up the fake engagement. Act in lurve."

Koi slows to a stop at a red light. "That's not bad news."

It's not? "So you don't . . . *mind* acting in love with a complete stranger?"

"But you're not a complete stranger. Not anymore. We're old friends now."

A car pulls up right beside us. The window lowers, and the two paparazzi inside snap photographs.

"Let's test out our acting skills." Koi puts the car in park and takes my hand into both of his so the paps beside us can get a full view.

I know Koi's only kidding around, but it makes about a thousand butterflies dance wildly in the pit of my stomach. Especially when he brings my hand to his mouth and presses his lips onto the tips of my fingers.

Whoa. I have to bite the inside of my cheek so I don't gasp. It's true, he's not exactly what I imagined he'd be. Slightly arrogant. A bit self-involved. However, this *is* Koi Kalawai'a. Pretty much every girl I know has had a celebrity crush on him at some point. Myself included.

"They're getting some great shots," Koi whispers. "And the ring is, like, glowing in the sunlight. Sweet."

He moves a strand of hair away from my face. Our eyes lock. Our hands intertwine. My heart rate kicks up a notch. I know this is pretend but . . . geesh. It's making the butterflies swarm. Someone behind us honks, breaking the moment.

"Oops. Green light." Koi lets go of my hand, and I exhale. He speeds off again. "Good work, partner."

Playing a game usually involves keeping your head *in* the game. In this particular game . . . that's not such a good idea! Snap out of it, Red.

"Earth to Red?" He waves a hand in front of my face.

"Hmm?" I turn to face him.

"I said, so what's the good news?"

He did? Oh. "Um, the good news. Diamond says Zay can't break up with you now. You get to keep your fake girlfriend. Well played, my friend."

"Told ya. Diamond loves me. She probably wishes *she* could date me."

I playfully punch his shoulder. He winces in mock pain. "Are you always so full of yourself, or do you save genuine moments for when you're alone?"

"Hey." He frowns. "I can be genuine."

I study him for a second, strands of his hair blowing in the breeze. Can any of these Hollywood types be genuine? "Ok, let's hear it, then. Share something real."

His hands grip the wheel as he seems to contemplate what *real* information I can be trusted with. "Ok, here's something. My mom dropped me off at a fire station when I was three days old. After changing her mind about tossing me in the garbage."

Whoa. "Are you being serious?"

"I would not make that up."

I didn't know. "I'm sorry that happened to you, Koi." I sit up in my seat. "So were you adopted, then?"

"I should have been. Multiple times it almost happened. But because my mom would go back and forth between wanting me and not wanting me, I ended up bouncing around from foster home to foster home for most of my young life."

I'm suddenly sick to my stomach, thinking of such a heartbreaking situation. A family falling in love with their foster kid, desperate to adopt, only to have the kid taken away. And poor Koi in the center of it all.

"You should have been protected from that. Seems really unfair."

"Eh, it's ok," he says. "Maybe the Universe tried to make it up to me. 'Cuz when I was twelve, I landed in a house with six other boys. Noah. Ori. Wilbert. Lono. Tahj. And Liam."

Wait a second . . . "The Six?"

He nods. "We became brothers. We *are* brothers. 'Ohana." He pounds his fist on his chest. "It means family. Family . . . beyond blood."

Another car pulls up beside us. The pap in the back seat is snapping photos while the driver navigates traffic. It makes me tense. What if they get into an accident? What if they *cause* an accident?

"I can't believe they pull up beside you at such high speeds. Seems dangerous."

"They never trail me this way when I'm alone. It's the price you pay when you're as talented as Zay-Zay Waters."

Speaking of Zay-Zay. "Does *she* know about what happened to you? The foster homes? Your mom?" Not sure I'll ever get over the image of a young Koi Kalawaiʻa being transferred around to different foster homes year after year. A loving and supportive family should be a guarantee in life. Like food and water and . . . oxygen.

He laughs. "Zay-Zay doesn't know anything about me. We're business partners. With my experience in Hollywood, I keep things light, drama-free, nothing sad. Basically entirely focused on the person I'm talking to. It's a key to success."

I sigh. That's what Diamond told me to do regarding Taylor Thompson Lee. "Well, I know *we're* business partners. But just so you know, a little drama never bothers me. Besides, your story isn't sad. It's empowering. Makes me love you and your band even more."

"You *love* me? I knew it!" He places a hand over his heart. "Is it because I got you the ring? You know you have to give it back, right?"

"Pipe down." I laugh. "You as a *performer.*"

"Oh, that's boring." Koi flips on his blinker, switches lanes, and merges onto a new freeway. There's a giant Ferris wheel on a long pier that stretches out over the ocean. It makes the Ferris wheel at the Strawberry Fest look downright minuscule. "Your turn, Red. Tell me something real about you."

Something real? Hmm. "Um. I was raised on a farm. Got two sisters and two brothers. The oldest are twins. Mom and Dad are alive and . . . happy. We're all really close."

"Alive parents and a happy family?" Koi groans. "That's not very interesting. Please try again."

"Hey." I playfully punch him on the shoulder again. "Don't be mean."

"I'm kidding, of course." He laughs. "What about a boyfriend? Got one of those back home, milking cows?"

I shake my head. "No boyfriend for me. What about you? Who are you *really* dating?"

"I don't think I'm the dating sort."

"What's that mean, Koi?"

"The girls I meet wanna go have ice cream and then see a comedy show at the Laugh Factory."

That seems like a fair-enough date. "What do you wanna do?"

"Maybe meditate on a mountaintop in a faraway land. Maybe discover the meaning of life." He points toward the sky. "Maybe convince the Universe to tell me all her secrets. C'mon, Universe!" he calls out like he's howling at the moon. "You gotta tell me something. I'm beggin'!"

"I thought I was the only one weird enough to chat with the Universe."

"A girl who talks to the Universe? Niiice. You're intriguing. I like you, Red."

"You *like* me?" I place a hand over my heart. "I knew it!"

We both laugh.

"Oh, hey, should we go over fake-date particulars? Me and Zay did that before we started dating. It helps."

Fake-date particulars? "What do you mean?"

"What's allowed, what's not. I know you said not to kiss you or you'd . . ." He pauses, rubbing his chin. "Karate chop me in the throat?"

I make a face. "That was harsh. Sorry about that."

"It's ok. I get it. Zay wanted things to seem believable, so she was ok with kissing. But it's fine if you're not."

"I mean, if Zay was." I think back to our kiss on the carpet, and a chill rushes up my spine. "Then I *guess* it's ok."

"Cool. So, like, the basics. I can touch your hair, hold your hand, kiss you. Oh." He reaches out and squeezes my knee. "What about pet names? Can I call you *babe*, or is that too creepy? How about *love*? I like *love*. Especially with you. It sounds sweet."

I like love, especially with you. Oh boy. Here come the Hollywood swoon lines again. "*Love* . . . works."

"I might tell you I love you. If people are close by. It always sounds good. Will you love me too? *Please* love me."

Omigosh. The heat has returned. Even though we're traveling down the freeway at sixty-five miles per hour and the wind is like a tiny tornado, I'm burning up. "Yes, Koi. I will love you."

"Sweet." He bops me on the nose like I'm his kid sister.

Riiight. Back to reality. Get your head . . . *out* of the game, Red. The Universe has gifted me a day of pretend. And Koi Kalawai'a's really not so bad after all.

I lean my head back and let the sun fall down on me like rain.

FIFTEEN

There is no red carpet when we arrive at the Getty. However, there's a lot going on, with massive amounts of security, lines of cars waiting, and a giant sign that says CLOSED TO THE GENERAL PUBLIC: INVITE ONLY CONCERT. Of course, there are paparazzi. I see them with their cameras and manic eyes, looking for celebrities to snap. Which they think they've found in us. The calls for Zay-Zay and Koi begin right away as we're ushered in past the long line. Plus, the two cars that have been trailing Koi's convertible this entire ride are pulling up behind us. They get stopped by security.

So far there's not much to see. Lots of concrete and a grand entrance to an underground parking structure. After we pull into a spot, Koi presses the button that lifts the soft-top roof. As it rolls into place, I watch him run both hands through his hair. Each strand falls perfectly into place. Not fair. I use the mirror to undo the wind damage to mine. It's taking a little longer than expected, especially with these long nails. How do people manage with these things? After a few minutes, I can feel Koi staring at me.

"Sorry. My hair doesn't fall magically into place like yours."

Instead of responding to my comment, he reaches out and runs his fingers down the side of my neck. It makes a chill rush up my spine. Is this part of the fake fiancée . . . touching?

"You have freckles right here. That's definitely different than Zay."

Oh. He's right. I do. I self-consciously cover them with my hand. "They get worse in the sun. Do you think people will notice?"

"Cute little freckles on your neck? So what if they do? Zay could have freckles. I mean, she doesn't. But she could." He pushes open the car door.

I think there are only about two people in the whole world who have noticed I have freckles right there. They're named Mom and Dad. I take a final glance in the mirror, decide the windblown look isn't so bad after all, smooth Randy's strawberry ChapStick across my lips, and step out into the dim parking structure.

"Have you been to the Getty before?" I ask as we move toward the elevators. It's a rare moment with almost no one around. No paparazzi. No fans. And of course, none of Zay's entourage.

"Too many times to count. You'll see. It's one of those places you can't ever get enough of."

We move into a small elevator room. We're alone, but I still look over my shoulder. I feel like strangers could be lurking in corners at any time. Koi grabs my hand as we wait for the elevator, studying the tattoos Randy took so much time to shade in.

"You're missing a detail on these," he says.

"Really? I think they're identical."

"Almost . . ." He traces the tattoos with his fingertips. His simple touch energizes me more than that Ethiopian coffee I drank the other night. "Zay was in a Broadway show when she was seven. *Persephone*? Not sure if you know that."

I know so much about Zay-Zay Waters. Starring in *Persephone* on Broadway was how she rose to fame. At seven years old, she became the youngest actress ever nominated for a Tony. The show closed after only one year, but that didn't matter. Zay-Zay was just getting started. "Yes. I definitely knew that."

"Well, what you probably *didn't* know was after Zay-Zay lost the Tony for *Persephone*, she was understandably devastated. She was crying. Afraid people were going to make fun of her, with all the cameras lurking around, desperate to document a seven-year-old's reaction to losing in front of the world. So her mom hid her in a backstage bathroom at Radio City Music Hall. That way no one could take photos of her while she was upset."

I actually remember reading an article on *Page Six*. It was about Zay-Zay's history of temper tantrums and meltdowns starting with *that* day, when she and her mom stormed out of the building in protest of her losing to Audra McDonald. I feel guilty knowing the details of such a private moment, especially since Zay's mother passed many years ago.

"They waited in the bathroom," Koi continues, "until they were presenting for the next award. Then she and her mom snuck out a side door and went and got ice cream at Van Leeuwen. Zay said it ended up being the best night of her life, 'cuz her mom let her stay up till sunrise. Audra McDonald sent her a cookie bouquet the next day too. Zay was a big fan of Audra. So anyway, the microphone tattoo, right here." He traces the shape. His fingertips feel warm. "Right on the side. Should be a tiny ice cream cone. It's hard to notice. It would be easy to overlook. But it's there. Yeah. In loving memory."

The story has made the hairs on my arm stand straight up. So Zay-Zay *didn't* throw a temper tantrum because she lost. She was a kid. And her mom, like moms do, was trying to tend to Zay's little needs in the midst of such a big situation.

"I thought you guys didn't talk," I finally say.

"One day we got stuck in a car together. Waiting to do a carpet. Her assistant at the time noticed the ice cream cone. I overheard."

The elevator doors slide open, and we step inside. Koi taps the button just as a guy calls out, "Hold the elevator!" Koi sticks out his hand to stop the doors, and a couple rushes in. "Thanks, buddy," the guy says to Koi.

I notice his girlfriend's jaw drop and hear her whisper, "Omigosh, babe, that's Koi Kalawaiʻa and Zay-Zay Waters. *Record* them."

Koi must hear it, too, because he tugs on my arm. I stumble into him, and he leans and speaks softly into my ear. "Love?" He's whispering, but it's loud enough for the couple to hear. I know he's putting on a show. "I'm cold. Keep me warm." Koi wraps a strong arm around my waist. I rest my head on his chest, surprised how comfortable it is to stand this way with him.

The elevator dings; the doors slide open. He whispers, "You're a natural at this."

A natural at letting Koi Kalawaiʻa shower me with attention and whisper words of love in my ear? I mean, who wouldn't be? We file out behind the couple, who is probably sending their little video to all their friends and posting it on social media.

"Where do we go now?" I glance around at the long line of people that leads to security checkpoints with metal detectors and guards checking bags. On both sides of the platform, train tracks extend far up a hillside.

"Excuse me, sir, you'll need to go through the check-in!" a deep voice calls out.

Koi and I spin around to face none other than Taylor Thompson Lee.

He's dressed eccentrically in a black top hat, maroon corduroy shorts, purple Crocs, and a yellow T-shirt tucked into his shorts. Koi lights up at seeing his friend, and they shake hands and bang shoulders the way boys do.

"Dude." Koi's eyes scan Taylor's outfit. "You look like Willy Wonka threw up on you."

"Exactly what I was going for." Taylor turns to me, tipping his hat and bowing. "Zay-Zay Waters. You're much more lovely in person. I mean that."

Does he really? I try to remember the YouTube videos from the research I did last night. I was never all that good at cramming for tests, though I watched his film *Gastar Saliva* twice when it came out. Cried both times. Should I tell him? I do need to keep things focused on him to feed his ego. Oh gosh, seconds have passed, and I'm standing here like an idiot!

"I'm . . . feelin' the hat." There. I said something.

"I found it in the garbage outside my office on the Universal lot." He takes it off and shows it to me, like it's normal for rich and famous directors to find clothes in the garbage. "What kind of moron would throw this away? Right?"

"As far as top hats go," I say, "it's pretty dope."

A sleek, soundless white space-age tram moves slowly down the tracks.

"C'mon." Taylor motions toward the tram. "We got the next tram all to ourselves. 'Cuz I tossed out stuff like *Universal*, *Motion Picture Association of America*, and *Zay-Zay Waters*. They decided we were important."

The people we're cutting in front of don't seem to mind. In fact, there are currently about twenty-two phone cameras pointed at us. Though there must be a sign somewhere that I can't see that says PLEASE DON'T SCREAM AT THE CELEBRITIES, because it's pretty quiet as we walk.

"Hi." A girl moves to stand beside me. "I'm Taylor's girlfriend."

Somehow I overlooked her. Though I can't understand how I did such a thing. It's like she was cut from the pages of a magazine. She's much taller than me. I put her at six feet, so she might even be a bit taller than Taylor in her heels. Wearing a cutoff shirt that shows her *ridiculously* toned abs, jeans with holes . . . everywhere, and stilettos. Obviously she does not care about the three thousand stairs I saw on the Getty's website.

"I'm Isabella." With her Spanish accent, it sounds like *Eesa-bay-a*.

"Nice to meet you, Isabella," I say.

"Oh crap, I'm the worst." Koi slings an arm around my shoulder so the smell of his cologne envelops me like the warmest hug. "Zay, Issa. Issa, Zay."

"No, *I'm* the worst." Taylor makes an overexaggerated frown. "I was so excited to meet you, Zay-Zay, that I forgot to introduce you to the love of my life."

"It's ok, we already met." Isabella smiles. "We're, like, best friends now."

The automated tram arrives, the doors slide open, and we all file inside. Issa and I have a seat on the sleek metal chairs. Taylor and Koi opt to stand, as Taylor is showing Koi something on his phone.

"Are you in college, Isabella?" I ask as the tram doors slide shut and the vehicle gently jerks to motion, climbing up the hillside.

"Call me Issa. No. I'm mostly a model. But when work is slow, I also work for a nonprofit. It's called the Friendship Circle."

"Do you help people . . . make friends?"

"It's for kids with special needs. And yes. Sometimes we do help with that. It's hard for them, you know. To make friends." She sighs. "Making friends is hard for anybody. Myself included."

Wow. Issa doesn't strike me as the kind of person who would have trouble making friends.

"I'll be your friend."

She holds out her hand. "Pinky swear?"

We link pinkies.

"Yay, I have a new friend." She claps excitedly. "You're not at all what I thought you'd be. I thought you'd be . . . scary."

"Scary? No way. I'm just a farmer. We're not scary at all."

She laughs. I quickly realize my stupid mistake. Geez, Red!

"I mean . . . sorry." I grimace. "I was playin' this Xbox game before I came here. *Farmer . . . in the Dell.* It's a fun one."

"I love video games! We should play together sometime. What's your gamer tag?"

"Um . . . ZlayZlayRiverwater."

"Cool. I'll find you." She crosses her legs, and I marvel at how comfortable she seems in stilettos. My feet hurt just looking at hers. "You're one of my favorite singers. I had to promise Taylor I wouldn't fangirl over you, but I'm failing. I adore you. Your voice is in my ears whenever I cross the Pacific. I get anxious when I fly, but you make it better."

Wow. What must Zay-Zay feel like with all this *constant* adoration. "Thank you, ma." I'm quick to turn the conversation away from . . . not me. "*I'm* tryin' not to fangirl over Taylor Thompson Lee. Did you? When you first met him?"

"I didn't know who he was. I had never seen any of his movies. I don't watch movies, really. I'm too busy with work and Friendship Circle. I thought he was homeless. He was lying on a bench under a blanket in Central Square in Paris. So I offered him the rest of my lunch."

"Wait, what? You're lying."

"He started eating it too." She laughs. "When I told him to have a good day, he said how could he when I gave him dry chicken marsala without capers."

Now I laugh.

"We been together ever since." She leans forward and whispers, "I know you and Koi aren't really together."

My eyes stretch wide. "You . . . do?"

She places a finger over her lips in the universal *shhh* symbol. "Your secret is safe with me. Although . . ." She lowers her voice more. "Are you sure he doesn't really like you?"

Koi? Really like . . . me? "What do you mean?"

"I know the way a guy acts when he likes a girl. I think your fake boyfriend likes you. Plus . . ." She grabs my hand and gazes at the ring. "This ring? For a girl he's *fake* dating?"

"It's just a loan. I gotta give it back."

"You have no idea how many calls he had to make and how much begging he did to get this loan. He was obsessed for the last two days. Taylor and I went with him. I tried on so many rings, but he kept saying no, no, no. He said it had to be *perfect*."

I'm speechless for a second. Issa moves on, as if she didn't just drop a huge bomb on me. She stretches out her long legs. "You know, they shot *Gastar Saliva* in Seville, Madrid, and Barcelona. Have you ever been to Spain, Zay?"

I definitely have not. Has Zay-Zay?

"Of course you have. Silly for me to ask." Issa sits up excitedly. "Last summer you performed at Andalucía. I'm *from* Málaga, you know." She calls out to Taylor. "Babe, remember Zay-Zay performed at Andalucía in Málaga? She was so near you."

"Oh yeah." Taylor lights up. "We were in Antequera that whole week, filming right down the road. We should've crashed your set."

"Man, I love Antequera." Koi slides into the seat beside me. "We shot a stealthy, somewhat illegal music video in El Torcal. It was wild."

El Torcal. Antequera. Málaga. I have no idea where any of these places are.

"So, Zay." Taylor plops into the chair directly across from me. Now I can see the Crocs he's wearing have tiny Donald Ducks all over them. "Did you stay at the Nobu while you were in Málaga? Or Puente Romano?"

It's tough to understand what's coming out of these people's mouths. I can make a good guess he's asking me about . . . hotels? I decide to toss the question right back at him. "Is that where you stayed? The . . . Puente Romano?"

"Taylor at a hotel?" Issa shakes her head.

"I usually sleep in the woods," Taylor says. "I find high levels of toxins at hotels. Plus, I think I'm allergic to the chemical refrigerant they use in air conditioners. In my little RV, it's just me, endless sky, and *fresh* air."

"Calling an EarthRoamer a *little RV*," Koi cuts in, "is like calling King Kong a monkey."

They all laugh. As they continue chatting, I make a mental note to google *El Torcal*, *Antequera*, *EarthRoamer*, and . . . well . . . everything else they're saying too.

"Yeah, but you were in Greece, babe," Issa says sweetly. "Traveling to Litochoro to climb Mount Olympus would have been fun."

Taylor leans forward and rests his elbows on his knees, smiling at his girlfriend with such life and light in his brown eyes. "We'll have lots of time to climb mountains together, I promise. Staring at all those blue rooftops in Santorini put me in a trance, that's all. I was over that whole location."

The group laughs again. This time I laugh too. Though I have no idea what that means or why it's funny. Blue rooftops sound kinda magical, to be honest. When it comes to travel, my list starts with Meramec Caverns in Sullivan, Missouri, and stops an hour away at Aunt Tiny's place in Iberia. I never even visited our distant cousins in New Orleans. I gotta get out more. Although, speaking of getting out . . .

Suddenly, I can see the city of Los Angeles in a way I never thought I would. I stand slowly and make my way to the window of the tram. Rows of skyscrapers off in the distance, grassy hillsides, layers of leafy green trees, cars whizzing by on freeways, and mountaintops piercing through the haze at the horizon. The Los Angeles skyline, in vivid Technicolor. We're *soaring*!

"You doing ok?"

I turn to face Koi, who is standing beside me now. "I'm doing *amazing*. Thank you for bringing me here."

"I knew you'd love it." He wraps an arm around my shoulder. "Technically we haven't arrived at the Getty yet. There's lots more to see."

"Hey," I say softly, since I don't want Taylor and Issa to know I'm not exactly one of them. "What's El Torcal? You said you shot a video there?"

"It's a national park in Spain." He whips out his phone and opens his photo app. Soon, I'm staring over his shoulder at all these surreal-looking limestone rock formations that feel straight out of Wonderland. I definitely remember seeing this in the background of one of Koi's music videos. "You're away from the city. Caught in the mountain breeze. One of the best days of my life."

"If I were to consider a best day of *my* life, this one might be a top contender."

"The day's just begun." He slides his phone into his back pocket. "Hey, when I go again, you'll come with me."

I give him a look, like *Yeah right.*

"I'm serious." Then he leans and whispers in my ear. "Don't you wanna see the world with me, Red?"

I look into his bright eyes and decide to pretend this moment is real. Koi Kalawai'a is here with me, not because I'm standing in for Zay-Zay Waters and he's using her to headline Lollapalooza, but because he wants to see the world . . . with me. "Count me in."

The tram slows to a stop.

SIXTEEN

There is a small red carpet on the entry-level plaza, with photographers and news reporters holding microphones. It's nothing compared to the chaos of Skybar, but it's enough to be a whole thing. When they catch sight of us exiting the tram, the calls begin immediately.

Taylor Thompson Lee!

Hey Taylor, can we get a quick interview?

Zay-Zay Waters!

Zay-Zay, could we get a few pictures of you?!

Koi Kalawai'a, are you here with the Six?

Koi calls back, "They're on vacation! I was working them too hard."

Taylor marches right over and assumes his position as the center of attention, with Issa at his side. Despite rocking Donald Duck Crocs, a top hat he admittedly found in the garbage, shorts, and a simple yellow shirt, he looks more like a star than anyone I've ever seen in designer duds. There is something about him. Like he's utterly and completely comfortable in his own skin. Like, if all the adoration, fame, and fortune left him tomorrow, he'd assume his position on a bench in Paris and happily accept handouts from folks passing by in Central Square.

"I'm not doing red carpet," Koi says.

I exhale, relieved. "Me either."

"Let's check out the gardens and pretend we're regular folks here to enjoy all there is to see."

"Pretending I'm regular folk is gonna be real easy for me."

"There you go again." Koi grabs my hand. "Thinking you're regular."

As the carpet press focus their attention on Taylor, the tram lurches forward and back down the hill. Koi drags me away from the platform.

"Geez, this place is like nothing I've ever seen." Our view opens to an expansive terrace at the base of white stone stairs. The stairs lead to the main Getty building, an architectural masterpiece atop this hillside. Can a building be art? This one certainly seems to fit the bill, with its asymmetrical structure and walls that curve as if bending in the wind. Probably what the nomads of yore felt like when they stumbled upon the pyramids at Giza for the first time. It's beautiful, otherworldly . . .

We climb the stairs, and the *click-clack* of Zay-Zay's boots against the white travertine tiles echoes. The serene atmosphere on this hilltop kind of reminds me of time on the farm with Dad. When he and I are the only ones with the energy to wake up at 4:30 to feed the chickens in the quiet of the early morning.

After doing a horrible job of pretending I'm *not* out of breath, we reach the top of the staircase and follow a tree-lined path around the main building. Though there are a few people meandering about, they seem more interested in taking pictures of the outdoor sculptures and vast landscape than looking around to see who is passing them. So Koi and I move about without any intrusions, upstaged by the sheer scale and magnificence of the Getty's outdoor experience.

Quite a few buildings make up this massive property. I've counted four so far. Some bend and curve; some have a random square or other geometric shape added into the architecture. The whole thing sorta reminds me of pictures I've seen of the Maison Carrée in Nîmes, France, with its columns that could have easily been built by otherworldly beings. When Jack climbed the beanstalk, *this* might be what he saw in the giant's backyard.

172

Our pathway opens to another skyline view of Los Angeles. I can even see the Pacific Ocean from up here! "By the way," I say as we pass a large grassy area where a few people lie on blankets beside picnic baskets. There are also men setting up a sound system and small platform stage for the lawn concert. "Who's performing?"

"Zay-Zay Waters?" He smiles. I cock my head to the side and give him a "Yeah right" smirk. He laughs. "What? You could do it. You should."

"I've already taken this stand-in job to unknown territories by getting fake engaged. Let's not push it."

We continue our stroll, moving under the shade of the trees that line the path, the breeze blowing ever so gently across our skin.

"*Was* that you singing in the video? Or Zay?"

"It was me," I confess.

"You've got a good voice. *Really* good. You know that, right?"

"Eh. That's what they keep telling me." There's a London plane tree with branches that arch out in perfect formation for climbing. I pause for a moment to step off the path, reaching to touch the base of the tree. It's surprisingly soft, like I could peel the bark off with my long pink fingernails. "*You've* got a good voice. You know that, right?"

"Of course I do." Koi crosses his arms under his chest. "But we were talking about *you*, and then you veered."

"Did I veer?" I raise an eyebrow.

"Oh, you veered."

We continue walking. Down below, the lower gardens are constructed in a circular shape with a cute maze of bushes in the center of a large pond. There are flowers, too, hundreds of flowers in all different hues of pink, and there's this insane waterfall sculpture that flows into the pond. Water pours out over an artsy stone staircase. Have I walked into the pages of a storybook?

"I figured something out about you." Koi crosses his arms under his chest. "You're a *deflector*."

"Is that like the Dementors from Harry Potter?"

"Red, you know you deflect. I don't think you like talking about yourself. Why? You seem fascinating."

Do I? "How can I, Red Morgan from Orange City, Iowa, be fascinating to you, Koi Kalawaiʻa? Who vacations in places I've never heard of. You know where I vacation? Nowhere." I laugh. "I don't even go on vacation."

"J. Paul Getty. The man responsible for this place originally." Koi extends his arms. "The guy lived most of his life in Europe. Never really went overseas. He was *afraid* to fly. Afraid of the sea, too, so boats were out of the question. Can you imagine? He never saw the original Getty Villa he worked so hard to create. Too scared to get over here."

Wow. "Is that true?"

"It's true. You think that makes him *not* interesting?" He steps in front of me, and the sun shines down on him in a way that makes him look like one of the art pieces in this garden. "Just because you haven't been anywhere doesn't make you less fascinating. So no more deflecting. Let's talk about you. You're an amazing singer. Let's say I was in Iowa. Where could I hear you sing?"

"In the shower?" I shrug. "Kidding. I sing with my choir at home. They're called the Aca-pellets. But now that I've graduated, I guess . . . nowhere."

His face falls. "That's tragic."

Up ahead is a beautiful bench underneath the shade of pink flowers. The flowers reach ten to fifteen feet into the air, supported by metal poles that bend, stretching out like an umbrella. So it's like a giant bouquet.

Koi points. "Wanna sit under the flower tree?"

I nod and let him guide me. I don't know if he deserves an Academy Award for today's performance, but I'd say he at least deserves a nomination. The way he's treating me, talking to me, tending to me. Even the way he's holding my hand right now. It's different from the way he held my hand at Skybar. Today, it's like he's holding me tight, afraid that I'll run away. He takes a seat on a curved bench and pats the empty space beside him. The universal motion for *Please, sit beside me.* I'm happy to oblige.

"Can I make a confession?" Koi's green eyes shine bright under the Los Angeles sun.

The muscles in my stomach tighten. "Um, sure."

"I watched that video of you falling into manure like twenty times."

"Oh." That's not the confession I was expecting. "Yeah, people think it's hilarious."

"No, you don't understand. I wasn't watching it because I thought it was funny. It's because I never heard Zay sound that way before. It was raw, enchanting. Like an angel. It captivated me."

Ohhh. "Wow. That's a huge compliment, coming from you."

"With a voice like yours." He leans forward and whispers, "Red. You should be singing."

"Don't knock the stand-in gig," I say. "It has its perks."

"You know what I mean. I would pay to hear your beautiful voice again and again."

I pound on my chest like my fist is the defibrillator bringing me back to life, 'cuz, *whoa,* Koi's got me shook, and my heart hasn't had this kind of action . . . ever. "Can *I* make a confession now?"

He stretches out his long legs. "Sure. Yeah."

"I think either you're the greatest actor alive. Or the sweetest guy ever. Which is it?"

"I'm just being honest. You can sing."

"Thank you. I mean, I know I can sing. I sing at school. I never stop singing at home. My chickens get serenaded *every* morning. But Zay-Zay Waters and people like you? You guys can *sang.* I just . . . sing."

"Is that Iowa farm talk? I don't get it."

"You know. You guys belt. Sing from your chest. I sing in my head voice. Pretending to be Zay in the video was easy. Because I was singing a simple song, like 'Over the Rainbow.'" I don't know what possesses me to do it. But I start singing the song. The first few lines of the bridge. Koi leans into me, listening intently. "See? Zay belts. Pushes from her chest. I literally can't do that. My vocal cords don't work that way. It's a curse, I guess. A singer who can't belt."

"First of all." He grabs my hand and places it on his chest. His heart is *racing*.

"Whoa. Are you ok?"

"No." He continues to hold my hand against his chest. "You sang for me, and my heart got *excited*."

I pull my hand away, surprised it's tingling all over from touching him, like he's one of those plasma globes they sell with high-voltage electrodes in the center. "Koi, you of all people, the great belter, know there's no way I could pursue a singing career. I mean, even Disney princesses belt."

Two women walking in front of us are staring. I hear one of them whisper, "Holy crap, that's Koi Kalawai'a."

The second woman elbows her and says, "Forget Koi, check out who he's with. It's Zay-Zay Waters. Oh em gee. We have to put this on the Gram."

Koi calls out. "How about a pic *with* us?"

The two women slowly approach.

"You'd let us?" one of the ladies asks, tugging on the purse slung over her shoulder. "We had to sign papers that said we wouldn't ask for autographs or approach any celebrities here, but could we shake your hands? We're huge fans."

Koi amps up the charm and pops off the bench. "They made you guys sign papers. That sucks! Let's do this quick, before security throws all of us out of here."

The ladies are downright giddy as Koi moves to stand between them. One holds out her phone and snaps the pic.

"Let me see if it's good." Koi nods in approval. "Nice. Tag me in it."

Now the other lady steps timidly toward me. "Zay-Zay Waters?" She holds up her cell. "Can we break the rule with you too?"

I push off the bench and nod. Careful not to speak a word as I move to stand with the women.

"You know," she says. "I was at your concert at the Isleta Amphitheater in Albuquerque. Couldn't afford the meet and greet VIP tickets, since they were like a thousand dollars and I'd recently lost my job. I guess the Universe was looking out for me, anyway. What kismet to see you here now."

I'm not sure meeting a fake Zay-Zay Waters should qualify, but I'm thrilled to create a happy moment for her. Koi takes the cell and snaps a photo of the three of us.

"Omigosh, thank you so much!"

The two women move off, staring down at their phones and chatting excitedly.

"A thousand dollars for a *picture*?" I whistle. "I should take one thousand pictures of you, sell them on eBay. Boom. Retire at eighteen."

"That's a thousand dollars for pictures with *Zay-Zay*. Not me. My meet and greets are nowhere near that level. Plus, I split everything with my band, remember? We don't end up making much on meet and greets."

"That's very good of you. To split the money with them."

"It's not goodness. We write our songs together. We're a team. Also, deflector, we're not done talking about you. You do not have to push like Freddie Mercury to be a good singer. There are great singers who don't belt."

"Oh. We're back to this?" I focus on the waterfall on the other side of the railing. The sunlight reflects off the water like someone is pouring crushed diamonds into the pond. It's breathtaking. Koi crosses to stand beside me, and we both stare down at the coins glistening in the water. I wonder what sorts of wishes were made right here in this spot. "All right, Koi." I turn to face him. "You have my undivided attention. I will not deflect. Name the great singers who don't belt."

He seems like he wasn't expecting that. For a moment, I'm confident he doesn't have an answer, since he's standing so quietly. Finally he speaks. "Karen Carpenter. From the Carpenters. She sang in her head voice. The world loved her."

"The Carpenters? The ones who sing that Sesame Street song about singing a song, right?"

He laughs. "Do *not* knock the Carpenters. 'Rainy Days and Mondays' is my jam."

"Ok, fine. I'll give you Karen Carpenter. Any others?"

"Roberta Flack!" he says, a bit too loud. He lowers his voice. "For the most part, she's not belting. She's a crooner. Soft. Gentle. Melodic."

He's right. But still. "Maybe I'm wrong. I don't think Roberta Flack and Karen Carpenter would be popular if they were *today* kind of artists. Today, people wanna listen to Beyoncé. Bruno Mars. And . . . you."

"You *are* wrong. Bring back crooners! Seriously." Koi steps closer to me. "I'd pay to hear you sing again. I would." His fingertips brush my cheek. "Can I kiss you?"

Whoa. Definitely wasn't expecting that. "You . . . wanna kiss me right now?"

"I mean, a lot of people are watching us." He shrugs. "It would be sweet. Zoi is hot right now. Keep it trending."

Oh. That's right. Keep your head *out* of the game, Red. He's performing for the cameras. "Sure. Yeah."

"You sure?" His eyes cloud over, and he takes a step back, putting distance between us. "I don't wanna make you uncomfortable."

"I'm fine with it." I scratch at my elbows.

He places his hands gently on my hips. They feel heavy and light at the same time. "Pretend we're on set and the director said *Action.*"

Action? Omigosh. I'm not ready. Could I raise my hand and ask the director for a five-minute break?

Before I know what's happening, he's leaning forward and pressing his lips to mine. They feel warm. *He* feels warm. And though the kiss is basically pretty innocent, my heart is throwing itself against my ribs, and everything is spinning. My knees buckle.

"Whoa." Koi pulls away and wraps his arms around my waist. "You feel wobbly again. Like you did on the carpet at Skybar."

"Yeah?" I take a moment to steady my equilibrium. "Maybe, um, I'm not eating enough since I got here. Feel a bit light headed."

"Oh no." He pulls me closer and rests his head on top of mine. "I hate that feeling. Now I'm worried about you."

Oh gosh. Keeping my head out of a game like this is proving to be complicated! I need space. I need air.

But just as I'm about to put some distance between us, Koi says, "Oh, look. They're here."

I turn to see who *they* is. Lots more people have arrived. Guests are laying out blankets and finding spots on the lawn. I've been so caught up with Koi, I didn't notice the place was filling up for the concert. Also, I blink to make sure I'm seeing this correctly—I recognize them.

Noah.

Ori.

Wilbert.

Lono.

Tahj.

And Liam.

"It's the Six!" I spin back around to face Koi. "Aren't they supposed to be on vacation?"

"They are on vacation." Koi smiles. "Vacationing in Los Angeles. First stop. The Getty Museum."

"Wait a second." It suddenly dawns on me. "It's *you*. *You're* performing here? With the Six?"

"Yoooo, bro." Liam rushes to Koi, wraps his arms around his waist, and lifts him off the ground.

Koi cracks up laughing as Liam spins him around, and the boys reunite with Koi. Slapping each other on the back, banging shoulders. They're all talking a mile a minute. It's so loud. It makes me long for the sounds of the farm, my brother's shouting over an Xbox game, Daeshya crying, Mom hollering at us kids to do this or that.

"That tram security, bro." Noah carries his ukulele. "They tried to tell me I couldn't bring up Gretchen." He kisses the instrument. "I don't go nowhere without my baby!"

Koi motions toward me. "Guys, Zay-Zay Waters. Don't be rude. Say hi."

"Whoaaa!" Noah and Liam say in unison. Then Liam adds, "You know we know da kine. Hi, Zay-Zay."

I have no idea what *da kine* means. I assume it's something good. "What's up, y'all."

"Howzit?" Wilbert steps to me. It's easy to recognize Wilbert, because his hair hangs to the middle of his back. There are Instagram fan pages dedicated solely to his hair. "Would it be weird if I hugged you?"

"Do *not* hug her," Koi warns. "She has contracts that forbid smelly dudes from hugging her."

"I eat contracts for breakfast," Wilbert says before giving me the most gentle, big-brother hug. And unless you dislike oranges and strawberries, he smells just fine.

"Zay-Zay," Koi says proudly. "These are my brothers for life. We all grew up together. Ori."

Ori waves.

"Wilbert and Noah."

Wilbert tugs on his black blazer. Noah puts prayer hands over his heart and bows like a yogi.

"Lono and Tahj."

Lono and Tahj wear identical black T-shirts, except one says OBI WON and the other says OBI LOST.

"And Liam."

Liam waves. "Aloha, beautiful Zay-Zay."

The Six. How unbelievably *cool.*

"Please tell me that's not our stage." Tahj's hair is so spiked with gel it could injure someone. "I have three keyboards. How is it all gonna fit?"

Tahj moves off, and Lono, Liam, and Ori follow after him.

"Nice meeting you, Zay-Zay." Wilbert rushes to follow his brothers.

Which leaves Noah, who is texting. He looks up and sees the boys nearing the stage. "Oh shoot." He waves at us. "Bye." And now he's gone too.

I turn to Koi. "Why didn't you tell me you were performing?!"

"We're performing. There. Now you know." Koi points at the stage. "Wanna join us up there? C'mon, Red. Sing."

I shake my head. "I'm not allowed. You know that."

"Tell Diamond I made you. I'll take all the blame."

Would she actually go for that?

"C'mon, how cool would it be for you to get on stage with me and the Six? You'd be *amazing.*"

"Hey." Issa is out of breath as she makes it to our side. "Zay-Zay, you wanna see some art with us while the boys do their sound check?"

"You cool with that?" I ask Koi.

"Yes, but I'll *miss* you," Koi replies sweetly.

Issa reaches to take my hand, but Koi beats her to it. I stumble into his arms.

"Hey," he whispers in my ear. "Will you miss me too?" I don't have a chance to answer because he leans forward and presses his lips to mine. This time I make sure my legs stay planted firmly on the ground, even though the Getty gardens are *spinning.* When he pulls away, he says, "Goodbye, beautiful."

He rushes off toward the stage. I bring my fingers to my lips, still ignited from our kiss.

"Wow."

I turn to face Issa. She's smirking at me.

"What?" I say. "What's that *wow* for?"

"Remember when I said I think your fake boyfriend might have a *real* crush on you?" She places a delicate hand on her hip. "Well, I think the fake girlfriend might be crushing harder."

"What? No." I lean forward and whisper, "Issa, girl. We just actin'. You know that."

"Do I?" She links her arm around mine. "Don't take this the wrong way, Zay-Zay. But Koi has been complaining about you *all* year. He says you're insufferable and loathes every minute he's forced to spend with you."

I frown. "He said that?"

"Obviously he's been lying. First he makes us shop for hours for a fake engagement ring. And now, based on what I'm seeing, he's completely *smitten*."

"Ladies." Taylor Thompson Lee steps next to us. "I wanna see Fabriano, Pontormo, and Rembrandt. Not necessarily in that order. But let's go."

SEVENTEEN

Issa thinks Koi has a real crush on me. She thinks I have a crush on him too. Do I? I mean, ok. How could I not? He's acting like the perfect boyfriend. The hand holding, the kissing, the whispering in my ear, the . . . ring. This is like an entire season of *The Bachelor* scrunched up into a few days. Except there aren't any other girls to compete with. So *I'm* getting all the attention. But a guy like him wouldn't really fall for a girl like me . . . would he? I wanna bite my nails, but I can't. Because these aren't my nails! They're long and hard and plastic and pointy. Why do women get these things?

"Zay-Zay, what do you think?" Taylor stands beside me in the large art gallery. We're on the second floor of the East Pavilion, and getting here absolutely required us to use a map. The Getty is that big. "What are your thoughts on *Rembrandt Laughing*? Why is it so fascinating?"

I glance at the Rembrandt painting we've been staring at for so long. Why is it fascinating? "Why *do* people stand and stare at a picture of a human, when there are humans all around that pass us by in vivid Technicolor? Some of the Universe's finest creations are an arm's length away, every day, always. We don't make eye contact. Heck, we avoid it. Yet, here we stand, staring at a frozen . . . image. Why?" I pause, carefully choosing my next words. "I think it's because a true artist captures a moment. We all know real-life moments are impossible to capture. Right?"

Of course I'm right on that one. There are so many moments I wish I could have captured. Like the moment on the red carpet when Koi kissed me for the first time. A chill rushes up my spine at the memory. I go on.

"But we can't capture moments, can we? I mean, we can try, but as soon as you think you've figured out how to do it, the moment is gone. But here, the strokes of Rembrandt's brush have become a time machine. Transporting us. Giving us that thing we so desire—a moment captured." I shrug and turn back to face him. Issa now stands at his side. "That was a long ramble. I could be wrong."

Taylor and Issa are frozen. Like, seriously, they're not blinking.

Uh-oh. I forgot to be Brooklish!

"My bad. My bad. I was bein' too deep, huh?" I slap myself on the forehead. "Forget all that. I was bein' hecka dramatic."

"You're low-key genius." Taylor takes off his top hat, and his mess of hair falls into his eyes. He pushes it off his face. "Honestly, I wish I had *recorded* it."

"Why *do* we let people walk by us?" Issa whines. "I really hate that! I always want to stop and say hi. People are walking works of art. Oh my goodness, Zay-Zay, that's so true. Everything you said is *true*."

Issa rushes ahead of us, saying hi to every person that walks by her, pausing to stare deeply into their eyes.

"What if she never stops doing that?" Taylor asks.

"My bad. I hope I didn't break Issa," I whisper back.

"Hola." Issa stops a Latina mother walking with her toddler. *"Vos y su hija son tan bellas."*

The woman looks overjoyed. *"Muchas gracias. Usted también es muy bella!"*

A moment later, and the two women are happily chatting. Issa holds the little girl.

"She's pretty dope," I say to Taylor. "She told me you guys met because she thought you were a homeless Parisian. That true?"

"It's true. She took all the capers off her dry chicken marsala and then gave it to me. I still ate it."

I laugh. "What did she do when she realized who you are?"

"Who I am, Zay-Zay Waters, is a mere man. I've been hoping she doesn't ever figure that out." He leans closer to me and speaks softly. "I'm proposing to her tonight. A real proposal. Not that fake stuff that you and Koi get into. I got her a pink diamond. Koi made her think we were shopping for you. But it was mostly a decoy. I wanted to get her the ring she loved."

My eyes stretch wide. That's why Koi had them going on a wild chase for rings. It wasn't for me. It was for *Issa*.

"Do you think we're too young? Be honest, Zay."

"Nope. I wasn't thinking that at all."

"I'm twenty-five. My parents got married when they were twenty, and they've been married for thirty-eight years. Issa's parents got married young too. Also still together. Plus, Issa's wise beyond her years. By the time she was twelve, she was working full time and traveling the globe. She got emancipated from her parents when she was sixteen. Which many would consider foolish, considering her parents are worth about two billion dollars."

I bite the inside of my lip to make sure my jaw doesn't drop. Issa is a rich heiress? Didn't she tell me she works for a nonprofit in her spare time?

"I love her. Where's the rule that says we have to be a certain age before we go after what we love? She's the best thing that's ever happened to me. I thank the Universe for her every single day."

My eyes well up with tears. "My bad. That"—I wipe at them—"made me cry." I take a moment to really take in Taylor Thompson Lee, from the garbage top hat to the Donald Duck Crocs. I probably shouldn't say this to him, but I can't resist. "You realize you're like . . . a big deal, right? Ain't you supposed to be thankin' the Universe for how great *you* are? You know, I watched like six*teen* interviews of you the other day so I could be properly prepared to stroke your ego. You don't seem to have one."

"Don't tell anybody. It'll ruin my name in Hollywood."

I wipe at my eyes again and laugh. "You know what I mean. You are a great man."

"The day I realized what a lot of truly great men have in common, it changed my life. From the Buddha to Socrates, Isaac Newton to . . . Albert Einstein and more. Do you know what they all have in common?"

I could toss out a million guesses. The truth is, "I don't know."

"They're not here anymore."

I frown. "I'm not understandin'."

"That's what they have in common. They're *gone*. No matter how great you think you are, you can't stay here. Your time comes. Your time goes. Nobody can avoid it. Nobody. If that doesn't humble a man, then I don't know what will."

A chill rushes through my whole body.

Taylor extends his arm toward *Rembrandt Laughing* and adds, "However, in the words of the great Zay-Zay Waters, they leave their captured moments behind for us to gaze upon." He bows in my direction. "It's what you do, too, Zay-Zay Waters. Capture moments of greatness. With your music."

That is what Zay-Zay is doing, isn't it? "Yeah. I-I guess you're right."

"What's next? What's the next moment you're trying to capture?" he asks excitedly.

Even though he's asking Zay-Zay and not me, the question weighs as heavy as an iron anchor in the pit of my stomach. When it comes to me, I . . . haven't really been trying to capture any moments. What *are* my plans? "Um. I mean . . ."

"Why don't you come audition for my new movie?"

Wait . . . what? "Seriously?"

"I have a short list of girls I'm considering, since my original lead had to back out. She couldn't get on board with my vision. And also, she was asking for more money than the budget of the entire movie. I was happy to see her go. I never thought about you, honestly, though your name has come up lots of times. The character is a singer. She's got a pretty unique journey, and I thought maybe you were too . . . Zay-Zay. Too . . . big. If you know what I mean. I didn't think you'd understand the importance of desperately trying to capture a moment in time. Clearly I was wrong. You might be perfect to play Chanel. That's her name, by the way. The lead girl."

This is certainly a moment Zay's been trying to capture. A proper meeting with Taylor Thompson Lee. Do I play hard to get for her, or lurch forward, hug him, and tell him I can't wait to audition for his movie? I decide to keep it simple.

"That's what's up, Tay. Can I call you Tay?"

"Please don't. It sounds like someone with a broad Yorkshire accent saying the alphabet. *Q. R. S. Tay. You. Vay.*"

I play along with the worst British accent I can force out. "*Double You. Ex. Wwwhy. And Zay.*"

"*Why* and *Zay-Zay*, to be precise." Taylor tips his hat. "Cheerio, and that's how you say the *A, Bay, Say-Zays*. With a broad Yorkshire accent."

We both laugh. Issa is still chatting with the mom, and now bouncing the toddler on her hip. Issa found her real-life art for the day, live, in vivid Technicolor.

"You know we're shooting the movie in Tel Aviv, Netanya, Ramla . . . a few other places too," Taylor explains. "Oh, and Tzfat."

Tzfat? "You're shooting in *Israel*?"

"Most of it, yeah. It will be a six-month shoot. Not glamorous. I do real life. We get dirty. We often skip hair and makeup. Just a few of the things that make me different. You up for an adventure? You ever been to Israel?"

"No. But . . ." Would it be weird to say I've been wanting to visit since this morning? Ever since Zay's chef, Caleb, planted the seed. "I'd *love* to visit Israel." I really would. I won't let the sad longing show on my face. He's offering Zay-Zay this amazing opportunity. She'd be grateful. She'd smile. So I do, too, then add in Brooklish, "I'm wit' it, Taylor."

"I'm wit' it, too, Zay-Zay Waters."

~

"I can't believe it!" Aish is so excited she sounds out of breath.

I'm hovering on the side of the stage, whispering, though I don't really need to be. The Getty Museum has provided a nice area for our group. Three guards stand in front of our setup as an added security measure. No one could get near me if they wanted to. I'm watching Taylor onstage, chatting it up with Koi and his band, holding tightly to Issa's hand as more people find spots on the lawn. Unsuspecting Issa. She has no idea that hand will have a diamond ring on it very soon. One she won't have to give back.

"He said his people will probably be calling my people. Or, her people." Which is the only typically Hollywood thing Taylor has said all day.

"Zay is going to go absolutely bonkers when she returns from Brazil. What a wonderful surprise. Red, you're amazing."

"Eh . . ." I pause, staring at the stage. A few hours ago, I thought one of the worst things that could happen would be Koi dragging me up there. Now, I kinda think the worst thing that could happen would be if he *didn't*. Taylor asked me what my next captured moment is. I didn't have an answer then. I do now. "There's a caveat," I blurt, not recognizing the sound of my voice.

"A caveat," Aish repeats. "What do you mean?"

"I mean . . ." Oh gosh! What do I mean? "Zay needs to sing." I exhale. "*I* need to sing." I really do. I simply cannot let this moment pass me by. I must attempt to capture it. I *must*.

"Let me make sure I'm clear." Aish speaks slowly. "He wants Zay to sing live. Right now? As sort of a . . . prerequisite for her audition?"

Sure? "Um, yep. That's exactly what he said."

"I should add Diamond to the call. I need her input. You don't mind holding?"

"Not at all." I scratch at my elbows.

I wait. A few seconds later, I hear Diamond's voice. I listen in as she and Aish discuss Zay's fake dilemma. To be on stage with Koi and the Six would be like 92 percent of all the childhood wishes I never knew I had even wished for coming true. Could this happen? I guess the better question is, Am I . . . *ready*? Would it lead to something good? Oh, please, Universe. Let it lead to something good.

"Did you hear that, Red?" Aish says.

"Sorry." I check back in. "Could you repeat it?"

"You're a good singer." Diamond's voice sounds like she really means that. "But you don't have the same power in your voice as Zay. Taylor Thompson Lee might notice the difference."

She's right. Zay-Zay belts like Mariah Carey. "What if I sing something light?" I offer. "Like in the video. 'Over the Rainbow,' even."

It's quiet for a moment before Diamond speaks. "Are you prepared to sing that?"

"Yes, I'm . . . prepared. But. I should add that—"

"Good." Diamond cuts me off. "Call us back to let us know how it was received."

She and Aish are gone before I can tag on the extra bit of info: "I should add that . . . I'd be singing *with* Koi. In front of *other* people." Should I call them back?

Koi's moving off the stage. "Hey. Show's about to start." He stops in front of me. "What's going on with you? I see a glint in your eyes. Something's up."

"Is the offer still on the table? For me to sing?"

"Sure. Are you allowed?"

"I mean, yes. Technically." I tell him about the conversation I had with Diamond and the very important parts of the story I left out. "What should I do?"

"Take the gamble. What's the worst that could happen?"

"They fire me. Sue me. Zay tries to kill me."

"It was a rhetorical question." Koi laughs. "If you make Zay look good, it won't matter. Plus, you can always tell a little white lie. You thought they knew you meant onstage with me and my band. Honest mistake."

Not sure how honest it is. But it's not like I've been a perfectly behaved stand-in since I've been here. So far, they haven't complained. "I told them I would sing something light. I suggested 'Over the Rainbow.'"

"You know Israel Kamakawiwo'ole's version of it?"

"Yeah, of course I know it. It's one of my favorites."

"Cool. We'll play it in a higher key so it sits in your range."

This is real. This is about to happen. I'm about to capture a moment. Or . . . at least try.

EIGHTEEN

oi and his band are already three songs in to tonight's free lawn performance. I should be shaking in my leather boots—well, Zay's leather boots—knowing at any time he could be calling *me* onto that stage. But dancing to the eclectic sound of new-age folk pop, under the Los Angeles stars, on this magical hilltop, beside Issa and Taylor Thompson Lee . . . I think I've momentarily forgotten my anxieties. Especially at this very moment, with Wilbert rocking out a sick rhythm on a djembe and Liam on the bansuri, an instrument that looks like an extra-long wooden flute and sounds like a chorus of boy sopranos. The real star of the show is Tahj, on *three* different keyboards. I can't leave out Ori on the bass, Lono on the electric guitar, Noah bringing in the sweet sound of the ukulele, and Koi. Koi Kalawai'a himself, belting out the lyrics to their hit song "Storm."

I pull my eyes away from Koi's enigmatic energy to glance out at the lawn. Everyone is so in tune and focused. No one is checking texts or making calls. In fact, phones are only being used as lights, held high over people's heads, or to record the onstage magic. Koi belts out the final phrase, the song ends, and the small audience erupts into wild applause. With a guitar slung over his shoulder, Koi speaks into the mic.

"I wanna pause for one moment, because I gotta explain why we're here at the Getty doing this free concert for all you lovely people."

Oh boy. Is this where he's about to introduce me? Or, well, Zay-Zay?

"A friend of mine said he wanted to do something really special. He had this whole weird thing planned that included mountain tightrope walking, skydiving and, like, an underwater escape room, and I was like, bro. That all sounds terrifying."

The crowd laughs.

"Then he came up with *this* idea. Something *relatively* safe. He said one of his favorite places was the Getty. And one of his favorite bands is . . . us. He was, like, if I could have my favorite band at my favorite place with . . . well . . . you know what? I'm gonna let him tell you the rest. Here he is. Everybody, please welcome to the stage . . . Taylor Thompson Lee."

Of course I'm trying to act nonchalant and unknowing as Taylor moves to the stage and takes the mic.

"I'm usually behind the camera, so this will be quick." He pauses. "When I was a kid, I use to talk to the Universe."

I can certainly relate to that.

"I would say to it, like, almost taunting, 'I'm going to be a director, and there is nothing you can do to stop me!' And then, like, a bird would poop on my head."

The crowd laughs.

"So, I thought the Universe had a pretty good sense of humor. Anyway, years passed, and I was directing the neighborhood kids. Directing plays at school. I borrowed money and made my own movie with nothing but a few iPhones, and suddenly things were going my way, and I was in. I was the director I told the Universe I'd be." He pauses for a moment, as if he might be a great director but he's not so great at public speaking. He wipes his palms across his shorts and clears his throat. "I was a bit shocked to discover, in the midst of all my success, I had this overwhelming underwhelm. All my dreams were coming true. Why should I feel such . . . longing? So I asked the Universe."

Everyone is silent, so eager to learn this uncommon bit of information from this world-famous director. Yeah, why should Taylor Thompson Lee feel any sort of underwhelm? He seems to have it all. I sneak a peek over at Issa, and her brow is furrowed. She's trying to make sense of what's happening but doesn't seem to have figured it out yet.

Taylor continues. "Instead of a bird pooping on my head, I got a very *clear* message. That dreams are pretty much useless if there is no one beside you to share in all the madness and also to tell you that you're really not as cool as you think you are. Someone to sit on the couch with, or on the beach with, or on the . . . floor with."

The crowd laughs.

"Someone to laugh with and complain with, and talk about how utterly ridiculous the world can be."

And now I'm a hundred percent sure Issa gets it. Because I see her lift her hand and wipe away tears.

"So, I placed a new order with the Universe. And because the Universe still has a sense of humor, a bird literally pooped on my head. I kid you not."

The crowd laughs again.

"Very soon after that, this enigmatic, beautiful, ethereal human angel showed up in my life. I had all these weird ideas, ways to tell this human angel how I feel about her, but thankfully my best friend, Koi, said, 'Bro, whoa. You might die on a mountain tightrope.' So here I am. Still on a mountain. But attempting to be normal, even though I abhor normality."

He pulls a ring box out of the pocket of his shorts, and the crowd gasps. A few cheer, and some, including me, wipe away tears.

"Isabella Cortina?" Taylor holds up a pink diamond that should be hanging with the rest of the stars in the sky. "I would like to live to be a hundred and twenty. I would like to live all of those years with you by my side. Will you completely abhor sameness with me, for the rest of our lives?"

I look over at Issa. She's kinda wobbly in those heels now. In fact, *her* legs are a bit like strands of spaghetti. Her face is red and flushed, as tears slide down her cheeks. Taylor moves across the stage and down the small set of stairs toward her. He gets down on one knee and grabs her hand. He's talking softly, but the audience is so quiet it's like his voice is echoing, even without the microphone.

"Would you be ok to change your last name to Cortina Thompson Lee or . . . I can change my last name. Taylor Thompson Lee Cortina? Whatever. We can figure it out later." He blinks away his tears. "Will you please, please marry me? Be my wife for the rest of our lives."

She nods and chokes out, "Of course I will. I *love* you."

The crowd erupts into cheers as they embrace and kiss. It's pretty much the sweetest thing I've ever seen. Also, I just decided . . . I abhor sameness too. He places the pink diamond on her finger, and they kiss again.

I could continue staring at these two lovebirds, but I hear a familiar soothing ukulele solo, the intro to Israel Kamakawiwoʻole's "Over the Rainbow." Koi is frantically waving at me. Oh shoot. That's my cue. Omigosh, that's my *cue*!

Deep breath. You got this, Red.

I make my way to the stage, a thousand thoughts crashing around inside my brain. I focus on only one. One thought. I want to *sing*. Koi hands me the mic. Dad always tells me two things that look contradictory on the surface can be simultaneously true. I know he's right, because at this moment, I can hear the screams from the crowd as they believe Zay-Zay Waters has taken the stage to sing for them. But also, I hear nothing. It's time to capture a moment.

I *sing*.

Though I've sung this song before, I don't believe I ever understood the meaning of it the way I do at this moment, with dozens of phones and cameras pointed in my direction, the Six as my supporting players and Koi Kalawaiʻa singing harmonies under me. This is a song about hope. It's a song about longing for escape. It's about taking a journey. But it's also a lament. A question to the Universe. Does somewhere over the rainbow exist? Or will I spend my life longing? Daring to dream? That's all some people ever do.

I gaze into Koi's eyes as we sing, and decide that *over the rainbow* is right here at the Getty. His voice is a gentle hum under mine, but we are connected in a way that is so powerful. It reminds me of what Taylor said. An enigmatic, beautiful, ethereal human angel showed up in his life. I wouldn't admit it to Koi, I'm barely admitting it to myself, but . . . one has showed up in mine too.

Someone's standing at my left. I turn to see Noah, with his beloved Gretchen in his arms. He's a wizard on that thing, his fingers expertly strumming the Jawaiian version of this classic song. To my right stands Wilbert, with a djembe slung over his shoulder, pounding out the gentle rhythms.

The crowd sways their arms from side to side. Some sing along. A few people call out.

Zay-Zay!

Zay-Zay, we love you!!

There are claps. Cheers. Mostly the biggest, brightest smiles. I'm singing my heart out in a way I didn't know I could. Plus, the song poses such a good question. If birds can fly over the rainbow, why *can't* I? Well . . . at this moment . . . I am flying. Heck, I'm *soaring*. With a seven-foot wingspan. With majestic presence and courage. With a magical ability to rise high, even above the storms.

Even above the rainbow.

NINETEEN

Omigosh, and then the people cheering like that! It was insane."
I know I've been rambling this entire ride. I can only hope
I'm not driving Koi insane as he weaves through traffic. "They
were screaming for Zay-Zay like I've never seen before."

"They were screaming for *you*," Koi corrects me.

They *were* screaming for me, weren't they? And suddenly a brand-
new feeling arises. All the other emotions that have been living deep
within my body, existing with*out* this new feeling for so many years,
seem thrilled to have it around. Cheering and celebrating. Welcoming
it with open arms. Hoping it stays. Can it? Or does bliss like this run,
once it realizes it's been spotted. Like a mythical mermaid who can't
allow herself to be seen, lest she be captured.

Koi merges onto Pacific Coast Highway, and I lean my head back,
staring up at the diamonds in the night sky, every part of me still ignited
from tonight's otherworldly experience.

"You guys were unbelievable. You and the Six. No, I'm not deflecting or veering. You just were. I truly love Koi and the Six."

"Whoa, whoa, Red. Not sure we're ready for *true* love in our fake
engagement."

I laugh. "How about Taylor and Issa?" I turn to face him, smiling.
"Did seeing a real proposal inspire you to do better for your next fake one?"

"It inspired me, all right." Koi reaches for my hand, interlocking his fingers with mine. "I decided I don't want a fake fiancée anymore."

Oh? I stare down at my ring. Not quite ready to let Starshine go. We were just getting to know one another. "So are we becoming *unen-*gaged?" I frown. "Or a grammatically correct *disengaged*?"

"Disengaged. Unengaged. However you wanna say it. Yeah. Let's stop. It was stupid anyway. It's like when Aladdin freed the genie. You're now free, Red. Sorry I forced you to go through with that."

"I-I didn't feel forced. It was fun. We were . . . having fun, right?"

He shrugs and pulls his hand away from mine to grab his chiming phone. He taps the screen, and I tune out his conversation.

I mean, *I* was having fun. A shiver moves through me, so I wrap my arms around my waist. Without Koi's warmth, the Malibu breeze is downright *freezing*. All the bliss I was feeling seems to be waving good-bye, the way Alice waved to her cat when she fell into the rabbit hole.

"Did you hear all of that?"

"Hmm?" I turn to face Koi. His face is lit up. "Hear what?"

"The Lollapalooza short list got shorter. We're *in*." He grins. "Koi Kalawaiʻa and the Six are in!" He grips his steering wheel and screams into the night. "Red, we're in!! *Ahhhh!*"

My heart feels like it weighs a thousand pounds. Koi's dreams are coming true. I force a cheerful tone. "That's great, Koi. I'm really happy for you."

"*Whoa.*" Something has caught his attention. He whistles. "That's amazing." He slows the car, and I shift to see what he's suddenly gazing upon.

The Pacific Ocean is to our left, and the waves crashing into the shore, are . . . glowing. *Whoa* is an understatement. It's *the* most magical thing. "What is it? How is it doing that?"

"It's bioluminescence. We have beaches like this in Hawaii on rare occasion, but I've never seen it here in LA. Wanna get a closer look?"

"Sure, yeah. Let's do it."

He makes a quick U-turn and parks on the side of the street. My eyes are super focused on the neon-blue, glow-in-the-dark ocean waves. "How is it glowing like that?"

"It's algae." Koi puts the car in park and presses the button to raise the roof.

I note the few cars that have been trailing us are parking too. Haven't they gotten enough photos for the day?

"Why it's glowing and twinkling like stars?" He shakes his head. "That, I can't tell ya."

We cross into an empty parking lot. The night air feels cool, so I wrap my arms around my body to block out the chill.

"You cold?"

I shake my head. "I'm fine."

Koi extends his arms in the universal "Need a hug?" gesture. "My strong arms can keep you warm."

A few paparazzi stand on the edge of the parking lot, cameras pointed in our direction. Koi got his prize. He's gonna be performing at Lollapalooza. He doesn't need to pretend with me anymore. "It's fine. I'm good."

"Suit yourself."

We walk in silence. When we step onto the dark sands, it suddenly occurs to me that I've never . . . walked across sand before. My boots sink with each step. It's sort of a sink, lift, step, sink, repeat. I'm moving like a snail. It makes me laugh.

"What's so funny?" Koi asks.

"This sand thing. It's tricky." I laugh again. "I'm struggling here. Never done this before."

"You've never walked in *sand*? You really are fascinating." He stops. "I could carry you."

"No, that's—"

Oh gosh. Koi has somehow maneuvered one arm around my back and uses the other to sweep me off my feet. He's literally carrying me in his arms now.

"Koi!" I'm laughing so hard. "Please put me down. This is ridiculous."

"I'm a human rideshare," he calls out. "Uber on foot!"

"Omigosh, put me down!"

"Never." Only now he's struggling too. With the weight of me, and the whole sink, lift, step, sink, repeat situation. He's wobbling all over the place.

"Koi, I'm serious—"

He takes another shaky step, and suddenly we're both falling in slow motion. I can't even feel afraid, because I'm laughing *so* hard as we tumble, sand flying *everywhere*. I laugh, lying flat on my back, staring up at the night sky.

"I thought your ancestors threw javelins and lifted stones with their bare hands, pretty boy!"

He crawls to my side and lies beside me, out of breath and laughing hysterically. "I mean, that was like a thousand years ago. Plus, their wives were naked, not wearing heavy boots! Easier to carry."

"Suuure." I turn to face him. "Blame it on the boots, weakling."

We both sit up, dusting sand off our clothes. Koi pulls at my hair. "You have so much sand in your hair."

I look at his hair. "So do you."

I don't know what makes me do it. It's obviously not for the cameras, since our fake relationship just . . . ended. I can't resist. I run my hands through his hair, letting my fingers linger for a moment, holding the silky strands off his face as our eyes connect. He's such an interesting contrast to the dark night. So bright, so warm. And yet his eyes seem to blend in with the stars. I'm going to miss him.

"What are you thinking, Red?" he asks softly.

"Nothing." There's a new feeling now, being welcomed by the others as it settles in. Heartache. My heart . . . aches. Not just for Koi. But for all the magic in Wonderland. I don't want it to end.

A crashing wave steals my attention away from Koi. Under the light of the full moon, it's like a thousand silvery-blue stars have fallen into the ocean and are now washing up onto shore, glowing and pulsating with all the power of the Universe.

Koi pulls himself up and offers me a hand. I take it, letting him help me to my feet.

"You gotta admit." He dusts the sand from his shirt and jacket. "The Universe can be pretty cool sometimes."

That's an understatement.

Koi kicks off his sneakers, rolls up his jeans, and moves toward the water. I slide off my boots, hike up my boho skirt, tie it in a knot, and follow close behind.

"Look at this!" he calls out.

As his feet touch the water, his footprints glow in the sand.

"I feel like we're on another planet." I watch as my own feet leave glowing footprints, wishing I had a camera to capture this moment, but also deciding that the best moments in life, maybe, can't be captured.

Another wave crashes in. Neon-blue water washes over our feet.

"Ahhh," I cry. "It's like ice!"

Koi moves to stand beside me. "I could pick you up again."

"Don't you dare." I place my hands on his chest, surprised I can feel his heartbeat through his thin shirt. Also surprised it's beating so . . . fast. "Why is your heart racing?"

"It does that on rare occasion," he says. "When it gets excited."

Excited? "Oh, because of Lollapalooza?"

"Because of you."

Me? We stare into one another's eyes, neither of us saying a word, the sound of the ocean the most soothing serenade.

"You really are fascinating, Red," he whispers. "I promise you are."

This time I let the words sink in deep and gently touch my soul. "I think you're fascinating too."

"Can I make a confession?" Koi reaches to brush sand from my cheeks.

"Let me guess." His fingertips feel cold and warm at the same time. "You want to kiss me one last time. For the paparazzi in the parking lot?"

"Speaking of that." He sighs. "You know, I've always hated kissing Zay-Zay. Being around her in general always felt like such a chore."

That is what Issa said to me. Another gentle wave of bioluminescent waves splash around our feet.

"But I knew," he goes on, "when I kissed you the first time, that something was very different. Because . . ." He pauses for a deep breath. "I liked kissing Zay on the carpet at Skybar. But it wasn't Zay, was it? It was you. So that's my confession. I like kissing you. I . . . like you."

It feels like I'm holding his confession in my hands. Because it's piled on top of all the many gifts the Universe has given me these last few days, it's in danger of falling and shattering like glass. I can't move. I can hardly breathe. I wanna keep it safe. I wanna keep his confession forever. Of course reality rushes in like the icy waters over our feet.

I hold up my hands. "My nails are never professionally done."

He frowns. "Huh?"

"And my hair?" I pull at my curls. "It's never this bouncy and shiny." I extend my arms. "And I don't have the courage to get a tattoo. I hate needles!"

"Red, what are you talking about?"

"How can you like me, Koi?" I ask seriously. "You don't know me. You don't understand me. What if this is just an illusion? You know, like on *The Bachelor*?"

He raises a confused eyebrow. "*The Bachelor*?"

"Yeah. When the fantasy-suite dates are over and they're, like, shopping at Costco buying toilet paper." I shake my head. "Most of those couples don't make it in real life. 'Cuz real life is real. *This* isn't . . . real."

He stares at me, contemplating. "Let me ask you something. You like this ocean water? The way it glows, I mean."

I glance down at another gentle wave of bioluminescence lapping over our feet. I nod. "Sure. Of course."

"You don't know a whole lot about this water. You don't know *why* it's glowing. It could be an illusion. It might not last long. And yet . . . you like it. How can you not?"

I exhale. That's a pretty brilliant point.

"Red." He takes both my hands into his. "You're like the mystery of this water. I don't know why you glow the way you do. It doesn't matter. You're not an illusion. I see you. I *like* you."

I take the deepest breath, careful not to inhale *all* the oxygen. I wanna leave some for Koi. "I like you, too, Koi." I say it softly, even though I'd rather scream it from the Malibu mountaintops.

Suddenly our lips connect. And though everything around us is cold, we are warm. He is warm. The gentle, glowing icy waves splashing around our feet are warm too. In this moment, he is very much like the mystery of this bioluminescent water. I don't know why he glows the way he does.

I like him just the same.

TWENTY

Our fingers are intertwined as Koi expertly navigates traffic on Pacific Coast Highway. My head is leaned back against the seat, staring up at the night sky and the twinkling stars.

"Tell me things," Koi calls out over the sound of the rushing wind. "Let's go back and forth. Confession time."

Ohhh. I love these games. Except there's so much he doesn't know about me. What should I confess first? I hold out my hand. "I know you only picked out this ring to deflect Issa and get her the ring she loves. But I *really* love it. It's so pretty. I named her Starshine."

"It was to deflect Issa." He squeezes my hand. "I still really got into it. I felt like Starshine was made for you."

I squeeze back. "Ok, your turn. Confess something."

"Hmm. Ok, this one time, my manager convinced me to go on a series of dates. Real dates. With Blaze from Necessity. You know the group?"

"Oh yes." Necessity is, like, if K-pop went multicultural American. Five girls. All different ethnicities. They dance like strippers. They sing with autotune. They dress similarly to . . . anime dolls. I have a hard time imagining Koi out on a real date with a girl like Blaze, who wears swimsuits on the red carpet and carries a red leather whip and a backpack purse shaped like a snake.

"Worst dates ever. She was mean, demanding, screamy. She yelled at a waiter once for refilling her coffee cup too soon. She said, and I quote, 'I'm not here so you can feel like you have something to do. Let us enjoy our meal!' That was the moment I decided I would never date another girl my manager set me up with. I was like, nothing is worth this torture. But no matter how hard I tried, she wouldn't back off. It felt stalker-y. Anyway, I came up with this ridiculous story to get away from her for good." He pulls his hand from mine to switch lanes. A few seconds later, our hands are intertwined once again. "I told her there was this shaman in the Brazilian jungle who was known for helping people change their lives."

My ears perk up.

"And that the shaman had, like, an aversion to celebrities, and wouldn't let me come to his village and see him unless I could guarantee I'd be alone and without paparazzi or phones. I mean, the lie was pretty elaborate and—"

"Sorry to interrupt . . ." The similarities between Koi's made-up story and Zay's actual one seem way too much to be a mere coincidence. "Did this shaman run a business that was low-key illegal? And he didn't want people to find out about it?"

"Wait, Zay told you? I told *her* about it when she asked how I was able to get rid of Blaze. She thought it was pretty clever. In fact, she said she was gonna use it someday when she needed to pull one over on somebody."

Oh.

My.

Ga.

I am screaming. Not audibly. But in my head, I'm screaming at the top of my lungs. Anger rises to the surface. Koi did tell me she was president and CEO of the master-schemer club. And I . . . "I think I got played."

"Played?" Koi repeats.

"Zay-Zay is not in the Brazilian jungle. I can't believe I ever thought she was."

"Wait . . . *what?*" Koi's voice changes. He actually sounds pretty spooked. "What did you just say?"

I turn to him. "Am I violating the NDA if she's not in Brazil? 'Cuz that's where she told us she was."

Koi groans. "Zay told you she's in the Brazilian jungle?"

"With a shaman who was gonna help change her life. So long as she didn't bring the paparazzi with her. The shaman apparently hates working with celebrities."

"A shaman who reads TMZ in the jungle? That's *my* dumb, made-up story. Zay-Zay stole my story!"

As far as stories go, this one *is* pretty far fetched. And yet we all fell for it, hook, line and sinker. Zay-Zay for the win. We slow to a stop at a red light.

"So where is she really?" My temperature continues to rise on this very cool night.

"Definitely with a guy. Whoever he is, she clearly doesn't want *anyone* to know about it. Which does not speak well for this situation."

So Zay isn't off trying to discover the meaning of life. She's messing around with some *guy*. She dragged me away from my home, got all these people involved—lawyers, Aunt Diamond, my *parents*, and more—so she could sneak off to date some rainbow-haired dude with copper-plated teeth!

Aish's phone rings in my lap. I decline the call.

"You sure you don't wanna answer that? You gotta tell them Zay is not in the Amazon jungle. If she's playing with fire, everybody's about to get burned. They need to find out where she actually is."

Suddenly a car pulls up beside us. He lowers the window and starts snapping photos with a professional camera.

"I hate to do this." Koi flips on his blinker as the lights turn green. "I have to stop and get gas. I'm on *E*."

Koi pulls into a Shell station, and the paparazzi cars trailing us pull in behind him, one after another. He hands me a pair of sunglasses and presses the button to raise the roof.

"Don't look over at them," he suggests.

A few have gotten out of their cars and are walking right up to Koi's, snapping like crazy, no shame in their game.

"Hey." Koi lowers his window. "Can you guys back up a bit?"

The closest of the paparazzi bends his whole body, peeking into the window. "Is that Zay-Zay?" the pap asks. "Or the stand-in?"

I gasp.

Koi immediately raises the window, taps the button to turn the engine back on, and pulls out of the spot beside the gas pump. My heart is pounding louder than the djembe.

"Koi," I whisper. "What's happened?"

He speeds out of the gas station and back onto the highway so fast his tires screech.

"I should be able to make it back to Zay's. But they're gonna have to help me get gas. If we don't run out before we get there. Cross fingers. Toes. Everything."

I twist around to see the cars trailing us. "How do they know?"

"Go online," he says. "Check TMZ. They usually have the top celebrity story. This would be a top story."

With shaking hands I manage to type *TMZ* into the search engine of Aish's phone. I breathe a sigh of relief when I see the top trending story isn't about Zay. "It's not about her. It's about some married football player having an affair."

Koi exhales. "Ok, so it's not common knowledge. Yet. Check a site called 'What's on My Block.'"

In a few seconds, I'm on the site. And yikes. I pound on my chest like my fist is a defibrillator. This is not good. The headline pierces through me. It actually guts through me. I'm *shook*.

Does Zay-Zay Waters . . . Have a Stand-In?

There are two photos under the headline. One of me, onstage, under the stars at the Getty. The other, of Zay-Zay, under the stars, on a lake beach, kissing a guy. The same time and date are stamped on both pictures, with small print that says, How can Zay-Zay Waters be in two places at the exact same time?

Of course I recognize the guy Zay-Zay is with. Because he was the top trending story on TMZ. It's the married athlete. The one having an affair!

I hand the phone to Koi.

"Zay-Zay." He sighs. "Why did you do this?"

Aish is calling again. I tap the screen to answer the call. "We know what's happened."

"Red, this is bad." Aish's voice sounds raspy, like she's been crying. "Please tell me you're almost here. Please."

"We're almost there. We're being trailed by about seven paparazzi, though. And Koi's gonna need someone to run and get him gas."

"Speaking of Koi. Let him know there are close to forty-five paps at the gate. Phones are ringing off the hook. It's a freaking *nightmare*. There's drones too. Brace yourself. And I might not be here when you arrive."

Oh, I'm braced. "Why won't you be there? Where are you going?"

"I've been fired."

"Aish, *no*." My heart feels like a heavy stone sinking to the bottom of the sea. Somehow I know this is pretty much all my fault.

"Get home safely, Red."

She ends the call before I have a chance to respond. I lean my head back against the seat. The brightest day of my life has gone dim. Though Koi grabs my hand and holds it tight, he says nothing. Because really, what is there to say?

~

Is this the doppelgänger?!

   Is your name Red Morgan?

   Red?

   Is this Zay-Zay or Red?

   Koi, did you know Zay-Zay was cheating on you?

   Are you aware you're with the look-alike?

   Red, how long have you been standing in for Zay-Zay?

They know my name? "How do they know me already, Koi?"

One of the security guards is screaming at the paparazzi to back up. We finally make it through, and the gate shuts behind us. Koi drives slowly through the quiet property. I don't care about breaking the rules anymore. With fumbling hands, I dial Mom's phone. She answers right away.

"Mom?"

"Red? What's happening? We got a call asking for an exclusive interview. How did they get our number?"

Koi can obviously hear her. "Red, tell her not to talk to these people. Tell her don't answer her phone unless she knows who it is."

I repeat what Koi said. Except it freaks Mom out.

"There was a guy on the property taking pictures. Dad scared him away, but . . ." Mom groans. "Are you safe, Red? I'm worried."

"I'm safe." I fill Mom in on what I know, begging her not to repeat a word of it to anyone except Dad. When we've made it up the hill and Koi's moving slowly around the fountain in Zay's driveway, Aish and Randy are coming out the door.

"Mom, I'm back at her house. Do not talk to these people. Love you, ok?"

"Love you, too, Red."

Koi says, "I just ran out of gas."

"Well, we made it. So the Universe isn't completely unkind."

We push open our doors as Aish approaches with a bag slung over her shoulder.

"Aish." I step forward. "Why are you *fired*?"

"Zay-Zay wasn't exactly pleased to see your performance at the Getty and blamed me entirely."

How is that fair? "Aunt Diamond said I could!"

"Well, she can't very well fire Aunt Diamond, now can she? Apparently, I'm . . ." She pauses, as if in deep thought. "'Useless if you can't see through the schemes of a basic opportunist like Red Morgan.' End quote."

My jaw drops. Basic?!

"It's fine. Back home to Middlesbrough I go. My grandparents will be thrilled to let me sleep on their couch for a bit. Me? Not so much." Aish is putting on a brave face, but I can tell she's been crying. "I'll land on my feet. You know I will." She leans forward and hugs me tightly. "It was an absolute pleasure getting to know you, Red."

This feels worse than when I saw Tony getting fired. Because Tony getting fired had nothing to do with me. This is *all* my fault!

"Koi, I'll run and get you gas," Randy offers.

"No." Aish rests a hand on Randy's shoulder. "Allow me. I'm on my way out anyway. I'm nobody, so the paps won't follow me. I'll leave the gas tin with security."

"I'll Cash App you for the gas." Koi reaches into his pocket and removes his phone.

A moment later, Aish replies, "Koi? Uh, you just Cash App'd me fifteen hundred dollars. Are you wanting the diamond-chain premium platinum brand?"

"Consider it your severance pay. Now landing on your feet just got a whole lot easier. Plus, I know *tons* of folks looking for assistants. We'll be in touch, all right?"

Aish wipes tears as they slide down her cheeks. "Who knew you were one of the good ones? Thank you, Koi." She moves toward the garage, her large duffel bag slung over her shoulder, her head low.

Koi and I follow Randy toward the house. When we step inside, we can hear Diamond arguing on the phone. Maybe *screaming* is a better word.

"You signed a forty-five-million-dollar deal with the Clothing Company! It's a family company. I'm begging these people not to cancel your contract."

I hear Zay's voice through the speaker on Diamond's phone. In spite of what's happened, she's calm.

"My career will be fine without the stupid Clothing Company. Don't beg nobody for nothin'. Period. I'm not about ta' be arguin' wit' you like this. You makin' a big deal. I'll fix it. I always fix it."

"Oh, it's that simple, huh, Zenaria?" Diamond says through clenched teeth. "Make a big mess, and you'll just fix it? You could be canceled for this."

"I'm almost twenty years old. What I do in my private life is none of your business," Zay claps back. "Or anybody else's, for that matter. Their obsession with my life is *sick*. I'm grown. I can do what I want."

"Niece, their obsession with your life keeps your million-dollar mortgages paid. You can't just do want you want. Life doesn't work like that. There are always things to consider. *People* to consider."

"People like the people on my payroll?" Zay's voice drips with sarcasm. "People like you? I wish I could fire you too."

"Take me off your payroll!" Diamond barks. "Guess where I'll be? Still right here. Because that's what family is all about. I'm here because I want to be. Not because I have to. Maybe one day you'll get that through your thick skull. Not everyone wants to be bought and paid for."

"And yet everyone *can* be bought and paid for," Zay-Zay replies coldly. "Facts."

"I'm done arguing. Big Bear is three hours away. Get your bags packed, get in a car, and get home. Now."

"I'm on my way," Zay mumbles.

"Zay, he's married," Diamond almost whispers. "Why would you *do* this?"

"He's separated," Zay articulates slowly. "Legally separated."

"Niece, I have been on this earth for forty-seven years, and I can assure you that *legally separated* is a fancy phrase that means *still married*. You have potentially destroyed your clean image and trashed the face of this sweet little girl standing in for you. You should be ashamed of yourself. You really should."

"Sweet?" Zay-Zay laughs. "She bought and paid for too."

It makes me gasp. Diamond turns to see us standing behind her. She sighs heavily.

"I can fix this." Zay speaks calmly, with an even tone. "You know I can."

"You better. Good*bye*." Diamond ends the call, tossing her phone and slamming herself down onto the couch. She rubs her temples. "Koi, I apologize for *all* of this. Obviously, this is not Zay. She's a hired stand-in."

"Right. Um." He tosses me panicked eyes, like he's not sure what he should be saying here. "I'm stuck here until Aish gets back with gas. If there's anything I can do to help, let me know."

"Thank you, Koi," Diamond says. "This is our mess to fix. Randy, take Koi to the pool house and have him wait there until Aish returns. Please see them both out after that."

Koi turns to me.

"It was nice to meet you . . ." He scratches his head. "What was your name again?"

Oh, he's good. I can play along. But first. I slide the borrowed ring off my finger and hand it to him. "Thanks for letting me wear this. It felt nice. Felt like . . . mine."

He takes it carefully into his hands.

"And my name is Red. It was nice to meet you too."

"Red, huh?" He sighs. "I really had no idea."

Bless this boy. Always thinking of others. He follows Randy out the back patio doors.

"Red," Diamond says. "Zay will arrive soon. We will both need to speak with you. Wait upstairs until then. Maybe try to get some sleep too."

"Yes, ma'am."

"And Red?" She attempts to straighten out the wrinkles on her shirt. This morning she looked so together, so crisp and clean and sophisticated. Now, with her shirt untucked and wrinkled, her makeup smeared, and dark circles under her eyes, it's like Zay-Zay's latest escapade has thrust Aunt Diamond into an instant wreck. "Zay-Zay does have a way of fixing messes. Whatever she's dreamed up, go along with it. It might not seem like it, but I can promise you, it *will* be in your best interest."

TWENTY-ONE

Outside the sun is beginning to rise. I cover my ears in a strange attempt to drown out the silence of the house. Who knew quiet could be so all-consuming? Sitting in the front row of Zay's theater room staring up at the fiber-optic-star ceiling feels like gazing at the enchanted ceiling at Hogwarts, bewitched to match the sky outside. I tried to sleep, but the anxiety wouldn't allow it. Tried to watch a movie, but couldn't manage to get the projector to work. So many instructions . . . it was worse than trying to operate the combine at home. Instead, I opted to walk around Zay's upstairs closet and stare at all her expensive clothes, read some of the books she has in her library, and teach Tyrone a few of the tricks Norman was so good at. But Koi was right. This house went from the most thrilling Malibu castle to a dungeon of doom and gloom. Who ever thought loneliness could pack such a powerful punch? All that glitters is definitely not gold.

"Play dead, Tyrone."

He stares up at me and raises his paw.

"No, that's shake."

He lies on his belly and scoots across the floor.

"That's crawl." I laugh. "It's ok. You're a good boy." I slide off the chair and sit on the plush navy-blue carpet that feels like spun silk. Tyrone snuggles up on my lap, and I scratch under his ears. "All right boy, it's five a.m." I rub my eyes and yawn. Tyrone yawns too. "Can't believe you pulled an all-nighter with me."

"Tyrone, come!"

I look up. The prodigal celebrity has returned. It's Zay-Zay Waters, seeming like she actually has been in the Amazon jungle. Her face is flushed and splotchy, her red curls pulled into a messy bun on top of her head, and she's wearing yoga pants, an oversize sweatshirt, and flip-flops. Her eyes are super swollen, like she's been crying for a decade.

Tyrone stands, staring at Zay with his sad puppy-dog eyes, and then looks back at me. Back to her. Now back to me. The zoomies set in. It's the craziest case of zoomies I've ever seen. He just runs back and forth in front of the large screen, spinning around in circles so he's a blur of white fur, barking, trying to dig a hole in the carpet. He's an absolute mess.

"Tyrone!" Zay-Zay calls out to him. "Stop it right now before I put you in your crate."

Which one? I think with an eye roll. There's, like, a crate in every room in this house. Or stuff him in the garage, like Aish and Randy do. Is this a Malibu mansion or a dog prison? The threat of doggie jail does make Tyrone stop spinning. He still seems confused. Finally, he crawls over to me, lays his head in my lap, and whimpers, like this game of Guess Who the Real Zay-Zay Is at Five in the Morning has completely depressed him.

"I think he's got sensory overload. He's exhausted too." I'm speaking softly so I don't upset him any more. "Maybe take him for a quick walk anyway. Reconnect with him."

"I've been gone for a few days, Red. You're not the dog whisperer." She marches over, grabs a whimpering Tyrone by the collar, and leads him out of the theater, leaving me alone again.

"Hello."

A man has entered the room. He's Black with smooth brown skin and kinky curls cut low. He takes a seat in one of the chairs in the back, crosses his legs, and adjusts the jacket of his gray suit by undoing a few of the buttons. Double-O Seven wishes he was as cool as this dude.

"Hi," I reply.

"Don't mind me. I'm Zay's lawyer, Mark Stone. Pretend I'm not here."

Oh gosh, they've called in a *lawyer*? What exactly is about to happen? "Um, I'm Red."

He nods coolly. "Yes. I know."

A second later and Zay returns, sans Tyrone. Clearly she decided not to take my advice. She's texting on her phone, or maybe she's sending an email, or heck, maybe she's doing a Google search for the most effective ways to get rid of unwanted doppelgängers.

"Apologies for the long wait, Red." Diamond rushes into the theater and takes a seat beside Zay in the front row. Facing me as I sit on the floor. "Did you sleep ok?"

Sleep? Ha! Good one. "Yes. Thank you."

She twists around and motions toward Mark. "The man seated behind us is Mark Stone. He's one of Zay's lawyers."

"We met," Mark calls from the back. "We're already good friends."

"You can't fire Aish," I blurt as I sit up nice and tall, ready to save Aish by any means necessary. "She's the best assistant. Me singing at the Getty was not her fault. I asked permission to sing. Sorta left out that it would be onstage. With Koi and his band."

"Aish is fired for more reasons than getting played by you." Zay cuts me off. "But speaking of the Getty. What the actual hell were you thinking?"

"Taylor Thompson Lee asked to hear you sing." I scratch at my elbows. That's not really true, but she doesn't know that. "I thought a light-sounding song would be ok. I did ask Aish if—"

"Aish can approve my DoorDash order," Zay-Zay interrupts. "That's about where her authority begins and ends."

"And me?" Diamond turns to her. "Where does my authority begin and end? I also gave Red permission to sing."

Oh wow. Is Aunt Diamond . . . standing up for me?

Zay ignores her aunt and continues speaking directly to me. "If Taylor wanted to hear *me* sing, he could. YouTube, Spotify, Amazon. I mean . . . pick one."

"Live," Diamond cuts in again. "He wanted to hear you *live*."

"Kinda hard to hear me live when I'm not there, Auntie!" She pauses for a moment, sitting back in her chair. "So now because of her, and Aish, and *you*, there's like a thousand videos of that wack performance circulatin' on the internet! People even sayin' my Super Bowl performance might have been her!" She turns and glares at me. "They say I got you chained up in the basement, writin' for me too. Or it's some weird Illuminati type stuff and we the same person. All this BS nonsense. This *all* coulda been avoided if you had just kept ya' mouth shut like you was hired to do."

"*Wack performance?*" Diamond folds her arms under her chest. "I understand your anger, Zenaria. But her performance was mesmerizing."

Oh my goodness. Diamond *is* defending me!

Diamond speaks pointedly. "And obviously if you *had* been in the Brazilian jungle with the imaginary shaman, *none* of this would have happened. This is not Red's fault. It's yours."

"How you figure?" Zay cocks her head to the side.

"Niece, there was a photographer in Big Bear trailing you. You were going to be outed regardless."

Zay sucks her teeth. "I disagree. So what, I had a stand-in standin' on red carpets. She's not the first celebrity stand-in. Red decided to pretend she was on *American Idol*, and now everybody's takin' shots at me. This has blown up because of her. Period."

Zay stares at me. Well . . . glares. For a moment, I imagine her leaping off that chair and attacking me like we're on *Real Doppelgängers of Malibu Hills*.

"Let's not play the game of who is most at fault," Diamond declares boldly. "Because Zay, I can assure you, you'd win. Let's simply let Red in on the particulars of the new agreement."

New agreement?

"Do we return the money?" I'm trying my hardest to hold back tears but failing miserably. "You end my family's chances at a distribution deal for our oats? What's next? Let me know so I can be prepared to break the news to my family."

"Your family don't gotta give back the money," Zay says. "In fact, since today is your last day, I have Mark ready to pay the remainder of what's owed to Morgan Family Farms LLC."

I wipe a tear as it slides down my cheek. "You do?"

"You just gotta agree to the new terms." Zay-Zay crosses her legs coolly.

I brace myself. It suddenly feels like not only has the seat belt light come on during the flight but the little plastic oxygen masks have dropped too. What is about to happen here?

"We want you to chemically straighten your hair, dye it black, and cut it short," Zay boldly declares.

Say what?!

"So you no longer are so similar to me." Zay's talking so nonchalantly. Like asking someone named Red, with red hair, to dye her hair black makes good sense! "I don't want you walkin' around with the ability to represent me. Plus . . ." She pulls at her messy bun. "I like the red. And the curls. I've decided to keep it for a while."

I wipe at my eyes again. This is beyond unreasonable. "If I refuse?"

"You *can* refuse," Diamond cuts in. "But technically, you *were* in violation of the NDA the moment you stepped onto that stage at the Getty. I understand why you did it, but you didn't let us know it was a live performance on stage with Koi's band. We could essentially make your family pay back the money you already received. We *could.* We don't want to do that. Work with us so we don't have to."

It suddenly dawns on me what's happening here. They're *blackmailing* me. "To be clear. If I don't cut, color, and straighten my hair, my family suffers? Shouldn't you be stroking a white cat and twisting your handlebar mustache when you blackmail someone?"

"This ain't blackmail," Zay snaps at me. "I gotta fix the mess you made!"

"Correction, *Zenaria*." Diamond speaks so sternly it scares *me*. "The mess *you* made."

"It's like you're taking her side!" Zay-Zay whines. "She got on a stage in front of people. In front of cameras. In front of the world, and *sang* as *me*. This is *our* family name. My legacy! We gotta protect that."

Diamond ignores Zay's outburst and focuses on me instead. "It's not blackmail, Red. Please remember what I told you."

Oh, I remember. She told me Zay knows best and to do what needs to be done. Like I have a choice here? Tears are streaming down my cheeks as I stand here alone, facing this . . . tribunal armed with scissors and hair dye. "It's not like I have a choice. So, whatever. I'll agree to it."

"There's always a choice, boo," Zay replies coldly.

"When it comes to the well-being of my family, there is no choice." I wipe at my nose. "You're protecting your family. Your legacy. I'm protecting mine."

"I'm glad you feel like that." Zay's smiling now. "Because there's more."

"More?" I repeat.

"Yeah. You also gotta agree to *keep* your hair changed. For at least a year. Randy will tend to the upkeep."

I'm hot and cold at the same time. "That's ridiculous and unreasonable, and you know it."

"No, you getting on stage at the Getty was ridiculous and unreasonable! This is necessary."

"And until everything has officially blown over," Diamond interjects, "you'll need to agree to stay away from press."

"Not talking to press will be easy," I say dryly. "I live in Orange City, Iowa."

"Don't be naive, Red," Zay chimes back in. "Everybody is gonna be clamorin' to talk to you. To get your side of the story. We're askin' you not to give it to them. We're contractually obligatin' you to not speak to them. Do you understand what's happenin' right now? I don't think you do."

"Just because we *grow* corn doesn't mean my brain is made of it." Dang these stupid tears. "I get it. I won't look like you. I won't answer the phone or return emails. Anything else, or can I go home now?"

"Do you understand that they will offer you money?" Diamond scoots to the edge of her chair. "Maybe not a lot of money, but there will be perks."

"They'll offer me money?" I repeat.

"They gonna offer you fame, Red. Five raggedy minutes of it." Zay shakes her head. "This is what everybody wants, ain't it? To be famous?"

"I . . . have never wanted that," I say simply.

"We were counting on that," Diamond continues. "Which is why we decided—"

"*I've* decided," Zay cuts in.

"Right." Diamond shifts in her seat. "Zay has decided, because it's her money, to sweeten your deal. And offer you more money than they ever would. Since fame is not what you're after."

"If you agree to all the terms Mark laid out in a new contract, then I'mma pay you, on top of what I already owe, one hundred and fifty thousand dollars."

Oh.

My.

Ga.

I think my entire life is flashing before my eyes. Here I am, essentially winning the lottery, enough money for me and my family. I could save the farm. Heck, I could save a bunch of farms. And all I can hear in my head is Koi's voice saying, *It's not give and give. It's give and take. What do you want, Red?* If Zay-Zay Waters is offering me close to a quarter of a million dollars, she's *desperate*. I gotta protect my family. I peel myself off the floor and stand.

"I will agree to the terms of your new contract, but only with an additional . . . agreement."

Zay smacks her lips. "Nah, boo. We not bargainin'. The deal is the deal. Take it or leave it."

"*You* take it or leave it," I repeat. "I want Tyrone."

Zay's eyes narrow. *"What?"*

"I want Tyrone," I repeat. "Give him to me. Or there is no deal."

Zay laughs. "You *trippin'*. I'm *not* giving you my dog. Sorry yours *died*. But, nah. Not happenin'."

"He's miserable here. As beautiful as your home is, he doesn't belong trapped alone with a dog walker while you're away all the time. Let me take him. Why can't he live out his dreams too? I have two brothers, two sisters, and a farm filled with people. They would love Tyrone. He would have acres of land to play in every day. He'd be in dog heaven."

"*This* is dog heaven. He has acres of land here," Zay points out.

"Acres of land he can barely access. You're keeping him sheltered, just so he can be here for you when you need him. That's not fair. You gotta let him go and seek out a life for himself. I can tell you, if he had a voice, he'd say, *Let me go.*"

"It's a deal." Diamond stands. "Zay-Zay, I'm going to call the vet and see what Tyrone needs to travel."

"No!" Zay bolts out of her seat, her eyes brimming with tears. "I am not lettin' her take my dog! Auntie, you can't let her take Tyrone."

"Zenaria Waters." Diamond places a hand on her hip and turns to face her niece with the saddest eyes. "You have bigger issues to deal with. Like fixing your new, tarnished, adulterous image. This meeting is over. Now we have one with Shannon and the others at the public relations firm. They've opened early for you. Get ready. We need to be in Beverly Hills in an hour." Diamond turns to Mark. "Please include Tyrone in the new contract. Review the fine print with Red."

Mark nods. "Will do."

"But how can we believe her?" Zay cries. "She could be lying. What if she changes her mind and talks to the press?"

"She gave you her word." Diamond turns to me. "For some reason, I believe that means something to Red."

Diamond crosses to the door and exits the theater, leaving me standing in front of Zay-Zay. Mark waits off to the side. Should I tell her I'm sorry? I really am.

"You know what bothers me the most about you gettin' up on that stage." She angrily wipes a tear as it slides down her cheek. "Koi."

"Koi?" I repeat.

"He tolerates me because it benefits him. I know the boy don't like me. He would never invite me to sing with him. I saw the photos of y'all kissin'. He had to know you weren't me. He had to."

I'm sure my silence says it all. He knew. Of course he did.

"I hope *you* know, never speakin' to him again is in the new contract." She turns, crosses to the door, and exits.

Never speak to Koi again? I wipe my own tears. Now I'm glad I didn't say sorry.

"Excuse me?"

I look up. Mark holds his briefcase.

"Let's finish this meeting in Zay's office, shall we?"

"Yes," I say. "That'll be fine."

TWENTY-TWO

Zay's got a whole setup with a shampoo bowl, vanity, and manicure-and-pedicure station with massage chairs. It's a room in her house, but it's designed to perfectly resemble an actual beauty shop. Which has come in handy to de-Zay-Zay me. On the floor are piles of my red curls that Randy hasn't taken the time to sweep yet, since we're rushing so I can make my flight. Without a proper ID, the check-in will be a lot longer since I'm flying commercial this time. I'm trying not to look down at the hair, because every time I do, I feel like throwing up. I focus on my nails instead. Which Randy took the time to return to their former short, nonpainted state.

I feel the cold shampoo as it's massaged into my scalp. A few moments later, the burning begins to subside as warm water from the handheld nozzle cascades over my head. Normally, when I wash my hair, it feels so heavy, but 80 percent of it is now on the floor, so I'm currently as light as a feather. Or at least my head is. I feel a wad of tissues being thrust into my hand and open my eyes to see Randy sadly staring down at me.

"Thanks." I blow my nose and dab at the flow of tears. "It's just hair," I choke out.

He squeezes my shoulder. "It's . . . just hair."

I don't actually think he thinks that, because his hands have been shaky this whole time. Plus, he's not his usual chatty and fun self. He's solemn and melancholy, like cutting off my hair is a crime against humanity and he is the guilty party. Only *he's* not the guilty party. It's Zay! She's the crime against humanity! To think I memorized TikTok dances in her honor. I'd take it all back if I could.

"What I'll do is blow-dry it after this. And set it with the flat iron." He doesn't sound like himself either. He's talking so softly. Almost whispering.

"Flat iron?" I repeat as he wraps a towel around my head. "You gave me a relaxer. That *chemically* straightened my hair, right? Why do I need a flat iron?"

"I used a gentler chemical." He tucks the towel so it's tight around my head. "One of my own personal creations. I recommend setting it with a *bit* of heat. How's the skin on your hands and arms?"

"My skin feels a bit tingly, but fine other than that."

Randy used a special blend of ingredients—baking soda, lime juice, cinnamon oil, plain white flour, and a few other things—to remove his Better-Than-Henna tattoos. "After you treated it with all that stuff, it came right off."

"My Better-Than-Henna is like *magic*. It's gonna change the world. Once I finalize the formula, hopefully it'll send me into early retirement. You wanna come with me?"

"I can't retire." I sniff. "I haven't even started working yet."

"Suit yourself."

Randy motions for me to take a seat in the styling chair. I twist the chair around so it's not facing the wall-mounted mirror.

"I don't want to see right now. Not ready."

"Better to see at the end." He cranks up a blow-dryer. I decide to focus on the terms of the new contract while he works. Mark explained everything to me thoroughly.

I am not allowed to talk to press about the particulars of this experience. Ever.

I am not allowed to talk to anyone about the particulars of this experience. Ever. Because should personal information, privy only to me, get out, I will be held responsible for the leak.

I *am* allowed to reply, if absolutely necessary, *Yes, I am the girl who stood in for Zay-Zay Waters.* That's it. The information starts and stops there.

I have to keep the short black hair for up to one year.

My social media accounts have to be deleted for up to one year.

I am not allowed to perform onstage for up to one year.

I'm essentially . . . deleted . . . for up to one year. At least, that's what it feels like.

Last but not least, with the exception of Randy traveling to Orange City for my hair appointments, I am not allowed to keep in personal communication with any of the people I came into contact with while working for Zay. Including Koi Kalawai'a.

Should I find myself in violation, all moneys will have to be returned, and I open myself up to possible lawsuits, financial damages, and legal costs.

"Randy, I'm so sorry," I say. "But . . . can we take a five-minute break to clean my hair off the floor? It's like staring at a dead body."

"Of course, doll."

He sets down his tools and begins attacking the bright white squares of tile with a broom, stuffing my precious curls into a trash bag. There really should be somber music playing. My heart feels like one of those Fourth of July fireworks that you look at, waiting for the big explosion, but it just makes a *pffft* sound before emitting a tiny spark, and everybody groans and says, *Welp, that one was a dud.* That's my heart. It's not thumping; it's just going *pffft, dud.*

"There." Randy leans the broom up against the wall.

Randy continues blow-drying, flat ironing. A few sprays of this. A few pumps of that. I get lost in my thoughts as he works. Of course I'm thinking about Koi. Never speaking to him feels unfair. Maybe I can use some of the money Zay's giving me and fly to Lollapalooza. We might not be contractually allowed to talk, but at least I can see him perform again. As I stand there among the screaming fans, only I'll know that we shared a special bond for a short while.

"Would you like to see now?" Randy asks.

"Nope." I wipe at my eyes again.

"Honey, I'm done. You gotta. I'm a stylist to the stars. I wouldn't do you wrong."

"But—"

He's spinning me around, and suddenly I'm facing the mirror. My face is red. My hair . . . is not. Randy didn't lie. It's not *horrible*; it's just . . . not me. As far as short cuts go . . . it's . . . fine. It's black. And it's *straight*. It sits just below my ears. I look like that girl from *Tron*. Quorra was her name, I think. It makes my light-brown skin seem paler than ever. There's bangs, so . . . that's weird. "I don't hate it."

"You don't have to wear the bangs when you're not out and about." Randy lifts the hair off my forehead. "See. Add a little gel, and it's off your face."

My heart is slamming up against my chest—*pffft, dud*—over and over again. I burst into tears. "I'm sorry, Randy. You did a really good job. I look like a totally different person, that's all." I stare at my reflection, and it's a stranger staring back at me. "I think I lied. I do hate it."

He rests a hand on my shoulder. "I promise, this, too, shall pass. Focus on the silver lining. Because of the contract, I get to fly to Orange City, Iowa, every few months to do your hair. I'm excited. Maybe you can teach me how to tie up a hog or whatever y'all do on farms."

Only Randy could make me laugh at a moment like this. I sniff and wipe my nose with the back of my hand. "I don't know who I am, if I'm not Red."

He rubs his bald head. "You think I'm not Randy 'cuz I don't have no hair? Girl, bye. I'll be Randy for as long as I'm here." He leans up against the counter, studying me with his kind eyes. "And you'll be Red as long as you are too."

"Randy, you're so nice." I take a deep, calming breath, then whisper, "How can you work for Zay-Zay? She's a monster."

"You know, sometimes I imagine . . . ," Randy starts, "that in heaven, before we come down here, we have to go to this, like, buffet. You ever been to those restaurants where you pay at the counter, and then you can go and pick out whatever you like?"

I nod.

"I imagine heaven is something like that. We all gotta enter into the buffet room and pick what we want. Blue, green, or brown eyes. Pretty hair. Tall. Short. Intelligent. Whatever we want. It's there for the picking. And, honey, Zay-Zay walked into that room, and she picked *insanely* talented. But the thing about it—everything we pick comes at a cost. There's a price. You wanna walk around with a face like Taylor Thompson Lee's girlfriend? What's her name?"

"Isabella."

"Folks is probably gonna be jealous of Isabella. I'm guessing that girl don't have many close girlfriends."

I remember Issa saying something like that. That it was hard for her to make friends. I never thought about it like that. Since for me, her insane beauty only seemed to add to her qualities.

Randy goes on. "You wanna be rich and powerful? Oh, that comes with a whole host of problems. A cost. Wanna be as smart and innovative as Elon Musk? Folks is gonna wish you dead. I think that man got, like, fifteen bodyguards. So Zay-Zay picked being one of the best singers in the world, and I can't pretend to know or understand the price she's paid for her insane gifts. But *she* knows. Sometimes that means she don't come across as the nicest person." He pauses. "So is she a monster? To you, maybe. But Red." Randy crosses his arms under his chest. "Zay has made it her business to mitigate and tend to the heavy burden that comes along with *all* it takes to be Zay-Zay Waters. She's turned her heavy plate of goodies into a bountiful blessing. Maybe it's time for you to do the same."

"I have been doing that! I help at home. On our farm. At our store. I'm there for my family. My sister, my brothers too. I do so much. The Universe knows. I do all I can!"

"That sounds like stuff you do for other people, though. What do you do to tend to you?"

The question throws me. What *do* I do to tend to me? "I-I don't know."

"You really need to figure that out."

He extends his arms. I stand and let him wrap them around me. What is it about hugs that makes you just . . . cry even harder? So I do. I cry and cry and cry onto his shoulder. And my heart that's been going *pfft, dud* for the past few hours might be picking up a *bit* of speed. Heck, I think I hear a *thump-thump* trying to resurface.

"Red, listen." Randy lifts my chin so I'm staring into his big brown eyes. "Most of us on this planet ran through that heaven smorgasbord."

I laugh.

"Honey, at warp speed." He laughs too. "We didn't realize we had to strategically plan our trip here. We just landed on Earth and got in line. We do what we're told. We march around like zombie robots, doing and saying all the things we think will make us special. *Other* people, they stayed in that smorgasbord room for hours, weeks, months . . . *years*. Making sure they picked all the right things and understood how to mitigate the effects of their choices. You planned well for your trip here. You gotta remember that you did. Remember who you are and why you came here. Ok? Remember that everything can lead to something good. *If* we make the effort. That's the part folks leave out. It's gotta be an effort. With the effort, it can always lead to something good."

I think of Caleb, Zay's chef. The way he grabbed onto his tzitzit, the little tassels hanging from his pants, and declared they are his daily reminder of who he is and why he came here. Maybe I need a daily reminder too.

Randy wipes away my fresh tears. "Promise you gonna try to remember? Promise you gonna make the effort?"

"I promise."

"Good." He moves across the room and reaches under a cabinet to remove a small wrapped package. "This is for you. To *help* you remember. And to assist your effort. But I can't give it to you unless you promise not to open it. Not until it's the right moment."

I scratch at a head that doesn't feel like mine. "How will I know it's the right moment?"

He smiles slyly. "You'll just know. The Universe is magical like that." He hands it to me. "Keep it somewhere safe until then."

Hmm. I shake it, the way Elijah and Jax do with presents on birthdays and holidays, but whatever is in the box is packed tight. It doesn't make a sound. "Thank you, Randy."

"Thank *you*, Red. For showing me beautiful you."

TWENTY-THREE

I stare out the window as the commercial flight travels slowly across the runway at the Sioux Gateway Airport. When the small aircraft slows to a stop, the lady sitting beside me taps me on the shoulder. I turn to her, ready to declare that I am not actually Zay-Zay Waters.

"I dropped my pen." She points. "Could you grab it for me?"

Oh. I reach for it and hand it to her.

"Thanks." She stuffs it into her purse before lifting her phone to her ear. "Hey, hon, yeah, we landed. I know . . ."

I tune out her conversation and sigh. While it's pretty official that Zay-Zay's plan to make me unrecognizable again has worked, I'm still not quite convinced I've fully accepted it. Celebrity is a powerful drug. Adoration fuels you like nothing I've ever experienced. It would be hard not to fall under the spell of a world like Zay's. But being invisible—it's not without its perks. For starters, you can cry on a flight, like I've been doing. And though the setting sun is peeking through the airplane windows and seems to be shining on me alone, like a spotlight, no one has noticed my tears.

As we all stand to file off the plane, I tug on my old Wranglers. Zay returned my jeans, my dusty leather boots, and my She-Ra T-shirt too. She also kept her word and sent me off with one hundred and fifty thousand of her dollars. I'm pretty sure the folks at Northwestern Bank in Orange City are scratching their heads, looking at my account and wondering what the actual heck. Little does Zay know . . . I would've kept her secrets for free.

As we file off the plane and into the airport, my phone rings. I see it's Mom and tap the screen.

"Hi, Mom."

"Red, Red, Red!" She sounds so excited. "Where are you?"

"I'm headed toward baggage claim right now. There should be a car service waiting for me. I'm almost home."

"Hi, Red!" I can hear Elijah in the back.

"Last day of Strawberry Fest," Jaxson yells. "Get here."

"And the Ferris wheel at night is so pretty," Loren adds. "I think it's bigger this year. Wait till you see it."

"I can't wait." My heart feels refueled at the thought of reuniting with my family. "I should be home in an hour or so." My siblings cheer. It makes my heart happy. "I brought a surprise back for everyone. Something the whole family can enjoy." The thought of my siblings' faces when they get a look at Tyrone makes this whole experience absolutely worth it.

"Is it Monopoly with real gold pieces from Zay-Zay?" Loren asks.

"Shhh!" Jax says. "You know she's not allowed to talk about she-who-must-not-be-named."

Mom must've filled the siblings in on the fine print. I'm glad they understand. "Guys. I'm almost at baggage claim. I'll see you soon."

"Wait, Red," Mom says. "We have some news for you later about our oats. But we wanted to share it with everyone. We were waiting for you to get back."

News about the oats. I think I have an idea of what it might be. "Is it good news?"

"Red, it's *amazing* news," Mom says breathlessly.

I'm not sure why it makes my eyes well with fresh tears. Something about Mom and Dad's dreams coming true, while mine are contractually obligated to be on hold, seems like a swift kick to the gut. "Can't wait to hear all about it."

I hear a chorus of goodbyes before I end the call and stuff the phone into my pocket.

"Excuse me?" I say to two female workers standing near baggage claim, chatting away with one another. One of them turns to me. I recognize her! It's the same woman who hugged me and cried. The one who said Zay's song "Believe" was her story.

"Yes?" she says. *Unbelievable.* She has no clue I was the girl standing in for Zay-Zay that day. "Can I help you?"

"Um." I tuck a strand of my strange straight black hair behind my ear. "My dog traveled with me. Could you show me where I pick him up?"

"Out the front doors, follow the path around the main building, and you'll see cargo pickup." She gives me a warm smile. "Have a nice day." She and her friend return to their conversation.

"Sure. You too."

~

The car company has rules, and so after a short walk with water and a snack, Tyrone is back in his crate, the crate is in the back of the SUV, and we are speeding across the highway toward Orange City. I stare out the window, studying the different hues of green on the oak and hickory trees as we whiz by. The last time I traveled this highway, I was with Randy, Aish, and the infamous Zay-Zay Waters, getting prepared to embark on the most thrilling ride. So many emotions were coursing through my veins, pumping me up like a hot-air balloon getting ready for takeoff. The excitement had grabbed me, convinced me anything was possible. Now it's like that moment when the roller coasters are shut down for the night and you're headed home after a day at the theme park. Everyone is silent, exhausted, sweaty, and . . . smelly. The fun is over. The only thing possible now is getting back to real life.

The hour-long drive seems to fly by, and suddenly the small SUV's tires are making that crunching sound on the gravel as the driver pulls into our massive parking lot. Tyrone whimpers and scratches at the bars on his crate. He's been such a good boy, but I know he's absolutely over this long day of travel.

"Thank you, sir," I say as the driver lifts the heavy crate and places it on the walkway, with Tyrone barking like mad.

"Not a problem, miss." The driver looks around. "Wow. Nice farm."

"Thank you." Guilt washes over me like a surge of Malibu seawater. Normally when people compliment our farm, I feel puffed up with pride, but a strange disconnect has formed. I force a cheerful tone. "We have a grocery store, too, if you're ever in the neighborhood. And we sell pigs born on-site."

"Very nice. My family and I live in Storm Lake. My wife grew up on a farm. She'd sure get a kick out of this place." He gives me a wave. "Enjoy the rest of your evening, miss."

In a moment, he's in his car, pulling out of the parking lot and back onto the highway. I kneel to unlock the crate, and Tyrone steps out timidly, head low, ears rolled back. Like he knows this is his new home but he's nervous to see it.

"Check it out, bud. It's *all* yours," I say softly.

He finally takes in all there is to see. His tail starts wagging like crazy. He barks and spins around in excitement, like he's arrived at dog Disney and isn't sure if he should head toward Tomorrowland, Adventureland, or Critter Country.

"Shhh." I laugh. "Tyrone, you'll spoil the surprise."

I note all the setup for the Strawberry Festival as I make my way toward the house, with Tyrone trotting happily beside me. Food stands. A giant jumping pillow nicknamed the Blob, where hundreds of kids will be jumping high and squealing like pigs in the pigpen in an hour or so. Our game section with the popular ball toss, and the Ferris wheel too. Loren said it was bigger this year. I'm surprised to see it's . . . small. Nothing compared to the one on the pier near Malibu. That thing stretched high into the sky, somehow making the Ferris wheel we rent for the Strawberry Fest seem tiny and unimportant. Or maybe I'm projecting—maybe it's *me* that seems tiny and unimportant.

I tug on the strap of my lone gifted duffel bag from Randy. The only thing inside is the gift he told me not to open until I know it's the right time. What if it's never the right time? What if Randy's mystery gift remains sealed and unopened forever?

I continue on toward our house, and the familiar smells of the Morgan Family Farm waft to my nose, warming me up inside. Freshly mowed grass, the smell of the evergreens that border our property, and whew—I fan my hand back and forth in front of my nose—I can *absolutely* smell that hog barn. I chuckle to myself, thinking about when Diamond first saw me and asked what to do about my smell. If I smelled like hog barn, I guess I can see what she meant.

"Are you the lady with the falafel food truck?" a tiny voice calls out. "'Cuz you can park on the field."

I turn around to face my little sister Loren. She's carrying two bags of trash and stares at me like I'm a stranger.

"Do I really look old enough to own a *falafel* truck, Loren?" I tug at the hair. "C'mon, sis."

"Oh. My. Gaaaaa!" Loren drops her trash bags and rushes into my arms.

I laugh as she hugs me so tight we both fall over. Tyrone thinks it's a game and jumps on top of us, barking and trying to lick our faces.

"Who the heck?" Loren sits up and rubs Tyrone's belly. "Who is this?" She covers her mouth with both of her hands and turns to me. "Is this the surprise? We have a new dog!"

I wipe tears at the corners of my eyes and nod yes. Loren screeches, lurches forward, and hugs me again.

"We will talk about your hair crimes later." Loren's out of breath from screeching. "First things first . . ." She gives Tyrone her full and undivided attention. "I must get acquainted with my new furry brother. *Bro*, I love you already. You had me at *ruff, ruff*."

Tyrone attacks her with doggie kisses, and I do believe he already likes her more than me.

"Loving the brown patch over your eye." Loren pats him on the back. "Hey, what's your name, fella? Huh?"

"It's Tyrone." I stare down at him like a proud mama. "He's basically brand new. Only seven months old."

"Who's seven months old?"

I turn to see Mom wiping her hands on her apron. I wave. "Hi, Mom. This is Tyrone. He's seven months. He's . . . ours."

"Red!" She rushes to my side and wraps her arms around me, like she's trying to fill me up with all the love I may have lost during my time away. She pulls back and reaches to play with my new *Tron* haircut.

"You hate it? Be honest," I say.

"I don't . . . love it." Mom gives me her "Sorry, I'm just being honest" eyes. "You're my red baby." She sighs. "I'll get used to it." She leans forward and whispers, "You gotta stay like this for a *year*?"

I nod.

Mom makes the grimace emoji face and turns to Tyrone, who is going zoomie crazy with all the attention he's getting from Loren.

"Mom." Loren's eyes plead. "We can keep him, right?"

Mom places a hand on her hip. "Is he trained, Red? 'Cuz I am so not in the mood."

"Oh, he's trained. In fact, he's been living in crates for the last few months, so he definitely won't pee or poop in the house. He loves people. He's such a sweet boy."

"Then he can stay." Mom smiles.

"Who can stay?"

I'd recognize that big, booming voice anywhere. I turn to see Dad, and Tony, too, moving across the field. Dad and I lock eyes, and for a second I see the wheels turning as he tries to decide if this person standing in front of him is his daughter.

"It's me, Dad." I pull at my hair. "It's ok if you hate it. Mom does."

Mom shoulder-bumps me. "I said I didn't *love* it."

"That's Mom-talk for *hate*," I reply.

Dad rushes to me, wraps his arms around my waist, and lifts me off the ground. "Red."

I laugh as he spins me around.

"My baby girl is back." He sets me down and gives me a once-over. Thankfully he doesn't mention the new haircut. However, he does say, "You look skinny. What happened?"

"Dad, I'm *starving*. They drink green water for breakfast."

"We have that raisin challah bread," Mom offers. "Plus tons of eggs, potatoes, and maple syrup. Make yourself some breakfast for dinner. Or you could wait till things get started here. The food trucks are amazing this year."

"I can wait. I'll make the rounds with the food trucks." Besides, breakfast for dinner reminds me of my first date with Koi and the "Breakfast for Dinner" menu at Sun and Sand. I hope my family can't see the sadness in my eyes. With all the amazing things that have happened to me, including the small fortune now sitting in my bank account, I don't have the right to be anything but grateful.

"Hi, Tony." I wave. "Do you hate my hair too?"

He gives me the grimace emoji face. "It's . . . interesting. That's for sure."

"I saw Zay-Zay with *your* hair," Loren calls from the ground, Tyrone snuggled up on her lap. "She was on TikTok with a little girl in a hospital, singing 'Believe' to her. It made me cry. Weird how similar you two are. I mean, not anymore, though."

Zay-Zay and her public relations team must be getting right to work. First stop, the children's hospital. Tomorrow she'll be building orphanages. By this time next week, she will be the first person granted saint status while still alive, and everyone will have forgotten about her salacious affair with the half-married man. If all goes according to her plan, in a year, they will have forgotten me too.

Dad takes notice of Tyrone. "Who is this? He could be Norman's little brother."

"It's our dog, Dad," I say. "Well, now he's ours."

"'Bout time we got us a new dog." He bends down to rub Tyrone's belly. "I hate to find out I have a new furry kid and run." He pats Tyrone on the head. "Tony and I need to grab a few things at the hardware store before tonight." He stands and kisses the top of my head. "Welcome home, hon." He kisses Mom on the cheek, and he and Tony move off toward the parking lot.

"I gotta get back to the food trucks," Mom says, "or they won't know where to park. We have eight this year. Can you believe?"

"I can help, Mom," I say. "Let me drop this bag off and—"

"No, no." Mom waves me off. "Take a moment. Get your bearings. Make a tea or a coffee. Lyndia's watching Dae. We hired four part-timers for the fest. Plus, we have a new stock boy too. You'll meet him. His name is Henry."

"Henry has red hair like you, Red." Loren frowns. "Oops. I mean, like yours *used* to be."

"*Loren.*" Mom turns to face me. "Oh, hon, before I forget, Doug Meyers called for you. Asked you to call him back ASAP, about some paperwork you signed in the wrong spots. He needs you to re-sign and said to call as soon as you arrive."

"Doug Meyers?" I frown. "The man who inseminates our pigs?"

"Mm-hmm. I told him I could help, but he said it had to be you, since you're the one who signed the papers in the first place. I texted you his number."

"Forget about pig insemination." Loren adjusts her thick glasses before placing a hand on her hip. "You guys know *Oh, So You Think You Can Sing Live?*, right?"

"What about it?" I ask.

"Next week they have their last stop for this season. In Des Moines. *Iowa.*" Behind her thick glasses, Loren's eyes are lit up like a string of backyard lights. "You should *audition.*"

Me? Audition? For *Oh, So You Think You Can Sing Live?* I'd be lying if I said the thought has never occurred to me. I can almost see the silver confetti raining down on my head as the crowd erupts into thunderous cheers and the judges hand me my ticket to New York City. But . . . I shake my head. Loren doesn't understand. "I'm not interested."

"What do you mean you're not interested? Has your brain turned to pencil shavings? Why not?! I saw you perform as Zay. At the Getty. Everybody saw it. Mom *cried.*"

"Wasn't just me," Mom says. "Dad cried too."

"Red." Loren still has her arms wrapped around Tyrone. "I couldn't believe that was my sister on that stage. I was so freaking proud of you."

Now I'm crying. I wipe at my eyes. "Can we drop it?" I sniff. "I'm gonna go make a call to Doug. Two of the pigs are in heat. If we don't get those pigs inseminated—"

"Forget those stupid pigs!" Loren untangles herself from Tyrone and stands. "Mom, tell her. Tell her what you told me."

Mom seems like she wasn't exactly prepared to be having this conversation. At least not right now.

"Um. Maybe this isn't the right time, Lo."

"What is it, Mom?" I wipe at my eyes again. "What did you tell Loren? Tell me."

"Well, you know." Mom wrings her hands together nervously. "Dad and I both think . . . that you've helped so much . . . and got this place running so smooth . . . and you've been so amazing . . ."

"*Mom.*" Loren groans. "Spit it out."

"Ok, fine." Mom sighs. "*We*, not just me, think you should take a break from helping on the farm. For a year. At least. I'd prefer two."

It's like all the oxygen has left my body. They don't want my help? They don't need me? My vision is blurry from all the tears. Mom reaches to wipe them from my cheeks.

"Red, please don't cry. 'Cuz then *I'll* cry." Mom points at Tyrone, whose ears are rolled back. He's staring up at me sadly, whimpering. "Now your new brother is crying too."

Tyrone steps forward and lays a paw on my boot. I bend down and rub behind his ears. "It's ok, Tyrone. I'm not sad. My family doesn't need me anymore, that's all. Nothing major. I'm useless around here, is all it is."

"You're not useless, Red." Mom pulls me back up. "You're maybe our most important team player."

"Then I don't get it. I love being here with my family. This farm . . . it's *everything* to me."

"That's impossible, Red." Mom crosses her arms under her chest. "I *own* this farm, and it's not everything to me. Let me retire on an overwater bungalow in Fiji and I'll be very happy."

"Mom, be serious." I wipe at my nose with the back of my hand.

"Red, I am serious. You have no idea how tired I am. Besides," she adds, "you're too young for *any*thing to be everything. I think we all are."

"Excuse me? Mrs. Morgan?"

We turn to see our part-time farmhand, Jacob, covered in . . . slime?

"Omigosh, Jacob?" Mom covers her mouth with both hands. "What happened?" Now she covers her nose. "Ugh. You *stink*!"

I cover my nose too. He really does stink.

"Two of the pigs are sick and puking everywhere," Jacob explains. "What should I do?"

"Quarantine them! In the other barn. We'll have hundreds of people here soon." Mom waves Jacob off. "And go wash and change. You'll get everybody sick!"

Mom must've forgotten we were having a very important, life-changing discussion, because she rushes off after Jacob without so much as a *We'll continue this conversation later.* Leaving me alone with Loren and Tyrone.

I turn to face Loren.

"Pig puke." Loren nods. "The glamorous lifestyle ya' just can't get enough of, huh?"

"Loren." I'm desperate to change the subject. "I can take Tyrone with me while I tend to my chores."

"I already did all your chores."

I frown. "You did?"

"Of course I did." Loren hugs Tyrone. "And this boy is coming with me." She kisses him. "Wanna help set up for Strawberry Fest? Of course you do!"

Tyrone trots beside her as she rushes off, like he's forgotten me already. Does *any*body need me around this place?

I tap on the contact info for Doug Meyers as I move toward the house, waiting while the phone rings.

"Yeah?" a voice that sounds strangely familiar finally answers.

"Um, Doug. Hi." I pull my bag back onto my shoulder. "This is Red Morgan from Morgan Family Farms, returning your call."

"Red." The familiar voice breathes a sigh of relief. "It's Koi."

TWENTY-FOUR

I'm tucked around the side of the house, hiding in the shadows under our old, dusty wooden awning, gripping the phone so hard my knuckles are losing color. This might be the last time we talk. I don't want anyone or anything to interrupt this.

"Koi, there's so much I can't tell you."

"You don't have to. *She* told me. About everything. I convinced her I didn't really know you weren't her. I told her that when we were alone, you mostly sat in silence and scrolled through Aish's phone with your sunglasses on. Not sure if she believed me. It definitely calmed her down."

I breathe a sigh of relief. "And the singing? The performance?"

"I told her it was *all* my idea. That part cooled her off a *lot*."

"Did she tell you about the new contract? The hair? Tyrone? I mean, she told you *everything* everything?"

"Pretty much. I think she needed someone to talk to. The whole conversation was pretty surreal, considering we've never really talked before. She was crying about Tyrone."

Ugh. The thought of Zay missing Tyrone doesn't feel amazing. The thought of him stuffed in his crate in her Malibu mansion doesn't feel amazing either.

"Why did you let her cut and dye your hair?"

"I didn't have much of a choice, Koi. I was terrified of what she might do."

"Who cares? Stand up for yourself."

"That's easy for you to say!" I press the phone to my ear as I pace back and forth across the back patio; I can see cars pulling into our parking lot. Strawberry Fest is about to begin. "By standing up for my family, I did stand up for myself."

"There you go again. Always thinking of others over yourself. You're *such* a saint. It's so boring."

"Are you being sarcastic?"

"Of course I am! 'Cuz you know where all the saints are now? Dead. Super dead. Stop playing the martyr. What do you want, Red?"

"What difference does that make right now?" This is not how this conversation is supposed to be going. He's supposed to be telling me he misses me. And I tell him I miss him. And then he tells me that he likes me so much. And I tell him I like him too. And then we cry, 'cuz we both know we'll never see each other again. It's a good cry. Satisfying. Sweet. Romantic too. But this . . . this call is not giving me *The Notebook* vibes. Like, at all. This call is making me want to scream, like I'm stuck watching that weird movie Dad forced us to watch with him last year, about an intelligent duck named Howard, from a duck planet, beamed down to Cleveland, Ohio, of all places. That movie gave me nightmares for weeks!

"If you don't think it makes a difference, then I guess it doesn't, Red."

"Why are you being so hard on me right now? Do you not know what she did to me? She cut off my hair."

"No. Randy cut your hair. You let him."

"They blackmailed me! I can't sing for a whole *year*. At least not in public. Talking to you right now, I'm risking getting sued by her. She's a blackmailer. She's a master *schemer*."

"And you taking Tyrone was what? *Not* a scheme?"

"No." I shake my head. "I was protecting him."

"Red, did you not hear me when I said that Zay made seventy-eight million dollars last year? She has like three different dog walkers. Tyrone would've been fine."

"He's better here," I shoot back. "He's happier here."

"In your opinion. Maybe you're right. Maybe you have really good opinions. Maybe you should search yourself for *more* opinions."

"You wanna know my opinion?" I'm not worried about anyone hearing me as I shout. "I think this all *sucks*. I loved being on stage with you." I wipe at my nose as words start pouring out like hot lava flowing down a mountainside, barreling over and destroying everything in its path. "I loved all the different people I met. Like Zay's chef, Caleb. He told me I should visit Israel, and now I can't stop thinking of it! Or Greece. Or El Torcal." I kick at the grass at the edge of the patio. "I wanted to join in on your conversation with Taylor and Issa on the Getty tram. Did you know that? I felt envious. I wanna know why staring at blue rooftops in Santorini is funny! I wanna climb Mount Olympus with Issa. I wanna be her *friend*. She was so nice. I don't care that she's beautiful. I liked her." My eyes well with tears that instantly spill over. "You know what else? I wanna practice my Creole with Lovelie. I wanna visit family I've never seen before in New Orleans. I wanna stare at more captured moments. I wanna capture my *own* moments. Heck, I wanna start an Instagram page for my hair. I mean, why not?"

Koi laughs. "Sorry. I don't mean to interrupt, but an Instagram page for your . . . hair?"

"Sorry. That was random." I pause to take a deep breath. "Koi . . . I wanna sing." I'm basically standing in one spot, but I'm still gasping for air, like I've run half a marathon. Then something wet and cold plops down onto my head. *Ahhh!* "Eww. Eww! *Eww.*"

"Are you ok?" Koi sounds concerned. "Red? Hello?"

"Yeah. Yeah. Sorry." I reach to feel the slimy sploosh . . . of bird poop. "Koi." I stare at the white disgustingness on the tips of my fingers. "You are not gonna believe what just happened to me."

"What happened?" he asks.

"A bird pooped on my head."

He laughs. "You're *lying*."

"I'm not." I laugh too. "Literally just now."

"Dude." Koi whistles. "The Universe *hears* you. Taylor would be so happy to know he's not the only one with birds pooping on his head."

Taylor. Oh, the mention of his name makes my stomach twist into knots and my heart jump into my throat. "How did he handle the news? Knowing that he was interacting with a fake Zay?"

"I've been calling and calling. He's not answering. He never reads the news, though, and he's been in auditions to replace the lead in his movie. Zay told me she'd let him know, though. She's auditioning too."

Of course she's auditioning. *I* got her the audition.

"Listen." Koi sighs. "I'm glad you know what you want, Red. You know what?"

"What's that?" I reply softly.

"The Universe should hear you. I hope all your dreams come true."

Why does it feel like he's saying goodbye? I don't want him to say goodbye. A deep longing rests in the pit of my stomach. Longing for the magic of glowing waves on a cool night in Malibu as Koi holds my hand and kisses me so sweetly. Longing for all the magic of "over the rainbow" to return.

"Hey, maybe I can fly out for Lollapalooza," I offer. Though I don't actually believe I'll do that. Being lost among a crowd of raging fans suddenly doesn't sound like such a good idea. Besides, what if Zay goes too? What if she sees me?

"Yeah, yeah. We'll figure something out. Red . . ." He sounds sad. "I gotta go."

I knew it. I knew he was getting ready to say goodbye.

"I've got press and a red carpet, and I'm traveling with the band this week too. I'll try to call when I can. But we have back-to-back shows. It might be hard."

"Oh sure. Yeah. Me too. Very busy." I stare at the bird poop on the tips of my fingers. "Back on the farm. They need me a *lot* around here."

"I'll leave you to it, then. You have my number. We'll try to connect, yeah?"

I say, "Yeah." It feels like I'm saying goodbye forever.

"I promise I won't tell Zay you're violating her dumb contract by talking to me. A hui hou."

"What's that mean?"

"Until we meet again. Aloha, Red."

And then he's gone. Why did Taylor Thompson Lee make me realize that I abhor normality? I really do. I scratch at my head again, right where the poop landed. Under my nails is white *and* black. I don't think the black stuff is poop. It kinda looks like . . . hair dye. But permanent hair dye doesn't come off. Does it? A thought suddenly occurs to me. An unbelievable, unimaginable *thought*.

I race around the house and push into the side door to the kitchen. I toss my bag on the table, unzip it, and take out Randy's package. With a pair of kitchen scissors, I cut the tape and lift the flaps. Inside are a few items: a box of baking soda, two limes, Epsom salt, a pack of flour, cinnamon oil . . . I stare down at all of it. Could what I'm thinking be real? There's an envelope too. With shaking hands, I remove the letter inside.

Dear Red,
Better-Than-Henna works on hair too. Honey, I told
you, it's like magic.
Love, Randy

I fold the letter and hold it to my chest. Randy didn't dye my hair! He Better-Than-Henna'd me! I grab all the products and toss them into a bowl the way Randy did when he removed my tattoos. I slice the limes and use a handheld lemon juicer to squeeze out all the juice. I pour in the flour, add Epsom salt, cinnamon, and baking soda. I mix everything the way I remember Randy doing it. Once I've made a sufficient paste, I rush over to the sink, dip my head under the faucet, and massage the mix into my hair. A few moments later, I'm grabbing the handheld nozzle and letting warm water pour over my head. Right away I see the black draining into the sink. Bless this man. I feel the curls coming back too! *That's* why he blow-dried and flat ironed my hair. There *was* no chemical straightener. Randy said he would never do any of his clients wrong. He absolutely stuck to that word!

Once I see the water is clear, I grab a kitchen towel and attempt to dry my hair. There is the biggest mess in the kitchen: water on the floor, table littered with cut limes, baking soda, flour, the oil . . . everything. Mom would scream if she saw this mess. I'll deal with it later. I rush to the half bath with the broken toilet just off the kitchen, yank open the door, and step to the mirror.

It's red! And curly! I mean, it's short. Short hair is not something I've ever had. It's still me. It's red. "I'm *Red*!" *Ahhh!!* I dance around the small bathroom. "Randy, you schemer!!"

Water is dripping down my back and onto the floor. I don't care. I rush out of the house and sprint across the fields to the greenhouses. I can hear Tyrone barking happily and Loren laughing as I approach. I yank open the doors and stumble inside. Loren turns to me, holding a water hose in her hand.

"Oh, thank the Universe!" She places her free hand over her heart. "Was that a wig you were wearing earlier? I didn't wanna tell you, it was hideous."

"Loren, he didn't dye or straighten my hair. It's still red. It's still curly." I pull at it. "It's still . . . me."

"I mean, major Orphan Annie vibes right now. But sure."

I laugh. "Loren, you guys are right. I'm too young for *any*thing to be everything." I square my shoulders. "I'm auditioning for *Oh, So You Think You Can Sing Live?* Wanna help me prepare?"

TWENTY-FIVE

A re you nervous?" Loren asks as Mom lays on the horn on a busy highway in downtown Des Moines.

"Why do you ask?" I stare out at the traffic, biting the tips of my fingers one by one.

"'Cuz you're biting each individual finger!" Loren calls out.

Ok, fine. I'm nervous! "It's not fair," I cry. "I've been practicing nonstop for a week. I cannot miss this audition!" There's a giant hood on the black leather jacket I borrowed from Melissa. I've had it pulled over my head for this whole ride, carefully disguising who I am, as if paparazzi still chase me around. But I'm officially over sweating like crazy. I yank it off. "Mom, can't you get around this somehow?"

"You want me to fly?" Mom tosses me a side-eye. "Or you gonna pay for my ticket if I drive on the shoulder?"

Mom knows I'm back to being broke. Because she's the one who helped me get the cashier's check from the bank. Made out to Zay-Zay Waters. All one hundred fifty thousand of the dollars she gave me now rest in the purse slung over my shoulder.

"C'mon, Ma," Jax calls out from the back of the van. "If you don't do something drastic, Red's gonna miss her audition! And her life will be forever ruined because of *you*."

"Y'all are so dramatic." Mom grips the steering wheel like she's actually considering veering off onto the shoulder. "Hold on tight, kids. Here we go."

She swivels to the left and onto the shoulder so we're now bumping along *past* the heavy traffic. Cars and trucks honk and give us dirty looks as we zoom past them.

"Mind your business!" Elijah calls out, even though the windows are all raised and nobody but us can hear him.

"Woo-hoo!" Loren lifts her hands like she's on a roller coaster. "Floor it!"

"Loren, be quiet!" Mom yells. "I'm up here sweatin'. I could get arrested for this."

Mom expertly navigates the shoulder; after a few minutes, we finally move past the accident. Traffic picks up speed. Mom pulls back onto the highway, and my siblings all cheer.

"That was epic!" Elijah shouts. "Mom, you ready for the Monaco Grand Prix!"

"Hardly." Mom flips on her blinker and switches to the exit lane. "I'm just glad no cops were around."

"Uh." Jax leans forward. "What if I told you cops *are* around, and right behind us?"

"No way." Sure enough, a cop car is *right* behind us. *Crap!* "Uh, it's ok, Mom. The lights aren't on."

I spoke too soon. We hear the familiar *woop, woop* of the sirens, and the red and blue lights begin to twirl and flash. We hear the cop's voice through speakers. *"Please exit the freeway and pull over."*

"Mom, floor it!" Elijah calls out. "This minivan can move. We got this!"

"Boy, are you crazy?" Mom puts on her hazard lights and exits the freeway. She immediately pulls off to the side of the road.

My heart sinks. It's over. Getting to the Des Moines Broadhurst Theater to audition for *Oh, So You Think You Can Sing Live?* . . . is over. I turn to Loren, Eli, Jax, and Daeshya, who is strapped into her baby seat, eating out of a box of Cheerios. It's like Cheerios exploded all over her.

"Wed." She giggles and kicks out her little feet.

"Don't be sad, you guys." I force a cheerful tone. "We tried. It's ok."

Loren points at all the traffic. "We wouldn't have made it in time. Even if Mom *wasn't* getting arrested and headed off to jail."

"I am not getting arrested! Getting a very expensive ticket? Probably." Mom places a hand on my shoulder. "I'm sorry, Red. We really did try."

Traffic is bumper to bumper and hardly moving at all. And Mom probably *is* about to get a very expensive ticket. I still can't give up. At least not yet. "C'mon, Universe. Maybe you can't show me something good. Crap happens. I get it. But I dunno. Can it *lead* to something good? I'll put in the effort. I promise!"

"Red, who the heck you talkin' to?" Jax calls out.

A few seconds later, a female cop taps on Mom's window. Mom lowers it.

"I did a stupid thing. I know." She points to the back of the van. "My kids got me on these streets thinking I'm driving in the Indy 500. Never take advice from your kids."

"Not quite the Indy 500. And yes, I have two kids. They tend to give the worst advice." The cop peeks inside the van. "Luckily nobody got hurt. License and registration, please?"

Mom hands her the requested items.

"Hi, Officer." I wave. "Any chance you could let us off with a warning so I won't miss my audition? I'm auditioning for *Oh, So You Think You Can Sing Live?*"

She studies Mom's license and registration before looking over at me. "At Broadhurst Theater?" She whistles. "They had a line wrapped around the block earlier today. I heard on the radio they're all inside. It's quiet over there now."

I feel like crying. In fact, I wipe at my eyes. I am crying. "This is awful. There's gotta be a way they'll still admit me."

"We got caught behind an accident," Mom explains to the police officer. "For like three hours. It was a nightmare." Mom grabs my shoulder again. "Red, it's ok. Don't cry, hon."

The cop studies me. "Anybody ever say you kinda resemble—"

"Zay-Zay Waters?" I finish her sentence, still wiping at my eyes. "Yes, they have."

The cop snaps her fingers. "Wait a minute. You're the stand-in! The girl from the farm video. I *know* you."

She recognizes me? "Yes! Yeah, I'm her."

"Oh, my kids *love* you! Wait till I tell them!" She looks down the street and shakes her head. "It's gonna take you folks another half hour to make it over to Broadhurst. *I* could get you there in less than ten minutes. Which would make me a hero to my kids. You guys like fast rides?"

Wait, what? "You're gonna . . . take us?"

"Least I could do. My kids watching you falling in manure over and over again gave me time to clean the kitchen and get all kinds of work done. I owe you." She peeks into the car again and speaks to my siblings. "Feel like taking a ride in a cop car?"

A moment of silence passes; then Loren, Eli, and Jax burst into wild cheers. The whole van is literally shaking. They don't wait for Mom to answer. They're already sliding open the door.

"Wait! Don't you dare get out of this car!" Mom turns to the cop. "I'm sorry. I can't let you take my kids. No offense, but I don't know you."

"I should introduce myself, then." The officer points to her badge. "Police Lieutenant Rivkah Vazquez."

"Ma, c'mon." Jax has unbuckled his seat belt and is kneeling beside Mom. "She's a *lieutenant*. Not a serial killer. She captures those."

"And here's my Instagram account too." Lieutenant Vazquez presents her phone to Mom and scrolls through her feed. She's married, has twins. Boy and a girl.

"Aww." Now Loren is leaning over Mom, staring at the feed as the lieutenant scrolls. "Me and Jax are boy-girl twins too. I'm older, though."

Jax snorts. "By like half a second."

"Mom, please." I might make this audition after all! I tap my feet excitedly. "I'm sure Lieutenant Vazquez will get us there safely. I'll text you the entire way. And of course we'll link back up once you arrive with Dae."

Mom seems like she's giving it serious thought. Finally she speaks. "Ok. All right. Fine. You can ride with the lieutenant."

More cheers from my siblings as they exit the car.

"I'll try to get them there in one piece." Lieutenant Vazquez tips her hat.

Mom frowns.

"Sorry. Bad joke. Let's go, kids." As she moves off, I hear her say to Jax, Eli, and Loren, "Did you guys know there's no seat belts in the back of most cop cars?"

"Wow, really? So cool," they reply.

Mom groans. "Text me the *entire* time, Red."

"I will." I push open the car door. "Mom, I might still make it. I *might*."

"You will." Mom reaches out to squeeze my hand. "I just know it."

～

Lieutenant Rivkah Vazquez is true to her word. We're all in one piece, scrunched up in the back, but in one piece. We've been flying through the city, blazing through red lights, onto shoulders, and around traffic. Cars move out of the way for us like the parting of the Red Sea. The siren feels like it's piercing right through me, melding with the beat of my heart. *C'mon, Universe! May it lead to something good! Please.*

"There it is!" Loren calls out, gazing out the window. "I see it!"

The theater has come into clear view. Lieutenant Vazquez was right. There should be hundreds and hundreds of people lined up outside and wrapped around the block. But there are only a few workers, wearing headsets and cleaning up.

"You want me to scare them into letting you in?" Lieutenant Vazquez slows to a stop in front of the theater and flips off her siren.

"That's ok." I pull my hood back over my head. "I have a few tricks up my sleeve."

The lieutenant pulls open our door, and we all file out with a chorus of thank-yous.

"I'll be watching for you, Red." She waves to me and my siblings. "Good luck!"

In a moment she's back in her car and speeding away, leaving us alone on the city street. A girl with a headset stands at a stage door, barking orders. I rush toward her, and my siblings follow. A security guard stops us at a row of metal crowd-control gates.

"Sorry, kids." He holds out his arm. "Sign-in ended about an hour ago."

"We got caught behind an accident," I plead. "Isn't there someone I can talk to?"

"You can talk to me," the security guard says. "I'll keep tellin' you the same thing. Sign-in ended."

Jax, Loren, and Eli toss me worried looks. I use my two fingers and whistle so loud the production person at the door stops what she's doing and turns to us. I wave at her.

"You'll want to talk to me!" I call out. "I promise."

She heads over.

"What?" she says. "Security should have told you. Everyone who is allowed to audition is already inside. I'm sorry."

I yank off my hood and run a hand through my short curls. Her eyes widen, then narrow.

"Remember me?" I say. "I'm the girl who stood in for Zay-Zay Waters."

"Whoa." Her jaw drops. "You're her. Red Morgan."

I grin. She knows my name!

"I saw you singing. It was on TMZ. With Koi and the Six. Was that really you singing? You were good."

"It was me. So . . . see? I can *absolutely* sing live. You know this show would not be the same without me." I'm standing here, the picture of confidence. I'm actually a bundle of so many nerves I might need to run to the bathroom here in a second. "You *have* to let me through."

"Production loves a good drama story. Zay-Zay's look-alike is a pretty good one." The girl taps the security guard on the shoulder. "Let her through."

Omigosh!! It's happening! I exchange excited hugs with my siblings as the crowd-control gates are pulled to the side. We all move around to step onto the sidewalk.

"Only you." The girl shakes her head. "I'm just a production assistant. Which translates to essentially nobody. I'm pushing it letting you in. The others can't come."

What? "No. These are my siblings. They're all under eighteen; I can't leave them on the street."

"Yeah," Jax echoes, shaking his head so his long dreads sway from side to side. "She can't leave us on the street!"

I elbow Jax and whisper, "Boy, be quiet."

The production assistant groans. "All right, gimme a sec." She speaks into her walkie. "Hey, Luke, can you jump over to line three?" She twists the knob on her walkie before she speaks again. "It's the Zay-Zay stand-in. Red Morgan. Yeah, and she's got three siblings with her." She pauses, listening in her ear set. "I know. I told her. All right, copy that." She points at me. "He said you can come in, but not them. I'm sorry."

My siblings standing beside me. Seeming so small. No matter how much they grow up, they will always be like Daeshya, crawling around in diapers, struggling to pronounce my name. But they're not like Daeshya. Not anymore. They're grown up. And maybe they don't need me so much anymore. Maybe *I* need them. Didn't Koi say that sometimes you gotta *place* your order with the Universe? Well, Universe . . . I need my siblings with me. I need them!

"Forget it," I say to the production assistant. "I would never leave these kids alone. What kind of person would I be?" I turn to my siblings and wink, then stretch out my eyes like, *Play along.* "Let's go, kids."

They catch on to what I'm trying to do. Loren pretends to cry. Jaxson and Elijah do too.

"I'm so sad!" Jaxson wails. "Why is life so cruel?"

"First our house fell into a sinkhole, now this!" Elijah wails.

I wrap my arms around them. "There, there, children. There, there."

"Hopefully Mama has more gruel back at the shelter," Loren adds.

"Omigosh." The production assistant motions to the guard. "They can all come. Just let them all in. If I get fired for this, so what. I hate this job anyway."

My siblings cheer, and fake tears instantly dry as we step onto the sidewalk.

"Adrian!" she calls out to another person wearing a headset and carrying a walkie. "Taking this one straight to the greenroom."

We follow the production assistant, and the heavy door slams shut behind us, drowning out the noise from the street.

"My name's Millie." We trail behind her down a wide hallway with a shiny concrete floor. "I can't promise they'll let you audition, but one of the production managers . . . he's letting the higher-ups know you're here. This show is all about drama. You being here . . . is exactly the kinda drama they go crazy for."

"Thank you, Millie. I appreciate you helping." I grip tightly onto my purse as we approach a door that says **BACKSTAGE** in bold. Millie yanks it open, and we follow through to the other side. The backstage area is chaotic, but Millie seems to know exactly where she's going as she skirts around workers, stacks of boxes littered here and there, light fixtures, and more. We move up a small set of metal stairs. Now we're *on* the stage. Literally standing right in the back. I sneak a quick peek. The theater is filling up. There are workers everywhere, guiding and keeping things in order. And the stage. Omigosh, it's like . . . glowing from underneath. I see where the judges will be seated too. The high-back chairs seem ominous with no one sitting there. But soon they will be there, sipping from their giant plastic cups, strategically stamped with **COCA-COLA** in bold, deciding the fate of the masses.

"Sissy," Loren whispers, tugging on the sleeve of my leather jacket. "It's the *stage*. How cool is this?"

"It's so cool!" I whisper back. Standing on the red carpet as Zay-Zay wasn't as exciting as this. Because that was all about her. *This . . .* is about me.

We journey on, underneath scaffolding and through a side door that brings us to another long hallway bustling with people. Lots like Millie, talking into walkies, seeming super busy while they tend to this or that, pushing multitiered carts, guiding young nervous performers from one room to the next. It's organized chaos. At the end of the hallway, we file into a large room where a few people are sitting and waiting. It's not green, but Millie stops and tells us to find a seat, so it must be the greenroom.

"Millie," I say, "I know I'm pushing it. But my mom. She'll have my baby sister. Can they come in too?"

"If they say you can audition, I'll work it out." She snatches her walkie off the pocket of her jeans. "I'll be out front. Tell her to find me." She points to a sign. "And log on to that website and e-sign the documents. You're not in yet, but if they bypass protocol and let you through, you'll need those signed."

We find seats on white folding chairs that are scattered around the room. Directly across from a girl with long black hair shaved on one side, a large nose ring shaped like a half moon, and a larger silver septum piercing that makes me wonder if she can breathe ok. Her whole getup makes mine seem simple. I'm wearing blue jeans, boots, and a leather jacket over a white T-shirt that says **INSPIRE** across the front. She is dressed like a goth-punk bride, in a short, frilly black dress, knee-high socks, plastic platform boots, and eyes so heavily lined with black and red she could be a character in a scary movie.

"Omigosh. You're that girl." In spite of her exotic getup, she sounds normal. "The one who was pretending to be Zay-Zay Waters."

"I am the girl who stood in for Zay-Zay Waters." I repeat the sentence like I'm reading from the contract I signed. "And you are?"

"I've heard you sing." She crosses her legs, and I wonder if her feet feel heavy in her giant boots. "You're amazing. You're totally gonna get a ticket to New York City. We'd be so lit in a group together."

I frown. Group?

"I mean, you've already got an in, right?" She winks at me. "They say Zay-Zay keeps you locked in her basement. I guess that means you're friends? Kinda anyway."

Ha. Good one. "I don't think *friends* would be quite the word to describe me and Zay's relationship. Also, she doesn't keep me locked in her basement. TMZ made that up."

"She's gonna be in Taylor Thompson Lee's new movie." The girl reaches to grab her phone. "Did she tell you?"

The girl fiddles with her phone before spinning it around so I can see the headline.

Zay-Zay Waters in Negotiations to Star in Taylor Thompson Lee's New Drama

"Wow." My voice sounds weak. Zay is going to be working with Taylor Thompson Lee. It's fine. I'm like . . . 48 percent happy for her. I mean, sure, *I* was the one who bonded with Taylor, not Zay, but it's her dream come true. "Good for her," I finally manage to squeak out, though I now feel like throwing up. "She deserves it."

"Red," Loren whispers. "That girl over there. Her name is Genesis Cromwell. I literally follow her on TikTok. She's so good. Should I go and say hi, and that I'm a fan?"

The room is super low key. Everyone seems pretty relaxed and nonformal. "I don't see why not."

"Hey, I'm coming too." Jax pops off his seat.

"Wait for me." Eli follows after them.

I watch my siblings move across the room. Genesis invites them to sit beside her. She seems more than happy to talk about herself.

"So, what number are you?" The goth girl holds a yellow card with a number on it.

"I, uh, didn't get a number," I reply, resisting the urge to snatch goth girl's card from her hands and hold it tight.

She frowns. "You have to have a number, or you can't audition."

Oh gosh. I need a number!

"Red Morgan?"

There is a woman dressed like she's someone important. I raise my hand. "Yes?"

"Please follow me," she says.

I wipe my sweaty hands on my jeans, stand, and follow her. We move back out into the hallway and travel a few doors down. We push into a small rehearsal room with music stands and instruments like pianos and guitars covered with nylon and stuffed into corners. The woman takes a seat at a small table with two other people.

"Have a seat, Red," a man with white hair and glasses says to me.
I sit in the chair in front of their table.

"Red." The lady who brought me here leans forward. "My name is Nori Aubert. I'm one of the executive producers on *Oh, So You Think You Can Sing Live?* We'd like to know if Zay-Zay Waters knows you're here."

I shake my head no. I can't tell if they're *excited* at the prospect of Zay-Zay dropping dead when she sees me, or horrified.

"We have to make sure there's no favoritism," Nori explains. "If you and Zay-Zay are friends, there is *absolutely* a conflict of interest in your being here and we can't let you audition."

I decide to be honest. "Not only are me and Zay-Zay not friends, she might call security and have me carted off stage when she sees me. I wish I could say more. I'm choosing to honor the contract she had me sign."

I wait for one of them to say, *Sorry, kid. It's not gonna happen today.*

Instead, the white-haired guy speaks up. "Can you sing for us now? Would that be all right?"

My leg bounces like it's attached to a marionette string. Asking to hear me sing is a good sign, right? That means they're considering letting me perform. Deep breath, Red. Stay calm. "Can I sing 'I Have Nothing,' by Whitney Houston?"

"That's a good song," the third person at the table says. She's a pretty dark-skinned lady with a coiffed natural fro. "Written by David Foster and Linda Thompson. If you sang this live, who would you dedicate it to?"

That's easy. "Me."

The pretty lady with the fro raises an eyebrow. "Care to explain?"

"Well, the song is a love song," I start. "About a girl who has nothing if she doesn't have this guy. That's not my story. In my case, I have nothing if I don't have . . . me. I'd be singing it to myself. Is that weird?"

"Not at all." Nori smiles warmly.

"Are you ok being interviewed?" white-haired guy asks. "The show is live, but we like to have things to cut to. We also like to do backstories for future shows. On contestants who we think have great potential."

"If we allow you to audition and you move forward," Nori adds, "we might send a crew to your house after the taping today. Interview family. That sort of thing."

Oh, that's right. They do those stories sometimes. Loren says when they do a backstory, you just know the person is gonna be good. "That's . . . fine. I think. Only if Zay-Zay approves. I can't explain that now. Just . . . hopefully it'll make sense soon." I imagine Jax with sunglasses, popping his collar and brushing literal dust off his shoulder as he gives the camera crew a tour of our machine shed.

Nori motions for me to begin. "Whenever you're ready, then."

I wring my hands together and clear my throat. A few seconds later the melody to the Whitney Houston song fills the small rehearsal space. It's such a beautiful composition. Soft and sweet to begin, but because of the acoustics in the room, my voice sounds much more powerful than normal. Nori stops me after only a few measures, a hand over her heart.

"Oh my," she says.

"Stunning," fro lady adds.

"Absolutely enchanting." White-haired guy smiles. "You're quite talented."

Wow. If these were my judges, I'd be off to New York City! I tap my feet, eagerly awaiting their decision. "Please let me sing live!" I blurt. "It would mean so much to me. It would be a dream."

"The show wouldn't be the same without you." Nori stands. "Good luck onstage today."

"I'm in!" I bite at the nail on my thumb. "Omigosh!" I shoot off my chair. "Do I get a number?" I can't help it. I'm literally jumping up and down. "Somebody told me I need a number."

"You need a number." Nori hands me a yellow card with black bold numbers: 613.

It's *my* number. I take the card and hold it against my chest like it's a brand-new puppy and I'm welcoming it to its forever home.

"I'll lead you back to the greenroom, and you can finish signing all the online paperwork." Nori moves toward the door.

"Thank you so much!" I follow after Nori.

"And Red?" fro lady calls out.

I turn back to face her.

"We have high expectations." She tosses me a thumbs-up. "Don't let us down."

TWENTY-SIX

R ed, are you breathing?" Mom elbows me in the side.
"Ow." I look at Mom like *Why are you elbowing me?*
"Sorry." She squeezes my shoulder. "I thought you passed out."
"Standing? With my eyes open?"

We're all in a tiny area off the stage: me, Mom with Daeshya on her hip, Loren, Jax, and Eli. We're waiting beside the show's host, Abstract Realitee. Though I'd guess that's not on his birth certificate.

Abstract Realitee grabs my hand and does a little dance with me. I think he's required to keep the contestants amped and excited. Except all the extra is making me nauseated. Or maybe it's the two cameramen who have set up camp beside us for the last five hours. With a camera pointed *directly* at my face, every grimace, smile, frown, tear, and deep sigh makes me question if I'm doing it for show or because it's how I really feel. It's bad enough watching Eli, Jax, and Loren get on board with the performative aspect of all this. Who knew these kids were so ready for Hollywood?

"Red, Red. Are you ready, ready?" Abstract wraps an arm around my shoulder.

This is also a thing with him. Repeating words.

"Ready . . . spaghetti!" I reply.

Since the cameras are recording, I'm trying to match Abstract's energy, but I'm failing miserably. Who says *Ready, spaghetti?* Honestly, if I can make it out of here without throwing up or passing out, I'll consider this day somewhat of a success.

"You guys excited for your sister to smash this audition? Gimme a *yeah e yeah.*" Abstract busts out another dance move, and Loren, Jax, and Eli all happily reply.

"Yeah e yeah!"

"Dope, dope. Nice. Nice." Abstract gives them all daps. "I'm not leaving you out, lil miss." He pinches Daeshya's cheek, and she giggles. "All right, all right." He turns his attention back to me. "They about to call you to the stage, Reddy Red."

I place a hand over my stomach and take a deep, calming breath. My hands are shaking. I ball them into fists. Someone wearing a headset taps Abstract on the shoulder. He turns to me and says, "Good luck. You got this."

I swallow like it hurts. Actually, it does hurt. I swallow again, hoping it loosens up my throat as I pull the hood to cover my hair. My dusty boots click-clack on a stage that seems as though it's covered with glass and somehow lit blue from underneath. When I make it to the lone microphone at center stage, I look up to face the crowd. The theater seats are tiered. So there's a balcony, and then a balcony *above* the balcony. Each and every seat is occupied with a human . . . staring at me. I slide the hood off my head, and the crowd gasps. A low murmur erupts, like the sound of thunder rumbling in the distance.

Seated in high-back chairs, behind their Coca-Cola cups, at a long table are the judges. In the first seat is none other than Blaze, from Necessity. Koi's nightmare date. Blaze has dark eyes and dark skin like Aish's. She's ethnically ambiguous, gorgeous, and a hundred percent terrifying. Her silky-straight hair is pulled into a long ponytail that hangs over her shoulder, and she's wearing a skintight orange leather bodysuit. Beside Blaze is the one judge on this show who never changes. He retired from his K-pop group at the ripe old age of twenty-six and now runs a popular podcast and stars on this show. His name is Eun Ho. He's wearing blue-framed sunglasses that match his blue suit. Finishing up the three is the lady herself, Zay-Zay Waters. Dressed in a cream-colored (also skintight) dress with spaghetti straps that matches the color of her skin. Her hair is fluffed and shiny, like Randy is somewhere hiding in a corner. She's also wearing an icy expression on her face. If looks could kill, I'd drop *dead*.

I take a step closer to the mic. "Hello."

My voice booms through the giant theater. Honestly, it echoes. I think I'm still saying hello on the third-level balcony.

"Wow." Blaze tosses a sly grin toward Zay. "Zay, you untied your clone and let her out the basement?"

The crowd laughs. Zay-Zay does not appear amused.

I decide to chime in. "Yes, I am the girl who stood in for Zay-Zay Waters. But she didn't know I was going to be here. I don't live in her basement. I live on a farm, in Iowa. And I'm here to audition. That's all." I reach into my back pocket to remove the envelope, now folded in half. "Though I did bring something for you, Zay. Before I sing, you'll need to see it."

She hasn't spoken. But Abstract Realitee has appeared at my side.

"All right, all right," he says. "I can be the postman. Lemme take that."

He rushes off the stage and hands the envelope to Zay at the judges' podium. Two cameramen move to her side to record her reaction. She peeks inside. Will she call for security? Will her Double-O Seven lawyer, Mark Stone, appear and have me whisked away faster than I can say *NDA*? I'm giving her the money back. Surely that means the contract . . . isn't a contract anymore. Or is that not how these things work?

"Zay-Zay?" I'm speaking softly, but my voice still booms. I know that there are only two things inside the envelope: the cashier's check for $150,000 and a note that says *I no longer wish to be bought and paid for. Sincerely, Red.* "Since technically I'm still on the payroll. I won't sing unless you accept that envelope. It's my official resignation."

Her eyes meet mine. It's quiet for a long moment before she leans forward and speaks, breaking the tense silence.

"Consider your resignation accepted, ma." She folds the envelope and places it beside her. "No favoritism. I hope you came here to impress. Good luck."

Omigosh. She's gonna let me sing? I'm bouncing on my toes. I'm about to sing!! "Thank you!" I grip the mic and think, "Gosh, I hope I don't pass out." Only I actually say that. The crowd laughs. I have really, *truly,* got to stop speaking my thoughts.

"Before you pass out . . ." Eun Ho is speaking now. "Tell us a bit about you. I mean, aside from the fact that you recently face-planted in a pile of poo." He laughs. The crowd does too. "What are you singing and why?"

"Well, like I said, I'm Red Morgan, from Orange City, Iowa." My hands are sweaty. I wipe them across my jeans. "I'm singing 'I Have Nothing,' by Whitney Houston."

The crowd erupts into cheers.

"Nice," Eun Ho replies. "Except wait. Trying to sing like Whitney? You sure that's wise?"

I shake my head. "I sing like me. I wouldn't dare try to sing like anybody else."

"Why that song, though?" Blaze cuts in. "It's a crazy-intense love song. Are you in love with somebody? Maybe Koi Kalawai'a?" The crowd oohs and aahs. Blaze blinks dramatically. "I mean, we all saw *you* kissing him at the Getty Museum."

"They were kissing all over the place," Eun Ho adds with a grin. "That was *her* at the restaurant when pretty boy Koi 'proposed.'"

I clear my throat. "Like I said before, I am the girl who stood in for Zay-Zay Waters. That's pretty much all I have to say about that."

Zay's eyes meet mine, and—I could be imagining it, but—she gives me the tiniest nod with the *tiniest* smile. Almost like she's secretly saying, *Thank you, Red. For keeping at least part of our agreement.* I toss back a tiny nod and the *tiniest* smile too. I hope it says, *Of course, Zay. I got you!*

I go on. "The song I'm singing, it's about learning to love myself. If you can do that, then you have *everything.* That's what it means to me, anyway."

"Aww," Abstract says. He's still onstage.

I look over at him. "Abstract, aren't you supposed to be backstage by now?"

The crowd erupts into more laughter. It makes me smile.

"Oh, my bad, my bad, Reddy Red. Let me disappear, like I'm supposed to."

He moves offstage. I turn back to face the judges and the audience.

"I like you, Red." Blaze takes a long dramatic sip from her Coca-Cola cup. "Even though there are now way too many women in this room who have dated Koi Kalawai'a." She rolls her eyes. "So you think you wanna be the next big pop star?"

"I . . . just wanna sing," I boldly declare. "Most of my life, I thought I couldn't. Now that I know I can, I don't ever wanna stop."

"Let's hear it, then." Eun Ho sits back in his seat. "Red Morgan from Orange City, Iowa. Good luck, doll."

I turn to my left and see my family huddled backstage, watching me with hopeful and supportive eyes. Jax and Eli hold up prayer hands. Loren forms a heart with *her* hands. Daeshya waves like she's wondering why I'm so far away. Her tiny voice pierces the silence. "Wed!"

Mom bounces her on her hip. "Shhh."

I turn back to the judges and the audience as the stage lights up from underneath. Not blue this time, but red. Pretty sure they did that one on purpose. With the stage now glowing red, the beautiful, haunting, melodic piano intro to "I Have Nothing" begins. I sing the poetic words, timidly at first. As I sing, I begin to realize that giving up the right to be Red is something I've been doing way before Zay made me. But on this stage, right now, I am so aware of what a privilege it is to be . . . me. Singing is one of the things I came here to do. From here on out, singing will be *my* daily reminder. A connection to my purpose in life.

I add as much passion as my voice will allow. By the time I reach the bridge, and the song transitions to a new key, the crowd cheers and bangs their hands together. My voice remains strong, even as my eyes spill over with tears.

I hold the last note for as long as I can, until the music fades, the red lights under the stage dim, and I'm left standing in silence. Only for a moment, though. Because the crowd is on its feet, cheering *so* loud. I wipe at my tears and turn to see Mom and my siblings jumping up and down and spinning around in sheer joy. Abstract is getting in on the action, too, doing a dance and high-fiving Jax, Elijah, and Loren. The energy is so high it's as if I'm pumped up with helium and could float up to the ceiling. Happiness has returned, high-fiving all the other emotions within me. Pushing them to the side so it can take center stage. I mean . . . this is the *dream*. This is *my* dream. All that's missing is the confetti. The silver should be raining down on me by now. I wonder if it's hard to sweep it off the stage after it falls and what I will do if it gets in my eyes. Only . . . I don't see any confetti. And in a few moments, the crowd has returned to their seats. Another moment—it's silent. The judges just . . . stare at me.

Why aren't they saying anything? Why didn't they push the platinum buzzer yet!

"Wow." Blaze finally speaks. "You definitely have a very . . . um . . . pretty voice. Yeah."

Eun Ho nods. "Yeah. It was cute."

Pretty? Cute? Oh geez. This is not a good way to start a critique.

"But," Blaze adds.

I knew there was a *but* coming!

"It's almost too pretty."

"Too pretty?"

"And too cute," Blaze goes on. "You do know that this season we're putting together a three-girl pop group. Right?"

Ohhh. *That's* why the goth girl said we'd be good in a group together. "I didn't know that."

"Well, now you know." Eun Ho leans forward to speak. "We want each girl to be—"

"A star," Blaze cuts in. "A *lead*. We don't want background singers."

"She's so not a background singer." Eun Ho waves his hand at Blaze like he's flitting away a pesky fly. "*But* I'm not entirely convinced you'd be able to stand the spotlight, Red."

"Sing somethin' else." Zay-Zay finally speaks. "Sing a song where we can see what you really got. Give us somethin' fun and poppy and, like, belty."

Belty? Uh-oh. I clear my throat and speak into the mic. "But there's great singers who don't belt. Like . . . Roberta Flack."

"Roberta who?" Blaze snaps her fingers. "Oh, I know. What about Katy Perry's 'Roar.' Sing that."

"No." Eun Ho shakes his head. "Her voice is too light for Katy Perry songs. What about Meghan Trainor. Or Tori Kelly. Tori's fun and light, but she's got a showstopper sound. Give us a bit of 'Don't You Worry 'Bout a Thing,' the Tori Kelly version. You know that song?"

The Stevie Wonder remake. "I know it."

"Sing that one." Eun Ho sips from his Coca-Cola cup. "Give us some fun, poppy vibes. We want more energy. How old are you, Red?"

"I'm eighteen."

"You're young, honey." Eun Ho sets his cup down. "'I Have Nothing' is a good song for when you're forty-two. Right now, you should be singing about parties and fun and . . . twerking. Be more twerky, Red."

The crowd laughs.

Eun Ho laughs too. "I'm kidding, of course. You know what I mean, though."

"Let me review all my notes." I count on my fingers. "Fun. Poppy. Energy. Twerky?"

The crowd laughs again.

"Now we're talkin'." Eun Ho shifts excitedly in his seat. "Hit it a cappella."

I look over at Mom, and she gives me a "You can do this" nod.

I start the cute pop song. It's originally Stevie Wonder, so it feels pretty close to my skill level. Though I can't belt like Tori Kelly, I can absolutely hit all her runs. The crowd is getting into it. They're clapping along, some standing on their feet. Halfway through, Eun Ho raises his hand. I stop singing and grip the mic so tightly I fear I might crush it. What does he think? What will he say?!

"Was that . . . better?" My voice sounds timid. Afraid.

"*Much* better." He nods. "I mean, I think you need a bit of work. We want Ariana. We want Queen B. We want Lady Gaga. I think with a makeover. New clothes. Dance lessons." He claps his hands together like he's starting to see it, and it's getting him pumped up. "I'm gonna say yes to you, Red. I say *yes* to your ticket to New York City."

Omigosh.

The crowd erupts into cheers; a giant green check mark lights up on the table under Eun Ho. I hold my breath. I want to be excited that I'm one vote away from a trip to New York City. But . . . did he say he wants . . . Lady Gaga? If humans were planets, I'm Earth and Lady Gaga is the exoplanet Arkas. And Arkas is a mere 259 light-years away. Didn't Lady Gaga once wear a meat suit on the red carpet? I don't even eat meat! The cheering dies down. Blaze leans forward to speak again.

"Red. You're *super* cute. I love the red hair. I'm all for genetic mutations. I wish my Vietnamese-Indian-Black-multiracial self had some red hair. Or, like, one green eye or something weird. Anyway. One thing for me that's hard to get past. You look like Zay-Zay Waters. We already have a Zay-Zay Waters. The world does not need another Zay-Zay Waters."

"She looks like me, but she's different enough," Zay-Zay cuts in.

Whaaa? Is she defending me?

"But you two have similar features." Blaze grabs onto her long ponytail, twirling the hair around her fingers. "She legit fooled the world when she was kissing your man."

"He's not my man," Zay snaps back.

Blaze smacks her lips. "He *was* your man. That's a fact."

That's actually not a fact, but the crowd oohs like Blaze just burned her. I can almost see the producers backstage, clapping their hands at the drama unfolding.

"We all believed it was you singing at the Getty, Zay-Zay," Blaze continues. "So, I dunno. We already have a Zay-Zay. And Zay-Zay, you're fabulous. You can't be matched."

Zay frowns at the compliment. "She's not tryin' to match me."

It's official. She *is* defending me!

Zay goes on. "Lots of singers and actors resemble somebody else. It's very common."

"It's really not that common, but I'll move on." Blaze flips her silky-straight ponytail, and I imagine her screaming at a waiter 'cuz they tried to refill her coffee too soon. "My bigger issue with you, Red, is that I don't think you're a good fit for a *pop* group. Maybe hone your skills. Take a pole dancing class. Add some sexy to your style. Loosen up. Let that Katy Perry roar out, and maybe come back and audition for us next year. You're young. It's a no from me, babe. Sorry."

The crowd boos. I feel my knees buckle. I try to widen my stance, to give myself more stability, as the sign on the table turns to a bright-red *X* underneath Blaze.

Her *no* feels like a punch to the gut. I stand strong regardless. It's up to Zay now. She *was* defending me. She's gotta say yes. She *has* to.

"All right, Zay." Eun Ho turns to her and slides off his glasses. "I say yes. I think this competition wouldn't be the same without Red. She's innocent. Fresh. Young. Adorbs. I think, with a little work, she could absolutely be in a pop group. Blaze says no. Now you're the deciding vote. What say you? Is Red moving on to New York City?"

The room goes silent. All eyes are on Zay-Zay Waters as she runs a hand through her hair. I can almost see the wheels in her brain turning, trying to decide if sending me back into obscurity is a good idea, or a great idea.

"Before I say what I think." Her Brooklish voice booms into the mic. "I'm very, curious. What do *you* think, Red?"

Huh? I point to myself. Which . . . probably looks really stupid. "I don't know what you mean."

"I mean, do you understand what you signin' up for? This is a pop group. How you feel about that?"

The words are on the tip of my tongue. *Sure, I wanna be a pop star!* I can say that. Right? *I wanna go to New York City!* I can say that too. *I can be whatever you guys want me to be!* That could easily roll off the tongue. But the truth is . . . I'm standing here not saying . . . anything.

"Red?" Zay-Zay leans back in her chair. "You aight?"

Am I? I mean, the thought of being Lady Gaga'd? I'm not quite sure what that means. "I wanna sing. Can't I just sing?" I've finally found my voice again. "I know I'm not a big belter. I'm not Katy Perry. Or Lady Gaga. I couldn't be Beyoncé if I tried. I still think what I have to offer is good."

"Obviously it's good," Zay-Zay says. "You're better than good. Nobody here disputin' that."

Wow. Have I traveled into an alternate dimension, or is Zay-Zay Waters giving me huge, *huge* compliments in front of the whole world? Isn't she supposed to be a monster? That is what I called her, after all.

"However," Zay goes on.

Ahhh. The *but*. There is always a *but*.

"You literally sang a song about havin' nothin' if you don't have you. Being in a pop group, I mean, *is* that you?" She drums her long fingernails on the table. "Did you come all this way to take some pole dancin' classes and channel the spirit of all the out-of-work pop stars that came before you? Here's the thing . . ." Zay-Zay crosses her legs, and I swear in this moment, all her star quality is shining through. She is confident and so *sure* of herself. It comes rushing back. I remember why I've always loved her. Because she's Zay-Zay Waters. "There's all kinda stages to workin' this business. Because of what happened, and how you blasted onto the scene, *maybe* you got an opportunity to skip some of the worst stages. I'm not knockin' what we tryin' to do. I mean, I'mma be writin' songs for this group. This group is gonna be fire. I'm not sayin' it's not. I'm just sayin'. I'm *askin'* . . ."

"Is this what I want?" I finish her sentence.

"Yeah." Another drum of her nails. "Exactly. Is it?"

Who would have ever thought such a simple question would send my mind blasting off into outer space. I gotta get back down to Earth. I'm standing on the stage, quiet. Contemplating. Once again . . . not speaking.

"Red?" Zay speaks my name into the mic. "You still with us?"

"I'm here." I wring my hands together, wishing this show wasn't live. "Can we take a commercial break or something?" The crowd laughs at that one. I really wasn't trying to be funny. "Can't we?"

"I'mma do somethin' I ain't never did before on this show," Zay says. "I'mma leave it up to you."

What? I'm pointing at myself again. "You can't do that, can you?"

"Girl, I think you know me well enough to know that I do what I want."

I actually do know that about her.

"For the first time in this show's history. The vote comes from the contestant. The vote comes from you," Zay says.

Suddenly the room is super loud as everyone attempts to process what Zay's . . . giving me.

Eun Ho raises his hand. "Quiet, everyone. Please. This show *is* live. Thank you very much."

"Red Morgan." Zay smiles. "It's all on you. Yes? Or no?"

I turn to my family. Mom is grimacing like an emoji face. Jax's eyes are closed tight, his hands folded in prayer over his chest. Loren is mouthing, "Say yes!" And Elijah is jumping up and down like he's already celebrating, like he knows I'm no fool. Of *course* I'm gonna take my ticket to New York City. Except . . . now my life is flashing before my eyes.

Me in a pop group.

Wearing a leather catsuit and plastic platform boots.

Doing synchronized dances with an anaconda around my shoulders.

Swinging on a wrecking ball with devil horns.

Twerking.

"Um." My tiny voice booms, and words spill out that I didn't know I had in me. Like a derailed train. I couldn't stop them if I tried. "I came all this way because I decided I wanted to sing. I mean, I know I can sing, but I've always wondered if the way I sing was good enough. Singing here, on this stage, in front of you all, proved that it is. I can *sing.*" I take a deep breath. "But . . ." I chuckle to myself. "Why is there always a *but*? Anyway, but. The truth is . . . Zay-Zay, you're right. I took a shortcut to get here. On the way, maybe I found myself a bit sooner than most people do. I'm not meant to roar. I'm meant to . . . soar. Like an eagle. And so." I speak softly and slowly, articulating every single word. Maybe so they understand what I'm saying. Maybe so I understand too. "You can take my ticket to New York City. Give it to someone who's got that roar inside them, ready to burst free. 'Cuz there is absolutely nothing wrong with a good roar. It's just . . . I'll be somewhere perfecting my flight skills."

I hear a collective gasp from the crowd.

"Thank you all for this amazing opportunity. Thank you for letting me sing. It's really all I wanted to do today."

It's quiet now. Deathly quiet. For a moment, I wonder what it would have been like to have the crowd cheering, the confetti raining down on me, and Abstract handing me my ticket to New York City. Instead, all I can see is the giant red *X* that is now shining on the table under Zay-Zay. Now all I can hear is the *click-clack* of my boots on the glowing stage as I walk off with*out* a ticket in my hand. I wipe at my tears and rush into the arms of my mom. I don't care about the cameras in my face. I lay my head on her shoulder and cry.

Abstract Realitee is patting my back and saying, "Aww, Reddy Red!"

"Mom," I whisper. "That was the hardest thing I've ever done."

She rests her forehead on mine. "The hardest battles go to the toughest soldiers. I'm proud of you."

"Red?"

I turn. *Whoa.* Zay-Zay Waters is standing in front of me. Elijah almost topples over.

"Dude, be cool." Jax shoulder-bumps Eli and waves at Zay. "Zay-Zay. Yo. Big fan of your work."

"Nice to meet y'all." She holds up the envelope. "Thank you for this, Red. Means a lot. It really does. I happily accept your resignation."

"Thank you." I wipe tears away. "For everything. I found my voice because of you."

"You always had your voice, Red. *Girl,* that's how I found you. How's Tyrone?"

"You can have him back," I blurt. "I never should've—"

"Red." She shakes her head. "After we finish my episodes with the show, I'm about to go off and shoot a movie for three months. You were right. He's better off with you. Please give him my love, though. Give him all the love, ok?" She waves at my siblings. "Y'all got a good sister. Y'all should treat her right."

Jax steps forward. "She is treated like a queen in our house. I prom-ise. My parents prefer her over *all* of us."

"No, we don't." Mom pushes Jax on the shoulder. "Boy, stop lying on national TV." Mom reaches out and squeezes Zay's shoulder. "Hi again."

Daeshya grabs at Zay-Zay's hair and says, "Wed."

Zay turns her attention back to me. "Soar like an eagle, aight? I'mma be looking for you in the sky. You better be there."

She gives me a hug, and I'm enveloped by the scent of her, straw-berries and vanilla and, like, a giant bouquet of fresh lilies from the Getty. She disappears back onto the stage, leaving me alone with my family. A moment passes as they stare at me in silence. Are they dis-appointed? Sad? Mad? I get my answer quickly, because a second later they're attacking me with hugs. Shouting "Congrats" and "Omigosh, you did so good" and "Yay, Red!"

Zay said she would search for me in the sky.

Feels like I'm already soaring.

TWENTY-SEVEN

"Why are you packing so many pairs of socks?" Eli asks. "Isn't New Orleans hot?"

Eli's lying on my bedroom floor beside Tyrone, who is chewing a dog toy. Jax sits on the floor beside them.

I slide another pair of socks into my suitcase. "You can never have too many socks, little brother."

"It's true." Loren's feet are dangling off the side of our bunk bed. She's actually wearing one solid-green sock and one striped orange as she stares at her phone. "Duuuude, it's only been one week since you were on the show. You now have fourteen *million* followers on TikTok. You haven't posted anything new!" She turns her phone around to show me. "Your fans are *waiting*."

"She'll post when she's ready," Jax declares.

"Right. I don't wanna bore folks." I put a plastic case of toiletries into the suitcase. "Maybe once I get to New Orleans, I'll have something cool to show."

"Can't believe my sister is famous. Like, for real." Eli whistles. "Guess that means I'm next."

Jax laughs. "What are you gonna be famous for? Having the ashiest ankles in Iowa?"

Eli throws a pillow at Jax's head.

"I'm so jealous you're going to New Orleans," Loren says dreamily.

"Who cares about that?" Eli cuts in. "Sis was the top trending story on TMZ for like three days. That's way cooler than a trip to New Orleans."

Jax moves over to the window, staring out at our oat fields. "Why are you going to New Orleans, anyway? You're taking a gap year. Go to Cancún. Cabo. *Rio.*"

"I'm volunteering with the Friendship Circle down there. I got in touch with the director. They could use the help," I explain. "Plus, it's where our ancestors came from. I wanna see our history."

"Oh wow. Zay-Zay's making big moves too." Loren's still staring at her phone. "She signed on to do a new movie."

I tense but force a happy tone. "Yeah. I saw that."

"She's so lucky. I'm *obsessed* with *The Fast and the Furious.*"

Huh? I pause in my packing. "What do you mean? *Fast and the Furious?*"

Loren presents her phone for me to see. "It's on the *New York Post.* TMZ. Everywhere."

I read the headline.

Zay-Zay Waters joins cast of *The Fast and the Furious: Aerodynamic Drag.* Production slated to start this month in Dubai.

What? Didn't she say she'd never be in that movie? What happened with Taylor?

Lyndia comes into the room, Daeshya on her hip. "One of your friends is here from school. He's kinda . . . geeky. Brown hair. Weird vibe."

Oh no. "That's probably Brad." Melissa and Eileen told me he'd be stopping by to say goodbye.

"Isn't that the boy that's secretly in love with you?" Loren asks. "Better let him down easy. Tell him your type is Hawaiian hottie millionaires."

I zip up my suitcase and laugh. Except the mention of Koi makes my heart ache just a bit. We text sometimes. He was so happy about my audition. It still feels like we said goodbye forever. "Thanks, Lyndia. Is Brad in the living room?"

Lyndia shakes her head. "No, no. I didn't let him in the house. He was giving me space-alien vibes. He's on the back patio."

"Copy that." I pull my suitcase onto the floor. "Be right back, guys."

I move into the hallway, down the stairs, and into the kitchen, where Mom is layering lasagna ingredients into a glass dish. "Making your favorite for dinner tonight. Vegetarian lasagna."

"You're the best mom ever."

Mom tears open a bag of cheese and smiles. "I know."

I push out the door and move around to the back patio. I can see Brad sitting. Back to me. Hands resting on his lap. Wearing a wide-brimmed hat made out of . . . papier-mâché?

"Hey, Brad."

He turns around to face me and . . .

Oh.

My.

Ga.

"Who is Brad?"

It's Taylor Thompson Lee! Sitting on one of our patio chairs in a trench coat, purple cotton shorts, and rubber boots. My knees buckle, and I reach out to grab onto something so I don't fall. Only nothing is around. So I stumble. Taylor pops off the seat and rushes to my side.

"Red." He helps me stabilize. "Your legs look like strands of spaghetti."

"Funny. Koi said the same thing to me once." I stare at him in awe. "What . . . are you doing here?" I wanna lurch forward and hug him but decide it might be too much. I opt to playfully punch him in the shoulder. "Seriously! What are you doing here?"

He gazes out at the fields. "I can't believe you live here. This place is . . . neat." He turns back to face me. "The smell starts to grow on you too." He sniffs his clothes. "Literally."

"Taylor Thompson Lee." I am practically jumping out of my boots. "If you don't tell me why you're here, I'm gonna scream."

"Fine. I'll tell you." He removes his phone from the pocket of his coat. "I put this together, and I wanted to show you in person. To see what you thought."

He hands me his phone. A video is playing. The video is actually a compilation of . . . me. Me on the red carpet at Skybar. Me and Koi being interviewed. Me and Koi at Sun and Sand. Me singing at the Getty, and *lots* of me during the audition with *Oh, So You Think You Can Sing Live?* The video ends with me crying on Mom's shoulder.

Why does Taylor Thompson Lee have a video compilation of me?

"I edited it," he says, as if reading my mind. "I needed something to present to the studio. I mean, I wanna hire you. But they have to approve my pick." He exhales dramatically. "Thankfully, they did."

Hire me? "I . . . don't think I understand."

"Red." He stares at me like he's back at the Getty, studying the Rembrandt. "I came here to ask you in person if you would be my Chanel. I want *you* to star in my new movie."

I can't breathe. Or see. Or think. And dang these spaghetti legs. What is happening right now? I push Taylor gently on the shoulder, and he stumbles back. This is more than a dream. This is being transported to an alternate dimension.

"Do you often push people who offer you jobs?" He laughs.

"I'm sorry." I cover my mouth with both hands. "But . . ." This can't be real. I mean . . . "I thought you already hired Zay-Zay. I read it on Deadline. Why is she doing *Fast and the Furious*? What happened?"

He holds up his hands in the universal symbol for *How the heck should I know?* "I'm pretty sure that announcement about her being 'in negotiations' for my movie was part of her Operation

Clean-Up-My-Image." He adjusts his papier-mâché hat. "She did come in and audition. Obviously she was a whole different person. I wasn't getting Chanel vibes the way I was with you. I never offered her the part."

I'm trying my hardest to formulate some sort of response but only coming up with *Ahhhhhh!* Thankfully Taylor saves me from screeching.

"I saw quite a few girls. In the end, I couldn't get you off my mind." He scratches at his head. "Not weirdly. Just work . . . ly. Isabella says hi, by the way. She's singing to your pigs. She likes them."

"Issa is *here*?!"

"Yep. We've decided to elope in New Orleans tomorrow. Wanna be in our wedding?"

"New Orleans?!" I slap the palm of my hand against my forehead. "*I'm* going to New Orleans tomorrow."

He grins. "What are the *odds*?"

Omigosh. The overwhelm of all that's transpired in these few seconds has got pints of blood rushing to my head. I know there's a lot of fresh air out here . . . I need more.

"So?" He folds his arms under his chest. "What say you? Yes or no?" Now he grimaces. "Hopefully this isn't giving you flashbacks of *Oh, So You Think You Can Sing Live?*"

"Taylor . . ." I shake my head in astonishment. "I've never acted before. What if I let you down?"

"You'll have me as your guide. Besides, I don't want a seasoned actor thinking they have all the answers. This film requires something raw and real. We'll figure it out together. I want . . . you." He groans. "Sorry. Not weirdly. Work . . . ly. You get what I'm saying. I want you to star, and sing, in my movie. You up for a trip to Israel?" He scratches at his forehead. "We're shooting in some other places too." He sucks his teeth. "It's gonna be a rough shoot, so make sure you're up for it. Remember, I don't do Hollywood glamour. Not my style."

My life suddenly flashes before my eyes.

Dana L. Davis

In a dusty dune buggy traveling over the sandy hillsides of all the greatest cities in Israel.

Floating in the Dead Sea.

Filming at historic sites.

Singing.

I'm going to sing. I'm going to see the world. I lurch forward and hug Taylor.

"Yes!" I'm laughing and crying and trying not to explode. Has a person ever exploded before? "Yes, yes, yes!!"

"All the girls say yes to you, Taylor."

I pull away and spin around. Koi Kalawai'a is leaning against the old, rusted metal table in jeans and a simple T-shirt. His long hair rests just above his shoulders. His bright-green eyes shine brighter than they *ever* have.

"Koi?" My jaw drops.

"I mean, I wasn't sure you'd say yes, to be honest," Koi says. "You did decline being in a pop group produced by Eun Ho." He smirks. "That's like . . . every girl's dream."

"I would have said yes to Eun Ho," Taylor cuts in. "I've always wanted to dress up like a blow-up doll and parade around the world in spandex leotards." Taylor tugs on the belt of his trench coat. "By the way. Do you guys have a bathroom? Or since this is a farm, do I . . . pick a field? How does it work here? I'm down for whatever."

"We use toilets." I point toward the house. "You may or may not be attacked by my family members."

"Nice." Taylor moves toward the house. "I've always wanted to meet an American farm family. Bucket list, check."

Taylor disappears around the corner. Koi steps closer to me.

"Do I get a hug? Or are you too big-time now that you're starring in a movie written and directed by Taylor Thompson Lee?"

I rush into his arms, and he lifts me off my feet. I laugh as he spins me around. "Koi Kalawai'a." He sets me back down.

"You can just call me Koi." He smiles. "Hi, Red."

"I *missed* you," I say.

He grabs at his chin, as if he is a supersleuth who has at last solved a great riddle. "You're right. Your hair *isn't* all that shiny."

I pull at it. Then hold up my hands. "No tattoos either. And check out these nails."

"Red," he says softly. "It wasn't an illusion. You're *still* glowing. I still like you."

And suddenly our lips connect, and I swear it's as if the Universe is expanding. Shooting out new planets and galaxies and asteroid belts and tesseracts so that it can continue listening to the deep wants and desires of all the people residing within.

"I have a new proposal to . . . propose."

I laugh. "You better have a ring I can keep this time."

He pulls a candy Ring Pop out of the pocket of his jeans. "Will this do?"

"Koi." I shake my head. "You spent too much."

"I can afford it." He tears off the wrapper and gets down on one knee. "Red Morgan of Orange City, Iowa, who glows as bright as a sun from a distant galaxy." He slides the ring onto my finger. "Will you . . . date me? Get to know me? Maybe see the world with me?"

I lift the Ring Pop to my mouth and take a taste. *Yum.* It's strawberry. My favorite. "Yes. *Yes!*"

He stands, wraps his arms around my waist, and kisses me again.

I am currently surrounded by all things good in this world.

There really are *so* many good things.

EPILOGUE

*R*ed!
Red, over here!
Red Morgan! This way!
Red!
Red, we love you!
Red, give us a wave!

The calls are almost deafening, the flashes of light so bright. I step from the limo onto the plush red carpet at the Dolby Theatre in Hollywood, California. There are at least a hundred cameras pointed in my direction and maybe more than a thousand fans standing behind crowd-control gates. Screaming, waving their cameras and phones. I am steady on my feet, even though I'm wearing three-inch diamond-encrusted stiletto heels. The train of my indigo ball gown flows behind me like running water as I enter into the chaos of the red carpet at the ninety-eighth annual Academy Awards.

"Are you nervous, babe?" Koi speaks directly into my ear.

"Not with you by my side." I'm thrilled to have his hand gripping so tightly onto mine. He is my rock, my oak. I love him.

Red Morgan!
Red, this way!
Congratulations on your nomination, Red!

Good luck to you!

I wave at the fans calling out to me from the streets and wipe discreetly at a tear forming at the corner of my eye, as the cameras go *click-click-click* and the shouts and cheers vie for my attention. These tears are the sort that Cinderella probably had when she showed up at the castle the day after the wedding. The kind reserved for moments when dreams you didn't even know you had come true.

"Who let *you* in here?"

I turn and look into the bright eyes of Taylor Thompson Lee. Dressed in a yellow tuxedo . . . and beret to match.

"Taylor!" We laugh and embrace.

"Hey, share the love," Issa calls out.

Issa is a vision of perfection in her sparkly silver gown, a hand placed over her giant belly.

"Issa!" My best friend and I embrace, as if we haven't seen one another almost every other day for the last two years. "How's my god-daughter today?"

"Driving me crazy!" Issa places both hands on her protruding belly. "March cannot come soon enough." She motions toward my left hand. "How's Starshine?"

I stare down at the engagement ring Koi bought for me. Recently reuniting with Starshine after two years apart . . . it's certainly been a highlight. I knew she was mine from the moment I saw her. "She's good." I smile. "She's *perfect.*"

"And how did *you* get in here?" Taylor turns to Koi. "Academy Awards security should have you on the *no* list."

"Dude." Koi shakes his head at his friend. "I'm with the future Best Actress. Chill."

As Koi, Issa, and Taylor laugh and catch up and the chaos of the red carpet maintains its deafening roar, I adjust Starshine, glistening under the lights, and sigh dreamily. My heart in my throat, my stomach in the type of excited knots that might never untie. I am fully aware that this is the most magical ride. I plan to enjoy my special evening.

My publicist approaches. I've only been working with her for six months, but so far . . . I'm *impressed*.

"Red, you're simply stunning in indigo!" Aish extends her arms, and we embrace. She pulls away and gives me the once-over. "I love the hair up. It makes you classic, like Dorothy Dandridge."

I pull at the little tendrils around my hairline. "Dorothy's *so* classic."

"This is a bit unorthodox," Aish starts, "but hear me out. Genevieve Thatcher is dying to get an exclusive with you and Taylor. Can we start there? Then we'll have you run the whole gamut? I hope you had a sufficient dose of evening caffeine. It *will* be a long night."

"I'm ready," I declare with a broad grin. "And you're the boss."

"Actually, no." She laughs. "You're the boss."

"Over here!" a reporter from MSNBC calls out. "It's Genevieve Thatcher from MSNBC. Can we have an exclusive with you and Taylor?"

Aish grabs Taylor by the elbow, and I follow them over to Genevieve.

"Red Morgan." Genevieve extends her sleek gold microphone. "Yours is a true Cinderella story. What was it like filming with the great Taylor Thompson Lee?"

"Well . . ." I glance over at Taylor as he adjusts his yellow beret. "I slept in dust for months. Ate bugs—"

"Not on purpose," Taylor interrupts. "They just sorta flew into our mouths."

"I caught dysentery," I say.

"I *did* tell you to use my water filter during those three days in Liberia." Taylor innocently holds up his hands.

"I should have listened." I laugh. "I mean, it's funny now. It wasn't then. A few weeks after that, I spent two days at the Ziv Medical Center in Tzfat with a *mystery* stomach bug. They took good care of me, though." I pause, reminiscing on so many unbelievable experiences.

I even got to see the blue rooftops of Santorini. "And you know what? I'd do it all over again. And again. Times infinity. It was the greatest experience of my whole life."

"Beautiful." Genevieve turns her attention to Taylor. "Taylor, tell me about your inspiration for *Chanel* and how it came to be?"

While Taylor speaks eloquently about one of the highest-grossing movies of last year, I take a quick moment to observe all there is to see. I know the Morgan clan is packed around the TV in the living room back home. Loren is probably biting her nails, jumping up and down shouting *There she is!* Jax and Eli are arguing over who gets to sit in the lounger. Dad's probably asking a hundred questions. Mom shushing him so she can focus. They're not here, but I can absolutely feel their loving energy stretching out over the thousands of miles.

At the far end of the carpet, near a giant clump of reporters, I see her. Zay-Zay Waters. Her long blonde braids are pulled over her shoulder. She's stunning in a black silk gown with a plunging neckline and matching heels. She's speaking animatedly beside Bowie Jameson. Their once-scandalous affair turned a lot *less* scandalous when Zay-Zay and the NFL quarterback got . . . married. Though I can't help but wonder if it's another one of Zay's schemes. With Zay-Zay Waters . . . you just never know. Tonight she's once again nominated for best original song and flying high as always. Soaring with the eagles.

She turns, and our eyes meet. She smiles at me. I smile too.

"Well, Taylor and Red," Genevieve says. "We over at MSNBC wish you the best. Thank you so much for taking the time to speak with us this evening, and congratulations on both your nominations."

"Can we get the Fantastic Four?" a cameraman calls out. "On the carpet together!"

Suddenly we're all together—Issa and Taylor, Koi and me. *The Fantastic Four* is what they've been calling us in the press since, in spite of our busy schedules, we manage to spend tons of time together. There is power in numbers, because, here with my friends, I am as mighty as an oak, standing tall after a heavy storm, where other trees lie uprooted beside it.

For me, it doesn't matter what it says on the envelope tonight. I've already won. With the lights flashing, Koi holding tightly to my hand, people shouting my name, and my eyes welling with tears, I realize that sometimes we prepare for rain. Other days the sun shines so bright. A heart can break . . . a heart can heal. A friendship can face a trial or stand the test of time. But whatever obstacles or pleasant surprises show up along the way, I remind myself to take my moments to look up at the sky, smile, and think my favorite mantra. The words are my umbrella in the rain . . . my joy under the rays of sunshine.

Thank you, Universe. May it somehow lead to something good.

ACKNOWLEDGMENTS

I have to start these acknowledgments by thanking the Universe for having a very strange sense of humor. While I was writing this book, a bird never pooped on my head. However, I did fall—SPLAT—just like Red. Not into a pile of manure (that actually would have been preferred), but I face-planted pretty hard nonetheless. Like Red's dad, I "broke" my arm in the fall. Not off a combine, but I fell just the same. Big thanks to the sling that helped me get through my final edits. Basically a ton of weird similarities connected my life and the lives of the characters in this story. Some very funny. Some . . . not so much. *None* of which involved a Malibu mansion or a private jet . . . or a Koi Kalawai'a. But maybe the Universe is still working on those. I'm grateful for it all. May it somehow lead to something good.

I'd also like to thank my agent, Uwe Stender, and the entire team at Triada US, a.k.a. the best agency in the land. My phenomenal editor at Skyscape, Carmen Johnson. With additional thanks to my extended team of editors, Jason Kirk (you have no idea how much your guidance meant to me). And Jenna Justice—your attention to detail is quite impressive. Additional thanks to Stephanie Chou. Appreciate you! My hardworking team over at Alloy: Viana Siniscalchi, Josh Bank, Romy Golan, and president extraordinaire Les Morgenstein. I appreciate you all.

Thank you to my extremely talented cover team: Alison Impey and Erin Fitzsimmons.

Fake Famous had only a few beta readers in its earlier drafts. Those readers really helped shape and form this story. I'm so grateful to my tiny team: Michael Willuweit, Uwe Stender, Diane Magras, Sanjita E. Thank you for comments that helped guide Red's journey.

Thanks to Skyscape for being the best publisher in the land. My Skyscape team—Jillian Cline, Emma Reh, Stef Llama, Kristin Lunghamer, Alison Impey, and Caroline Sun. You all are fabulous and deserve all the beautiful things.

This book is dedicated to Carmen Johnson and Viana Siniscalchi, because without them, Red would still be in an alternate dimension, wondering why I wasn't finishing her story. Thank you both.

Many friendships kept me sane during the year and a half it took me to complete this novel. My mom, Candy Jo Cheers. My sister, Shona Davis. Mikey and Kiki Shivers. Ava, Jaxson, and Zyaire. My daughter, Cameron, who continues to put up with me staring at my laptop for hours a day, year after year—love you so much. And thanks to my dad for always reading my books and offering editorial critiques, even after the books are already done. Can't wait to get your edits on this one! ☺

This book was my first venture into a new way of plotting. *Save the Cat!* will be my forever go-to. So thank you to Katya Lidsky for helping guide the journey into learning story beats. I will never plot any other way.

Thank you to the Friendship Circle organization (please research them . . . best organization in the land) and Chabad of Studio City. Also, big thanks to Rabbi Zvi Block for your support. You are one of the kindest humans I have ever known. Thank you for caring about me and others. May G bless you for all you do.

And to my readers. Thank *you* for taking this journey with me. I love you all. May the Universe send lots of birds . . . to poop on your heads.

Until next time,
Dana L. Davis

ABOUT THE AUTHOR

Dana L. Davis is an author, actress, and voice-over artist who lives and works in Los Angeles. She has starred in *Heroes, Coach Carter, Franklin & Bash, Veronica Mars,* and countless other film and TV productions. A few of her animation credits include *Star vs. the Forces of Evil, Craig of the Creek,* and *She-Ra and the Princesses of Power.* Dana is a classically trained violist and the founder of the LA-based nonprofit Culture for Kids, LA, which provides inner-city children with free tickets and transportation to attend performing arts shows around LA County.